ALSO BY BRIAN KLINGBORG

Thief of Souls

WILD PREY

BRIAN KLINGBORG

MINOTAUR BOOKS
NEW YORK

First published in the United States by Minotaur Books, an imprint of St. Martin's Publishing Group

www.minotaurbooks.com

Designed by Omar Chapa

All translations of classical Chinese poems are rendered by the author.

Library of Congress Cataloging-in-Publication Data

Names: Klingborg, Brian, 1967- author.
Title: Wild prey / Brian Klingborg.
Description: First Edition. | New York : Minotaur Books, 2022. |
    Series: Inspector Lu Fei series ; 2
Identifiers: LCCN 2022001168 | ISBN 9781250779076 (hardcover) |
    ISBN 9781250779083 (ebook)
Subjects: LCGFT: Novellas.
Classification: LCC PS3611.L5629 W55 2022 | DDC 813/.6—dc23
LC record available at https://lccn.loc.gov/2022001168

Our books may be purchased in bulk for promotional, educational, or business use. Please contact your local bookseller or the Macmillan Corporate and Premium Sales Department at 1-800-221-7945, extension 5442, or by email at MacmillanSpecialMarkets@macmillan.com.

First Edition: 2022

10 9 8 7 6 5 4 3 2 1

This one is for Sophie and Sylvie

WILD PREY

PROLOGUE

The man and the boy wait until dark—then they go in search of something to kill.

They hide their motorbikes in the thick underbrush and enter the forest by foot. The bikes are Frankenstein machines—chimeras cobbled together from Chinese, Thai, and local Burmese parts, whatever keeps their motors running and wheels turning.

The man's gun is no different. It's an ancient AK-47, weathered and battered and held together by scrounged hardware and a silent prayer. Threaded to the muzzle is a jury-rigged sound suppressor the man has cleverly manufactured from an old oil filter.

Aung is the man's name, and he is thirty-five, but looks fifty. He wears a ragged shirt, a traditional Burmese sarong known as a *longyi*, a hat, flip-flops, and carries a canvas bag slung over his shoulder. He smokes a thick cheroot and as he trudges through the brush, clouds of sweet-smelling smoke waft into the verdant canopy overhead.

Aung was once a soldier, fighting in the endless conflicts between the central government and separatist groups. Sometimes he fought on the side of the *Tatmadaw*—the government's armed forces. Sometimes on the side of the separatists. Whoever paid more. He had a family, and they had empty bellies to fill.

Given his past, Aung figures he has accumulated enough bad karma for ten lifetimes and will be reborn as a snake, or perhaps a fish. But he wants to avoid making things worse and coming back as a grub or a cockroach, so more recently, Aung has turned to hunting animals instead of people. In doing so he continues to incur a karmic debt, but that can't be helped. He still has a wife and children, and they still have bellies to fill.

He could, of course, return to the *Tatmadaw* and earn a paycheck killing teenagers and university students who have taken to the streets to protest the latest coup—but there are some levels to which Aung will not stoop for money.

Besides, there is plenty of gold in the forest if you know where to look. Turtles. Marbled cats. Lorises. Hornbills. Pangolins, but those are increasingly rare. For a python, Aung might earn 50,000 kyat. For a moon bear, 500,000 kyat. A leopard will bring in upward of 700,000 kyat. That's more than five times as much as he can earn in a month doing honest work, even if there was honest work to be had—which, in these increasingly desperate times, is severely lacking.

Often, Aung returns home empty-handed or only with enough bushmeat to feed his immediate family. But when he is successful in making a valuable kill, Aung gives money to others in the village who are in need and donates to the nearby monastery. His motives are not entirely altruistic—he hopes his generosity will earn him merit to partially offset his bad karma. Still, he enjoys great status in the village, and if not for him, the local monks would lack a decent television for viewing football matches.

As night blankets the forest, Aung navigates through the brush using an old flashlight with a cracked lens. He stops every so often to shine the light upward, looking for a telltale twin glow that indicates the presence of something worth expending a bullet.

The boy follows along dutifully. His name is Zaw, and he is Aung's nephew. He's just turned thirteen and this is his first time on a hunt. Aung did not want to take him along, but family is family, and after the boy's father begged him incessantly for months, Aung finally gave in.

"Just keep your eyes open and your mouth shut," Aung told Zaw before they left the village. "Don't make a move unless I say so. Don't cough, don't sneeze. Don't even fart loud enough to scare the animals away, or I'll skin you alive and sell your hide in the market."

Zaw knows that Aung's bark is worse than his bite. But he also knows what's at stake here—a great deal of money. More money than Zaw has ever seen in his brief life. So, he has followed his uncle's directive to the letter and not uttered a single sound since they left the road.

They walk for more than an hour before Aung stops to rest. Zaw lowers himself to the ground with a sigh of relief. His shirt is drenched with sweat. The trees are alive with the sound of insects and nocturnal birdcalls.

Aung tosses the remains of his cheroot into the dirt. "Very close now."

Zaw opens his mouth, then shuts it again, unsure if this means he has permission to speak. Finally, curiosity outweighs caution. "Close to what, Uncle?"

Zaw can't see Aung's face in the night, but he can hear the mischief in his voice. "You'll see."

They continue on.

Twenty minutes later, they come to a fence made of chicken wire. Zaw suddenly realizes what his uncle intends.

And that realization terrifies him.

"Hold this," Aung says, handing Zaw the AK-47. Zaw takes the rifle. Aung produces a pair of ancient bolt cutters from his bag and snips at the wire. He makes a hole just big enough for a skinny thirty-five-year-old and an even skinnier thirteen-year-old to slip through. He takes the rifle back before he enters. Zaw follows nervously.

They are greeted by a piercing sound: *wak-wak-wak-wak-wak!*

Zaw nearly jumps out of his flip-flops. Aung shines the flashlight— Zaw sees a peacock boldly confronting them, its eyes glittering. The peacock spreads its tail feathers, displaying a pattern of iridescent eyelike orbs. Aung hisses at it. The peacock turns and trundles away haughtily.

A few meters ahead they come upon a second fence made of thick steel mesh. Zaw knows this one isn't intended to hold peacocks. As they approach, he hears a low rumbling growl that shrinks his testicles deep into the cavity of his belly.

"Uncle!" Zaw starts.

"Shh!" Aung clicks off the flashlight. He pulls Zaw close and breathes in his ear, "Listen carefully. The rifle will make a loud noise, so we will have to move quickly. You hold the light. I'll do the rest. We'll take what we can sell for the most money. Whiskers. Paws. Skin. And most of all, the *lee*."

"Uncle, these animals must belong to the Lady. It's too dangerous!"

"The greater the danger, the bigger the prize."

"If we're caught—"

"Do as I say and we won't be." Aung can feel Zaw's shoulder trembling beneath his palm. "Be strong. Think of what you will buy with your share." He leans the rifle against the mesh and hands Zaw the flashlight. "Hold it up so I can see what I'm doing." He grunts as he cuts through the mesh with his bolt cutters.

Something coughs in the darkness. Zaw points the flashlight into the enclosure. He sees a pair of glowing orbs staring back at him. "Uncle!"

"Give me light!" Aung hisses. He finishes making a hole and returns the bolt cutters to his bag.

Another growl raises the hairs on the back of Zaw's neck. The glowing orbs are nearer now. Zaw starts to shake in fear.

Aung takes a package wrapped in newspaper from his bag. He unfolds it to reveal a hunk of pig liver. He tosses it into the enclosure. Then he sticks the barrel of the rifle through the hole in the fence.

"What if it ignores the meat and attacks?" Zaw whispers, his voice cracking.

"Then you'd better hope the rifle doesn't jam."

The beast slinks from the underbrush. It bares its teeth. Bloodred gums, yellow daggerlike canines.

"Steady," Aung says. He knows he'll only have time for one shot, maybe two. And the sound suppressor will greatly reduce the accuracy of the rifle. He needs his prey to be close. Close enough to smell its rancid breath.

The greater the danger, the bigger the prize.

The tiger roars. Zaw nearly drops the flashlight and runs. But he's never been this far from the village before. He wouldn't even know in which direction to flee. His fate is intertwined with his uncle's. They will either get rich together—or die horribly.

The tiger sniffs at the chunk of liver, blowing motes of dust into the air. Keeping a baleful eye on the two humans, it pads forward, opens its mouth to take the bait.

Aung fires. He fires again.

The tiger mewls, scrabbles in the dirt, then lies still.

"Come on!" Aung says. He slips through the hole in the mesh and yanks Zaw in after him.

"Light!" Aung orders. Zaw sees one of the tiger's eyes is now an empty hole, leaking gore. Blood stains its teeth. Aung draws a knife from a sheath on his belt. He works quickly, severing the tiger's four paws and wrapping them in twists of newspaper. He plucks out a handful of whiskers, valued as good-luck charms and a remedy for toothaches. He amputates the penis and proudly shows it to Zaw. "Look at this beauty!" Aung wraps the member in newspaper and slips all the body parts into his bag. "Lift the leg for me."

"We have enough, Uncle," Zaw says. "Let's go. Before someone comes."

"But the skin!"

"Please, Uncle. Please."

Aung considers. The hide will fetch an astronomical sum. But the boy is right. Every moment that passes increases the risk of being caught. He sheathes his knife and picks up the AK-47. "Give me the flashlight."

They slip through the hole in the mesh and make their way out through the bird enclosure, then into the open forest. Zaw breathes more easily with each step. Before long, his fear turns to exultation. He and his uncle will be legends! And the money earned will be enough to feed the extended family for months. To buy a new motorbike. Ten new motorbikes! Zaw battles an urge to giggle deliriously by stuffing his knuckles into his mouth. He nearly bumps into Aung, who has abruptly stopped walking. "Uncle?"

Aung doesn't answer. He sweeps the darkness ahead with his flashlight.

"Uncle?" Zaw whispers.

"Shh!" Aung unslings the AK-47 from his shoulder.

A shrill whistle comes from the rear. Zaw and Aung turn. Aung's flashlight reveals a man standing five yards distant, a rifle raised and point-ing at them. "Drop it!" the man says.

Aung hesitates.

"There are many of us," the man says. "Drop it or we'll shoot."

The darkness is immediately transfixed with multiple beams of light. Men, holding flashlights under the stocks of their rifles, converge on Aung and Zaw from all directions.

Aung knows they will kill him for sure, regardless of whether he chooses to fight. But the boy . . . perhaps they will allow him to go free if he doesn't resist. He sets the AK-47 down and raises his hands. "The boy is only thirteen. Take me but let him go."

One of the men steps forward. "That's for the Lady to decide." He smashes the butt of his rifle into Aung's face.

Dawn finds Zaw and Aung kneeling in the dirt of a narrow path that cuts through the forest. Their hands are bound behind their backs. Dried blood from his ruined nose stains Aung's shirt.

Half a dozen soldiers in green fatigues lounge in the shade of a broad-leaf evergreen tree, smoking cigarettes and talking idly about the things that such men do—the quantity of alcohol they have consumed, the women they've slept with, the men they've killed.

A jeep approaches along the path and pulls to a stop a few meters from Zaw and Aung. The soldiers toss their cigarettes down and stand at attention.

A man hops out of the jeep. He's short and stocky and wears a pair of aviator sunglasses and a holstered .45 automatic at his hip. The soldiers salute him. He returns the salute, scowls disdainfully at Zaw and Aung, and lights a cigarette.

A young woman climbs out of the jeep. She wears a dark blouse and knee-length *longyi*. Her hair is cut boyishly short, and her face is creased with a lattice of tiny scars across the bridge of her nose, her eyebrows, her cheekbones. She unfurls a parasol and holds it up to shield the third pas-senger from the morning sun.

This passenger is an older woman, dressed in loose, flowing clothing, her face obscured by a wide hat and enormous sunglasses, her fingers, wrists, and earlobes sparkling with precious gemstones. Red earth crunches beneath her boots as she approaches Aung and Zaw, the younger woman shadowing her with the parasol. "So," she says, a hand propped on her hip. "You shits killed one of my tigers."

"Mercy," Aung says, his voice hoarse with thirst and fear. "I beg your mercy, Lady."

"I'll show you the same mercy you showed my tiger. How would that suit you?"

"If I'd known it belonged to you—"

"Enough. You will only make things worse by lying."

Aung hangs his head. "I'm sorry, Lady."

"You are now." The woman lights a sizable cheroot and blows smoke from the corner of her mouth. "Since you are fond of tigers, I will introduce you to my favorite. Contrary to their fearsome reputation, tigers are intimidated by humans. They will rarely attack unless they are absolutely starving, or they mistake a person for some other kind of prey. But this one is different. He has killed at least eleven people. We call him 'Throat-Ripper.'" She motions to the soldiers.

The soldiers set their rifles down, march over to Aung and Zaw, and haul them to their feet.

"Please!" Aung shouts. "Please, Lady! Mercy!"

There is a mesh-lined enclosure set half a dozen yards inside the forest. The soldiers drag Aung, kicking and screaming, toward it. Zaw allows himself to be conveyed along limply, unresisting, like an empty sack.

"The boy is only thirteen!" Aung shouts desperately. "It was all my idea! He didn't even know what I was planning to do!"

One of the soldiers unlocks a gate in the fence. He swings it open, and the others toss Aung inside, then Zaw. The first soldier closes and locks the gate.

Aung lurches to his feet and presses his face against mesh. "He's only thirteen!"

The woman watches as the tiger slinks from a tangle of underbrush in the corner of the enclosure. It pads back and forth warily. Aung tries to frighten it off with kicks and shouts. The tiger retreats, and then circles back around a few moments later. Aung curses at it. The tiger snarls.

Zaw remains curled up on his side, face buried in the dirt.

The tiger pounces. It drags Aung down to the ground. It savages his body, tearing skin and cracking bone. After swallowing a few chunks of flesh, its hunger appears satiated. It licks its chops and saunters over to Zaw, sniffs him curiously, and then, seemingly bored, walks off in search of shade.

The woman smokes her cheroot and waits for the tiger to return and kill Zaw, but when it does not, she grows impatient. "Just shoot the boy and deliver both heads to their village in a basket," she orders.

The matter settled, she, the young woman, and the man with the holstered .45 return to the jeep and head back the way they came, leaving a cloud of red dust in their wake.

ONE

Four thousand kilometers to the north, Inspector Lu Fei is hunting a beast of a different stripe.

Hunting is perhaps the wrong word—conjuring, as it does, the image of a man in camouflage, toting a high-powered rifle, pursuing his prey with a single-minded determination, undeterred by bad weather, rough terrain, hunger, thirst.

Lu, on the other hand, is sitting idly on a cement bench in a tiny plaza outside the entrance to an open-air market in Raven Valley, a modestly sized township seventy kilometers from Harbin, the capital city of Heilongjiang Province. The July sun beats mercilessly down upon on his shoulders like droplets of molten lava. His armpits are soaked with sweat. His toes are swimming in his shoes.

He badly—desperately—needs a beer.

On the edge of the plaza is a food cart selling cold sesame noodles and tofu pudding. The vendor is—a tad gratuitously in Lu's opinion—flaunting a cooler filled with Harbin lager. Row after row of emerald-green bottles, beaded with condensation. What joy it would be to place one of those glass angels against his feverish brow. To sip that crisp golden nectar!

But no. Duty calls.

Duty, in this case, being a fugitive named Chen, wanted for peddling black market animal products—meat, bones, teeth, skin, scales, genitals; anything that can be eaten or processed as a medicinal remedy—to various restaurants and apothecaries in the area. Marketing exotic wildlife to gastronomes and men who suffer from erectile dysfunction is an old story in the People's Republic, but in the wake of the coronavirus and intensifying international pressure by conservationists, the government has finally gotten serious about cracking down on the trade.

Chen has thus far managed to keep his center of operations secret, no small feat in a country where two hundred million surveillance cameras monitor its citizenry, but he was recently spotted on CCTV cameras buying groceries at Raven Valley's Ding Hao market.

Hence, the vigil under the blazing sun. The sweaty armpits. The unrequited desire for a beer.

As deputy chief of the township's Public Security Bureau, this kind of grunt work is below Lu's pay grade. However, in the interests of egalitarianism, and because the *paichusuo* only has so many constables to position at strategic spots around the market, Lu volunteered to take an afternoon shift.

Lesson learned. Next time outdoor surveillance is required in July, Lu will pencil himself in for a four-to-midnight shift.

The phone in Lu's pocket vibrates. It's a text message from Chief Liang: *What's the latest?*

Lu pictures Liang, sitting in his office, air-conditioning unit on full blast, smoking a *Zhongnanhai* cigarette. Relaxed and drowsy after having enjoyed a lunch of grilled lamb and Johnnie Walker over ice.

He texts back: *Avocados are on sale, three for the price of two.*

Liang's response: *What's an avocado?*

Lu shakes his head silently and puts the phone back in his pocket. He stands and massages some feeling back into his right buttock.

Where the hell is this turtle's egg?

He needs a spot of shade and something refreshing to drink, so he heads into the market. Three thousand square meters of food stalls, open on all four sides, with a corrugated roof overhead in case of rain, offering a bewildering variety of fresh produce, seafood, cuts of meat, sweets, drinks, snacks, and sundries. Post-epidemic, it's as packed as ever, but live animals are no longer permitted to be sold, much to the dismay of grannies who prefer to watch their dinner get slaughtered, bled out, gutted, skinned, and chopped into bite-sized pieces before their own eyes.

Lu pauses at one of the stalls to admire the brightly colored skewers of candied hawberries, bloodred, cheerfully delicious. If it wasn't for the buzzing gnats, he might be tempted to buy one. He moves along and rummages through a bin of *longyan*—"dragon eye" fruit. Sweet white flesh, a wonderful treat on a summer's day. But he doesn't want to bother with peels and pits. Another two aisles over is a smoothie stand. Perfect. Lu gets in line. There are two women working the stall, one of whom is Constable Sun. She's wearing civilian clothes, plastic gloves, and a dirty apron.

"Watermelon, please," Lu says.

Sun hesitates. She generally addresses Lu as Deputy Chief, but as they are both working undercover, that would be inappropriate. And yet, she doesn't want to be disrespectful. She comes up with a workable compromise. "Sure thing, *shuai ge.*"

Lu nearly laughs. This term literally means "handsome brother," and it is a polite, yet casual way to address a stranger. Given his hierarchical relationship with Sun, and the fact that it's been a very long time since anyone called him handsome, Lu can't help but be amused.

When Sun returns with Lu's smoothie, he hands over his money and leans in: "You're supposed to be keeping your eyes peeled, not peeling oranges."

"It's been really busy, and I felt guilty just standing around, so I decided to help out."

"Don't get distracted."

"I won't. Promise."

Lu returns to the plaza, only to find that two middle-aged men, their shirts pulled up to their nipples to expose their ample bellies—a budget version of air-conditioning that some wag has dubbed the "Beijing bikini"—are lounging on his bench.

Fair enough. Lu goes over to lean in the shade against a wall. He sips his smoothie and scans the market.

The small portable two-way radio attached to his belt chirps. Lu pulls it out: "Leader One, go ahead."

"This is Red Two." Red Two is Constable Huang's designation. He's stationed on the west side, opposite Lu's position. "I see him. At least, I think it's him!"

"Red Two, what code?" Lu says.

Huang is good-natured and honest, but as dumb as a petrified tree stump. For his benefit, Lu has kept the radio transmission codes as simple as possible. Code One means the suspect has been sighted, alone, entering the market. Code Two—in the company of others. Code Three—he's in the process of departing the market.

"Code One!" Huang says.

"Copy," Lu says. "What's he wearing?"

"White shirt. Green shorts. Black hat."

"Copy," Lu says again. "All units, observe, but keep your distance. Remember, we want to see where the suspect goes. Over."

Lu watches the market, but the crowds make it impossible to spot Chen. He speaks into the radio: "Leader One to Red Four."

Constable Sun answers. "Red Four, over."

"Do you have a visual?" Lu says.

"Not yet, over."

"Go look. But be careful. Over."

Lu waits. A moment passes and then the radio crackles.

Sun: "He's buying vegetables."

"Copy," Lu says. "Keep watching and keep your distance, over."

Two minutes later, Sun reports: "He's buying a load of fruit . . . now sliced beef . . . some liver . . . *feichang*." *Feichang* is the large intestine of a pig, a common addition to soups and stir-fries, infamous for its foul odor.

One of the other constables chimes in: "Is he making hot pot? In July?"

"Keep unnecessary chatter off the channel!" Lu hisses.

While he waits for further updates, Lu texts Chief Liang. He receives no reply. *Perhaps he's taking a nice afternoon siesta at his desk.*

Sun is back: "Now he's moving toward the exit. The south exit."

"Red Three, coming your way," Lu says. Red Three is Fatty Wang. "Wait for him to pass by, then follow. Don't lose him!"

"Copy," Wang says.

Lu hustles across the plaza and into the market: "All units, be advised, target is moving south." He spies Constable Sun several aisles over and zig-zags between stalls to fall in line behind her. They emerge from the market onto a side street that is chockablock with food carts and sidewalk vendors. Lu doesn't see Chen. "Red Three, do you have eyes on the target, over?"

"He's turned left," Wang says, breathless. "Er, west. No, east! On Renai Road."

"Stay with him."

Lu takes a quick backward glance—constables Huang and "Yue-han" Chu are bringing up the rear. That's everyone on the team accounted for.

Lu and Sun turn left on Renai Road. Lu figures Chen is just taking the long way around as a precaution and will eventually circle back to his point of origin. He sees Fatty Wang weaving through pedestrians up ahead and jogs to catch up, Sun at his heels. Fatty Wang makes a sudden right turn before Lu can reach him.

"Suspect turned right on Xinsheng Road," comes Wang's report. "Suspect entering residential building."

By the time Lu rounds the corner, Chen is already safely inside. He huddles with Sun and Fatty Wang against the side of the building. Wang is sweating heavily, whether from exertion or nerves, it's hard to say. "I wasn't sure if I should follow him in," he says, sheepishly.

Lu glances up—the building is six stories of gray cinder block. He counts windows—ten per floor. That's twenty apartments per floor, or one hundred and twenty apartments altogether. *Ta ma de.*

"I'm sorry," Wang says. "I thought he'd get suspicious if I just walked in right behind him."

Lu nods tersely. Wang is right, of course. But now what?

Constables Huang and Chu arrive. "Which apartment?" Chu asks.

"We don't know," Wang says.

"Great," Chu grouses. "Are we supposed to knock on every door in the building?"

"Why don't you go around and watch the back entrance," Lu tells him.

"Why me?"

"Because you're big and tough," Lu says.

Chu snorts and stalks off. Constable Sun looks up at the building and runs the same calculations as Lu. "*Are* we going to knock on every door?"

"Should we call for backup?" Constable Huang asks.

"I already alerted the chief." Lu checks his phone. Liang has responded. "He's on the way."

"Oh, good," Fatty Wang says, with obvious relief.

Lu adjusts the revolver stuffed into the back of his pants. He is the only member of the team carrying a gun. Given the paucity of weapons training among police in the People's Republic, he is concerned that issuing firearms to the constables is a recipe for disaster. They are as liable to shoot a bystander, or each other, as hit the suspect.

Chief Liang, Sergeant Bing, and Constable Wang Guangrong arrive ten minutes later. All three are in uniform and both Liang and Bing carry holstered revolvers.

Lu sends Wang Guangrong around back to wait with Constable Chu. He prepares to enter the building but Chief Liang motions for him to wait. Liang is smoking a cigarette and he takes a few last puffs, then tosses it onto the street.

"That was a *Chunghwa*," Liang says, by way of explanation. *Chunghwa* cigarettes are a luxury brand that cost five times as much as the *Zhongnanhais* Liang usually consumes by the truckload. "If I get my ticket punched today, at least I got to enjoy one last good smoke."

"You sure that's sufficient?" Lu says. "We'd be happy to wait while you finish the pack."

"Don't be impertinent," Liang says. "Which apartment is he in?"

"We're not sure," Lu says. "But he's making hot pot. We should be able to smell it."

Chief Liang is incredulous. "That's your plan? To stick your nose under every door until we find him?"

"He bought *feichang*. If you detect the odor of spicy broth and pig shit, you've probably got the right place."

"Unbelievable!"

"If you have a better idea, Chief, I'm all ears."

Liang doesn't.

The front door is locked. Lu randomly chooses an apartment on the first floor—he hopes this isn't where Chen is hiding out—and presses the call button. When the resident answers, Lu says: "Health Department! Buzz us in!"

After a brief pause, there is a click, and the electronic lock disengages. Lu opens the door and enters. The others file in behind him. Constables Sun and Fatty Wang stay downstairs to guard the entrance. Lu, Chief Liang, and Sergeant Bing work their way up, floor by floor.

There are a couple of false alarms—turns out, the building is a potpourri of smells, some pleasant, many not—but they finally converge outside an apartment on the fourth floor that betrays the telltale scent of red-pepper hot pot broth and the stench of *feichang*, overlaid with the cloyingly sweet odor of incense. Lu knocks while Liang and Bing flank the door.

"Health Department!" Lu says. "Temperature check." There is no response, but Lu is not surprised. Loud music blares inside the apartment. Lu could probably operate a jackhammer in the hallway without the occupant hearing. He tries again anyway, shouting this time: "Open up or we'll have to call the Public Security Bureau!"

The volume of music suddenly decreases. Lu hears a click as the door is unlocked from within. He reaches under his shirt for the revolver.

The door opens, just a crack. A man peers out at Lu. It's Chen, all right. Lu recognizes him from CCTV surveillance footage. Chen is shirtless and shiny with sweat.

Lu smiles disarmingly. "Good afternoon, Uncle. We have to come in and take your temperature." In the wake of the virus, this type of intrusion is unwelcome, but not uncommon.

Chen stares at Lu. Dressed in plain clothes, Lu doesn't look like a cop, but he doesn't look like he works for the Health Department, either. "Where's your uniform?" Chen asks.

"Don't give me a hard time, okay, Uncle? I have to check every resident in every single apartment on this entire block. Let me in and I'll be out of your hair in thirty seconds."

"Go ahead," Chen says. "Hold up your thermometer."

"I need to come in."

"No, you don't."

Lu pushes on the door. Chen tries to shut it. There is a struggle. Sergeant Bing adds his bulk and, together, he and Lu pop the door open. Chen sprawls onto the floor. When he sees Bing's uniform, he scrambles into the kitchen and snatches up a cleaver from the counter.

Lu draws his revolver, but then freezes, his mouth open in shock.

The cramped interior of the apartment has been converted to half animal market and half slaughterhouse.

A dozen wire cages placed against the wall hold a mini zoo's worth of animals. Lu sees cats, bamboo rats, birds, snakes, lizards, bats, and a pair of wolf pups. Meanwhile, the remains of some unfortunate creature are spread across the kitchen counter—bits of meat, bone, and a fuzzy pelt. Other animal skins dry on a rack near the window. The kitchen table is covered with bins holding dried animal parts, bones, and teeth. Four large pots boil on the stove, sending up huge clouds of greasy vapor. Lu assumes only one of them holds Chen's lunch.

Now that he's inside, he nearly gags at the combined stench of incense, hot pot broth, boiled meat, animal musk, and feces. He covers his mouth with his free hand and brandishes his revolver. "Easy, Chen. There's nowhere to go. You're outnumbered and we have sidearms. Put the cleaver down. Come quietly."

"*Qu ni de ma!*" Chen snarls. He hurls the cleaver at Lu's face. Lu ducks. The cleaver sails over his head and *thunks* into the wall above the doorway.

Chen turns to the stove and picks up a pot of boiling broth. Lu, who has recently recovered from serious burns sustained on a previous case, shouts, "Watch out!" and dives for cover. Chen flings soup across the room. Sergeant Bing hits the floor but takes a spray across his back. He cries out in pain. Chief Liang is a few paces behind Bing—Bing's body shields him from the worst of it, but the scalding liquid splatters all over his shoes.

The shoes are the nicest footwear Liang has ever owned, a gift he purchased for himself to celebrate his fifty-fifth birthday. Each night after work, he meticulously and lovingly polishes them to a high sheen.

Now he looks down at the precious Ethiopian leather, befouled with hot pot broth and bits of greasy meat. A thick white gelatinous ring of sliced pig's intestine lies directly on his right toe.

Liang roars. He draws his sidearm and aims at Chen. Chen holds the empty soup pot out in front of his body, then realizes it is no match for a bullet and ducks below the kitchen counter.

"Chief, no!" Lu yells.

Too late.

Liang fires. Crockery explodes. Glass shatters. Wood splinters. The sound is deafening.

"Get your ass out here with your hands up, you hemorrhoidal dog's anus!" Liang shouts.

Chen crawls out from behind the counter, arms raised in surrender. Lu can see shards of broken earthenware embedded in the skin of his palms. "Don't shoot! I give up!"

Liang holsters his revolver. "Cuff him." He sees Lu and Sergeant Bing exchange a stunned look. "What?"

They cuff Chen and hustle him to the *paichusuo,* where he is locked in a cell. Lu calls the county procurator to let him know Chen has been captured, then gets himself a cold drink from the canteen and walks down to the holding area. He enters to find Liang perched on a stool, in his stocking feet, smoking a cigarette—strictly against regulations—and Chen sitting on the floor of his cell, armed with a rag and polish, working Liang's shoes over.

"Rub firmly but gently," Liang instructs. "Just like when you're 'hitting the airplane.'" This phrase, *da feiji*, which refers to the motion of cocking an antiaircraft missile launcher, is a euphemism for pleasuring oneself. Liang sees Lu in the doorway and gives him a crooked grin.

Lu turns around and walks out. He's going to pretend he didn't just witness a blatant violation of a prisoner's rights.

TWO

An hour later, Lu relates this tale to Luo Yanyan over a glass of beer in her tiny bar, the Red Lotus.

Her mouth drops open. "*Tian!* He didn't hit any of the neighbors, did he?"

"No. He was damn lucky."

"What about the criminal?"

"He'll be sent off to the county lockup tomorrow."

"What's going to happen to the chief?"

"What do you mean?"

"He fired his gun in an apartment building. At a suspect armed only with a pot of soup."

Lu takes a long pull of beer and wipes his mouth. "Chen had a cleaver, too."

"Still."

"Nothing will happen. The neighbors won't dare complain. Liang might have to pay the landlord a few yuan to patch up the damage. That's about it. I didn't even put the weapon's discharge in the report."

"You cops really stick together, don't you?"

"Come on. Most folks detest the sight of us unless they are in some sort of crisis, and then all they do is complain that we didn't show up fast enough. We are like a third daughter when all you really want is a son. At best, an unwelcome burden. At worst, the object of intense resentment. If we don't stick up for each other, who will?"

"Hmph." Yanyan gets up from the table. "I have to make the rounds."

Lu reaches out and takes her hand. "Yanyan."

She pulls away and inclines her head warningly at the other customers.

"Who cares?" Lu says.

"Let me get you another beer." She leaves him to exchange pleasantries with a few young office workers, men in white shirts and black pants who are drinking *mao tai* liquor and snacking on a dish of roasted peanuts tossed with seaweed and salt.

Lu sighs. He's long carried a torch for Yanyan, and after the horrific case of the serial killer Zeng, in which he risked his life to save hers, their relationship finally seemed to be blossoming into something more than simple friendship. He is anxious to move things forward, but has taken a cautious approach, knowing that Yanyan is a widow who still carries the deep sadness of losing her husband. And he is mindful of the old story about a farmer who grew impatient with the slow growth of his seedling plants and decided to speed things along by tugging them a tiny bit higher each day. Naturally, he only succeeded in killing his entire crop.

But a man can only resist tugging for so long.

Just a few weeks ago, during the Dragon Boat Festival, Lu saw a chance to advance his case. The festival is a lively annual affair commemorating the ancient poet and statesman Qu Yuan, who drowned himself as a political protest. Or maybe he just got drunk and fell into a river—the exact details are rather hazy. In any case, citizens celebrate by gathering to make *zongzi*—sticky rice with various sweet fillings—drink wine, and watch teams of young men race colorfully outfitted boats featuring dragon-shaped prows.

Lu figured, a holiday atmosphere, alcohol, sunshine, laughter. A perfect recipe for romance.

He convinced Yanyan to take a day off and drive to Harbin to watch the boat races on the Songhua River. After a pleasant afternoon in the city, they had dinner and drinks at a seafood restaurant in Raven Valley—

followed by a nightcap at Yanyan's house. One thing led to another, as these things do, and they wound up in her bed, fumbling at each other's clothing. Lu had just managed to undo Yanyan's shirt and was eagerly kissing his way from the side of her neck down into the depths of her delectable cleavage when she suddenly stiffened and pushed him away.

"What's wrong?" he asked, alarmed. "What did I do?"

She sat up and shook her head, then glanced at a framed photo on the nightstand. Lu was all too familiar with that blasted photograph and its silent censure. It was a shot of Yanyan and her dead husband on the day of their wedding, him in his best suit—perhaps his only suit—and her in a red *qipao*, the long silk dress with a mandarin collar traditionally worn by Chinese brides.

"I'm sorry," Yanyan said. "I think . . . perhaps you should go."

"But—"

"I don't feel well. Too much wine." Lu could see tears rolling down her cheeks. He touched her shoulder, but she stood and walked to the corner of the room. "Please, Lu Fei. I need to be alone."

What else could he do but return to his tiny bachelor's apartment and stew in a toxic broth of confusion, dismay, disappointment, and unrequited lust?

Since that night, Lu has tried multiple times to reach out to Yanyan, both physically and emotionally, without success. She is like a brick wall. It's somehow worse than when he used to secretly yearn for her from afar. Whatever intimacy he has painstakingly cultivated over the past few months has been revoked, like membership in a private club that has returned his deposit and informed him it no longer accepts clients with his particular profile.

For Lu, this terribly unsatisfying situation is like that old poem "The Fortune Teller" by Li Zhiyi:

> *I live upstream on the Yangtze River,*
> *You live downstream.*
> *Though I cannot see you, I think of you every day.*

And we drink from the same waters.
When will the Yangtze cease to flow?
When will this regret fade?
I wish your heart was like mine
So, I wouldn't have to bear this desire for both of us.

THREE

The girl looks to be about twelve, maybe thirteen. She sits on a bench in the lobby of the *paichusuo*, dressed in baggy pants, a yellow shirt that was once white, and plastic sandals. Her hair is short and sloppily cut.

Lu has been summoned by Constable Huang, who is on duty this morning at the reception desk. "She says her sister's been missing since Friday," Huang tells him. "She fears the worst."

Lu nods for Huang to return to his post and smiles down at the girl. "How can I help you, miss?"

The girl's eyes are too large for her face, and when she opens her mouth, her teeth seem too big as well, lending her the look of a feral cat. It takes Lu a moment to realize these are not physical characteristics specific to the girl—they are the result of being underfed. "My sister. She's missing."

Lu joins her on the bench. "Since Friday, you said?"

"Something terrible has happened to her." The girl's eyes well with tears.

"Now, miss, you don't know that."

"She's dead or been kidnapped and sold to a brothel."

"Let's not get ahead of ourselves. Would you like some tea? Let me get you some tea." Lu assumes a female presence might prove reassuring, so he asks Huang to locate Constable Sun and have her bring some tea and biscuits. He returns to the bench and asks the girl her name.

"Meirong. Tan Meirong."

"Meirong. That's a pretty name. What about your sister?"

"Meixiang."

Lu asks her a few innocuous questions. Where Meirong lives, what school she attends, how old she is.

"Fifteen."

Lu is shocked. She looks much younger. "Where are your parents? Why aren't they here with you?"

"My mother is dead."

"Oh, I'm sorry. How?"

"Cancer."

"And your father?"

Meirong makes a face. "He couldn't come. He's . . . not feeling well."

Lu senses there's more to that story, but Constable Sun has arrived bearing a tin of almond cookies and a paper cup, so Lu makes introductions. "Now tell us about your sister," he says. "Meixiang, you said her name was?"

Haltingly, in between bites of cookie and sips of tea, the girl speaks. Her older sister Meixiang has been working for the past year in Harbin to support the family, which, following the death of their mother, consists of just the three of them—the two sisters and their father.

"What does your father do for a living?" Lu asks.

"Nothing," Meirong says. "He hurt his back and hasn't worked since."

She continues her story: during Meixiang's sojourn in Harbin, the sisters have kept in touch on an almost-daily basis through WeChat. Meirong pulls out her phone and shows Lu and Sun their text exchanges—it's like a foreign language, full of strange acronyms, emojis, and memes.

"Last Friday night, she texted me that she was going on vacation," Meirong says. "Here, look." She scrolls down to a message: *Little Sis, going to get some sun.* ☼ ☺. *Talk to you soon!* "But I know for a fact that she didn't write that herself."

"How?" Lu asks.

"First, whenever she had time off, she would come home. Not 'go get some sun'! She doesn't have time for trips to the beach. Or the money for it. Everything she makes goes into our mouths or to pay rent. And besides, she never calls me Little Sis!"

"What does she call you?"

"Brat. Turd. Little Devil. Lots of things. But never Little Sis!"

"Okay, you got this on Friday," Lu says. "And today is Tuesday. And between then and now—"

"I messaged her a dozen times and nothing. I called a hundred times and nothing. At first, her phone rang, but starting Saturday, it went straight to voice mail."

"Are you able to track her phone's location from your phone?" Sun asks.

"No. Meixiang says that's just being nosy."

Lu smiles. "Please give Constable Sun here all the relevant details. Don't leave out anything that you might feel would be useful. Friends your sister has mentioned. Boyfriends, ex-boyfriends. We'll start by requesting access to her phone records and checking with the Harbin police."

Lu returns to his office and conducts a quick review of Tan Meixiang's life using the various databases at his disposal. He discovers that she is a high school graduate, works in the service industry in Harbin, has committed no crimes, posted nothing objectionable on social media, paid her bills in a timely fashion, and therefore, left almost no discernable trace in the world.

He instructs Constable Sun to requisition Tan Meixiang's WeChat records. He determines the precinct where Tan Meixiang's Harbin apartment is located and gives the local *paichusuo* a call. He introduces himself and reports Tan Meixiang as missing.

"I'm wondering if you can check into any complaints she might have filed, that sort of thing," Lu says. "And can someone there call around to the local hospitals and morgues?"

"We're pretty busy," the sergeant says. "But we'll *jin liang*."

Lu groans inwardly. Aside from "no beer," *jin liang* are the words he hates most in the Chinese language. They mean "to do one's best," but when someone says they will *jin liang*, what they are really saying is they might—maybe—get around to entertaining the request if the gods decree, the stars align, and they have absolutely, positively nothing better to do.

But as Lu holds no sway over the Harbin PSB, all he can do is say thank you and hang up. Just then, Sergeant Bing pokes his head into the office. "Time for the study session."

"Oh, for the love of Buddha!"

"Come on. You're supposed to set a good example for the constables."

One of the many tools the Chinese Communist Party has used since its inception to indoctrinate citizens in Marxist theory—or, as the CCP calls it, "socialism with Chinese characters"—is regular study sessions. In a predigital era, this would entail a small group of individuals meeting on their lunch break or after regular work hours to discuss scintillating topics like "Mao Zedong Thought" and "Deng Xiaoping Theory." But in keeping with the times, the CCP Propaganda Department has recently created a phone app called Study the Great Nation featuring a long list of "educational" subjects and various quizzes to test whether users are paying attention.

The app is not mandatory, but its use has been strongly encouraged— very strongly—for Communist Party members and employees of government and state-owned enterprises. Likewise, many schools and private companies have jumped on the bandwagon. In a watered-down version of the old "struggle sessions" in which victims were forced to confess their supposed crimes against socialism and face public humiliation, some schools now openly shamed students with low scores, and company employees who do poorly on quizzes are forced to pen self-criticisms.

Even Raven Valley's sleepy little *paichusuo* has been caught up in the frenzy. The county's most senior cop is a grizzled old chief surnamed Bao. To curry favor with provincial officials, Bao has pitted all the PSB stations under his purview against one another in a competition for the highest collective score on the app. He has promised the winners an all-you-can-eat-and-drink karaoke bacchanalia. And he has threatened the head of the unit that earns the lowest score with a transfer to the most godforsaken stretch of the Heilongjiang-Russian border he can find.

This explains Chief Liang's sudden enthusiasm for "enhancing the Party's ability to use Marxist principles to solve the problems facing contemporary China." He has taken to convening a weekly gathering in the canteen where all the constables on duty pool their knowledge to answer some of the app's tougher questions.

As soon as everyone is assembled, Liang gets straight to the point. "Who's got the answer to this one? 'Our illustrious president emphasizes the goal of establishing a common destiny between the Chinese people and people around the world with a *blank*.' With a what? Money? Free booze? What?"

"The answer is 'a peaceful international environment,'" volunteers Fatty Wang.

"Good for you," Liang says, typing the answer into his phone. "You are excused from your next weekend duty."

Everyone in the room starts protesting.

"Silence!" Liang shouts. "You all have an equal chance to answer. Now, how about this one: 'The Chinese Communist Party was formally established in 1921 on a boat on what lake?'"

"Ooh, ooh, I know this one!" Constable Huang raises his hand. "The South Lake in Zhejiang Province."

Huang's reputation for general obtuseness is well-established, so Liang is initially hesitant to accept his answer.

"He's correct," Constable Sun chimes in.

"Well, all right, then," Liang says. "Constable Huang, you are excused from recyclables sorting."

And so on. This continues until all the outstanding quiz questions have been answered, after which everyone can return to their *actual* duties.

FOUR

Lu arrives at the *paichusuo* bright and early the next morning.

He goes to his office, grabs his thermos, fills it with hot water in the canteen, and walks up front to scan the night log. Yuehan Chu has worked the midnight-to-eight shift and when he spots Lu coming, he sits up a bit straighter, rubs sleep out of his eyes, and nods at the lobby. Lu peers through the glass partition and sees the girl, Tan Meirong, sitting on one of the benches.

"How long has she been here?" Lu says.

"Not sure. When I looked up, there she was."

"You mean, when you *woke up*, there she was."

"I went to take a leak. Should I piss in my thermos next time?"

"You'll want to watch that tone, Constable." Lu goes out to the lobby and stands in front of Meirong. "What are you doing here?"

"Waiting for you to find my sister."

"Aren't you supposed to be in school?"

"It's summer break."

"Oh. Right."

"When are you going to find her?"

"These things take time, Meirong. Go home and I'll call when I have news."

"I think I'd rather just sit here and wait."

"Don't be ridiculous."

"I know how it is. If I don't sit here reminding you, you'll forget all about her."

Lu grits his teeth. "Suit yourself."

He goes to his office and adds tea leaves to his thermos. While his tea steeps, he checks his messages. As expected, there has been no update from the PSB station in Harbin. He inquires with Constable Sun regarding the WeChat records. She tells him they won't be ready until that afternoon.

Lu spends the morning knee-deep in mind-numbingly dull administrative tasks. And he does, in fact, forget all about Tan Meixiang for a couple of hours. Eventually, a rumbling in his stomach alerts him that it's time for lunch. When he leaves his office to go buy food, he suddenly remembers Meirong and peeks through the reception window to see if she's still in the lobby.

She is.

Stubborn, Lu thinks. He exits through the back of the *paichusuo* and buys two Styrofoam containers of fried noodles at a street cart. He returns to the lobby and offers one of them to Meirong. She looks at him in confusion.

"I figured you must be hungry," he says.

"I don't need you to buy me food," Meirong says. "I need you to find my sister."

"I told you I'm working on it."

"Something awful has happened to her. She's been sold to a farmer in Qinghai Province who will rape and beat her all day long, or someone's cut out her kidneys and auctioned them off to the highest bidder!" Meirong bursts into tears.

Lu glances at the reception window, hoping for a rescue by Constable Sun. Instead, he finds only Li the Mute, so called because he can go weeks on end without uttering a single syllable. No help. No help at all. He sits down on the bench. "I understand you're worried. But you can't torture yourself with such thoughts."

"She's all I have."

"What about your father?"

Meirong shakes her head, her thin shoulders shaking.

Lu reaches out his hand to give her a comforting pat, withdraws it.

"Tell you what. You eat your lunch, and later today I'll drive to Harbin and talk to the local police myself."

Meirong knuckles tears from her cheeks. "Can I go with you?"

Lu digs into one of the food bags and hands her a napkin. "Wipe your nose. And sorry, I can't bring you on official business."

"Maybe I can be useful."

"No."

"How else will you know if anything's missing from her apartment?"

Hmm, Lu thinks. But no. "Strictly against regulations."

"Please?"

"No."

"I've never been to Harbin. I'll stay in the car. I won't make any trouble. Please?"

Lu is hungry and wants to go eat his lunch. "I'll think about it. Take your noodles."

Lu puts the container in her lap and picks up his own. He stands. Meirong clutches his sleeve. She gives it a quick, plaintive tug, then lets go.

In the early afternoon, Constable Sun informs Lu that Tan Meixiang's WeChat records are available. They include Meixiang's financial transactions, social media postings, texts. Most everything looks routine. But there is one item of interest: last Friday night, Lu sees the purchase of a ticket for the Saturday train to Dalian.

Dalian is a port city on the southern tip of Liaoning Province, about three and a half hours from Harbin by bullet train. Lu has been there on a couple of occasions. It's a popular destination for tourists, especially Russians, Japanese, and South Koreans. It boasts pleasant summer weather, good beaches, amusement parks, excellent seafood, and, best of all, an international beer festival in July and August featuring beers from around the world, live music, and food stalls.

If Tan Meixiang was truly going to take a vacation, Dalian would be a logical choice. But there is no record of any payments or debits after the purchase of the train ticket. No Dalian hotel, no restaurants, no taxis. Nothing. Not even an ATM withdrawal. Weird.

Lu might even be tempted to call it suspicious.

He checks the GPS tracking report for Tan Meixiang's phone. He sees a ping from a cell tower in Dalian at 12:15 p.m. on Saturday. He cross-references this with her train ticket. The itinerary was for an 8:30 a.m. departure from Harbin and 12:06 p.m. arrival in Dalian.

It's safe to say that Meixiang's phone, at least, made it to Dalian.

But after that final ping, the phone goes silent.

Lu calls the Dalian PSB headquarters and requests a canvass of local hospitals and morgues for any *wu ming nu shi* (no-name women)—i.e., Jane Does. This will take a few hours, at least. In the meantime, still no news from the Harbin PSB.

As useful as a dog's fart, Lu thinks.

He signs out a patrol vehicle and stops by the lobby. Tan Meirong is slumped on the bench, dozing, one of the plastic sandals dangling from her big toe. He should let her sleep, rather than rouse her to the harsh reality of a missing sister who more likely than not has met a terrible end.

Instead, he gently touches her shoulder. "Meirong?" Her eyes pop open, and they are filled with fear. "Easy," Lu says. "It's just me."

Meirong slowly returns from whatever dark place her dreams had taken her. "Did you find her?"

"No. But do you still feel like taking a ride?"

They merge onto the Tongjiang Expressway bound for Harbin. Traffic is moderate, but when the other vehicles see Lu's patrol car, they slow down, wary of being ticketed. Lu weaves in and out of traffic impatiently, seeking an open lane. He considers turning on the light bar, but that would be a violation of PSB regulations.

Meirong gazes in wonder at the car's elaborate console—the radio, the computer, the array of buttons. "What's this do?" she asks, extending a forefinger.

"Don't touch!"

Meirong quickly snatches her hand back. Lu feels slightly guilty for having snapped at her. "That controls the siren," he explains, after a moment. "These buttons are selectors for different sounds."

Lu continues to jockey for position on the expressway, but soon finds himself boxed in by a big flatbed truck in front and a Baojun SUV in the neighboring lane. After a few frustrating minutes, Lu says: "Want to see how it works?"

"Really?"

"Sure. Try that one."

Meirong presses a button. Lu honks the horn. Instead of a *beep-beep*, it makes a *whoop-whoop* sound. The truck, unsure if it's being pulled over, responds by further reducing its speed. Lu waves aggressively at the Baojun SUV. The Baojun drops back, and Lu pulls in front of it. He accelerates but quickly finds himself trapped behind another knot of traffic. "*Ta ma de.* Hit that one."

Meirong presses a button. Lu honks the horn. It makes the sound of a klaxon. The lane ahead clears remarkably fast.

"It's like magic," Lu says. Meirong giggles.

They drive for a bit and then Lu says: "What more can you tell me about your sister?"

"I don't know. Like what?"

"Does she have a lot of friends? A boyfriend? Is she pretty? Does she go out dancing, does she drink?"

"I don't think she has a lot of friends. She doesn't have a boyfriend. She's average-looking. She works most nights at a restaurant. She mostly drinks tea."

"That's not very informative."

"She's just a normal girl."

"The more details you can provide, the better sense I'll have where to search for her."

Meirong shrugs. "I don't know what to say."

"How old were you when your mother died?"

"Ten."

"And your sister was fourteen."

"Yes."

"Four years is a big age difference."

"After Meixiang was born, my dad had to travel far away to find a job. So . . . he and my mom didn't see each other for a long time."

"What kind of job?"

"Construction, mainly. He's not a professor or a policeman or anything. Regular work."

Lu gets the picture. It is not unusual for rural residents lacking a good educational background or specific skills to find employment in nearby cities where there are more opportunities. Some 228 million of these *nongmingong*—"farmer laborers"—currently work as couriers, construction workers, in factories, at restaurants, driving taxis, and other blue-collar or service-industry gigs far away from their homes and families, sometimes for years at a stretch. They are part of an unspoken pact the Communist Party has made with the citizens of the People's Republic: keep your nose to the grindstone and out of politics—and you, too, can become gloriously rich.

While this strategy has enabled the growth of a strong middle class and lifted millions out of abject poverty, in most cases, the promised riches have not materialized for the *nongmingong*. Because of their *hukou* status, they slave away for low wages and with zero job security, without the benefit of insurance, access to health care, pensions, or any of the other social welfare programs accorded to citizens with the dumb luck to have simply been born in a city.

"Tell me more about your father," Lu says.

"Not much to tell. He was gone a lot, and then he hurt his back and hasn't been able to work since."

"How long ago was that?"

"Three years."

"So, what does he do now?"

"He lies on the couch and complains about the pain and drinks a lot."

"Ah." Lu digests that for a moment. "That's why your sister had to move to Harbin? To make money?"

"Yes. After high school she worked in a supermarket, a coffee shop, a sheet metal factory. But then she heard you could get paid more in Harbin, so she went there."

"And how does she get along with your father?"

"Badly. That's part of why she went to Harbin."

"Did he . . . Was he mean to her?"

"They argued all the time," Meirong says. "He . . . well . . . he said she didn't respect him. Which I guess is true."

"Did he hurt her in any way?"

"Maybe a slap now and then. Same with me."

Lu can see possibilities here. An argument over money, perhaps taken too far. "Has he ever done anything inappropriate to her?"

"What do you mean?"

Lu struggles for the right words. "You know . . . touched her in some way he shouldn't have?"

Meirong is appalled. "He's not a pervert!"

"All right. I'm just turning over stones. That's what I do. Did they perhaps have a fight recently? Last week?"

"How could they? They hardly talk, and besides, she was in Harbin and he was in Raven Valley."

"He never goes to Harbin to see her?"

"He barely gets off the couch to go to the bathroom."

"Right. Does your sister know anyone in Dalian?"

"Dalian?" Meirong asks. "I have no idea. I doubt it. Why?"

"We traced her phone to there."

"You found her phone?"

"Not exactly," Lu says. "We just got a ping off a cell tower. We don't know where the phone is currently. It's either turned off, destroyed, or out of juice. But if she was going to take a vacation, Dalian might be a logical destination."

"I told you already, she *didn't* take a vacation! This is proof she's been kidnapped and sold to some mean old Russian gangster who reeks of vodka!"

"Calm down, Meirong. Before we get too caught up in wild conjecture, let's see what answers Harbin has for us."

FIVE

They soon reach the city and Lu locates the correct PSB station and double-parks in front. He considers having Meirong wait in the vehicle, but the July sun is blazing and that might be considered cruel and inhumane. "You can come in with me but sit quietly in the lobby and don't be a nuisance," he says.

He presents his credentials to the constable at the reception desk and asks to see a supervisor. He is kept waiting for twenty minutes. A tall, thin man eventually emerges. He's got one pip and two silver bars on his shoulder boards—that makes him one rank below Lu. He introduces himself as Supervisor Deng. "How can I help you?"

"I'm here about a missing person case," Lu says. "I called and left a message yesterday, but no one called me back."

"Sorry, we're very busy. And people go missing all the time. I'm sure whoever it is you're looking for will turn up soon."

"The person in question is a nineteen-year-old woman and she's been missing since Friday," Lu says. "The circumstances are suspicious."

"A nineteen-year-old woman?" Deng says. "Well, she's probably just run off with her boyfriend."

"She doesn't have a boyfriend," Meirong says.

Deng looks at her with disdain. "I'm sorry, who are you?"

"Her sister."

Deng frowns at Lu. "Is it generally your practice to bring relatives along when you investigate a missing person case?"

"Don't you even want to know her name?" Meirong says. "It's Tan Meixiang."

"Tan Meixiang," Deng says. He leans down, hands on his knees, and gives Meirong a patronizing smile. "Well, if I run across a Tan Meixiang, I'll be sure to ring you up immediately."

Lu is annoyed, but he knows taking a hard line with Deng would only make things worse. "Would it be possible to check your incident reports starting Friday night?"

"As I'm sure you were told on the phone, we'll get to that as soon as we can," Deng says. "We're very busy here." He waves a hand around the lobby. It is currently empty apart from one young man, dressed in rags, with an unkempt beard and several weeks' worth of grime darkening his skin, who is engaged in a deep philosophical discussion with the hot water dispenser.

"If you just log me in to your system, I'll do the work myself," Lu offers.

"Don't be ridiculous," Deng snaps. "How would you feel if I came to your station and asked to check through your records?"

"Brother Deng," Lu says, risking a tone of familiarity. "Imagine if it were your sister. Or your daughter?" Lu nods down at Meirong. She looks up at Deng and blinks her big round cat's eyes.

Deng clicks his teeth in annoyance. "I only have a few moments."

Meirong waits out front while Deng and Lu go to Deng's desk. It takes about half an hour for Lu to learn what he wants to know: no one in Harbin has reported Tan Meixiang missing; no bodies fitting her description have turned up in city morgues or hospitals; and she has no record to speak of with the local PSB apart from registering her Harbin address, as is required by law.

Lu thanks Deng profusely and offers to buy him a drink should Deng ever find himself in Raven Valley Township.

"Why would I go *there*?" Deng asks.

"Fair question," Lu says.

Tan Meixiang's apartment is not far, so Lu leaves the car at the *paichusuo* and he and Meirong walk. They soon arrive at an older building, five

stories, the exterior walls dotted with air-conditioning units and a rick-
ety zigzagging fire escape.

"Does your sister have a roommate?" Lu asks.

Meirong nods. "They're just roommates, though. Not friends. Meixiang barely ever talks about her."

Lu buzzes the apartment. No answer. He looks at his watch. It's almost 4:30. He hopes the roommate is home; otherwise he'll have to go
hunt down a building supervisor or landlord to gain admittance. He keeps
buzzing. Eventually an annoyed female voice comes through the intercom:
"What?"

"Public Security," Lu says. "Let us in."

Silence. Lu stabs the buzzer again. The lock on the front door clicks,
and he opens it. Lu eyes the elevator in the tiny lobby suspiciously. He is
claustrophobic and it is his general policy to regard every elevator in the
People's Republic as faulty. He'd rather get stuck in a dark basement with a
pack of zombified Red Guards than trapped in an elevator, but he doesn't
want Meirong to waste any of her limited physical resources on taking the
stairs. He summons the elevator and when they step inside, he presses the
button for the third floor and says: "Let me do the talking."

They are greeted at the apartment door by a young woman who is
dressed in a Starbucks uniform. She looks nervous, which is only natural.

"I'm Inspector Lu," Lu tells her. "I'm here about Tan Meixiang."

"Did something happen?" the woman asks.

"May we come in?" Without waiting for an answer, Lu pushes open
the door and enters. The apartment is small—a sitting and eating area and
cubbyhole kitchen, a bathroom, and a bedroom with two narrow beds.
The woman doesn't complain when Lu pokes his head into the bathroom
and bedroom.

"What is your name?" Lu says.

"Lin Qun."

"You and Ms. Tan are the only ones who live here?"

"Yes."

"When's the last time you saw her?"

"I don't know. Um . . . last week sometime. Thursday or Friday?" Lin looks curiously at Meirong. "You're her sister, aren't you?"

"Yes," Meirong says. "How did you know that?"

"You look alike. She has a picture of you." Lin points to the refrigerator. Lu sees a faded photograph pinned there with a magnet. It shows Meirong and Meixiang, aged around ten and fourteen, and a woman Lu assumes is their mother. The mother is dressed in a robe and looks thin and drawn. Perhaps, Lu thinks, it was the last photo of the three of them before she died.

"Is Meixiang okay?" Lin asks.

"We don't know," Lu says. "She's missing. You said you saw her Thursday or Friday. Is it normal for her to not come home for several days? I'm just wondering why you didn't worry about her and alert someone?"

"Well . . . uh . . ." Lin colors slightly.

"Yes?"

"I spent a long weekend at my boyfriend's." Lin covers her mouth with her hand.

"Ah," Lu says. "Good thing I'm not a vice cop." He smiles to show he's joking. He asks her a few more questions, but she doesn't have much information to impart. "You don't mind if I have a quick look around?"

"I—"

"Have a seat on the couch. It won't take long."

Lu takes Meirong into the bedroom to search through her sister's belongings. Lu notes that her keys, phone, and wallet are gone. Meirong does not identify anything else of importance that is missing. On the way out, Lu gives Lin his card and asks her to call if she hears from Meixiang.

"What now?" Meirong says in the elevator on the way down.

"We try the restaurant where she worked."

SIX

The establishment looks high-end. It's got a gleaming façade of glass and chrome with huge neon characters that read *Shu Qi Da Qi*—"Hoist the Big Banner."

Odd name for a restaurant, Lu thinks. Perhaps the owner is a patriotic sort.

He double-parks in front. The day's heat has dissipated, and in this case, Lu thinks it's better if Meirong remains in the car. He cracks the windows and tells her to wait quietly and not play with any of the buttons on the console. He enters the restaurant foyer, where he is greeted by an attractive young hostess. To her credit, her pleasant expression doesn't waver in the slightest at the sight of his uniform. He introduces himself and says he is looking into the disappearance of Tan Meixiang.

"Let me call the manager for you, sir," she says, picking up a phone.

"Do you know Ms. Tan?" Lu asks.

"Yes . . . I mean, not well, but she's worked here for six months or so . . ." She puts the phone to her ear and dials a number.

"Do you know what might have happened to her?" Lu says. "Where she might be?" The hostess gives him a plastic smile and shake of her head. "Was there any unusual incident involving Ms. Tan at the restaurant recently?"

"Not that I'm aware of, sir." She holds up a lacquered fingernail and speaks into the phone: "Mr. Fang? There is a policeman here to see you. He's inquiring about Ms. Tan Meixiang. Tan Meixiang. Yes. Right. Thank you, Mr. Fang." She hangs up. "He'll be right with you."

Lu tries to pump the hostess for more information, but she is not forthcoming. He doesn't necessarily view her reticence as proof of a conspiracy, but she is definitely guarded. "What type of cuisine do you serve here, anyway?" he asks.

"We are famous for our exotic meats and dishes that feature medicinal properties."

"Medicinal?"

"Yes."

"When you say medicinal . . ." Lu says.

"Balance the qi. Improve organ function. Clear up skin problems. Increase virility."

"Virility."

"Yes, sir."

Hoist the Big Banner, Lu thinks. Now the name makes a bit more sense. "And what types of dishes increase virility?"

"Various kinds of animal penises and testicles." Despite her refined appearance, the hostess manages to say this without a hint of embarrassment.

"Right," Lu says. "Well, I'm just going to poke my head inside, if you don't mind."

"Mr. Fang will be along very soon, sir, if you wouldn't mind just waiting—"

"Sure thing," Lu says. Then he walks past her and enters the dining room, where he stops abruptly to gape at the sumptuousness of the decor.

He sees wood-paneled walls adorned with bright red and gold accents; a warm pink glow courtesy of crystal chandeliers dangling from the ceiling; statues of bare-breasted Greek nymphs carrying jugs of wine; velvet banquets and tables with blindingly white tablecloths. The waitresses are wearing silk jackets and short skirts and appear to have been chosen for their looks; the same goes for the busboys, who are dressed in bow ties, white shirts, and black pants.

Lu is not very knowledgeable about interior design, but if he had to put a label on the aesthetic, he might describe it as whorehouse chic.

It's early, so the dining room is only about a quarter full. The clientele is largely older, male, and, judging from the gold watches and Burberry, Prada, and Louis Vuitton "murses" in evidence, rather well-off.

Lu listens in as a waitress gives her spiel to a table of men who are drinking *bai jiu*.

"Tonight's set menu," the waitress says, "starts with turtle soup in a ginger broth and carpaccio donkey meat served with a spicy wasabi dipping sauce. Both very good for yang essence."

One of the men reaches over and squeezes a handful of the waitress's left ass cheek. "I can feel it working already."

The other men laugh. The waitress smiles and disengages herself with a practiced move. She continues as if nothing has happened: "Next dish is Three Golden Kings. Bull, yak, and black dog penis. Followed by sheep fetus in brown garlic sauce, snake meat with mushrooms, chicken and herbs, deep-fried crab, sweet-and-sour tofu, eight-treasure vegetables, and, for dessert, three kinds of gelato. All for twelve hundred yuan per person."

"How about off-the-menu items?" the ass-grabber says. "Maybe something extra special?"

Lu sidles a bit closer and tries to blend in behind one of the Greek nymph statues.

"We have a few items," the waitress confirms. "I can bring you a list."

"Tiger?" the man asks. He makes a motion with his finger to demonstrate which part of the tiger he's referring to.

The waitress covers her mouth with a menu and lowers her voice. Lu cannot hear what she tells the men.

"I knew it!" one of them complains. "You have to be connected to get the good stuff."

The first man motions petulantly at the waitress. "Go fetch the list."

As the waitress complies, Lu spies a man in a Western suit coming down a flight of stairs at the back of the dining room. He quickly returns to the foyer. The man approaches with an easy smile.

"I'm Wilson Fang. How can I help you?" Fang is of average height and weight, neither handsome nor ugly, with close-cropped silvering hair. His suit is dark and muted, but of good-quality fabric. His shoes are made from animal skin, perhaps crocodile.

"You are the manager here?" Lu asks.

"Owner and manager." Fang doesn't appear nervous or intimidated to have a uniformed policeman standing on his doorstep.

"I'm looking into the disappearance of one of your employees. Her name is Tan Meixiang."

"Perhaps you'd like to come to my office?"

"Sure."

Lu follows Fang though the dining room, up the stairs, and down a corridor that is lined on either side with closed doors. Above the doors are plaques featuring grandiose titles: Golden Lotus Pavilion; Wine Pool and Meat Forest; Garden of Clouds and Rain; Fragrant Blossom Grotto; and so on. Lu assumes these are private banquet rooms and he recognizes most of the names as literary sexual innuendos.

Fang's office is at the far end of the corridor. Fang opens the door and waves Lu inside. The decor here is urban safari: a huge teak desk and leather chair with an array of antlers and horns mounted on the wall behind it; a couch upholstered in what Lu assumes is fake zebra skin—though it might be real, for all he can tell; a glass coffee table with yellowed tusks for legs; a pair of leopard-print chairs. A tiger skin—glassy eyes and bared teeth—lies in the center of the floor.

Fang waves toward the couch and makes a beeline over to a credenza behind the desk where a computer monitor displays a black-and-white split-screen view of the restaurant's interior. He switches off the monitor. "Can I get you a drink, Officer? Johnnie Walker Blue Label?"

"Inspector. Lu. And no thanks."

Fang takes a seat in one of the leopard-print chairs and pulls out a pack of cigarettes. He offers it to Lu. Lu shakes his head. He sees that Fang smokes 555s, the late Chairman Mao's favorite brand.

"So, Tan Meixiang." Fang lights up. "She's worked here for, oh, six months or so. Nice girl. Hardworking. Did she do something illegal?"

"She's gone missing. You didn't notice?"

"Well, she asked for some time off, so no, I wasn't aware."

"When was that?"

"Last week."

"What day?"

"Hmm." Fang blows smoke at the ceiling. "Thursday or Friday."

"You're not sure which day?"

"I have thirty-seven people working here. It's hard to keep track of everyone's comings and goings."

"Understood," Lu says. "How long did she ask for off?"

"If I recall correctly, a week. Said she was going through some emotional issues. Wanted to clear her head."

"Did she indicate what kind of emotional issues?"

"Sorry, no, and I didn't press for details. She can't have been missing long, though."

"Her sister hasn't heard from her since Saturday."

Fang taps ashes into a brass ashtray. "And is that unusual?"

"They exchange some form of communication nearly every day."

"Hmm." Fang takes a deep drag. "I can ask the staff if anyone's heard from her."

"Yes, please. And can you think of any other details that might help? How did she seem recently? Was she distraught? Do you know anything about her personal life or relationships?"

"She didn't have any issues with the other staff that I'm aware of. She was popular with the guests. I don't know anything about her private life. She just rather abruptly approached me, and although I don't usually look kindly on my staff up and leaving without notice, I figured, *All right, she's never even taken a sick day before, so I'll cut her some slack.* Do you suspect foul play?"

"I don't want to speculate. Did she mention where she was going?"

"She didn't say she was going anywhere."

"Nothing about Dalian?"

"Nope."

Lu can't get a good read on Fang. He seems sincere. But he *is* running a restaurant that specializes in donkey dicks.

Following the pandemic, the government instituted a new and comprehensive ban on the trade and consumption of wildlife. Most of the menu items Lu heard the waitress reel off were legal but talk of special menus was highly suspicious. And with private banquet rooms referencing fragrant blossoms and clouds and rain, who knows what goes on behind closed doors here.

"Your restaurant looks very successful," Lu says.

Fang waves his cigarette dismissively. "We scrape by."

"You are known for dishes with aphrodisiacal properties?"

"We offer a variety of foods that have health benefits. Not just in terms of libido, but also balancing vital essences, improving longevity, mental performance."

"All that from eating a tiger's wang?"

"We don't serve tiger 'wang' here, Inspector. That would be illegal. And I take it you are skeptical regarding traditional medicine?"

"I'm a cop, so I'm skeptical by nature. But I try to keep an open mind."

Fang stubs out his cigarette. "Is there anything else I can help you with?"

"You don't know a guy surnamed Chen from Raven Valley, do you, by any chance?"

"I know at least a hundred guys surnamed Chen, Inspector. It's a common name. But none that I can recall from Raven Valley."

"Right. Would you mind if I have a quick look around?"

"I'd prefer you didn't, Inspector. Sorry. We have a lot of high-end clientele here. Businessmen. Officials. They prefer to maintain their privacy."

"Why? Are they doing something they shouldn't be?"

Fang smiles thinly. "Shall I show you out?"

Lu isn't going to insist. Harbin is not his jurisdiction. Fang leads him downstairs and through the dining room. He shakes hands with Lu in the foyer. "I'll be in touch if I hear anything useful."

"Thanks." Lu turns to go, then stops and says rather casually, "I noticed you have cameras monitoring the restaurant. Do you archive video footage?"

"No, Inspector. I just use the live camera feeds to monitor things when I'm working in my office."

"Right." Lu imagines there are a lot of booze- and aphrodisiac-related hijinks taking place in those private rooms. Would Fang be smart to keep a video record of them? Or, given the clientele—as he put it, high-end businessmen and officials—smarter to *not* keep one?

Outside, Meirong is sweating impatiently in the patrol vehicle. "What did you find out?"

"Her boss says she asked for time off."

"He's lying!"

"We don't know that for sure."

"Maybe he was part of the plot to kidnap her and sell her organs!"

"There are no thieves running around China stealing organs, Meirong. The government has a monopoly on that business." Lu takes out his cell phone. "Let me make a quick call." He rings Monk, proprietor of the Black Cat, one of Harbin's most popular gay nightclubs.

Monk answers: "Inspector Lu. This is a pleasant surprise."

"How are you, Monk?"

"Hanging in there."

"Glad to hear it. Listen, I know you're tapped into the restaurant and bar scene in Harbin. Do you know a place called Hoist the Big Banner?"

Monk snorts into the phone. "A meat market in more ways than one."

"How so?"

"It stands to reason that a place specializing in aphrodisiacs is a breeding ground for bad behavior."

"Details, please."

"This is all hearsay, mind you. But a lot of rich and powerful people go there. I've heard they indulge in a variety of top-secret and completely forbidden menu items."

"Such as?"

"Tiger, pangolin, bear. Also, illicit products of the human species. Male, female, boy, girl, whatever you fancy."

"Really? How can they get away with that?"

"Which? The prostitutes or the wild animals?"

"Either. Both."

"I just told you—a lot of rich and powerful people go there. The owner has serious *guanxi*."

Guanxi. Connections. The oil that greases the wheels of nearly every aspect of Chinese business and politics.

"What do you know about him? Fang?"

"Nothing. He keeps a low profile. I don't think I'd even recognize him if I was sitting next to him on a bus."

"Can you ask around? See if you can dig anything up."

"Sure."

"Thanks, Monk. Oh, and . . ." Lu glances over at Meirong. "Er . . . do you know if the waitstaff are, you know . . . part of the menu?"

"I wouldn't be surprised, but no . . . I haven't heard that's in the job description. I imagine the restaurant might be a good place for a young woman to meet an older man who's looking for a mistress, though."

SEVEN

By the time they arrive back in Raven Valley, it's dinnertime. Lu offers to buy something for Meirong, but she shakes her head. "You can just drop me off at the station."

"I'll drive you home."

"You don't need to."

"I *want* to."

"Why?"

"I'd like to see where you live. You never know what might prove useful in an investigation."

"I'm pretty sure seeing where I live won't."

"I'd also like to talk to your father."

"That'll be a waste of time."

"Just give me directions."

"Do I *have* to?"

"No. I can just call one of the constables and have them look up your address, but that would put me in a bad mood."

Meirong huffs but tells him where she lives.

It is one of the more run-down sections of town. Her apartment building is five stories of gray cement everything: gray cement stairs, gray cement walls, gray cement floors, gray cement ceilings.

Lu parks the patrol vehicle out front, attracting the attention of a gaggle of children who are playing on the sidewalk. The children are not shy—they run right up to him and start asking questions:

"Are you arresting somebody?"

"Where's your gun?"

"How many bad guys have you killed?"

Lu seriously doubts he will ever develop a paternal instinct. "Scram!" he says.

A group of adults is also outside, sitting on stools, taking advantage of the evening breeze. They are just as curious but more circumspect than the children. They nod their chins at Meirong and whisper into one another's ears.

Lu realizes he's put Meirong in an awkward position. It's never a good thing to be seen coming home in the company of a police officer. "Show me the way," Lu tells her.

They walk up several flights of steps. The walls are pocked and discolored and strung with electrical wires. Meirong leads Lu down a hallway with apartments to one side, and on the other, a row of windows overlooking a central courtyard. The windows appear to have never once been washed and are so dirty they discolor what little sunlight they admit to a tobacco yellow. Brooms, dustpans, and garbage pails clutter the way. Laundry hangs from water pipes along the ceiling.

Meirong stops outside an apartment, unlocks a door, opens it and shouts: *"Ah Ba!"* She motions for Lu to wait, then enters. After a moment, she returns and beckons him inside.

The interior of the apartment is nicer than the exterior, but not by much. It displays the same cement walls, barely enlivened by a few paper good luck charms and old Lunar New Year posters. The main room is crowded with a couch, a couple of mismatched chairs, a low table, an old television, and a hot water dispenser.

Mr. Tan rises stiffly from the couch when Lu comes inside. He is red-faced and rheumy-eyed and reeks of the cheap *bai jiu* he's been drinking. Lu introduces himself and Tan offers him a seat. He indicates the bottle of liquor. "Do you want a drink? Meirong, fetch a glass!"

"No, no, I'm fine, thank you."

Tan pours himself a few fingers. He picks up his glass, sits on the couch, and winces in pain. "She's not dead, then?"

"Not as far as I know," Lu says. "Why? Do you have any reason to suspect she might be?"

"How about a beer? Or tea? Meirong, make some tea!"

"No, I'm fine, really," Lu says. "Can you tell me when you last heard from your daughter?"

"A while ago." Tan sips from his glass. "She talks to Meirong, but not to me."

"Why is that?"

Tan shrugs. "I don't know. She's disrespectful. Always has been."

Filial piety—respect, obedience, and concern for one's parents—is the cardinal virtue of an orderly Confucian society. But seeing Tan sitting there in his dirty T-shirt and with his unshaven face, three-quarters in the bag at seven in the evening, Lu can hardly blame Meixiang's rumored defiance. "So, you aren't on good terms with her?"

"Not really."

"But she sends you money for rent and so on," Lu says.

Tan is insulted. "I fed her from the time she was a baby. Put clothes on her back. A roof over her head. It's the least she can do. I got injured, you see. My back. I can't lift anything over ten kilos, or I might get permanently paralyzed."

"Do you receive worker's compensation?"

"Not a damn dime. And I have no insurance."

"Your employer didn't pay you?"

"I got a little money, but just one lump sum. Barely a pocketful of change. I was just a day laborer. Off the books, you know. I had to take what they offered. So much for the great 'Chinese dream.' What a joke."

"I suppose it's a good thing Meixiang is dutiful enough to send money home," Lu says.

"She does it for her sister. She doesn't give two shits about me."

"Seems like the sentiment is mutual."

Tan pours himself another slug. "What do you know about it? You probably had rich parents from good backgrounds. Went to college. Now you have a cushy government job, and a beautiful uniform with a shiny badge that allows you to tell people what to do all day."

"Perhaps. Yet here I am, sitting in your apartment, trying to find a young girl that only her sister seems to care about."

Tan starts to puff up like a wet hen, but then melts into the threadbare couch cushions. "I know how it looks. Here I am, drunk before dinner. While my nineteen-year-old daughter is living on her own in the big city, slaving her youth away to support the household. But it wasn't always like this. I was born unlucky. No fancy schools or uniforms with shiny badges for me. Just hard labor, sunup to sundown, from the time I was eighteen. I did my best for the family. Then my wife died, leaving me with two young kids. What the hell do I know about raising girls? And as if that's not bad enough, I go and break my back. Two months in a hospital. Now I can neither stand up straight nor bend over all the way. I can't sleep more than half an hour at night because of the pain. And I can't afford any medicine, apart from this cheap shit." Tan points at the bottle. "Yeah, we've had to depend on Meixiang these past few years. And the truth is, without her, I don't know how we'll survive. So, even though Meixiang and I don't see eye to eye, I want you—I need you—to find her. That's the truth."

Lu looks at the nearly empty bottle on the table. And then at Meirong, with her skinny arms and sharp cheekbones. The brand of liquor Mr. Tan drinks is inexpensive but given the choice between a sack of rice and a liter of *bai jiu*, Lu wonders which he'd choose to spend his money on.

"You must find a way to better your situation, Mr. Tan," Lu says. "A girl needs a father."

"What do you suggest? I miraculously heal my back? Win the lottery? Marry rich?"

Lu rises from his chair. "Thank you for your time."

"Of course," Tan says, insincerely.

Lu walks over to where Meirong is preparing a bowl of instant noodles. "Will you be all right?"

Meirong stirs her noodles with a pair of chopsticks. "I will be if you find my sister."

Lu goes downstairs, only to find some neighborhood scallywag has scrawled an obscene picture on the grime covering the patrol vehicle's hood.

Talk about a lack of respect!

The children are nowhere to be seen, but Lu grills the adults who are chatting on their stools. They claim to not know who the culprit was. Then they pepper him with questions. He tells them that Meixiang has gone missing, and they cluck their tongues and shake their heads but provide no useful intelligence, apart from the fact that Mr. Tan is a lazy drunk, which Lu already knows.

Lu wipes the picture off the hood with the heel of his hand. As he drives off, he predicts whichever juvenile miscreant drew that picture will pursue one of two future career paths: either he will become a criminal, or a government official.

Either way, in the end, he'll likely end up in jail.

EIGHT

After Lu has left, Fang returns to his office, closes the door, pours himself a measure of Johnnie Walker, and lights a 555 cigarette. He unlocks a drawer in his desk and removes a prepaid cell phone. He dials a number from memory.

After half a dozen rings, a voice answers: "What?"

"We might have a problem."

"What problem?"

"A cop was just here asking about Tan Meixiang."

"I thought you had Harbin Metro in your back pocket."

"He's not from Harbin. Raven Valley."

"Where the hell's Raven Valley?"

"A town about seventy kilometers from here. The girl's hometown, apparently."

"*Ta ma de*, he's got no jurisdiction in Harbin, does he? What are you worried about?"

"You're not concerned a cop is sniffing around? Not only was he prodding for information on the girl, he was making veiled accusations about certain items on the menu here. What if he goes to the Forestry and Grassland Administration?"

There is a pause. "That *would* be a problem. Who do you know at the NFGA?"

"Just a couple of low-level officials."

"Well, you'd better call and see if there's any internal chatter about you. And in the meantime, cool it with the contraband items."

"What about the cop?"

"Maybe he's just looking for a bribe. See what your Harbin contacts say about him."

"All right." Fang hangs up. He removes the SIM card from the phone, snaps it in half, and tosses it into the wastebasket. He locks the phone back in the drawer.

He hopes this Lu Fei is smart enough to just go away.

It's not that Fang's squeamish—it's just that dead bodies do have a way of creating a stink.

NINE

Thursday morning, Lu is in the *paichusuo* canteen filling his thermos with hot water when Constable Wang Guangrong shambles in. Wang has taken a turn at night duty and he manages to look like he's spent two weeks in a black ops detention center undergoing sleep-deprivation torture. Lu bids him a good morning but Wang can only manage a surly nod. He yawns and then says: "That girl is out there in the waiting room."

"Meirong?"

"Don't know her name. Same one as yesterday. Is she going to come here every day from now on?"

"Just leave her be, Constable."

"I am leaving her be. She's not leaving me be."

"How so? Is she bothering you?"

"She sits and stares and makes me feel like I've done something bad."

"Perhaps you have a guilty conscience. 'If you stand straight, you don't worry that your shadow is crooked.'"

Wang mutters something disrespectful under his breath. Lu pretends not to hear it.

He goes to his office and starts on paperwork. He does not go out to the waiting room to greet Meirong. If she wants to sit there all day, so be it. He's doing his best to find her sister, and he doesn't require an underfed fifteen-year-old in plastic sandals and a tattered shirt to act as his conscience.

When Sergeant Bing arrives, Lu asks him to appoint a couple of constables to make another round of calls inquiring about unidentified patients or corpses at Harbin hospitals and morgues. Sergeant Bing does, but the constables come up empty. Which is good news, but it doesn't bring Lu any closer to resolving the mystery of Tan Meixiang's whereabouts.

He now pivots to the next logical avenue of inquiry—the place where Meixiang's trail suddenly went cold.

Dalian.

Lu has been there only once, for the beer festival. He found it to be a pleasant city, situated at the tip of a peninsula, laid out with numerous open plazas, parks, and green spaces, the architecture an eclectic mix of Russian, Japanese, and Chinese, excellent seafood, and the worst of the summer's heat kept at bay by cool breezes off the waters of the Yellow Sea.

As for Dalian's famous beaches, Lu has not had an occasion to visit, but he has seen the photographs. Cerulean skies. Clear blue waters. Hills dotted with emerald pine trees. Neat rows of multicolored sun umbrellas. Gently breaking whitecaps.

And every square inch of sand covered by masses of tourists, seething like a colony of angry fire ants.

To be fair, this is no different from the scene at any other beach in the People's Republic. Comes with the territory. And the population of 1.4 billion.

It occurs to Lu that there is nothing to stop him from combining business with a little pleasure and taking a long weekend in Dalian to investigate Tan Meixiang's disappearance. And while he's at it, enjoy some lobster. Sample a few new beers. Maybe even visit one of those golden beaches. Perhaps he could convince Yanyan to come along.

He wonders if she might possibly possess a bikini.

He phones Yanyan and makes his pitch. "A weekend at the shore. Warm sand. Cool water. Good food."

"What about the Red Lotus?"

"Everyone needs some time off now and then, Yanyan. Besides, you've been doing big business lately. You can afford to shut down for a few nights."

"I don't know . . ." Yanyan says.

Lu can sense the ramparts rising. "You know they have a forest zoo there. With pandas."

"Pandas?"

"That's right." *Who doesn't love pandas?* "Tigers and lions, too."

"Hm."

"And as it so happens, there's the annual beer festival going on now. This could double as a business trip. You'll be able to sample some craft beers, and maybe add a few selections to your bar menu."

"I suppose."

"Tell you what. I'll book us a couple of tickets for tomorrow. We'll go down, see the sights, get a little sun, have some food and drinks, and be back in time for you to open up Sunday evening if you want."

"Well . . ."

"I won't take no for an answer. Life is short, it was a terrible winter, and we deserve to treat ourselves. I'll take care of everything. All you need to do is pack some clothes. I have to run now, but I'll pick you up tomorrow, say around ten?"

"I have to think about it . . ."

"Great! See you then. Oh, and Yanyan?"

"Yes?"

"Don't forget your swimsuit."

Lu calls around Dalian and, given that it's peak tourist season, discovers decent hotels to be in short supply. He finally manages to book a room at a midrange chain. The location lacks an ocean view, but breakfast and complimentary Wi-Fi are included. Lu is tempted to reserve a room with a single king-sized bed, but he doesn't want to push his luck. He books one with two queens.

Travel arrangements complete, Lu spends the afternoon on routine administrative matters and then elects to head out early and get a haircut. He stops by Chief Liang's office to tell him he's going to Dalian.

"What for?" Liang says.

"The missing person case."

"Can't you just talk to Dalian PSB over the phone?" Liang extracts a cigarette from a pack on his desk, lights it, and blows smoke at the ceiling.

"Not sure if you've read the latest Ministry of Health regulations," Lu says, "but smoking is no longer permitted in workplaces."

"This is my office," Liang says.

"You're right. It's not really a workplace, after all."

"Hilarious. Is it really necessary for you to go there?"

"It was the last place where we got a ping from the girl's phone."

Liang's eyes narrow mischievously. "I seem to recall the beer festival is happening now."

"Is it? I wasn't aware."

"No, of course you weren't. Anyway, don't you have enough to do here?"

"Sure. But the girl is from Raven Valley so she's our responsibility. And her sister sits out there in the waiting room all day long, looking for answers. I get the impression she'll do so until she gets some."

"That's her choice."

"I'd hate for the local media to get wind of it. Think of the optics. Destitute local girl, aged fifteen, single-parent home, missing sister, idling time away in the Raven Valley *paichusuo* while the police do nothing."

"Haven't you done what you can?"

"Apart from visiting the last known location of the missing girl, yes. But you know how the media loves these tear-jerker stories."

"Bloodsuckers." Liang puffs silently for a moment. "Have a nice trip."

Lu passes through the lobby on his way out. "Go home, Meirong," he tells the girl. "I'll be away for a couple of days, working on the case."

"Away where?"

"You don't need to know every detail. Rest assured, I'm doing my best and I'll let you know if I find out anything."

"You're going to Dalian, aren't you? Can I come?"

"Absolutely not. I shouldn't have even taken you to Harbin."

"I hear they have pandas at the Dalian zoo. I've never seen a panda."

"Try the internet. I'll call if I have news."

TEN

Lu and Yanyan meet Friday morning and catch a local train to Harbin, and from there, the high-speed rail to Dalian. The entire trip takes nearly six hours. Yanyan is wearing jeans, tennis shoes, and a white T-shirt. Her hair is pulled back in a ponytail, and, apart from a pair of earrings and the cinnabar bracelet—an ever-present reminder of her dead husband—she wears no jewelry or makeup.

She is the most radiant creature Lu has ever set eyes upon.

Which makes him sorry for what he must do next.

"I have to make a quick stop at the local police station before we check into the hotel," Lu says.

"Why?" Yanyan asks, suddenly suspicious.

"Just some minor business."

He offers to carry her bag, but she says no, with a touch of irritation. Lu sees that it is dawning on her that he hasn't been completely forthcoming regarding the reasons for their trip.

It only takes a few minutes to walk to the Qingniwaqiao PSB branch, where Lu shows his credentials and inquires about Meixiang. He is told to wait in the lobby.

Yanyan sits on a bench and crosses her legs. "I didn't realize you were here to work."

"I'm not. I'm spending time with you."

Yanyan looks around at the lobby. "Me, a half dozen cops, and some Korean tourists who have had their luggage stolen."

"It'll just be a few minutes."

Naturally, it requires more than an hour for Lu to pin down a supervisor and confirm that there is no trace of Meixiang in local hospitals and morgues or any police reports featuring a woman who fits her general description.

The supervisor confirms that the cell tower that recorded the last ping from Meixiang's phone covers the downtown district around the train station.

"In other words, Meixiang switched it off basically as soon as she stepped foot off the train," Lu says.

The supervisor shrugs. "Or perhaps someone pickpocketed it and turned it off so it couldn't be traced?"

"Do you know if the train station has a lost and found?" Lu asks. "Maybe her phone turned up there."

"I guess you'll have to ask at the train station."

It's now nearly six in the evening and both Lu and Yanyan are hungry, tired, and cranky. They check into the hotel—she remarks on the fact that he's booked only one room and says she hopes he doesn't snore—and decide to eat at a restaurant nearby. During dinner, Lu keeps the conversation light, but it takes Yanyan several drinks before she begins to loosen up and laugh at his dumb jokes.

"You have a lovely smile," Lu says.

Yanyan covers her mouth. "Stop."

"Why?"

"You're embarrassing me."

"No—why are you . . . What I'm trying to say is . . . Did something happen that I'm not aware of?"

"I don't know what you mean."

"Here, have some more wine." Lu has ordered them a French vintage to accompany their dinner. He knows nothing about foreign wines, but he was attempting to be sophisticated and romantic, a decision he now regrets—it tastes like old fruit fermented in battery acid.

"No more," Yanyan protests. "I'm getting tipsy."

"Okay." Lu pours anyway. "My point is, I thought we were getting along very well."

"We do get along well, Brother Lu."

"I mean, *very* well."

This is met with an uncomfortable silence. Lu breaks it by lifting his glass. *"Gan bei!"* They drink, Lu grimacing at the burning sensation in his chest.

"You don't like it?" Yanyan says.

"I like *you*, Yanyan."

She coughs wine into her napkin.

"Please tell me," Lu says. "Did I do something to make you angry?"

"No." Yanyan gulps water.

"What, then? I'm just trying to understand."

Yanyan looks down at her plate. Lu reaches over and touches her forearm. His fingers inadvertently brush against the hard, lumpy surface of her cinnabar bracelet.

"Talk to me," Lu says.

"If I'd known I was going to be the subject of an interrogation, I wouldn't have come."

"I want to know what's wrong. Why you no longer seem interested in . . . taking our friendship a step further."

Yanyan lets out a deep sigh but doesn't pull her arm away from his touch. As she meets his gaze, her dark eyes reflect the flickering candlelight. "I like you, Brother Lu. Very much."

"That's a good start."

"But you know I'm a widow."

"Yes. And you have been for a few years. Isn't it time you . . . moved on?"

"Moved on?" Yanyan says, with a flash of anger.

"I didn't mean it like that."

"Then how did you mean it?"

"You have mourned your husband as a wife should. Honored his memory. But it's been years. Don't you think he'd want you to be happy? To find . . . love . . . again?"

"It's not that simple. I still feel him everywhere. His presence."

Lu feels an icy finger trace a line down his spine. "You mean . . . like a ghost?"

"A ghost? No! Idiot!" Yanyan laughs and the contentious mood lifts. Lu laughs along at his own silliness, then casually pours the rest of the wine bottle into Yanyan's glass.

An hour later, they have both showered and climbed into their respective beds. The TV is on—some celebrity-studded variety show. Background noise.

Yanyan is wearing a dark T-shirt and pajama pants. Lu is dressed similarly. He wonders if she's wearing a bra under that T-shirt. He badly wants to climb under the sheets with her and find out.

Yanyan's comment about her dead husband is a tad eerie, but not surprising. The belief that some lingering aspect of the dead remains in this world and can have a very real and tangible influence on the fortunes of the living goes back thousands of years in China. Hence, the elaborate burial rituals, careful deliberation over the placement of grave sites, and regular offerings of rice, food, and drink.

Master Kong, the Great Sage, proclaimed the proper mourning period for a widow was three years. But even he, a real stickler for decorum, understood that the living eventually had to get on with things. *So,* Lu wonders, *how long is Yanyan going to sleep with a framed wedding photo on her nightstand before she decides it's time to let someone new into her bed?*

Yanyan yawns, stretches sleepily, kicks off her blanket, and rolls over onto her side. Lu stares at the curve of her hip. The splash of her dark hair on a white pillowcase. Her shapely calf, naked where the bottom of her pajama pants have ridden up, gleaming in the soft light of the television.

He suddenly feels overcome with desire. He tosses and turns and finally gets up and goes into the bathroom. He splashes cold water on his face. Brushes his teeth. Combs his hair with his hands. Brushes his teeth again. He leaves the bathroom and, heart hammering, walks over to stand at the edge of Yanyan's bed.

"Yanyan," he whispers, throatily.

Her eyes are dark pools hidden within impenetrable shadows.

"Yanyan?"

He reaches out to touch her. Pulls his hand back. Reaches out again. Withdraws.

He stands there for a moment, hoping she will look up. Spread her arms. Pull him into her embrace. Wrap her legs around his hips. Find his mouth with her own.

Instead, she begins to snore.

Lu switches off the TV and climbs into bed. He lies there for an hour before he falls asleep with the lyrics to "Song of a Pure-hearted Girl" by the poet Meng Jiao looping through his fevered brain:

Wutong-*trees grow old together*
Mandarin ducks mate for life
A faithful wife loves her husband until her death
To give up her own life in such a manner!
But even a tsunami cannot roil
A woman whose heart is like water in a deep well.

ELEVEN

Lu wakes determined to make a good day of it.

He and Yanyan have a leisurely breakfast and then take the light rail to Jinshi Beach. At first, Lu is disappointed to learn that Yanyan has not brought a bikini. When she emerges from the changing room in a dark-blue one-piece, compared to the smorgasbord of pale flesh on display around them, Yanyan looks positively chaste. Yet, for all her modesty, she is the living embodiment of the ancient beauty Wang Zhaojun, who was said to be so gorgeous that birds, upon seeing her, instantly forgot how to fly, and plummeted to the ground.

"'Peerless in her looks,'" Lu says. "'Yet she lives all by herself in a remote valley.'"

"Another one of your poems?"

"By Du Fu. To be honest, I can't remember the rest."

"What a shame."

They share a pleasant if chaotic afternoon. The crowds are fierce—nearly every square meter of sand is occupied by some mixture of Chinese, Koreans, Japanese, and lobster-skinned Russians. The water is a bit chilly for Lu's taste, but the Russians and Koreans like it fine, and suddenly so does Lu when Yanyan emerges with the waves exhibiting the effects of the cold through the thin fabric of her swimsuit.

When they have had their fill of the teeming multitudes and the sun and the sand, they take the light rail back to the hotel. They shower and dress for dinner and Lu suggests they check out the beer festival. As always, the jostling crowds are a challenge, but they manage to eat their fill and get moderately tipsy. On the way back, Lu reaches for Yanyan's hand and this time she doesn't resist. Their path takes them through the greenery of Zhongshan Square. Lu finally pulls Yanyan into his arms and kisses her, long and deep and hard. She kisses him back, the same way.

Although snogging in public is not as taboo as in years past, PDA in the People's Republic is still a relative rarity, and Lu and Yanyan earn themselves a wolf whistle from some dark corner of the park. Lu laughs, but Yanyan is embarrassed and breaks away. They continue to the hotel, where they share another kiss in the elevator. By the time they reach their room, Yanyan's inhibitions seem to have dispersed in a cloud of alcohol and pent-up desire, and they attack each other with animal ferocity. Lu has his shirt off and his hands on Yanyan's breasts when the unthinkable happens.

A knock at the door.

"Who's that?" Yanyan says.

"Who cares?" Lu growls.

The knock comes again. Insistent.

"See who it is," Yanyan says.

"It's just the turn-down service."

"This hotel isn't fancy enough to have a turn-down service."

"*Gan!*" Lu gets up, finds his shirt, shrugs into it. "Don't you move." He walks to the door and peeks through the peephole. He can't see anything. Confused, he opens the door.

Tan Meirong is standing in the hallway.

"You!" Lu barks. "What in the hell are *you* doing here?"

"I came to see if you found my sister."

"Are you kidding me? How did you even get to Dalian?"

"Bus. Did you find her?"

"NO!"

Yanyan comes up behind him. "Who's this?"

Lu grits his teeth. "This is Meirong, the sister of the missing woman I was inquiring about at the police station." He turns back to the girl. "How did you know I was here?"

"You asked me if my sister knew anyone in Dalian," Meirong says.

"No, I mean, how did you know which hotel? What room?"

"I'm smart."

"Find your own sister, then!" Lu says.

"How old are you?" Yanyan asks.

"Fifteen."

Yanyan's sisterly instinct kicks into gear. "And you're here all alone?"

"Yes."

"Oh, you poor girl. Do you want to come in?"

"She does not," Lu says. "Go home, Meirong. I told you I'd call if I found anything."

"Doesn't look like you're trying very hard," Meirong says, with a snarky glance at Yanyan.

"Good night." Lu begins to shut the door in Meirong's face.

"Brother Lu," Yanyan admonishes. She catches the door and opens it. "Come in."

"Yanyan, please," Lu begs.

"She's just a kid," Yanyan says.

Meirong is dressed in sweatpants and one of her better T-shirts and wearing a school backpack. She enters the bedroom and looks around curiously. Lu sees she's exchanged her plastic sandals for cheap tennis shoes. "Make yourself right at home," he says.

"Have you eaten?" Yanyan says.

"I brought some bread rolls with me, but I ate them all this morning."

"You must be starving. Brother Lu, let's take her down to the restaurant and get her some dinner."

"Don't encourage her," Lu says. "She's not supposed to be here."

"Where's your sense of compassion?" Yanyan asks.

"I left it over there on the bed two minutes ago," Lu says. "Maybe if Meirong goes home, you can help me find it."

"Gross," Meirong says.

Yanyan picks up her handbag and slips into her shoes. "I'll go down and find you some food," she tells Meirong. She gives Lu a disapproving look on her way out.

"Now look what you've done," Lu says.

"You're supposed to be here looking for my sister, not . . . you know."

"How did you know what hotel and room I was in?"

"I called the police station back home and told them I was Dalian PSB and was supposed to deliver some files to you."

Lu is extremely put out, but also impressed. "Let me guess—you spoke to a Constable Huang."

"I didn't catch his name. So, have you found out anything? Anything at all? Or have you been too busy with your girlfriend?"

"The local police have no reports regarding your sister or anyone answering her description. There's no record of her booking a hotel room or paying for a meal. It's as if her phone took a train here, but she didn't."

Meirong takes a seat on Yanyan's bed. "Maybe whoever kidnapped her and sold her to a Korean brothel stole her phone."

"You watch too many movies. What kind of phone did she have?"

"Same as me. A Xiaomi."

"Those phones are sold almost at cost. They're so cheap, no one would go to the trouble of stealing one."

Yanyan returns with dumplings. Meirong eats ravenously. Lu wonders how he is going to get rid of her and restart his romantic evening with Yanyan.

As it turns out, he isn't. Meirong has no place to stay, so Yanyan generously offers to share her bed for the night.

"You must be joking," Lu says.

Yanyan puts an arm around Meirong's bony shoulders, her eyes flashing. "I'm really disappointed in your coldheartedness, Brother Lu."

Lu grabs his key card and wallet. "I'm going down for a drink."

He sits in the lobby bar and fumes into a glass of beer. He's about to order another when a woman approaches him. She's thirtyish, teased and dyed hair, lots of makeup, short skirt.

"Hi," she says. "Drinking alone?"

He gives her a quick up-and-down glance, then turns back to his beer. "I'm a cop. Beat it."

The woman walks away, and out of the hotel bar, without another word.

When Lu returns to the room twenty minutes later, the lights are off and Yanyan and Meirong are asleep in their bed. Cozy as two little peas in a pod.

Lu changes into shorts and a T-shirt and plays a mobile game on his phone—one that involves lots of martial arts and slaying of bad guys—until he finally falls into a fitful sleep.

TWELVE

The next morning is Sunday, and Lu suggests returning to Raven Valley immediately after breakfast.

"I thought we were visiting the zoo?" Yanyan asks.

"I've had enough of Dalian." Lu knows he sounds petulant but cares not a whit.

"I hear the zoo has pandas?" Meirong says hopefully.

"Forget it," Lu grouses.

"Brother Lu." Yanyan puts a hand on his arm. He looks into her big brown eyes and finds himself unable to resist her insidious powers of mind control.

"Tell you what," Lu says. "I'll go back to the train station and check lost-and-found for Meixiang's phone. You two go to the zoo and I'll meet you at the station in the afternoon and we'll head home together."

He asks Meirong if her sister's phone has any distinguishing characteristics. Meirong shrugs. "Like what, a mustache? It's a phone. Same model as mine. Oh . . . she has a TNT case on it."

"TNT?"

"The music group."

"Never heard of them."

Meirong rolls her eyes. "I'm not surprised."

Downstairs, Lu puts them into a cab and tries to thrust some cash into Yanyan's hand, but she refuses. "I make my own money," she says. He watches the cab drive off, then catches one of his own to the train station.

Lu tracks down the head custodian and asks if he has a key to the lost-and-found room. "Of course," the custodian says, as if Lu is mentally deficient. "Who do you think puts all the lost stuff in there?"

The custodian unlocks the door, and inside, Lu finds shelves chock-ablock with old coats, scarves, hats, toys, earphones, glasses, and a huge bin of cell phones.

"This many?" he says in dismay.

"People lose phones all the time," the custodian answers. "Or some idiot steals one, and then discovers he can't unlock it, so he just tosses it."

Lu sorts through the bin, parsing out the Xiaomi models, of which there are more than a dozen, but none are the same model as Meirong's.

Another dead end.

He thanks the custodian and finds a noodle stand in the station for a quick lunch. As he eats, he notices a dirty and disheveled old lady digging through a nearby garbage can. He watches as she plucks out bits of uneaten food, recyclables, and anything else that catches her fancy. He sets down his chopsticks and approaches her with a friendly smile.

"Hello, Auntie. How are you today?"

The old lady gives him a suspicious look and starts to gather up her junkyard treasures and put them in a rolling cart.

"Don't be afraid," Lu says. "I mean you no harm. I'm looking for something. A phone that may have been thrown away last Saturday. Perhaps you found it in one of the garbage bins?"

She mutters to herself and starts to wheel the cart away. He catches up. "There's a reward."

The old lady stops. "Reward?" Her expression turns cagey. "How much?"

"Er . . . a hundred yuan?"

The old lady snorts and continues walking.

"One fifty," Lu says. He trots after her. "Two hundred. Final offer."

The old lady stops. "Let me see the cash."

"Really?" Lu sighs. He counts out two hundred. The old lady holds out a grimy hand. "No," Lu says. "I don't even know if you have the phone."

"I have lots of phones. *Lots!*"

"I'm looking for one in particular."

"I'll hold the money," the old lady says. "If I don't have the one you're looking for, I'll only keep half."

"Half?"

"For my troubles."

Lu almost laughs at her cheek. "Fine. Hurry it up, then."

He follows her outside the train station, across a busy intersection, and into a narrow alleyway where she and others like her have apparently made their makeshift homes—in most cases, little more than some corrugated or plastic sheeting over an old mattress or a threadbare rug. A few residents look up at Lu with eyes that brim with despair or are simply devoid of hope. Others ignore his presence altogether.

The old woman's spot consists of a reasonably clean cotton futon shielded by a tarp. An old man sits in the mouth of the shelter smoking a cigarette butt. He watches the old lady and Lu arrive with placid disinterest. The old lady takes a Styrofoam container of leftover food from her cart and gives it to the man. "Go away," she says.

"Who's this?" the old man asks, nodding at Lu.

"My boyfriend! Go on!"

The old man grudgingly takes the food and walks away. The old lady smiles at Lu, showing missing teeth. "He likes me, so he watches my stuff when I'm away." She crawls into the mouth of the shelter and rummages around in the back. Lu squats down and sees that she's got all kinds of bags and bins back there. She finds what she's looking for and drags it out into the light: a plastic shopping bag holding a variety of cell phones, chargers, power cables, and the like. She dumps the contents out onto the ground. "Look for yourself!"

Lu does. Among the pile he finds a Xiaomi that looks like it has been stepped on by an elephant, or perhaps run over by a tank. It is the same model and color as Meirong's phone. He turns it over in his hands. There's no case. He rummages in the pile and is elated to find one—it's a weird orange color and features a photograph of half a dozen skinny youths with tousled hair. There's a logo in the corner that looks like a white *N* superimposed on two black *T*s.

"Do you remember where you found this, and when?" Lu asks. "Did you see who it belonged to?"

"Maybe," the old lady says.

"Maybe yes, or maybe no?"

"Maybe yes." The old lady holds out her hand.

"Seriously?" Lu says.

"Seriously."

Lu counts out another hundred but doesn't hand it over. "First, let's hear what you saw."

"I don't remember what day it was. Could have been Saturday. Could have been Sunday. Could have been Thursday. I don't have a calendar."

"All right. And?"

"It was a man. I saw him step on it and throw it away."

"What did he look like?"

"My eyesight isn't so good these days."

"Then how do you know it was a man?"

"My eyes are good enough to tell a man from a woman!" the old lady snaps.

Lu asks in vain for a more detailed description, but one is not forthcoming. In any case, he can now be fairly certain that someone other than Meixiang carried the phone to Dalian. And he can think of only one logical reason why.

To create a false trail.

Two hours later, Yanyan and Meirong arrive from the zoo tired, hot, and happy. They tell Lu all about the pandas and the tigers and then Meirong remembers why everyone is in Dalian.

"Did you find the phone?"

"Um . . . no." He doesn't want to ruin what appears to have been an unusually pleasant morning for Meirong. Besides—until he knows for sure what happened to Meixiang, why worry her?

They board the train to Harbin. Lu buys everyone a box meal for dinner—rice, meat in a spicy sauce, oily vegetables. By the time they reach Raven Valley, the sun has set. Lu sends Meirong home in a cab and offers to drop Yanyan off on the way back to his apartment.

"That's okay," Yanyan says. "I'm going to swing by the Red Lotus."

"So late?"

"A few customers might stop in."

"It's more or less on the way."

"No, I've put you out enough this weekend." She summons a car on her phone. They wait in silence for a moment, and then she turns to him. "I realize the trip probably didn't go quite the way you'd planned."

"Understatement of the decade."

"That poor girl! I just want to feed her and take her shopping for some new clothes. Think of how sad she must be. And frightened for her sister."

"I'm thinking about it. How can I not? Wherever I go, whichever way I turn, she's there to remind me."

Yanyan takes his hand and squeezes it. "I like a man with a kind heart."

"Well . . ." Lu says.

Yanyan leans in and kisses him. Her car chooses this inopportune moment to arrive. "Good night," she says. Then she climbs into her car and is gone.

THIRTEEN

No surprise—when Lu arrives at work Monday morning, Meirong is sitting in the lobby.

He wishes he had an entire staff of constables with her same determination.

Lu enters the squad room. Sergeant Bing and constables Sun, Fatty Wang, and Li the Mute are working at their desks. Constable Sun greets him brightly. "Looks like you got some sun, Inspector!"

This tells Lu that everyone knows he spent the weekend in Dalian. Not that the trip was clandestine, of course, but Lu finds it disconcerting how quickly news of his every move spreads among the staff. And Chief Liang is the worst culprit of all. If the station were a ship, it would have sunk to the bottom of the ocean long ago.

Lu takes a seat on the corner of Sergeant Bing's desk. "I need you to file a request with Harbin Metro to review any available city surveillance footage in the vicinity of a restaurant called *Shu Qi Da Qi* for a week ago Friday through Saturday. For the purposes of investigating a missing person case."

Sergeant Bing sucks air through his teeth. "They'll never agree to that. Wouldn't it be better to just ask them to follow up themselves?"

"They won't. And you know it."

"I'll submit the request, but they won't respond for three weeks, and then they'll just say, 'Request denied.'"

"Don't worry about that. I'm going to roll out my secret weapon."

"What's that?"

"Deputy Director Song, head of Criminal Investigations Bureau, Ministry of Public Security."

"That's a sizable bomb," Sergeant Bing acknowledges.

Lu provides Sergeant Bing with additional details for the request, then goes into his office and calls Song. They have not spoken since the Mad Undertaker case, but they left on good terms.

"Inspector!" Song says. "How's business?"

"Quiet, Buddha be praised."

"As a representative of the state, Inspector, you should refrain from engaging in feudalistic superstitious practices such as worshipping Buddha. As Marx said, 'Communism begins with atheism.'"

"It was just an expression, Deputy Director."

"I'm yanking your chain. What can I do for you?"

Lu gives Song a quick rundown on Tan Meixiang and asks him to see what he can do about getting permission for Lu to review the CCTV footage he's requesting.

"Why make a big deal of this one missing girl?" Song asks. "Do you think it's related to a bigger case? A kidnapping ring or something? Is it the work of another serial killer?"

"No—I think it's just one missing girl. But her younger sister is right now sitting in our lobby and has been every day since her sister went missing."

"I hate when the relatives make you feel guilty for something terrible someone else did."

"Yes, but aside from that, I'm intrigued by the mystery of what happened to Ms. Tan. I suspect she's been murdered and someone has taken pains to cover their tracks."

Song sucks air through his teeth. "I'll make some calls."

"Thank you."

"Sure thing, but keep in mind—you've built up some credit with me through the Zeng case, but it isn't inexhaustible—so choose the chips you want to cash in judiciously."

"Understood, Deputy Director."

What follows is exasperating, but sadly, not at all surprising. Thirty minutes after he's hung up with Song, Lu is summoned by a shout from Chief Liang's office. When Lu pokes his head in, the chief says: "Shut the door." Lu does so. Liang is red-faced, and for once, not because he's been drinking. He leans down toward the phone on his desk. "Go ahead, Chief," Liang says. "Inspector Lu is here."

"Lu, this is Chief Bao," a voice growls through the phone speaker. *Ta ma de,* Lu thinks. "I hear you've been sticking your nose into Harbin police business."

Lu glares at Liang—it would have been nice to have received a warning before being tossed into the lion's den. "Well, sir, we have a missing girl's case—"

"Did she go missing in Raven Valley Township, Inspector?"

"No, sir."

"Where, then?"

Obviously, Bao knows where. "She was last seen in Harbin," Lu says.

"Ah, *Harbin!* Is your jurisdiction *Harbin*, Inspector?"

"No, sir, but—"

"Then stay the hell out of Harbin! Understand?"

"Yes, sir."

"Good. Problem solved." The line goes dead.

Liang turns off the speaker. "Nice work. You stirred up a big crock of shit."

"Something nefarious is going on here, Chief."

Liang holds up his hand. "I don't want to hear it."

"This missing girl is a nobody. So why does Harbin Metro care if I investigate? What are they hiding?"

"Do you understand the meaning of the words, 'I don't want to hear it'?"

"Someone's whispered into Bao's ear. Someone high up, because I had Deputy Director Song make a call on my behalf to get my request for surveillance footage approved."

"You called Song? What the hell were you thinking?"

"I was thinking that I'm investigating a missing person case."

"*Cao*, Lu Fei! Is this girl really worth all the fuss?"

"If she was your daughter, you'd probably think so."

Liang shakes his head angrily and smashes his cigarette into an astray. Lu takes a seat across from him. "I didn't ask you to sit down," Liang says.

"Listen, Chief—there's some kind of conspiracy going on here, and I think it's centered around this restaurant in Harbin that supposedly serves tiger penis and stuff like that."

"Ridiculous. If that were the case, the place would be shut down immediately and the owner tossed in jail."

"Officials go there. Rich people go there. The owner's got *guanxi*."

"If that's true, Lu Fei, then forget about the whole thing. If the owner has enough *guanxi* that someone feels they can ignore a direct request from Deputy Director Song at the Ministry of Public Security, you might as well try to dig up Chairman Mao and put him on trial for the Cultural Revolution."

Lu is aware that Chief Liang is not a cowardly man, but he's a seasoned vet who knows very well the risks of going up against the rich and powerful, and at this latter stage of his career, his main concern is surviving until retirement age with his pension intact.

"Chief—"

Liang massages his face with his palms. "Listen, kid. I admire your dedication. And you may be right. Perhaps the owner of this restaurant took a liking to your girl and raped her and when she said she'd go to the police, he had her killed and run through the restaurant's meat grinder. And now he's being shielded by some official who frequents the joint because he has trouble getting it up. It's a sad story, but by no means a rare one. And if you keep picking at it, you'll only end up getting yourself transferred to someplace even less exciting than Raven Valley—like the Gobi Desert. I know it's a bitter pill to swallow, but just wait a couple of weeks, mark the case as *unsolved*, and move on."

"Like I told you before, the girl's sister is sitting in our lobby. She won't quit coming here until we find Tan Meixiang."

"In a country as large and populous as the People's Republic, there are ten thousand equally tragic stories a day," Liang says. "If you obsess about every one that comes across your desk, you'll get eaten up from the inside out."

"So that's your advice? Let it go?"

Liang taps out another cigarette. "Don't go looking for trouble, kid. It will find you all by itself."

Lu goes to his office, shuts the door, calls Deputy Director Song, and gives him an update.

"I'm not surprised you're getting static," Song says. "The guy I called at Harbin Metro said the restaurant is popular with the city brass. People who might have something to lose if it's investigated."

"Who did you call?"

"One of the deputy directors. Good guy, but you know . . . he's a careerist. His number-one concern is his own ass."

"Who do you think he spoke to?"

"It doesn't really matter, Inspector. Whoever it was spread the word around until it got back to your boss's boss, which means it was at a high enough level to be dangerous for you."

"So, there's a conspiracy afoot."

"A conspiracy to shield the restaurant, yes, probably. Is there a conspiracy regarding the murder of a young girl who worked there? Who's to say?"

"I am," Lu says. "That's my job."

"Take your chief's advice, Inspector. Drop it. You'll get nowhere, apart from generating a lot of ill will and gaining some powerful enemies."

"Tall trees are known by their shadows. Good men are known by their enemies."

"Where did you hear that?"

"It's something people say."

"What people?" Song asks. "Americans? Russians? Idiots who live in a cardboard box down by the river?"

Lu sighs loudly into the phone.

"Are we done here?" Song says.

"Looks like it. Thanks for your help, Deputy Director."

"Don't get bent out of shape, Inspector. *Tang bi dang che.*" This idiom refers to a praying mantis that tries to stop a rushing chariot by holding out its tiny arms. In other words, *You can't fight city hall.*

FOURTEEN

Lu stews in his office until early afternoon and then signs out a patrol vehicle, slips out the back door of the station, and goes home to change into civilian clothes. Despite Chief Bao's angry directive, he drives to Harbin. He parks several blocks away from the *Shu Qi Da Qi* restaurant and canvasses the neighborhood, noting the position of cameras attached to light signals and utility poles. There are some blind spots, but for the most part, if Tan Meixiang left work Friday night under her own power, one of those cameras should have captured it.

Lu has brought along a Heilongjiang Lava Spring Football Club hat and he puts this on before he enters the restaurant. He hopes the hostess won't recognize him out of his uniform. He needn't have worried. There is a different, but equally attractive, hostess on duty.

"Do you have a reservation?" the hostess asks.

"No. Do I need one?"

"It's generally advised."

Lu glances over her shoulder at the dining room, which is barely one-third full at this hour. "Looks pretty empty."

"Most of the tables have been reserved."

Lu smiles sheepishly. "I understand. Please excuse me for not making a reservation. If you have a free table, I would be so grateful. Anywhere is fine, I'm not picky."

The hostess makes a show of checking her clipboard. "I can seat you now, but I'll need the table in an hour."

"No problem."

She shows Lu to a small table at the back, midway between the kitchen and the bathrooms. That serves Lu just fine. A busboy in a bow tie brings Lu a glass of water and tea. A waitress arrives. Lu orders the cheapest things on the menu. Deep-fried pork with cumin and sesame, tripe in chili sauce, and wood ears with garlic.

"Is that it?" the waitress says, her disappointment obvious.

"That's a lot for just one man."

"Depends on the man." She turns to go.

"Hold on," Lu says. He lowers his voice. "Would you happen to have any . . . specials?"

"We have the daily appetizer, main courses, and dessert—"

"No, not that. I mean . . . specials."

"Yes, we have a few. I'll bring you a list."

Could it be so easy? Lu wonders. "And a beer, please."

The waitress returns with Lu's beer and a printed sheet. Post-coronavirus, the Ministry of Agriculture issued an official directory of animals that can be farmed for meat, and others that can be farmed for fur. The first category includes the usual livestock, such as pigs, cows, poultry, and the like, and the second, foxes, racoons, and mink. Lu sees a couple of rarer items on the sheet—deer and alpaca—but nothing illegal. No tiger meat, bear paws, or pangolin.

"Is this it?" Lu asks. "Nothing more . . . exotic?"

"Sorry."

On his previous visit, Lu overheard the group of boorish men complaining that one had to be "connected" to get the "good stuff." Perhaps the *Shu Qi Da Qi* restaurant has a secret diner's membership, like a VIP club. Given the severity of punishments meted out to those who get busted violating the new restrictions, it would be prudent to thoroughly vet customers before offering them contraband dishes.

Lu drinks his beer and orders another. He notes the presence of several security cameras in the dining room. He leaves his table and goes into the bathroom. He sees nothing unusual inside, just the usual sinks and toilet stalls, and no cameras in view. He exits the bathroom and saunters by the kitchen just as a waitress comes out bearing a tray and manages to catch a quick glimpse of cooks in paper hats and aprons, steam rising from woks and pots of soup, cleavers dicing vegetables and meat with short, staccato chops.

He resumes his seat at the table and eats part of his meal and drinks his second beer. When that beer is done, he orders a third and attempts to strike up a conversation with the waitress, but she's busy and not interested in small talk. She rushes off and returns five minutes later with a Harbin lager.

"There was a girl who waited on me last time I was here," Lu says. "I don't see her now. Her name is Tan Meixiang."

The waitress shrugs indifferently. "She hasn't been here for a week or so."

"Is she on vacation?"

"I don't know. You want something else?"

"I take it you aren't friends."

"We work together, that's all. If there's nothing else—"

"Let me show you something." Lu takes his ID out of his pocket and gives her a quick flash, careful to keep a finger over his name. "PSB. Tan Meixiang is missing. Do you know anything about that?"

The waitress is suddenly wary. "No. Nothing."

"Are you aware of anything that might have happened to her?"

"Did you talk to my boss, Mr. Fang? I can get him for you."

"I spoke to him and he wasn't helpful. That's why I'm asking you. If you know something useful, you'd better tell me."

"Please don't cause trouble for me." Now she looks on the verge of tears.

"Was Ms. Tan sick?"

"I don't know."

"Was she stressed? Did she say she wanted a break?"

"We barely spoke. We only shared a handful of shifts."

"Did she mention going on vacation?"

"No . . . nothing. I hardly knew her."

"Do you have any reason to believe that Mr. Fang or anyone at this restaurant wanted to harm her?" Lu asks.

"No. I have other tables to serve." She backs away. Lu lets her go.

He figures he's got about two minutes before Fang finds out he's in the restaurant. He counts out some money and drops it on the table. He threads his way through the dining room and heads up the stairs to the second floor. He squeezes past a busboy bearing a tray of empty beer bottles on the way down.

He reaches the second floor and strolls down the corridor as if he belongs there. He hears laughter and conversation coming from inside one of the banquet rooms. The plaque over the door reads *Spring Breeze Chamber*. Another metaphor for sex. He tries the latch. It's unlocked. He opens the door.

Inside is a round table with twelve chairs, plates of pickled vegetables, shredded jellyfish, cold ham, beer, and *bai jiu* laid out neatly on its pristine white tablecloth. The walls are paneled in red and gold and inscribed with Chinese characters for health, longevity, and good fortune. An ornate chandelier hangs from the ceiling.

A half dozen men sit around the table. They are in their thirties and forties, white shirt sleeves rolled up to their elbows, and, judging from the flushed faces of some of them, several drinks in. Lu pegs them as mid-level bureaucrats, or perhaps sales managers for one of the local manufacturing or agricultural concerns. Conducting business, as business is generally conducted in the People's Republic, in an atmosphere of alcohol-induced conviviality.

There are also a few young women draped around the men. Tight dresses, painted lips, permed hair. Lu recognizes them as belonging to that class of female that has recently become as much a part of the status-obsessed culture of Chinese politics and industry as designer eyewear, Gucci loafers, and Montblanc pens: the *xiao san*, "little number threes." In other words—mistresses.

Having a woman on the side is a time-honored tradition in China. Given the cultural emphasis on having male heirs to propagate the patrilineal line, polygamy was a widespread and perfectly acceptable practice among the upper classes until the Communist Party took control of the mainland in 1949.

And old habits die hard. Nowadays, any self-respecting official or successful businessman has a girlfriend. Perhaps two. These women are known by different terms, such as *xiao san*, *xiao taitai*—meaning "little wife"—or *ernai*, a term that literally describes "a second breast to supply milk." The distinctions are a bit hazy, but these arrangements can be as loose as the occasional tryst without a specific economic compensation, or a long-term relationship in which the woman receives housing and a monthly stipend. In some first-tier Chinese cities there are even neighborhoods knowns as *ernaicun*—"*ernai* villages"—where kept women are housed near important services such as beauty parlors, clothing boutiques, and restaurants.

There is nothing illegal about having a *xiao san*, or making deals over drinks, and Lu is not taken aback by the scene in the banquet room.

One of the men turns around in his chair. "Yes?"

"Sorry, wrong room." Lu smiles and tarries a moment longer to run his eyes across the ceiling in search of a security camera. If one exists, it is carefully hidden.

The man grows annoyed. He rises from his chair. "Who are you? What do you want?"

"Apologies. Enjoy your dinner." Lu ducks out. He tries the next room. Locked. But one of the rooms farther down the hall is not, and Lu pokes his head in, ascertains that it's empty, and steps inside. He shuts the door and switches on the light. He sees the same red-and-gold-paneled walls, another round table and set of chairs. He conducts a search and, after a few minutes, finds what he's looking for, carefully concealed in the decorative molding of the ceiling—a tiny camera lens.

So, Fang *is* monitoring what transpires in these private rooms, with the customers presumably none the wiser. But the question remains—is he downloading footage from these surveillance cams? And if so, does he have a video recording that might shed some light on the fate of Tan Meixiang?

If Fang is downloading video footage, one thing's for certain: He'll now have some lovely screenshots of Inspector Lu Fei, deputy chief of the Raven Valley PSB, sticking his nose in where it's not wanted.

Lu hears voices coming down the hall. Angry, urgent. He switches off the light and huddles at the door. The voices pass. Lu gives it a moment, then opens the door and peeks out. The coast is clear.

Time to go.

Lu pads down the hall toward the stairs. As he reaches the landing, he hears the tromp of feet coming up from below. Lu makes a U-turn and rushes back down to the end of the hall. He's looking for an exit, but there isn't one. Just restrooms, more banquet rooms—and Fang's office.

The office door is open a crack. And Lu remembers there was a window inside, looking out from the back of the building. Perhaps there is a fire escape that will allow him to depart unseen. Lu ducks inside, shuts the door behind him, and locks it.

He rushes over to the window—and discovers that it is fixed. No way to open it.

Ta ma de!

Lu attempts to squelch the rising panic in his chest. It was stupid to come here. He's going to be caught red-handed, and there will be hell to pay.

What now? Lu looks around the office as if hidden somewhere within its tacky safari decor is the key to his dilemma. He sees the desk, the animal-print furniture. The antlers on the wall.

His attention is drawn to the monitor on the credenza behind the desk. It shows a split-screen view of the restaurant's surveillance feed. The dining room. The kitchen. Banquet Room #1. Banquet Room #2. And so on. Lu runs over for a closer look. Time stamps in the upper right-hand corner tick off the hours, minutes, seconds.

The office door jiggles.

Lu figures he's got one chance to get out of this office with a shred of dignity and his job intact—find something incriminating enough to warrant an illegal entry.

He checks under the desk and spies a computer tower. A line runs from the monitor on the credenza into the tower. Lu stabs the button for the disk drive. It opens to reveal—nothing. The tray is empty.

There is a second monitor on the desk, facing Fang's executive chair, this one with a screensaver featuring Fang in a series of photographs. The first shows Fang standing behind a table in one of the banquet rooms, a smug grin on his face. The table is ringed with various Harbin notables. Fang's hand rests easily on the shoulder of the vice mayor of Harbin. Seated to the vice mayor's left is Harbin's previous Communist Party deputy secretary.

If Lu recalls correctly, the vice mayor recently received an administrative demerit for his unsatisfactory response to the city's coronavirus outbreak, and the deputy secretary is currently in jail for corruption.

Still, it's clear that Fang does indeed have friends in high places.

Lu hears a key jiggling in the lock to the office door. Not much time now. He takes out his cell phone and captures the screensaver image.

The slideshow now advances to a picture of Fang in an exotic setting. Red earth, green vegetation, broadleaf evergreen trees. Behind Fang is a wire fence, and on the other side of that fence is a tiger. A big, beautiful tiger with orange fur and black stripes. Lu captures this one as well.

In the next photo, Fang is sitting at a table in a wood-paneled room. At the head of the table is a woman. The image catches her in the act of drinking from a cup, so Lu cannot see her face, just a bejeweled hand and a huge pair of sunglasses below a tangle of glossy black hair.

Lu is in the act of taking a snapshot when the office door bursts open with the force of a demolition blast.

FIFTEEN

Two busboys rush inside. Lu assumes they have been chosen for their size, as they are healthy-looking specimens. Behind them is a third man. He is tall and very thin, dressed in a white smock and pants that are sprinkled liberally with flour and sauce residue, and looks to be in his late fifties. A paper cook's hat sits on his head. Lu sees that the man is carrying a cleaver.

The last to enter is Fang himself.

Lu casually takes a seat in the chair behind the desk. "Hello, Mr. Fang. Fancy meeting you here."

"How dare you!" Fang says. There is no trace of his former smarmy politeness.

"Let me explain," Lu says.

"Get out of my chair."

"Of course." Lu stands. One of the busboys is holding a mallet of some kind—Lu assumes it's for tenderizing meat. His meat. The other has a knife. But they look scared. Lu slips his phone into a pocket and raises his hands. "I hope we aren't going to resort to physical violence."

"I've alerted the police," Fang says. "They'll be here soon."

"I *am* the police."

"That doesn't give you the right to break into my office and conduct an illegal search."

"I was looking for the bathroom and got lost."

"Fei hua!" Fang snarls. *Bullshit.* "I won't tolerate this kind of harassment. I have friends in the city government, you know."

"So it seems," Lu says, dryly. "In any case, I'm not here on business. I was curious about the cuisine. I found the pork a trifle salty, to be honest. I must be going now. I do apologize for the misunderstanding." Lu starts toward the door. The two busboys do not move to stop him. But the older man with the cleaver does.

"You're not going anywhere until the police arrive," Fang says. "And then we'll see what happens."

"I told you," Lu says. "This is all a misunderstanding. I was looking for the bathroom and got lost. The layout of this place is like a maze."

"Shen jing bing," Fang mutters. *Nutjob.*

"No need for insults, Mr. Fang." Lu takes another step forward. The cook blocks his way. He has arms like a racing dog—thin but corded with muscle. And covered with tattoos.

In recent years, Chinese hipsters, influenced by Western media and domestic rapper culture, have started to experiment with tattoo art—but for most Chinese, skin ink is a deplorable defilement of the body. Traditionally a method for identifying criminals, it remains in the public consciousness the mark of a gangster. A thug.

The cook's cleaver looks well-used and razor sharp. In contrast with the busboys, who are gripping their weapons so tightly that their knuckles are white, he holds it easily in his hand, without any signs of undo tension. And, Lu notes, he is missing one of his forefingers.

Cutting off a digit as an act of atonement is a Japanese yakuza tradition, not a Chinese one. But perhaps the tattooed man was inspired by his Japanese cousins. Or perhaps he just slipped when dicing some spring onions. Whichever the case, Lu is not concerned about the busboys, but the cook could be trouble. "You can't keep me here, Mr. Fang."

"I discovered you in the act of breaking and entering. That's illegal—even for a cop."

"If that were true—and it's not, because I told you, I was looking for the bathroom—we cops share an unspoken bond of brotherhood that leads us to treat one another kindly. If you get my drift."

"Oh, really?" Fang says, acidly. "It so happens, after you showed up at my door yesterday, I made some inquiries about you."

"Would that be because you have something to hide?"

"Not at all. It was because I wanted to know if you're the kind of policeman who goes around threatening people in order to squeeze a bribe out of them."

"I'm sure whoever you asked said that wasn't the case with me."

"Indeed, but that doesn't mean they were complimentary," Fang says.

Lu wonders who Fang might have been talking to. He pictures a jowly, liver-spotted face with pendulous lips. Xu, chief of homicide division, Harbin Metro PSB. Lu's nemesis. The man who had him booted out of Harbin and relegated to the relative backwater of Raven Valley.

If it's Xu who shows up at the restaurant, Lu will not be benefiting from the unspoken bond of brotherhood between cops. Quite the opposite.

"Move," Lu tells the cook. "I'm leaving. Now."

"You're not going anywhere," Fang says.

"What's your name, Uncle?" Lu asks the cook.

"Never mind his name," Fang says.

"I'm going to take a wild guess," Lu says, ignoring Fang. "You have a criminal record. Am I right?"

The cook doesn't respond, but his eyes flicker toward Fang, unsure.

"I'm sure you've done your best to keep your nose clean," Lu continues. "Even so . . . there's always something. Perhaps you developed a habit in prison. Amphetamines, say. And a search of your belongings might reveal some contraband."

"No," the cook says, slowly.

"I don't think you understand," Lu says. "A search of your belongings *will* reveal some contraband."

"He has no authority here," Fang says. "Don't listen to him."

Lu continues: "I'm sure you've paid your debt to society, but another black mark on your record—well, the ramifications could be serious, don't you think?"

"You have no friends in Harbin," Fang says.

"That's where you're wrong," Lu says. "I have plenty of friends.

Including some who are quite senior in the Ministry of Public Security. Don't you know I'm a bit of a hero for catching a serial killer?" Lu gives the cook a hard stare. "Get out of my way. Your cleaver's not going to stop me. And if you try, I'll put you back in a dirty hole for the rest of your natural life."

The cook stares back, but now he's fidgeting nervously with the cleaver.

"Get him!" Fang shouts at the busboys. They exchange a nervous glance, then reluctantly shuffle toward Lu.

"Don't even think about it," Lu snaps. He gives the cook a warning look and then cautiously edges around him toward the door.

"Lao Ping!" Fang protests.

The cook—Ping—doesn't move. Lu slips into the hallway. As he trots toward the stairs, he can hear Fang ripping into Ping and the hapless busboys.

Lu makes his way through the dining room and out the front entrance. Two police vehicles, lights flashing, are just now pulling up to the curb. Lu turns right and walks briskly down the sidewalk. He hears car doors slamming, the slap of boots on pavement. He half expects a heavy hand to clamp down on his shoulder, spin him around, but none comes. Lu zigzags for a couple of blocks and then winds his way back to his car. He starts the engine, cranks up the air conditioner—he's soaked with sweat—and heads for the expressway.

That was foolhardy. And although he managed to get out before he could be taken into custody, he hasn't heard the end of this. Fang will put a word into the ear of Xu or whoever his Harbin Metro contact is, and it will get back to Chief Bao. And Chief Bao will belch hellfire.

Lu decides the best way to handle the situation is just to lie his ass off. Minus a video recording of Lu snooping around, it will be his word against Fang's. And Fang has put himself in a difficult position by denying he is downloading footage. He can't very well produce evidence of Lu without admitting to the contrary. Given the drinking, the whoring, and the contraband dining that occurs in those banquet rooms, Fang's clients—his very powerful and connected clients—would be extremely dismayed to learn that Fang has been making home movies.

Lu hasn't even yet merged onto the expressway when his cell phone rings. Chief Liang.

That was fast.

Lu ignores Liang's repeated calls until he's on the outskirts of Raven Valley Township and then he picks up.

"Why the hell don't you answer your phone?" Liang shouts.

"Sorry, Chief, I didn't see that you were calling."

"Because you were too busy breaking into the one place you were told to stay away from?"

"What place is that, Chief?"

"Don't lie to me, Lu Fei. I know you signed a patrol vehicle out. And the owner of that restaurant caught you in his office, searching through his desk! Chief Bao is beside himself! He's going to castrate you with a soup spoon!"

"I categorically deny that I was at the restaurant, Chief."

"You . . . you . . ." Liang sputters.

"Does Fang have some sort of proof that I was there?"

"He saw your stupid face! *Ta ma de niao!*"

"No need to bring my mother into this, Chief."

"Damn it, Lu Fei! It's not a joke! Bao's really in a lather. Do you want to get your ass fired? Do you want to get *my* ass fired?"

"No, and no. I'm just trying to get to the bottom of this missing person case."

"And if you keep pushing, you'll see how far down the bottom really is and suck me down there with you. I don't know who the hell this Fang guy is connected to, but whoever it is, they've got enough weight to lean on Bao. And Bao would throw his own mother under a bullet train if it was politically expedient. Do you get me?"

Lu sighs. "Yes, I get you."

"I want you to call Chief Bao and kowtow your ass off."

"No, Chief, that I will not do."

"Lu Fei—"

"Listen, Chief. Tell Bao I denied ever being there. Bao won't believe it, but Fang can't prove anything without implicating himself in a dangerous lie, so he'll just drop it."

"So, you *were* there."

"I didn't say that, Chief. Perhaps it was someone who looked like me. Or Fang made the whole thing up."

Liang snorts. "I know you're trying to do the right thing, kid. But don't be a sap. Chances are the girl's just run off, or she got drunk and fell into the Songhua River."

"What about the fact that I found her phone mangled in Dalian and a witness says an unidentified male had it in his possession?"

"Who was your witness?"

"A, uh . . . homeless lady."

"Right. Good luck with that one. Maybe the girl's phone got stolen in Harbin and whoever took it got cold feet and decided to dump it. Did you think of that possibility? There's absolutely no evidence to suggest this guy Fang killed her."

"But he might have. Or someone in the restaurant, perhaps an official or rich businessman did, and Fang is covering it up. The fact that he's so concerned about me showing up on his doorstep is a sign of his guilt."

"Perhaps it's more straightforward. Fang doesn't want you nosing around because he's serving pangolin snouts to rich and powerful people. And *they* don't want to be caught doing something so flagrantly illegal. The girl isn't part of the equation."

"Fang's overreaction tells me different."

"Damn it, kid, back off. Give it some time. If there truly was a crime committed, somebody will get a guilty conscience and talk. Or make a mistake, implicate themselves. These scumbags always do, sooner or later."

"Meanwhile, what about the missing girl's kid sister who sits in our lobby every day?"

"You can't save the world."

"Then why did I become a cop?"

"Regular pay. Cool uniform."

"Nice, Chief."

Liang lets out a breath. "I'll see if I can cool Bao off. And I'll let him know about your suspicions regarding Fang. Aside from that, all we can do is wait for the other shoe to drop. In the meantime, you are under strict orders to leave Fang and his restaurant alone. I mean it. Full stop, or I'll put you on leave."

Lu hangs up, deflated and demoralized. He returns to the *paichusuo* and drops off the patrol vehicle. He collects his bicycle and rides to the Red Lotus where he attempts to drink away his angst. Yanyan sees that he's feeling down and tries to cheer him up with free snacks. But after two pots of Shaoxing wine, she cuts him off.

"Tomorrow's another day," Yanyan says. "Go home, drink lots of water, and get some sleep. Things will seem better in the morning."

Lu rides back to his apartment, drinks a liter of water, and flops into bed. Just before he drifts off, he remembers Chief Liang's words: "All we can do is wait for the other shoe to drop."

As it turns out, they don't have to wait long.

SIXTEEN

Following Lu Fei's escape, Wilson Fang viciously chews out Lao Ping and the two busboys, his verbal assault tempered only by concern that the guests in the banquet room down the hall might hear him cursing and yelling.

When he is finished, he wipes spittle from his lips and tells the busboys they have five minutes to collect their things.

"You're . . . you're firing us?" one of them sputters.

"Yes, genius!" Fang barks. "Piss off!"

The downcast busboys shuffle out of the office.

Fang turns to Lao Ping. "I'm very disappointed in you."

Lao Ping shrugs. "He was a cop. I don't want to go back to prison."

"He's a cop from some nothing township in the boondocks. He means nothing!"

"Then why are you so worried?"

Fang waves a hand angrily: "Get out."

Lao Ping leaves, shutting the office door. Fang slumps into his executive chair. He lights a 555 cigarette, unlocks a drawer in his desk, and takes out the prepaid cell phone.

That evening, he plays the dutiful host, greeting guests, doling out smiles and friendly pats on the back. Business is not bad for a Monday. Some notables from the Harbin Overseas Chinese Affairs office have taken over one of the banquet rooms and stocked it with cheap tarts in tight skirts and rivers of alcohol. They cajole Fang into drinking a round of *bai jiu*, then another. The deputy director, an arrogant young man who has obtained his position through family connections, takes advantage of the boisterous atmosphere to stick his hand up the skirt of one of the girls. She reacts by slapping him across the face. Everyone roars with laughter—apart from the girl and the deputy director, who wraps his hand around the girl's throat and starts to squeeze.

Fang quickly steps in and pries the two apart. He shoves the girl out of the room and calls for another round to be poured. He lights a cigarette for the young man, then toasts him with *bai jiu*. Everyone drinks, and order is quickly restored.

Fang finds the girl sniffling in the hallway. He hands her some cash. "If you're going to run with a pack of wolves, don't act surprised when they bite." He pushes her toward the stairs. "Get out. And I don't want to see you here again."

As it grows late and the last of the customers make their way home, Fang retreats to his office and pours himself a drink. He enters the password in his desktop computer and quickly reviews the daily footage from the restaurant's CCTV cameras. Aside from the incident with the tart at the Overseas Chinese Affairs dinner—and Lu's intrusion, of course—there's nothing worth saving. He downloads the most interesting snippets to his cell phone and erases the rest of the footage.

His nightly ritual.

He lights a cigarette and waits for his business manager to finish counting the day's take and bring it up to him. He yawns and blows smoke rings at the ceiling.

11:07 p.m.

He hears a loud pop from downstairs. He sits up in his chair, suddenly wide awake.

Fang has hunted wildebeest, buffalo, and warthogs in Africa. Monkeys and elephants in Southeast Asia. He knows a gunshot when he hears it.

Fang slips his phone into his pocket and runs to the office door. He looks out. He hears a scream—female. The only employees who are still in the building are the cook and the business manager, Ms. Zhang. The scream is undoubtedly hers.

Gan!

Fang considers locking himself in his office. The door is sturdy, but the lock won't hold up to a bullet.

More screams. Getting closer.

He sees Zhang stumble onto the landing at the far end of the hallway. She shrieks for help.

A figure, dressed in dark clothes, a cap and face mask obscuring their face, emerges from the stairwell behind Zhang. Zhang scrambles to her feet and sprints toward Fang, her face twisted in fear. Another loud *POP*. Zhang's blood splatters on the ceiling and walls.

There's a bathroom down the hall. A small window opens to the outside—Fang's not even sure he can squeeze through it, and it's a three-meter drop to the ground below.

It's his only chance.

He races to the bathroom door, wrenches it open, slips inside. He rushes into the stall, climbs onto the toilet seat, tugs the tiny window open. He squeezes his shoulders through the narrow space. It's tight. He's not going to make it.

He pictures the shooter coming through the door, putting a bullet up his ass.

This image spurs Fang to worm his way forward until his torso droops over the windowsill. He looks down—a concrete alleyway looms below. At this height, if he drops head-first, he'll break his neck.

Fang grips the sill underhanded and jackknifes his hips and legs through. One of his hands slips and he swings wildly by one arm. His shoulder cracks with the strain.

He hears the bathroom door bang open. It's do or die.

Fang lets himself drop the last couple of meters. He hits the pavement, rolls. He gets up—his ankle gives out and he falls. He looks up, sees a shadow framed in the bathroom window.

Fang pushes to his feet and, ignoring the pain, runs for his life.

SEVENTEEN

Lu is jarred from sleep by a phone call at 6:00 a.m. The caller is Chief Liang. Lu knows it's serious before he even answers—Liang is not an early riser.

"Please tell me you didn't do it," Liang says.

"Do what?" Lu can't issue a blanket denial because he has no idea what Liang is referring to, so he may *well* have done whatever it is.

"Where were you around eleven last night?"

"Asleep."

"Can you prove that?"

Lu sits up, suddenly alarmed. He doesn't like being on the opposite end of an interrogation. "What's going on, Chief?"

"There was a shooting at the restaurant last night. Fang's restaurant."

"Details, please."

"At least one employee dead, another wounded, and the gunman got away."

"What about Fang?"

"He's missing," Liang says. "So, you weren't involved in any way?"

"Hell, no, Chief. Do you think he's been kidnapped?"

"I don't know. I don't care. I'm worried about Bao, not Fang. He wants to meet with us."

"Fang?"

"Chief Bao, damn it!"

"You told him I didn't do it," Lu says.

"Of course I did. Not even you are dumb enough to go back there and get yourself into a shoot-out."

"Thanks for the vote of confidence."

"But just for the sake of discussion, do you have an alibi? Perhaps you spent the night with a pretty bar owner?"

"Sadly, no. As I told you, though—Fang has surveillance cameras all over the building. I bet there's footage of the shooting. And if Harbin Metro finds it, they might as well have a look at the tape from a week ago Friday night to see if there's any sign of foul play regarding Tan Meixiang."

"I'll be sure to let them know how to do their jobs," Liang says, sourly.

"If there's a dead employee, that makes it a homicide case. Which means that bastard 'Flounder Face' Xu will have oversight."

"You have bigger problems than your ex-boss, kid. Your own ass, for one. More importantly, my ass."

"Xu's dirty. And he's incompetent."

"Are you listening to me?"

"Maybe we can get the Criminal Investigations Bureau involved? Or at least have an honest cop put in charge?"

"Pay attention! Chief Bao! Noon, at his office. That's what you should be worried about."

"All Bao has to do is ping my phone," Lu says. "He'll see I was here, at my apartment, all night."

"Don't be a dope, kid. Any criminal worth his salt knows a phone can be tracked and plans accordingly."

"The surveillance footage, then. That will provide answers. As long as it doesn't 'accidentally' get erased by Xu."

"Noon! Bao's office!"

After Lu hangs up with Liang, he's too wired to go back to sleep. He makes himself tea and sits in his bed while he drinks it.

What to make of the shooting? Is someone trying to tie up loose ends? Are the rats starting to eat their own?

And is Fang dead, or just hiding out?

Lu finishes his tea, showers, dresses in his uniform, and rides his bike to the *paichusuo*. Naturally, he finds Meirong sitting in the lobby. The sight of her suddenly infuriates him.

"You can't do this every day," Lu snaps.

"Why not?"

"Because squatting here like a beggar isn't going to make things move any faster!"

"But you haven't found out a single thing!" Meirong says.

"Damn it!" Lu barks. "I don't know where your sister is. We may never know, and that's just how it is!"

Meirong bursts into tears.

"Wo kao," Lu mutters. He sits on the bench and puts a hand on Meirong's shoulder. Her bones feel as thin as a bird's. He wills himself to speak calmly. "I can't promise you that your sister is okay. That would be a lie. I know it's hard, but you have to prepare yourself for the possibility that she's . . . gone." Meirong's sobs redouble. "What I *can* promise you is that I won't quit looking for her. However long it takes. Weeks. Months. Forever."

Lu goes to the reception window, asks Fatty Wang to pass him over a box of tissues and to summon Constable Sun. He returns to the bench and sets the box beside Meirong. "I have your phone number and I will call the moment I have news."

When Sun emerges from the squad room, her face drops at the sight of the girl's distress. "Please take her home," Lu says.

Sun puts her arm around Meirong. "Come on, Little Sister." Lu walks them out and flags down a taxi. He watches them drive away, feeling both guilty and relieved.

Lu makes himself a thermos of tea and goes to his office. He logs in to a provincial crime database to have a look at the police report regarding the shooting at Fang's restaurant. It reads, in part:

On July 23rd, at approximately 11:21 PM, officers responded to reports of shots fired at the Shu Qi Da Qi restaurant, 233 Pingan Road. One employee was discovered shot to death in the second-floor hallway. A second employee was shot but survived and is in stable condition. The deceased was identified as Ms. Zhang Meitan, the restaurant's business manager. The surviving employee was Mr. Ping Xiong, a cook.

Mr. Ping maintains that he was finishing up in the kitchen at the close of business when a male suspect entered through the back door at approximately 11:00 PM. He confronted the suspect and sustained a gunshot wound to the chest. He lost consciousness and did not revive until after officers were on the scene.

The door to an office on the second floor belonging to the restaurant's owner and manager, Mr. Fang Da-an (A.K.A. Wilson Fang), was found open. It is not known if anything was taken from the office.

A single 5.8-millimeter projectile was recovered from each of the victims. No cartridge casings were present at the scene.

Mr. Ping maintains that he does not know if Mr. Fang was in his office at the time of the shooting. Mr. Fang's current whereabouts are unknown.

Appended to the report are a few grainy screenshots of the suspect taken from neighborhood surveillance cams. This pisses Lu off, as he was stymied in his effort to obtain similar photos dating to the night Tan Meixiang went missing. In any case, the screenshots don't show much. The suspect appears to be male, of average size, wearing dark clothes, a hat, and a cotton face mask.

Lu sips tea and mulls over the report. A single shooter using 5.8-millimeter ammunition. This caliber is unique to firearms manufactured in China for the use of the People's Liberation Army. But the theft and sale of PLA handguns is rampant on the black market, so the caliber isn't necessarily significant.

As for the surviving employee, Ping Xiong—Lu distinctly remembers Fang calling the tattooed man with the cleaver *Lao Ping*. *Lao* meaning "old," a term meant to denote familiarity, intimacy, rather than age. Ping is a common surname, but they must be one and the same person.

If Lu were a betting man, he'd wager his paltry pension that Ping knows more about the shooting than he's letting on. Unfortunately, he doesn't dare risk going to the hospital to question the old cook. He's already in hot water with Bao. Best not to push his luck.

Chief Liang comes looking for him just after 11:00 a.m. His shirt is ironed, his pants creased, and his expression grim. "Let's go, you dumb bastard."

They drive to the county PSB headquarters and are told to wait in a conference room. Chief Bao keeps them on ice for an hour, during which Lu's cell phone rings twice with an unknown number. He ignores it. Liang fiddles with an unlit cigarette. Lu doesn't recall ever having seen him so nervous.

"It'll be fine, Chief," Lu says.

"Will it, though?"

Bao finally appears. He slams the door and immediately starts yelling and doesn't stop for several minutes. Lu is taken aback by Bao's vehemence. He begins to suspect he's underestimated the trouble he's in.

"But Chief—" Lu protests.

"Shut it!" Bao shouts. "I don't want to hear your bullshit denials. And YOU!" He jabs a blunt finger at Liang. "Can't you keep your people under control?"

"But Chief—" Lu protests again.

"Aside from harassing an important member of the Harbin business community," Bao continues, "you conducted an illegal search of his premises! After I expressly told you in no uncertain terms to stay the HELL out of HARBIN!"

Lu opens his mouth, then shuts it, realizing that defending himself is a futile effort.

"And another thing!" Bao punctuates his words with fist pounds on the table. "I have it on good authority that you brought a twelve-year-old girl with you while conducting your unauthorized investigation."

"She's actually fifteen," Lu says.

"Never mind the flouting of protocol!" Bao's face turns an alarming shade of purple. "How about the liability risk? What if she'd accused you of rape?"

This is more than Lu can bear. "I would never!"

"That's not the point, you idiot!" Bao's fit has reached its crescendo. "I don't care that you caught the Mad Undertaker. Right now, I could give two shits if you solved every unsolved murder in Heilongjiang Province. I won't tolerate disobedience among my ranks. Understand? You are hereby suspended pending review."

"Chief Bao, may I just say—" Liang starts.

"Nothing!" Bao shouts. "You may say nothing! Be glad you, at least, still have a job! For the time being, anyway. Now both of you—get out of my sight!"

Liang seethes in the car on the way back to Raven Valley.

"Could have been worse," Lu finally says.

"How, Lu Fei? How could it have been worse?"

"You're still chief. And I didn't get fired . . . exactly."

"No," Liang says. "First will come the review. Then will come the firing. And I'll probably get a demerit. Thanks, kid. Thanks a whole boatload."

Lu knows Liang is right. He feels bad for putting him in a difficult position. And worse regarding his own potential fate. He cannot remember a time when he did not want to be a police officer. It's been his sole career focus and the one constant in his life. If he's cashiered now, what will he do with the rest of his life? Sell shoes? Raise pigs? Work in private security? "I'm sorry, Chief."

"I told you," Liang says. "I told you, but you never listen. It's a shame. You're a good cop. A great cop. But you refuse to play the game. So, you're bound to always lose."

"That's a bit harsh."

"Am I wrong? Am I?"

Lu glares out the window. He can't bring himself to say it, but no—Liang is not wrong.

Thirty minutes later, Liang pulls up to the front of Lu's apartment building. "That's it, then. I'll let you know when the review is scheduled."

"What about the cases I'm working?"

"Sergeant Bing will sort them out."

"So, I'm completely cut off?"

"That's what being suspended means, kid. Look it up if you don't believe me."

"But Chief—"

"Don't *but Chief* me. You have only yourself to blame. Get out of the car."

Lu steps out and slams the door hard enough to rattle the car frame. He catches sight of himself in the reflection of the side window. Who is this imposter in a police uniform?

The window rolls down and Liang leans over. "Listen, kid . . . I know you were just trying to do the right thing. Keep your nose clean until the review. Maybe we can get Deputy Director Song to speak on your behalf. All hope is not lost, but don't do anything stupid in the meantime. Get me?"

"Yes, boss."

"See you around."

Liang rolls up the window and drives away.

Lu goes upstairs and unlocks the door to his apartment. He strips off his uniform and sprawls on the bed in his underwear. He lies there, staring at the ceiling.

His phone buzzes. No caller ID, same as when he was waiting for his dressing-down from Chief Bao. He answers: "Lu Fei."

"Good morning, Inspector." A male voice, one he doesn't recognize. "Do you have a moment to speak privately?"

"Who is this?" Lu says.

"You can call me Mr. Jia."

"I don't like playing games, Mr. Jia. State your business, or I'm going to hang up."

"My business is Wilson Fang."

This stops Lu short. "I'm not sure I heard you correctly."

"Wilson Fang is a criminal. But as I think you've already discovered, he has some powerful friends."

"What crimes has he committed, specifically?"

"Not over the phone. Can we meet?"

"Who are you?"

"At the moment, all I can say is that I occupy an important position in a particular government ministry. And for that reason, I must be very cautious. I'm not going to say anything more over the phone. Do you want to meet or not?"

"Why do you want to meet with *me*?" Lu asks.

"I am aware of your queries regarding Fang and his restaurant. And I believe we can help each other. So, decide. Yes, or no?"

Lu thinks for a moment. Notwithstanding Liang's sage advice, what does he have to lose? "Yes."

"Harbin, Nangang District, eight p.m. I'll text you shortly before the appointed time to give you an exact meeting place. Come alone. No weapons, no recording devices."

"Why should I trust you?"

"You shouldn't. You shouldn't trust anyone."

The line goes dead.

EIGHTEEN

At the appointed hour, Lu sits in a rented car on a side street in Nangang District, keeping an eye on his cell phone. The minutes slowly roll past. Lu grows exasperated. This mysterious Jia character has gotten cold feet. At 8:25 p.m., he switches on the car ignition and prepares to go home.

Then his phone vibrates. A text: *Harbin Harmony Hotel. Room 302.*

Lu is unfamiliar with the Harmony Hotel. He looks up the location—it's not far. He drives there and discovers it is a nondescript establishment of the kind that businessmen take bar hostesses to for a night of drunken, fumbling sex.

Lu enters the lobby. There is a young woman in a white shirt and cheap uniform jacket seated at the reception desk. As Lu is wearing civilian clothes, she barely gives him a second glance.

Lu takes the stairs up to the third floor. He walks down the hallway to the far end, where he checks to make sure the stairwell is empty. He returns to room 302 and listens at the door. He can hear a TV, a snippet of music, a snatch of conversation, but these are all coming from the neighboring rooms. Lu lightly tries the door latch. Locked. He knocks and steps to one side.

He hears the click of a dead bolt. The rattle of a door chain. The door opens and a young man appears. He's a bit shorter than Lu, dressed in jeans and a short-sleeved shirt. His arms are muscular, his neck thick, jaw square, nose flat. His skull looks like it could take a couple of decent whaps with an iron bar and not suffer much in the way of consequences.

The young man glances both ways down the hallway, then motions for Lu to enter.

Lu hesitates. He was expecting a chubby middle-aged bureaucrat. This man has the look of a thug. "You're not Jia. Where is he?"

"You can speak to him inside. Don't linger out there in the hallway."

Lu has a decision to make. Walk into a hotel room with a stranger. Or turn around and leave. And forget about any dirt this Mr. Jia may or may not have on Fang.

"Back up," Lu says. The young man retreats. Lu enters the room. He pokes his head into the bathroom. It's empty, the shower curtain pulled aside. Lu closes the door behind him and follows the young man deeper into the room. He sees a queen bed, a nightstand, a dresser with a TV, a writing desk and chair. A window, curtains drawn. A closet, the sliding door open to reveal a few naked hangers and a hotel safe.

Lu checks the floor for plastic sheeting. He has seen Hollywood movies in which an assassin lays out a tarp before murdering someone to avoid making a mess. But there is no plastic here, just cheap brown carpeting with stains of undetermined source and vintage. "All right. Here I am. Now, where's Jia?"

The young man points to a laptop computer sitting on the desk. Lu's attention is momentarily captured by his hands. More specifically, his knuckles. They are swollen and discolored. Heavily calloused.

Lu once had a martial arts instructor with hands like that. The instructor's daily routine included slapping and chopping at canvas bags filled with sand, thrusting his fingers into a pot of metal pellets, and punching a wooden post. After each session he would massage his knuckles and fingers with a special liniment that smelled strongly of herbs and alcohol.

This form of training is known as "iron palm," and it is designed to generate strikes sufficient to break bricks and stones—and human bones.

Lu distinctly remembers that the instructor's hands were as rough as sandpaper, and even one of his lazy swipes felt like a blow from a sledgehammer.

A voice comes from the computer: "Inspector, please forgive me for not coming in person."

Lu walks over to the desk. A man smiles out from the computer screen. He's dressed in a suit and tie and sitting at a desk in an office somewhere. There's an elaborate departmental plaque on the wall over his right shoulder—yellow, blue, red, and green. Lu doesn't recognize the design. "You must be joking," he says. "A video conference?"

"I apologize," Jia says. "I have appointments in Beijing I could not reschedule. This is the next-best option. Can you step a bit closer to the camera? You're partially out of frame."

Lu hesitates. He glances at the young man warily. The young man stares back with a blank expression. Lu reluctantly moves in front of the camera. "Please tell me why I am here, Mr. Jia, and be quick about it."

"Of course," Jia says. The video feed freezes, pixelates, then resolves itself, catching Jia in the middle of a sentence: ". . . my trusted assistant. His surname is Bang and we need not fear having a candid discussion in his presence." Lu takes it that Jia is referring to the young man. "Perhaps you'd be more comfortable sitting down?"

"I wouldn't. Get to the point."

"The point, Inspector, is that you and I share a common interest. Wilson Fang."

"And what's *your* interest in him?"

"I am a highly ranked administrator in the National Forestry and Grassland Administration. My specific area of responsibility relates to wildlife conservation. Wilson Fang has made a small fortune serving his customers meat from endangered animals. And for this, he must be brought to justice. But he has many friends, as you have discovered. Some of my own colleagues, as well as those in other government ministries, are his clients. It is not in their best interest to have him exposed. Even now, they shield him. Consequently, although his hands are steeped in blood, I can do nothing through regular channels. Do you understand my dilemma?"

"Yes. You're looking for someone to do your dirty work for you."

"This is a dirty business, Inspector. I require someone to help me administer a cleansing."

The video feed freezes again, then restarts.

"Looks like we have a bad connection," Lu says.

"I'm routing this through a proxy server to avoid prying eyes, and it's causing some streaming issues. I consider poor video a small price to pay for security."

"Why have you reached out to *me*?"

"Despite the lack of official support, I continue to keep close tabs on Fang. Naturally, word of your investigation into the missing girl reached my ears. I was curious, so I did some digging into your background, and what I discovered was most intriguing. Graduate of Beijing People's Police College. Ten years serving various roles in the Harbin PSB. Promoted to deputy chief of the Raven Valley station."

"I'm familiar with my own résumé, thanks."

"Word is that your transfer to Raven Valley was related to a disagreement you had with your supervisor, a man named Xu, who is now chief of homicide in Harbin. Although the details of this disagreement are not a matter of public record, rumor is you caught Xu in a compromising situation, and he exiled you. So, in addition to your exemplary background and experience, I surmised that you are a man of principle."

"No need to slap the horse's ass quite so hard, Mr. Jia."

"I am just answering the question of why *you*, Inspector."

Lu doesn't trust a strange face on a computer screen, but he does want to hear what this Jia knows. "What can you tell me about Fang's involvement in the disappearance of the girl? Because that's why *I'm* interested in him."

"At the moment, nothing. But if we work together, we can kill two vultures with one arrow."

"And the shooting at the restaurant?" Lu asks.

"Ahh," Jia says. "That, I can shed some light on. Captain, if you please?"

Bang produces a folder and hands it to Lu. Inside is a photograph—in lurid color—of a dead man.

The man is dressed in dark clothing. There is a neat round bullet hole in his forehead. His eyes are half-lidded, and his mouth open as if he were killed in midsentence. Additional photos show the setting—an empty warehouse. A hat, cotton face mask, and gun lie on the ground next to the dead man. The gun is a black automatic.

"His name is Guo Ming," Jia says. "And he is—was—a contract killer. Among other things. You can read all about him in your law enforcement database, but for the sake of convenience, I've included a copy of his police record in the folder."

Beneath the photograph, Lu discovers two printed sheets detailing Guo's criminal history, which is extensive. "This is the guy who tried to kill Fang?"

"Yes," Jia says.

"How do you know?"

"Time-stamped CCTV footage shows Guo arriving and departing the area. Facial recognition technology confirms his identity. It's all there in black and white."

Lu sits on the edge of the bed and shuffles through screenshots taken from neighborhood surveillance cameras: a man wearing dark clothes, a cap, and a face mask on a motorcycle; the same man walking on a street; the man captured in the act of looking up as he adjusts his cotton face mask; the same shot, this time overlaid with a surface geometry map comparing his face to Guo Ming's official ID photo.

Lu shrugs. "I don't know what to make of this. Even if it proves Guo was the shooter, which it doesn't, it doesn't tell me why he was trying to kill Fang. And why he was subsequently killed."

"As you are no doubt aware, Inspector, the illegal animal trade and narcotics are closely related. Same smuggling routes, many of the same players. My guess is that Wilson Fang decided to diversify his portfolio and add heroin and methamphetamines to his menu and in so doing, earned the disapproval of a rival, so they hired Guo to kill him. Then they killed Guo, either because he failed, or because he was a loose end."

"Sounds like wild conjecture."

"A hypothesis based on evidence."

"Which rival?"

"I don't know. And honestly, I don't care. Narcotics is not my concern. My goal is to bring Fang down for peddling illicit animal products."

"How can you be so sure he got away?" Lu says.

"CCTV footage shows him leaving the district on foot following the shooting."

"And then?"

"And then nothing. It's like he vanished in a puff of smoke. Nobody knows where he is."

"But something tells me," Lu says, "you do."

NINETEEN

"Tell me, Inspector," Jia says. "What do you know about Myanmar?"

In truth, Lu thinks, *not much*. "It's a country south of China famous for opium, wild animals, and political instability."

"An accurate, if incomplete, assessment. Most Westerners know it as Burma, although it was officially renamed Myanmar in the 1980s. Hold on."

Jia disappears from the screen and is replaced by a map of Myanmar—a splotch of land squeezed between China, Laos, Thailand, the Andaman Sea, Bangladesh, and India. An enviable, but precarious, position.

"You know of the recent violence there?" comes Jia's voice.

"Vaguely."

"Beijing has economic and political interests in Myanmar, including the sale of weapons to the *Tatmadaw*, Myanmar's armed forces—so naturally, Chinese media sources aren't anxious to go into specifics. Suffice to say, the *Tatmadaw* engineered a coup—not for the first time—and hundreds of protestors have been killed in the ensuing conflict.

"This is adding fuel to an already highly volatile situation. Myanmar has been mired in nearly constant civil war since it achieved independence in 1948—mainly ethnic and religious groups fighting against the *Tatmadaw* to achieve political autonomy. As it stands, the country is currently a patchwork of mini fiefdoms ruled by these groups, all of whom are heavily militarized.

"One such region lies on the border of Yunnan Province. It's under the control of a Burmese militia group that is ethnically Chinese—the official language, street signs, TV broadcasts, and so on are all in Mandarin. Renminbi is even the currency of exchange."

On-screen, a portion of the map is highlighted in red. Lu sees it's a sizable chunk of the country that touches on Laos and Thailand and shares a few hundred kilometers of border with southern China.

"Fang's main supplier of animal products operates from a hidden facility in this region," Jia continues. "Her name is Daw Khaw. In addition to breeding endangered animals, she manufactures heroin, meth, and, lately, fentanyl."

Lu remembers the photograph he saw on Fang's computer—the woman sitting next to Fang, a cup lifted at just the right moment to obscure her face. "And you think Fang has run off to take shelter with this Khaw woman?"

"Yes. We don't know much about her, including her real name. *Daw* is an honorific, like 'Lady.' And *Khaw* is a Burmese form of the Chinese surname 'Xu.' It's said her father was Chinese and mother Dai."

Lu recalls that the Dai are an ethnic minority prevalent in Yunnan Province. He pictures beautiful women wearing colorfully embroidered sarongs and tall conical bamboo hats. "What *do* you know about her?"

Jia's face reappears on the computer screen. "She's around fifty years of age. Intelligent, well connected. Rumor has it she was either a prostitute who slept her way into a position of influence, or a guerilla soldier whose utter ruthlessness earned her the notice of local leaders."

"A whore or a killer, huh?" Lu asks. "No middle ground?"

"I'm just relating word on the street, Inspector."

"This sounds like a job for the Ministry of Foreign Affairs. Why can't they lean on the Chinese militia to shut down Khaw's operation and extradite Fang?"

"If only it were that simple. The militia is closely tied to Beijing and receives financial and material support in return for . . . a certain measure of loyalty. The militia currently denies Khaw's very existence and our government finds it convenient to believe them."

"Well, sounds like you're screwed, Mr. Jia. Thanks for wasting an evening I could have spent in a more productive fashion."

"Such as drinking at the Red Lotus?"

Lu is startled. "What do you know about that?"

"As I said, I've done some digging into your background."

Lu stands. "Goodbye."

"Don't be hasty, Inspector. Don't you want to know what happened to the waitress?"

"Yes, but the one man who can tell us is unreachable."

"No one is unreachable, Inspector. I have a plan."

"I'm sure you do."

"If I can obtain incontrovertible proof of Khaw's location and establish Fang's presence there—I just might be able to get him extradited and her shut down."

"How do you intend on doing that, short of me going down there and snapping some candids of the two of them lounging on a tiger skin smoking dope?"

"Why, it's like you're reading my mind, Inspector."

"I was joking."

"I'm not."

"But—" Lu sputters.

"I'm asking you to pose as a buyer of exotic bushmeat to infiltrate Khaw's facility and help us obtain its exact GPS coordinates. That will give me sufficient justification to requisition satellite images. If those images show evidence of drug manufacturing—which I'm sure they will—the National Narcotics Control Commission will take notice. And the commission is too large for any one bad actor to derail, so once that happens, a reckoning for Khaw is inevitable."

"And Fang?"

"Caught red-handed in a lie, the militia will do what's necessary to preserve Beijing's patronage, including handing over Fang. And once extradited, I promise you he will tell us whatever we want to know about this missing girl."

"Your man Bang here looks like he can handle himself. Why not just send him?"

"I told you . . . I don't know who I can trust even in my own organization. Out of an abundance of caution, I am assuming Khaw has access to the identities of NFGA employees. I need an outsider. Someone who has investigatory experience, and who is smart enough, motivated enough—and foolhardy enough—to yank a tooth from the mouth of a tiger."

Lu must admit Jia's plan has a certain crazy logic to it. "This kind of thing really isn't my cup of tea."

"Captain Bang will be watching your back the entire time, should you get into trouble."

"Captain of what? The high school ping-pong team?"

"Special forces," Bang chimes in.

"Which branch?" Lu asks.

"Classified."

"Naturally." Lu turns back to the computer screen. "Let's say I succeeded in this ridiculous plan of yours and made it to Khaw's location. Let's say, further, Fang is actually there. He's seen my face, you know. How long before he has me hung upside down and gutted like a pig?"

"You'd be surprised at what a haircut, a pair of glasses, and a change of clothes can do," Jia says.

"You can't be serious!"

"I can provide you with some research papers to prove my point, Inspector. Simple disguises are surprisingly effective."

Lu shakes his head. This Jia has an answer for everything. "Unfortunately, there's a monkey wrench in your plan. I just got sacked."

"Really?" Jia has the gall to sound amused. "Because of your investigation?"

"Correct."

"Then you can be assured you're sniffing around the right bush."

"Perhaps," Lu says. "But I'm no longer PSB."

"So much the better. Now you can pursue your mission without having to come up with an excuse for taking a leave of absence."

"You're kind of a selfish jerk, aren't you?"

"Let me offer you a bonus. If you succeed in bringing Fang to justice, I can get you reinstated."

"How do you figure?"

"Think of it this way. Once Fang starts talking, whoever has been running interference behind your back will either be up on conspiracy charges or, if they have any sense at all, will just fade into the woodwork. The heat will be off."

"Maybe, maybe not."

"And I can put a word in some ears. Who knows? You might even end up with a promotion!"

"I don't care about a promotion."

"Do you care about getting your job back?"

"Yes, but I'm no secret agent," Lu says. "I'm just a simple cop."

"Don't sell yourself short," Jia says. "Help bring Fang and Khaw to justice. And solve the mystery of the missing girl."

"I'll think about it."

"Don't think too long. What if the girl is still alive? The sooner we get Fang into a room and start squeezing him for answers, the better."

"I said I'll think about it."

"Very well," Jia says. "I'll be in touch." The video feed abruptly goes black.

Lu looks at Bang. "Is that it?"

Bang nods.

Lu stands up and moves cautiously toward the door, one eye on Bang. He opens the door and checks the hallway. Clear. He walks briskly to the stairwell, battling a sudden urge to run. He descends to the lobby and exits the hotel. He takes a circuitous route back to his vehicle, unable to shake the sensation of hostile eyes watching him the entire way.

TWENTY

First thing next morning, Lu calls Sergeant Bing and asks him to look up the police report on Guo Ming's murder.

Sergeant Bing whispers into the phone: "But you've been *suspended*."

"Just do me this favor."

"You're going to get us both in trouble."

"Nonsense. There's nothing wrong with a PSB sergeant looking up a police report."

"Inspector . . ."

"Brother Bing. Please."

Bing sighs into the phone. "I hope you know what you're doing."

"Don't I always?"

"No comment." Bing hangs up. He calls back ten minutes later. "What do you want to know?"

"Just the highlights."

"Guo Ming, aged thirty-five, criminal record as long as the Songhua River. Discovered by a security guard in an abandoned warehouse, Xiangfang District, early hours of Tuesday morning. Killed by a single bullet to the forehead, caliber pending forensics. A type 92 handgun was found at the scene, several rounds expended. Guo's prints were on it. No eyewitnesses, no surveillance footage of the area. Autopsy report pending."

"That handgun fires 5.8-millimeter rounds, correct?"

"Yes."

"No suspects?"

"No, but it appears Guo was involved in a lot of criminal enterprises—drugs, prostitution, theft. Seems like the kind of guy who was going to wind up getting shot sooner or later."

"Thanks, Brother Bing. When the forensics report and autopsy are available, please let me know."

Lu hangs up. He searches online for information about the National Forestry and Grassland Administration. There's no Bang listed, but he finds a photograph and bio of a certain Jia Zhanshu. According to the website, Jia is a deputy director in charge of conservation, based in Beijing. Lu recognizes the photo as the guy he saw on the computer.

Lu's door buzzes, causing him to jump. He's not expecting anyone. He clicks on the intercom. "Yes?"

"Delivery."

"I didn't order anything."

"Well, I got an envelope here with your name on it."

It's times like these Lu wishes the PSB issued cops sidearms as standard equipment. He goes downstairs, eyes peeled for trouble, but he finds only a motorcycle courier holding a package. Lu signs for it and the courier speeds off. Lu doesn't recognize the return address—someplace in Beijing.

Lu goes upstairs and tosses the envelope on the bed. He figures it's from Jia and if he opens it, he's committing himself to Jia's harebrained scheme. Especially if the contents are of a sensitive or classified nature.

What to do?

It's only midday, but he needs a drink. Through inebriation, insight.

Lu goes to a nearby restaurant and orders a bowl of cold sesame noodles and a couple of beers. He tries to clear his mind and allow thoughts, worries, emotions to float by, as if carried along by a gentle current of water.

But a vision of Tan Meirong, weeping in the *paichusuo* lobby, intrudes. Another of himself, selling shoes like the pair of which Chief Liang is so obnoxiously proud. "Yes, sir, the cordovan leather are an extremely elegant choice!"

Yesterday, the road ahead was steadily rising to a satisfying, if predictable, destination. Lu was destined to take over as chief of Raven Valley when Liang retired, or move on to a PSB command somewhere else. Get married. Have children. Retire at sixty. Enjoy a peaceful and contented old age.

Now, he's untethered and unmoored. Without anchor or direction.

Lu finishes his noodles and beer. He goes back to his apartment, rips the seal off the envelope, and shakes its contents out onto the bed. Inside is a printed itinerary for a flight to Kunming; an ID in the name of Long Ming, featuring a photograph of Lu; and a thick bundle of cash.

Lu waits for the call. It comes fifteen minutes later. "You received the envelope?" Jia says.

"Yes," Lu answers.

"That ID is valid. You won't have any problems traveling with it."

"Who is Long Ming?"

"You are Long Ming, Inspector."

"How?"

"I have certain resources at my disposal. Now, take note—your flight is scheduled for tomorrow at noon. That doesn't give you much time. I suggest you use some of that cash to buy new clothes, a pair of fake glasses, get a haircut. When you arrive in Kunming, you will no longer be Lu Fei, deputy chief of a third-tier city Public Security Bureau. You will be Long Ming, procurer of rare and exotic wildlife products for a casino owner in Macao."

"Macao?"

"We have an informant there who can provide a suitable backstory for you."

This is real. It's happening. Lu feels dizzy. He sits down on the bed.

"Are you there, Inspector?"

"I'm here."

"Do you have any questions?"

"When he's extradited, I want Fang to confess to whatever he's done to Tan Meixiang."

"You have my word."

"And I want my job back."

"You shall have it."

"Fine."

"So, we have an understanding?"

Lu takes a breath. "Yes."

"Very good. Captain Bang will meet you at the Kunming airport to-morrow. He'll brief you on the next steps when you arrive. Safe travels . . . Mr. Long."

TWENTY-ONE

Lu is going to need some help. He calls Yanyan and asks to meet her. "I'm at the bar," she says. "Just come on by."

Lu rides his bike to the Red Lotus and finds Yanyan inside, stocking the chiller with beer. She's wearing shorts and a sleeveless T-shirt and has worked up a bit of a sweat, which Lu finds terribly sexy.

She waves, a flash of red coming from her cinnabar bracelet. How Lu has come to loathe that simple band of resin and silk thread. "What's the emergency?"

"It seems I'm going on an undercover operation."

"How exciting."

"And dangerous." Perhaps, Lu thinks, Yanyan will be concerned enough about his welfare to give him a *proper* send-off.

"Doing what?"

"I can't really say."

"Mysterious."

"Did I mention dangerous?"

"You did."

"Right." Lu takes a seat at one of the tables. "I need to change my appearance. Do you have any ideas?"

"Hm. Tea?"

Lu glances at his watch. "Too early for a beer?"

Yanyan laughs and gets him a beer. They sit at a table and she pours for him. "Change your appearance how? Are you supposed to be someone in particular? Like a drug dealer? A corrupt official?"

"A guy who procures contraband items for his rich and morally bank-rupt employer."

"So, a gangster, but not the kind who robs banks or chops up people with a cleaver."

"Sounds about right. And I might come across a suspect who has seen my face. Which means I'll require a rather radical makeover."

Yanyan peers intently at Lu. "I never noticed that scar on your eye-brow. Did you get it in a fight?"

Truthfully, Lu gave himself that scar by falling off a bike when he was ten. The doctor who stitched him up was incompetent, hence the ragged white line that bisects Lu's left eyebrow. "Yes," Lu says. "A big fight. Huge brawl. I kicked a lot of asses that day."

"Maybe we need more of those. Scars, I mean. We can change your hair, that's easy enough. And you'll need new clothes."

"Can't I just wear what I'm wearing now?"

"When you're not in uniform, you dress like a cop who's not in uni-form."

"Ouch."

"I can do the hair myself," Yanyan says, "but I'm not really up on gangster fashion."

Lu drains his glass. "I think I know someone who can help with that."

Lu calls Monk and explains the situation. Monk is tickled by the idea. "How extreme do you want to go?"

"I don't want my own mother to recognize me."

"All right. You asked for it."

"I'll be there in a couple of hours."

Yanyan makes the rare concession of closing the Red Lotus and they go to her house after a quick detour to a pharmacy for supplies. Yanyan cuts Lu's hair with an electric razor, shaving close to his scalp around the back and sides and leaving a fringe on top. Then she bleaches the fringe at the top of Lu's head. When she's done, Lu is shocked by his own appearance. "I suddenly have an irresistible urge to slap my own face."

Lu calls a car service to take them to Harbin and pays with Jia's cash. He has never been to Monk's apartment, but it is exactly as he pictured. The furnishings are funky and minimalistic. The walls are hung with black-and-white photographs of beautiful—and tastefully nude—Chinese men. Yanyan gawps at them.

Monk grins when he sees Lu's hair. "Is it true what they say, Inspector?"

"What?"

"Blonds have more fun?"

"Who says?"

"I don't know. Americans. Europeans."

"I suppose that means ninety-eight percent of the world is miserable?"

Monk rolls his eyes. "Never mind." He smiles at Yanyan. "And who is this lovely creature?"

"Ah," Lu says. "This is Luo Yanyan. Yanyan, meet Monk."

Monk makes tea and they perch on his weird leather-and-chrome furniture. "So, you're playing a gangster who deals in contraband?"

Lu slurps tea. "Procures contraband, yes."

"What kind of contraband items?"

"I can't say."

"There's a world of difference between a guy who peddles drugs and one who sells stolen Roman antiquities."

"True. Okay—the backstory is, I'm buying exotic and endangered bushmeat for my boss, a casino owner in Macao."

"Thoroughly despicable," Monk says. "But that gives us something to go on. I'd say you're a bit rough and tumble, but not a violent thug."

"Exactly what I was thinking," Yanyan says.

"Might this be related to a certain restaurant you asked me about the other day?" Monk asks.

"Forget you ever heard about that," Lu says.

Monk smiles and jots notes on a pad of paper. "The hair is a good start, but if you're looking to really change your appearance, we're going to need more. A lot more."

"Such as?" Lu says.

"Let's start by fleshing out your character. Do you have a name?"

"Is that important to know?"

"Maybe."

"Surname is Long." *Dragon*—a common enough name in the People's Republic.

Monk nods. "Excellent. We can incorporate some dragon imagery into your character. Where is Mr. Long from?"

Lu shrugs. "I hadn't thought about it."

"Do you speak any regional dialects?"

"A smattering of Cantonese, and I understand Shanghainese, but I can't get my tongue around it."

"Let's keep it simple, then. Mr. Long is from Shanghai. It's a large enough city that whoever you run into won't necessarily expect to have crossed paths with you. And how did Mr. Long get into this racket? Did you start with petty crime and work your way up?"

"Is all this really necessary?"

"What if someone starts asking you a bunch of questions?"

"I'm the strong silent type?"

"Monk is right," Yanyan says. "In order to pull off something like this, you need to inhabit the role. Even if nobody ever asks you a question about your background, constructing a personal history will help you stay in character. Going undercover is like acting, only the stakes are not critical reviews—they're life and death."

"You two have a lot of experience with undercover work, do you?" Lu says.

"Yes," Monk says. "I'm a gay man in a country where being gay was classified as a mental illness until about twenty years ago."

"And I'm a woman who owns a bar," Yanyan says. "I wear a disguise every night." She smiles sweetly and pours tea for Lu with exaggerated politeness. "Why, yes, Brother Lu, I do find you incredibly witty and interesting. Tell me more about your amazing chicken farm."

"Point taken," Lu says. "Let's keep it as close to my real life as possible. My father was from Shanghai but was sent to Heilongjiang during the Cultural Revolution to grow wheat or whatever. He met my mother, they had me, and we moved back to Shanghai. Then . . . I don't know . . . my parents died, and I was orphaned and fell into a bad crowd. It was all downhill from there."

"Hardly compelling," Monk says.

"I'm not writing a romance drama. You two come up with something, then."

"I think we need a real drink for this," Yanyan says.

"Agreed." Monk disappears into the kitchen and returns with a bottle of Western wine and three glasses. "Sancerre," he says, by way of explanation. Lu has no idea what he's babbling about. Monk pours wine into two glasses, but Lu holds his hand out. "None for me. I'll have a beer if you've got one."

"Help yourself," Monk says. He and Yanyan clink glasses.

Lu wanders into the kitchen and opens the refrigerator to find only a few bottles of Snow Beer, which surprises him. By virtue of its cheap price and easy availability throughout China, Snow happens to be the world's best-selling brand, but it tastes like ammonia mixed with armpit sweat. Lu would have expected Monk to stock some foreign brands. Maybe the Mexican lager *Ku-luo-na*, or that American swill, *Bai Wei*, which is nearly as bad as Snow. But beggars can't be choosers. He grabs two and takes them back to his chair.

Monk and Yanyan decide Mr. Long was a spoiled youth heavily influenced by Hong Kong triad and American mafia movies who started a life of petty crime and low-stakes gambling while still in high school. From there, he segued into running underground card games. "When you started to make some cash, the first three things you spent your money on were a gold watch, a fancy motorcycle, and a tattoo," Yanyan says.

"But I don't have any tattoos," Lu says.

"We'll take care of that," Monk says, rather ominously.

"Later, you took a trip to Macao and loved it so much, you stayed," Yanyan says.

"Is that even legal?"

"You paid a local girl to marry you," Monk says.

"And then you found work in a casino," Yanyan continues. "Where you came to the attention of the owner. He liked your style and decided to make you his assistant."

"So now you handle various tasks on his behalf," Monk says. "Entertaining guests. Keeping an eye on his mistresses. Procuring whatever needs procuring. Drugs, prostitutes, cars, luxury goods. Exotic delicacies."

"But you're not muscle," Yanyan says. "In fact, you're a bit of a fop."

Lu sips from his bottle of Snow and grimaces. "I am?"

Monk nods. "Tough guys have a reputation to keep up. You might find yourself getting tested. That's the last thing you want. Mr. Long operates on his brains, not his brawn. Hopefully, that will keep you out of trouble."

Lu is offended that Yanyan would concoct such a wimpy persona for him, but he sees the logic in it.

"Now, your employer," Yanyan says. "He's recently developed a . . ." She giggles and covers her mouth with her hand.

"His equipment is no longer functioning the way it should," Monk continues. "Thus, the urgent need for you, his lackey, to source some medicinal remedies."

"I'm not a lackey," Lu protests. "I'm a valued assistant."

"That's the spirit," Monk says.

Lu notices Yanyan looking at him. "What?"

"You need an earring."

"An earring? No way."

Monk agrees. "Mr. Long would definitely have bling."

"Look at this as an opportunity to explore a different side of your personality," Yanyan says. "Have fun with it. Go *wild*." She's getting tipsy.

"I can do the piercing," Monk offers.

"Absolutely not," Lu says.

"It doesn't hurt," Monk says. "Much."

"I'll hold your hand, if you like," Yanyan offers.

"I'm not a baby!" Lu snaps. He immediately regrets his hasty words. It would be nice if Yanyan held his hand.

Monk boils water and heats a needle, then extracts it with a pair of chopsticks. He cleans the needle with alcohol and swabs Lu's earlobe. "Ready?"

"Just get on with it!"

Lu feels a quick, sharp jab, which quickly turns to a dull ache. A wet trickle runs down his neck. Monk grunts.

"What?" Lu asks.

"There isn't usually this much blood. Yanyan, can you grab me a dish towel from the sink?"

"No surprise," Yanyan says. "He's had a couple of Snow beers. That stuff is laced with formaldehyde."

"Well, this should take care of it," Monk says. He applies pressure with a towel soaked in cold water.

"What kind of earring would Mr. Long wear?" Yanyan muses.

"I have just the thing," Monk says. He goes into his bedroom and returns with a beautiful piece of bluish-green jade in a gold setting. "This earring cost me almost three thousand yuan. Please don't lose it."

"Three thousand?" Lu says. "I can sell it for a bus ticket home if I run out of cash."

Monk fits the stud into Lu's lobe. "Clean your earlobe twice a day with alcohol." He stands back and smiles approvingly. "Now—let's go shopping."

Monk takes them to a district known for trendy clothes and thrift shops. He is friends with many of the proprietors and manages to load Lu up with a variety of secondhand shirts, pants, and accessories from several famous Chinese and foreign brands—SEVEN, Shanshan, Fendi, Burberry, Zara. Lu spends a sizable chunk of Jia's cash on this shopping spree.

Next up, Monk suggests a tattoo parlor.

"No," Lu says. "I have to draw the line there."

"Don't worry," Monk says. "I have it all worked out."

Monk leads them down an alley to a basement-level storefront. A young woman, perhaps midtwenties, answers the door. She has what beauty bloggers call a *dao sanjiaoxing lian*—an "inverted triangle-shaped face." Each of the major face shapes—square, round, diamond, and so on—is believed to have its own associated personality. A woman with an inverted triangle-shaped face can be charming, but also sometimes cruel.

Lu finds this woman to be more on the charming side. Perhaps it is her warm smile. Her large, animated eyes. Or maybe it's her halter top and denim cutoffs.

She gives Monk an affectionate hug and waves them all inside. She goes by the English name "Lily." Monk doesn't tell her the reason why Lu needs her services, and she doesn't ask.

For a tattoo artist, Lily doesn't display a lot of ink. A ring of flowers around her ankle, a cat chasing a butterfly down one thigh, a red, gold, and green dragon across her shoulder.

Monk explains what he wants. "Something that suits a person who is into fast cars and money. A bit of a poseur."

Lily considers. "Like a female samurai warrior holding a katana, with bared breasts."

"Would that be one of your specialties?" Yanyan says.

"Nothing permanent," Lu says. "I can't have a permanent tattoo."

Lily ignores Yanyan. "Don't worry. I'll use special inks that won't wash off easily but fade over time."

"How long?" Lu asks.

"Depending on wear and tear, one to two weeks."

"That should work."

"Ready to get started?"

"No needles, right?" Lu reflexively touches his ear, which still throbs.

"It won't hurt a bit," Lily says. "Take off your shirt."

Lu does as requested. Lily has him recline in a chair and lays out her ink and brushes. Yanyan folds her arms, her lips pressed tightly together.

Lily dons a face mask and a pair of latex gloves. "You look pretty fit for a guy your age."

"I'm not that old."

"What's this from?" Lily traces the edge of a burn scar with her forefinger.

"I spilled tea on myself."

Lily picks up a brush. "Open your mouth and say *ahh*."

"What?"

"Kidding."

"How long is this going to take?" Yanyan asks.

"At least an hour and a half," Lily says. "Perhaps you prefer not to wait?"

"Well, you're scribbling on my ride home."

"This is not scribbling. And I don't like people hovering while I work."

Monk steps in. "Come on, Yanyan. Let's grab a bite to eat."

Yanyan is reluctant, but Monk tugs her toward the exit. When they are gone, Lu feels a touch embarrassed. "Sorry about that."

Lily smirks behind her mask. "I'm used to it."

All told, it takes Lily more than two hours to complete the work. She paints a fierce dragon of black, green, and gold coiling sinuously around Lu's right biceps, its snarling head glaring out from his right pectoral. She also inscribes a line of characters along the back of Lu's arm, carefully blended with the dragon's scales. The characters read *yi*, *zun*, *xin*—righteousness, respect, trust. Buzzwords favored by Chinese triads.

"Nice," Lu says.

"I know." Lily has Lu stand in front of an angled mirror so he can see the Japanese female samurai she has illustrated on his back. The samurai wields a katana sword, and her gorgeously rendered kimono is parted to reveal a single pert breast.

"You're talented!" Lu says.

"Your girlfriend might not like it."

"She's not my girlfriend."

Lu pays Lily an exorbitant fee and puts his shirt back on. She escorts him to the front room, where Monk is waiting.

"What happened to Yanyan?" Lu asks.

"It's late and she had to get back," Monk says. "She took a car service."

"Uh-oh," Lily says. "You're in *trouble*."

"Sorry." Monk shrugs.

"It's okay," Lu says. "This was a good idea. Thanks for setting it up."

Lily hugs Monk goodbye and tells Lu: "Don't shower for twenty-four hours."

"Got it."

"And if you decide you want some permanent ink, you know where to find me."

Outside, Monk looks Lu up and down and nods in satisfaction. "When you put on one of your new shirts, leave it unbuttoned so that the dragon peeks out. With the tattoo, the hair, the clothes, the earring—you look like a completely different person. One last suggestion: quit shaving for the time being."

"It takes me a long time to grow a beard."

"You don't need a beard. Just some scruff."

Lu rubs his chin. *"Jin liang." I'll do my best.*

TWENTY-TWO

Thursday morning Lu rises early and dresses head to toe in athleisure—track pants, a Guangzhou Evergrande soccer club jersey, a hoodie, and a pirated pair of highly coveted Air Jordan sneakers. He grins ruefully at his reflection. He looks like an aging boy-band wannabe.

He packs his remaining clothes and incidentals in a duffel bag and pockets his new ID card, Kunming plane ticket, and the leftover cash supplied by Mr. Jia. He leaves his real identification and cell phone on the kitchen counter.

Goodbye, Lu Fei. Hello, Long Ming.

Lu takes a taxi to the train station. He buys a breakfast of steamed pork buns and tea and catches the train for Harbin. As he rides, he attempts to settle into his new persona. *How would Long Ming eat these pork buns?* Apparently with his mouth open, smacking his lips with pleasure. When a pretty woman takes her assigned seat beside him, he openly leers at her legs. She notices his gaze, but keeps her knees pressed together and her eyes averted, too intimidated to call him out.

At the airport, Lu is nervous when passing through security, half expecting the fake ID to set off bells and flashing lights. But he breezes through the line without incident. Lu's ticket is for business class—a nice touch. The flight attendants are young and attractive. In keeping with Long Ming's personality, he flirts with them shamelessly.

"I didn't catch your name," he tells one of the attendants, when she brings him his second perfectly chilled beer. She has long hair pinned up in a bun and a red silk scarf around her neck.

"I'm Xiaowen."

"Hi, Xiaowen. I'm Long Ming. Want to have dinner when we get to Kunming?"

"I'm sorry, Mr. Long, we're not allowed to have dates with our guests."

"What? How do they expect you to find a rich husband?"

"Excuse me, Mr. Long, but I think you misunderstand. We are professionals and this is our career, not just a way to meet men."

"Okay, gorgeous, I stand corrected. If you change your mind, I'll be right here. I mean, where else would I be? Ha ha ha!"

The plane lands an hour late and by the time Lu has made it through the baggage area and into the arrivals hall, it's late afternoon. He finds Captain Bang standing among a group of drivers holding placards bearing their client's names. The placard in Bang's hand reads *Mr. Long*. Lu walks up to him and points to the sign. "That's me."

Bang does a double take, then realizes that it is, in fact, Lu. He does not comment on Lu's much-altered appearance. He jerks his head toward the exit. "Let's go."

They catch a taxi and ride in silence. After a reasonably short drive, they arrive at their destination—the Kunming Crowne Plaza. "You have a reservation waiting for you inside," Bang says. "There's a restaurant down the street—it's called Dong Feng. Meet me there in one hour." Lu grabs his bag, gets out, and shuts the door. The taxi speeds off.

Lu enters the hotel lobby, checks in at the front desk, and rides the elevator up to his room. The accommodations are more than satisfactory. A queen-sized bed, with sheets as white and smooth as fresh cream. A massive flat-screen TV. A love seat and coffee table and writing desk. A bathroom with a cavernous tub. Thick, luxurious bath towels. A range of free shampoo, soap, and skin-care products.

Lu cranks up the air-conditioning and collapses onto the bed. He's exhausted, although so far, he's done nothing aside from take a train, an airplane, and a taxi.

After thirty minutes, Lu pries himself out of bed. He washes his face and hands in the bathroom sink, brushes his teeth, and takes off his shirt to check his tattoos. They look, if anything, even more vibrant than when they were freshly inked.

Lu goes downstairs and inquires with the concierge as to the location of the Dong Feng restaurant. Although it's still a bit early, he walks there and hangs around outside, getting the lay of the land. Five minutes before the appointed time, he enters and finds Bang already sitting at a table in the back. Lu takes the chair across from him. Bang slides a menu over. Lu opens it and discovers a manila envelope inside.

"Did I forget our anniversary *again*?" Lu says.

Bang slurps tea. "Inside you'll find a list of dealers here in Kunming. Tomorrow you'll start making the rounds, asking about supply."

Lu places the envelope on his lap. A waitress comes by. Lu orders the only dish he knows Kunming is famous for—Across the Bridge Noodles: a savory broth made of chicken and pork bone, served with fresh vegetables and paper-thin slices of turkey and chicken skin, rice noodles, and bean curd.

And, of course, a beer.

Bang doesn't order anything.

"You're not eating?" Lu says.

"I ate earlier."

That suits Lu just fine. He guesses Bang would make for less-than-scintillating dinner conversation.

"A car will pick you up at ten." Bang hands over a business card. It reads *Kunming Delight Car*.

"I'm almost out of cash."

"There's more in the envelope. But don't spend it frivolously. Those are government funds."

"Yes, Mother. Where are you going to be while I'm making the rounds?"

"Watching."

"Creepy."

"The expectation is that your inquiries will attract a certain amount of attention and eventually a higher-level player will make contact. When that happens, you *must* insist on being taken to the source of product so you can personally verify its quality and provenance."

"*Provenance* is a big word for a grunt."

"I'm not a grunt."

"No, in fact, I hear you're a captain in the special forces. Tell me how you came to be in the employ of Mr. Jia."

"I'm not going to answer any personal questions, so don't bother asking. Also in the envelope is a dossier on a man named Alex Ho. He is an investor in Macao casinos. And a crook. Mostly white collar, but he occasionally dips his toe into drugs, sex trafficking, and the like. We have a mountain of evidence against him. Rather than going to prison, he's agreed to act as a cooperating witness. And pose as your employer."

"Why doesn't Alex just make introductions to Khaw's people?" Lu asks. "Wouldn't that be easier? Why waste time waiting for them to approach me?"

"Alex doesn't have any personal contacts in the illegal animal trade. He doesn't know any of Khaw's people."

"So, what good is he as a cover story? If he doesn't know them, and they don't know him, why would they give *me* the time of day?"

"They will know his name. They will share some mutual business associates. And they will consider it plausible that he wants to buy bushmeat. Aside from that, it's up to you to convince them you're worth the risk."

"Great," Lu says. "Brilliant." The waitress arrives with Lu's beer. A Myanmar lager. He pours and sips. Not bad.

Bang removes a cell phone from his pocket and sets it next to the beer. "Password is ten-zero-one-one-nine-four-nine."

It takes Lu a moment to process. 10/01/1949. The official date of the founding of the People's Republic. "Very patriotic, comrade."

Bang swallows the rest of his tea. "Any questions?"

"Is your number preprogrammed in case I need to reach you?"

"You don't reach me. I reach you."

"I'm sorry, this relationship just isn't working for me anymore."

Bang wipes down his cup with a napkin, then stands. "Good luck." He walks out of the restaurant.

Lu unlocks the cell phone. It's clean—no contacts, incoming or outgoing calls or texts. He considers dialing a random number in a faraway place—Uganda or Jamaica—to run up Jia's phone bill. But he doesn't know anyone in Uganda or Jamaica, so he puts the phone in his pocket and waits for his noodles to arrive.

TWENTY-THREE

At ten sharp the next morning, as instructed, Lu is waiting outside the Crowne Plaza. He's wearing jeans, tasseled loafers, a Gucci hoodie, and holding a knockoff Louis Vuitton murse. His car pulls up—a black Geely Boyue SUV with a placard in the window that reads *Mr. Long*. Lu climbs in the back and introduces himself to the driver. He consults the list of addresses given to him by Bang and tells the driver to take him to the nearest one.

This turns out to be the Eternal Spring Pharmacy. Unlike your average Western drugstore with its shelves of mass-produced pills, cold remedies, prophylactics, bags of candy, and the like, the walls of Eternal Spring are honeycombed with cubbies holding apothecary jars filled with roots, powders, dried berries, herbs, insects, and preserved animal parts. Lu waits until an old lady digging around in a bin of dried jellyfish leaves the store before he approaches the counter. The proprietor is a moon-faced man in his sixties wearing a bracelet of prayer beads that smells cloyingly of sandalwood.

"Nice shop you've got here," Lu says. "May I ask your name?"

"My surname is Tong."

"Mr. Tong, how're you doing?" They make a bit of small talk and then Lu leans an elbow on the counter. "The truth is, Mr. Tong, I'm in the market for something special."

"Everything I have is right there on display." Mr. Tong waves at the cubbies.

"What I'm looking for wouldn't be in one of your jars."

"I have jade. Good quality."

"No," Lu says. "I'm not interested in jade. I have jade coming out of my ass."

Mr. Tong shrugs. "Sorry. What you see is what you get."

Clearly, Tong is the cautious sort. Prudent, given the increasingly draconian penalties for selling illegal animal parts. Lu opens his murse and shows Tong a wad of bills. "Price is absolutely no object. No object whatsoever."

Tong coughs into his hand. "Rhino horn? I don't sell rhino horn. But I've heard of someone who does . . ."

"Not rhino. I have a client, you see. He has many rich and important friends that he enjoys entertaining with rare and exotic delicacies."

"Sorry," Mr. Tong says. "I can't help you."

"I realize I just walked into your shop off the street. You don't know me. But I assure you, I'm serious. If you know where I might go . . . I'll pay you a finder's fee."

Mr. Tong shakes his head. "I'm sorry."

Lu visits half a dozen more shops. Most of the proprietors are as circumspect as Mr. Tong, but his last call of the day is a bit more promising. He speaks to a Mr. Yang, who invites Lu into a back room and summons a pretty girl in a short skirt to serve tea. Yang lights up a Red River cigarette and offers the pack to Lu.

"No, thanks," Lu says. The girl finishes pouring tea and sits on the couch beside Lu, her knee pressed up against his.

"So, what do you want?" Yang asks. "I've got rhino horn, elephant ivory, highest-quality jade."

Lu sips his tea. It tastes of cocoa and black pepper. "I'm more interested in edible items."

The girl places a hand on Lu's thigh. "Do you like to eat tofu?"

The girl is flirting. Hard. In this context, to *chi dofu*—eat tofu—has the meaning of take advantage of or sexually harass a woman.

"You like her?" Yang says. "She can entertain you later."

Yang's offer disgusts Lu, but he is careful not to show it. "You have what I'm looking for or not?"

"Destination? Somewhere in China? Hong Kong? Taiwan?"

"Macao."

Yang takes a deep drag on his cigarette. "No problem. Only a small extra charge for delivery."

"It's not the delivery I'm worried about. It's the quality of the product."

The girl touches the back of Lu's neck. Her fingers are warm and soothing. "I like your hair."

"What *exactly* are you looking for?" Yang says.

"Anything sufficiently exotic and tasty."

"I may know a guy," Yang suggests.

"Make an introduction."

"Better I act as go-between. You tell me what you want, I'll get it for you."

"My employer values *yewei*," Lu says. This means "wild taste" and refers to the preference for wild-caught animals over those farmed for the meat. Because it is expensive and difficult to come by, eating wild meat is a valued form of conspicuous consumption. It is also considered more efficacious in its medicinal effects and ability to boost male virility.

"Mr. Yang says I'm *yewei*," the girl coos into Lu's ear.

"Come now," Lu says. "I'm sure you taste better than a bamboo rat."

The girl laughs and slaps Lu's shoulder playfully. Lu turns to Yang. "Can you set up a meeting for me with your source?"

Yang waves his cigarette. "He won't meet with you directly. I'm sure you can appreciate why."

"And I'm sure you can understand why I prefer to speak to him personally."

"Don't worry, Mr. Long, I'll take care of everything." Yang thumps his chest. "I'm your number-one guy!"

The girl brushes her lips across Lu's earlobe. "I'm your number-one girl."

"I'm sorry, I really must insist on meeting your source face-to-face," Lu says. "Not that I don't trust you. But my employer is very particular about the source of his *yewei*. If you can arrange it, give me a call. I'm staying at the Crowne Plaza."

"Drinks later?" the girl says.

"Perhaps next time I'm in town," Lu says. He stands. "Hope to hear from you, Mr. Yang."

Feeling thoroughly soiled after his day of subterfuge, Lu has the driver take him back to the hotel. Upstairs, he takes a long shower—his first since receiving the fake tattoo—then dresses in an Adidas tracksuit and heads down to the lobby bar for a cold beer.

He hasn't seen a trace of Bang all day. If Bang is keeping tabs on Lu as promised, his covert surveillance skills are first-rate.

Lu finishes his beer and wants nothing more than to go back upstairs, watch some TV, and go to bed, but he knows Long Ming wouldn't spend an evening watching variety shows in his hotel room. Lu inquires with the concierge as to dining and clubbing options. The concierge provides several choices.

Lu returns to his room and changes into something more suitable for a night on the town—an Italian stretch linen suit, tan in color, and a blue shirt. He straps on a fake Piaget watch with a dragon clockface—the better to suit his fake surname.

Lu takes a taxi to a famous restaurant called the Shiping Guild Hall. Its setting is a two-hundred-year-old residence decorated with antique furnishings and lit by paper lanterns. A woman dressed in flowing silk robes plays classical music on a zither near the entrance. Lu is shown to one of the least-desirable tables, but the restaurant is so packed, he's lucky to get any seat at all. He orders the local specialty—Yunnan bean curd, a bit sour and spicy. He tries a local beer—Black Yak—recent winner of an international prize. It tastes of chocolate. Lu dislikes it, but drinks it anyway, and then shifts to a lager.

The tofu is delicious and spicy enough to warrant two more beers. When Lu leaves, he nearly trips over the raised threshold of the front gate.

Lu looks at his watch. It's not yet 9:00 p.m. He wants to go back to the hotel and get some sleep but asks himself what Long Ming would do. He decides Long Ming would keep the good times rolling.

Lu catches another taxi to one of the clubs recommended by the concierge. He waits in line for thirty minutes, then pays an exorbitant entrance fee. Once inside, he sits at the bar and orders an incredibly overpriced beer.

The focal point of the club is a stage where a DJ twists dials and pushes buttons and dances like an idiot. A crowd of beautiful young hipsters jerks spasmodically in time to a booming beat and pulsating light show. Lu has at least a decade and a half on most of the clubbers, and the incessant noise, the jarring lights, put his teeth on edge.

The girls are dressed in spaghetti-strap tops and short skirts and glitter eye shadow. The boys wear baggy jeans and designer T-shirts that look like rags and cost as much the average monthly salary of a factory worker. As Lu watches the boys chase the girls and the girls chase other boys, and everyone desperately struggling to appear like they are having the time of their lives, he feels sorry for them. Being young and cool is hard work.

Lu tries to flirt with some young women, as he believes Long Ming would do. He is roundly rejected, which comes as something of a relief. He doesn't even attempt to dance. There are some levels to which he will not stoop, even in the pursuit of a higher objective.

Lu remains for as long as it takes to have two drinks and then leaves. Outside, he breathes a sigh of relief at the cool air and relative quiet.

He's waiting for a taxi when a black SUV with tinted windows pulls up to the curb. The back door opens. Lu feels something jab him in the back. It feels suspiciously like the barrel of a gun.

"Get in the car," a voice growls into his ear.

Lu considers his options. Fight? Or flee? Lu calculates his odds at fifty-fifty that he can turn and whip his elbow against the gun to deflect it without taking a bullet. From there, perhaps disarm the gunman, or at least run away.

But this is what he's been waiting for. Contact.

"I'm unarmed," Lu says.

"Move," the voice says.

Lu climbs into the SUV.

A man sits in the back. Young, handsome. He smiles at Lu. "Mr. Long," the man says. "Welcome to Kunming."

TWENTY-FOUR

The young man introduces himself as Mr. Cho. He speaks Mandarin with a slight accent. Cho is extraordinarily—for want of a better word—pretty. His skin is flawlessly smooth, his hair rakishly tousled. And if Lu is not mistaken, he is wearing eyeliner and a touch of lipstick.

Lu has heard of the recent trend among young Chinese men to beautify themselves with cosmetics. Whereas in the West, a male wearing makeup might be perceived as effeminate, among the status- and appearance-obsessed youth of the People's Republic, it's less a matter of sexual identification and more just a case of wanting to look one's best. And a little foundation and blush are far cheaper than plastic surgery.

Cho's associate, the one with the gun, climbs in beside Lu and shuts the door. He's a big guy with long hair in a ponytail. The driver of the SUV shifts into gear and they pull away from the curb.

"Where are we going?" Lu asks.

"Someplace where we can talk," Cho says.

"Starbucks?"

"Not exactly."

"How do you know my name?"

"Word has been getting around town. A big spender. Looking for something exotic. It arouses a certain level of curiosity."

"If there's something you want to know about me, just ask. No need to threaten me with a gun."

Cho smiles. "That was just to let you know we mean business."

"That's why I'm here. To do business."

Lu isn't too familiar with the layout of Kunming City, but he recognizes Dongfeng Square when they pass it—an enormous plaza where morning crowds gather for *taijiquan*, dance, theatrical productions, and games of badminton. Soon after, they cross the Panlong River. Lu sees the top of the Crowne Plaza in the distance and, for a moment, thinks that is where they are going. Perfect. A civilized drink at the hotel bar.

But no. The driver keeps driving.

Lu wonders if Bang is somewhere behind the SUV, in a taxi, or maybe a motorcycle. He resists the urge to turn around and look through the rear window. "So, where *are* we going?"

Cho shakes out a cigarette and offers it to Lu. Lu waves it away. Cho slips it between his lips and lights it with a gold Zippo. "Relax, Mr. Long. You've been telling everyone how rich your boss is. And I'm not the kind to bite the hand that feeds me."

Five minutes later, the SUV pulls to a stop. Everyone but the driver disembarks.

"If you'll come with me," Cho says. He heads down a narrow alleyway. Ponytail Thug motions for Lu to follow. Lu does. The shops along either side are closed, but Lu sees signboards advertising teahouses, restaurants, clothing boutiques, a bar, a convenience store. He hears odd sounds burbling up ahead. Coos. Whistles. Hoots.

"What's that?" he asks.

"Birds," Cho says, over his shoulder. "The bird market is down at the end of this lane. Closed for the night, of course. Those sounds you hear are probably the night owls." He laughs, but Lu doesn't get the joke. *Night owls?*

They stop outside a shop. Cho unlocks a metal shutter and raises it, then opens a door and disappears inside. Lu doesn't relish going into that dark, enclosed space. Ponytail gives him a little push of encouragement. Lu doesn't resist. This was the plan. Beat the bushes. Rouse some snakes. He steps inside.

The lights are off, but the long, narrow room is suffused with a dim green glow that ripples and undulates across the ceiling. It's chilly and there is a pungent smell—a bit like the bonito flakes you sprinkle on top of Japanese food. As Lu's eyes adjust, he can see the walls are lined with water tanks. Dark shapes flitting back and forth.

Fish.

"Come along," Cho says.

Lu trails Cho toward the back. Behind him, the metal shutter crashes down.

That's it, then. Lu's on his own. Bang's not getting through that shutter without a blowtorch.

"You like fish?" Cho says.

"Yes. Especially steamed sea bass with ginger, garlic, and scallion."

"I have a very nice selection. Angelfish. Seven species of betta. Shrimp. Ten kinds of goldfish. Koi. Lucky fish, good for feng shui."

"You make your living one guppy at a time, is that it?"

Cho opens a door. "In here is where I keep the real treasures." He switches on a light.

This room is likewise filled with tanks, some quite large, and all containing a variety of brightly colored fish, eels, and other aquatic life. It hums with the sound of water pumps and an air-ventilation motor.

Cho waves Lu over to one of the tanks and points to a fat little creature with a grayish yellow-and-white body. "You know puffer fish? The most poisonous fish in the world, and the second most poisonous vertebrate after the golden dart frog. Their internal organs, muscle, and skin contain a neurotoxin that is a hundred times more powerful than cyanide. If ingested by a human, it paralyzes the diaphragm. Death results from suffocation within an hour."

"Remind me not to lick one."

"A delicacy in Japan," Cho says. "But only chefs who have several years of special training are allowed by law to prepare them. Look here." Cho points at the bottom of another tank.

Lu sees nothing but sand. "What am I supposed to be looking at?"

"A grayish blob."

"Ah. Yes." The gelatinous creature neatly blends into its surroundings.

"Without you pointing it out, I would have taken it for a mossy rock. Or a piece of coral."

"Exactly," Cho says. "That is the stonefish. The most venomous fish in the world."

"I thought you said puffer fish were?"

"Puffer fish are toxic. Meaning if you eat them, you die. The stonefish is *venomous*. It carries thirteen spines on its back. Step on it and, well . . . it's a bad way to go. Shock, paralysis. Necrosis."

"Necrosis?"

"Tissue death. Your flesh rots on the bone."

"Nasty."

"Even if you survive the sting, you may suffer permanent nerve damage."

"Have you got any boxes of fluffy kittens back here, by chance?"

"You don't want to admire my electric fish?" Cho says. "I have eels. Rays. Catfish."

"I want to get down to business, Mr. Cho."

"As you wish." Cho pulls out a couple of stools. He sits on one and motions for Lu to sit on the other. He crosses his legs and pulls out his pack of cigarettes. He slips one between his glossy lips. Ponytail leans against a wall at the back of the room. Lu turns to look at him. "I don't think we've been introduced properly."

"Ah," Cho says. "That is my associate Bullethead."

"I guess your parents ran out of normal names like 'Illustrious Dragon' or 'Little Peace'?" Lu asks.

Bullethead smiles. He's got gold caps on his front teeth.

"Well, don't lurk in the background," Lu says. "Pull up a stool."

"Just pretend he's not here," Cho says.

"Oh, but he is," Lu replies. "And right behind me."

Cho lights his cigarette. "I really hate to ask, Mr. Long. But would you mind taking off your clothes?"

Lu laughs. Then he realizes Cho is serious. "Listen, I know it's Friday night and all, but that isn't exactly my idea of a good time."

"We have to check you for a wire," Cho says.

"Can I check *you* for a wire?"

"Either take off your clothes or this meeting is over. The choice is yours."

Lu can't see any way out of it. He stands and shrugs out of his jacket. "At least tell the fish to cover their eyes." He drapes the jacket over the stool, unbuttons his shirt, removes it.

Cho raises a plucked eyebrow. "Nice tats."

Lu slips out of his shoes. Bullethead holds out his hand. Lu tosses them over, one by one. Bullethead runs a finger around inside them. "Better wash your hands when you're done," Lu says. "I have a communicable fungal condition." He steps out of his pants, adds them to the pile on the stool. Then he unstraps the fake Piaget watch. He spreads his arms wide and turns in a circle. "Satisfied?"

"Not quite," Cho says.

"You must be kidding."

"Believe me, Mr. Long . . . I don't take any personal enjoyment in this exercise."

"Ta ma de!" Lu drops his underwear to his ankles and stands angrily, and embarrassed, with his hands on his hips.

"Okay, thank you," Cho says.

Lu pulls his underwear up. Bullethead collects the articles of clothing from the stool and checks their pockets and seams. He lays Lu's hotel key card, watch, cell phone, cash, and ID on the floor in front of Cho. Lu hurriedly dresses.

"I apologize for that," Cho says. "Please makes yourself comfortable."

Lu sits and Bullethead resumes his place against the wall.

Cho holds Lu's ID up to the ceiling light. Then he drops it back onto the floor. "You've spent the day making the rounds, making quite a spectacle of yourself."

"Well, I'm new in town."

"Are you new to this business, Mr. Long? Don't you have your own suppliers already?"

"As a matter of fact . . ." Lu hears Bullethead's shoes scrape on the cement floor. He snaps his head around. Bullethead shows him a flash of golden teeth. Lu turns back to Cho. "As a matter of fact, yes, I'm new to this. And so's my employer. Alex Ho. Perhaps you've heard of him?"

Cho doesn't react to the name.

Lu continues: "Alex is looking to host a regular dinner for friends and business associates. You know how it is with these guys—keeping up with the Chens. And—his health has recently taken a downturn." Lu holds out a forefinger and then lets it droop. "So, he's looking for some remedies that will help him find the steel in the silk. That last bit's confidential, by the way."

Cho flicks ash from his cigarette. Lu hears the scrape of shoes on cement again, but before he can turn, Bullethead has a wire garrote wrapped around his neck and a knee in his spine. Lu's fingers scrabble at the garrote, but it's sunk tight.

"Who are you really working for?" Cho asks.

Lu tries to speak—only a wet gagging sound emerges.

"Give him some air," Cho says. Bullethead loosens the garrote.

"You bastard—" Lu starts. Cho nods and Bullethead yanks hard, nearly hauling Lu backward off the stool. Black spots crowd his vision. Just before he goes out completely, Bullethead gives the garrote a little slack. The blood flows back to Lu's brain, but he remains immobilized, helpless, on the stool.

Cho picks up Lu's cell phone and drops it casually into one of the fish tanks. He walks over to a row of aquariums lined up on metal racks placed against the wall. "What do you know about jellyfish, Mr. Long?"

Lu gurgles.

"No need to answer," Cho says. "That was a rhetorical question. In any case, they are exceedingly odd creatures. Ninety-five percent water. No brain to speak of. They eat and shit from the same hole. A sexually mature jellyfish is said to have entered the *medusa* stage. Are you familiar with the word *medusa*?" Cho opens the lid of a tank. "Not unless you are a fan of Greek myth, I suppose." He uses a large plastic soup container to scoop up water. "Medusa was the daughter of Phorcys and his sister Ceto. A product of incest—so you know she's going to be nothing but trouble. She was gorgeous—and deadly. Instead of hair, her head was covered with a carpet of venomous snakes. One look at her face was sufficient to turn a man to stone."

Cho roots around in the tank with a handheld net. "The reasons for the taxonomy—medusa—are obvious. A beautiful creature . . . half goddess, half demon. In place of long, flowing tresses, venomous snakes. Or, in the case of jellyfish, tentacles. Tentacles rigged with stingers. Here we are." Cho nets a tiny creature and dumps it into the plastic container. He sets the net down, comes over, and pulls his stool closer to Lu. He holds the container up. "See that tiny little thing, there?"

Lu can just barely detect a floating whitish blob about the size of a fingertip.

"Have you ever been stung by a jellyfish, Mr. Long?" Cho asks. "If so, my guess is you encountered an ordinary moon jelly. Very common. Their sting is relatively mild, but still quite painful. Raises a nasty welt. What I have here, however, is something completely—entirely—different." Cho gives the container a shake. "This is an Irukandji. They come from that unfortunate country where it seems every living creature and plant evolved with the sole purpose of killing humans."

Lu manages to choke out a guess: "Sweden?"

Cho smiles. "Australia." He gives the soup container another shake. "Don't be fooled by the Irukandji's small stature. This little guy is one of the most efficient murderers on the planet. Nearly invisible in water. Its stinger leaves no trace. Its victims suffer a range of symptoms collectively known as Irukandji syndrome. Initially, only a mild irritation. Ten to thirty minutes later, severe cramping in the arms and legs. Then, an excruciating pain in the lower back. Followed by vomiting and difficulty breathing. The unbearable sensation of millions of tiny insects crawling beneath your skin. A blinding headache. Elevated heart rate and blood pressure. An unshakable feeling of impending doom. And then, eventually, death resulting from a brain hemorrhage or heart attack."

Bullethead shoves his knee harder into Lu's back, sharply arching his spine. Cho catches Lu's left wrist and clamps it between his elbow and hip. Lu feels his fingertips touch lukewarm water. He fights to pull his hand away.

"Don't flail about, Mr. Long," Cho says. "You might piss off our little friend."

Lu freezes.

"Who do you really work for?" Cho asks.

"Alex Ho," Lu rasps. He feels a tickle against his forefinger.

"And who is Alex working for?" Cho says.

"Himself! *Ta ma de*, let me go!"

"Why are you in Kunming?"

"To buy! Take my hand out of the water, you prick!"

"Why here?"

"Everyone knows Myanmar is the source, and Kunming is the doorway to Myanmar."

"What does this Alex Ho want with these products?"

"Impress his friends! Get his dick hard!" Lu grits his teeth. "*Gan ni niang*, take my hand out of the *water*!"

"You are a police informant!"

"I'm not! I swear."

"What is your address in Macao?"

"Three thirty Zhongshan Road, flat number twenty-three." Lu is making this up on the spot, but he figures any city with Chinese street names has at least one Zhongshan Road.

Cho rips off a series of rapid-fire questions—about Lu's parents, where he attended high school, how long he has worked for Alex Ho. He peppers his verbal assault with accusations that Lu is working for the PSB, the Macao Security force, Interpol, and a variety of acronyms that Lu has never heard of—USAID, ICCWC, CITES, UNODC.

Lu denies everything.

Cho abruptly removes the plastic container. "I will make a call," he says, and walks out of the room.

Bullethead unwinds the garrote. Lu bends double on the stool and coughs. His throat burns. He glares furiously at Bullethead. Bullethead pulls his jacket aside to show Lu the butt of the gun in his waistband.

Minutes pass. Lu rolls his neck and massages the deep crease around his throat. Finally, the door opens and Cho returns. "All right." He hands

Lu a bottle of water. Lu drinks, each swallow going down like a pellet of hot lead. "I hope you won't be too angry with us."

"You're a couple of bastards."

"This business is filled with bastards," Cho says. "One cannot be too careful. The good news is, Mr. Long, you just made your first friends in Kunming."

Cho tells Bullethead to fetch a round of beers from a cooler out front. While they drink, Cho confirms that he can procure whatever Alex Ho is looking for. Tiger, civet, pangolin, every kind of snake and bird, bamboo rat, fox, wolf pup, alligator, otter, ostrich—the list goes on and on.

"The thing is," Lu says, "Alex wants me to visit the source myself."

"Why?"

"He's particular about *yewei*. He wants me to vet the quality and confirm he's not being sold substandard fare from a meat mill."

"I can't take you to Myanmar."

"Why not?"

"For one thing, perhaps you're not aware, but it's another country, Mr. Long."

"I'm sure you have ways of crossing the border without a visa."

"The suppliers there rely on me to service customers in China. They don't work direct."

"But you'll vouch for me. We're friends now, right?"

Cho smiles. "Why don't you just give me a shopping list and I'll handle everything? You can stay here in Kunming and sample all the pleasures the city has to offer."

"Alex told me to personally vet the source. End of story. If you can't take me to Myanmar, I'll find someone who can."

"Mr. Long . . ." Cho shakes his head. "You don't want to go there. It's not a place where outsiders are welcome. It's extremely dangerous, especially now."

"You're an outsider."

"No, I'm not," Cho says. "I'm Burmese."

"Well, Alex was very specific. I don't want to disappoint him."

"It would be too complicated to make arrangements."

"*Gei wo mianzi*, Mr. Cho." *Give me face.* In other words, show me some respect. A request that cannot be refused without grave insult.

Cho sighs dramatically. The magic words have been spoken. Now he's in a bind.

Lu swallows the rest of his beer. "Either I go to Myanmar personally or there's no deal." He stands. "I'm tired. Take me back to my hotel."

Cho and Bullethead escort Lu to the mouth of the alleyway, where the SUV awaits. Cho opens the back door. "I'll see what I can do."

"You know where to reach me."

The driver wordlessly returns Lu to the Crowne Plaza. Lu walks on unsteady legs through the lobby. He rides the elevator up to his floor.

It's nearly three in the morning. He has never felt more worn out. He enters his room and locks the door behind him, then goes into the bathroom and takes a long piss and splashes scalding-hot water on his face. He strips off his shirt and dumps it on the floor.

He stumbles out of the bathroom with one goal in mind—bed.

He finds two men sitting in the dark, waiting for him.

TWENTY-FIVE

One of the men switches on a desk lamp. He has a wide, square face with a broad expanse of gleaming forehead leading up to a receding hairline, reminiscent of the late Chairman Mao. Thick forearms. Wide shoulders, a broad chest, and a substantial belly. He's wearing a maroon polo shirt and black trousers and he looks like a moderately successful businessman dressed for a weekend golf trip.

The second man is Bang.

"So much for watching my back!" Lu yells.

"I saw you make contact," Bang says calmly. "That was the plan."

"Do you know what they did to me?"

"Inspector," the man with the receding hairline says. "Please lower your voice."

"Who the hell are you?" Lu snaps.

"I am Jia."

Lu is confused, but he knows one thing—this is not the person he spoke to on the video feed in Harbin.

"I must admit I haven't been entirely honest with you, Inspector," Jia says.

"Oh, really?"

"I don't actually work for the Forestry and Grassland Administration."

"Who, then?"

"The Ministry of State Security."

"Ah," Lu says. *Ta ma de.*

The MSS is the most feared government agency in the People's

Republic. Its stated mission is to ensure "the security of the country through effective measures against enemy agents, spies, and counterrevolutionary activities designed to sabotage, destabilize or overthrow China's socialist system." In practice, it is akin to the CIA, FBI, and NSA of the United States, all rolled into one supersecret, all-powerful faceless entity.

Now it all makes a bit more sense—the fake ID, wads of cash, access to intelligence regarding Khaw and Wilson Fang.

"But I spoke to you—to Jia Zhanshu—on the computer."

"You spoke to *me* through the medium of a deep-fake video."

That perhaps explains the glitchy nature of the feed. Lu shakes his head in amazement. The capacity for technology to pull the wool over one's eyes has become absolutely terrifying.

"What's your real name?" Lu asks.

"For now, you can continue to call me Jia."

Lu walks over to the mini fridge. "I need a beer. Anyone want a beer?"

"Sure," Jia says, taking Lu by surprise.

Lu extracts a can and tosses it across the room, hoping to bean Jia in the head, but instead Jia catches it one-handed. Lu is grudgingly impressed. He offers a can to Bang, who just gives a short shake of his head. Lu takes a can for himself, pops the tab, guzzles, and belches loudly.

"Better?" Jia asks.

"They stuck my hand in a bowl with a deadly jellyfish!"

"You have to give them points for creativity."

"Do you find this amusing?" Lu shouts. "Because I'm not laughing!"

"Inspector," Jia says. "We knew they would be wary. We knew they would interrogate you. This was a dangerous, yet crucial test. And you passed. Congratulations!"

"A killer jellyfish!"

"Please sit down and let's discuss this like civilized people."

"I'm not going to Myanmar." Lu sits on the edge of the bed. "Get yourself another sucker."

Jia props a meaty elbow on the desk. "You are on the verge of accomplishing something no law enforcement agent in the People's Republic has ever managed to do: penetrate the inner circle of an insidious global animal-trafficking network. Think of the good that will come from your efforts!"

"If I survive."

Jia flicks an imaginary speck from his pants and crosses one leg over the other. He has committed the cardinal sin of wearing white socks with dark pants, but that's not what attracts Lu's attention—it's his shoes. Loafers. Leather. A foreign luxury brand, easily costing fifteen hundred yuan a pair. A bit steep for a public servant's salary. Either Jia comes from a rich family, or he's got an alternative source of income.

"You'll be fine," Jia says. "As long as you stick to your cover story. And should something go awry, Captain Bang will be there to extract you."

"Given what happened tonight," Lu says, "I'm not sure Bang is capable of extracting a big brass ring from a dead dog's asshole."

"We could not intervene during this first contact," Jia says. "Otherwise, the whole operation would have had to be scrubbed before it even began in earnest."

Lu grunts into his beer.

"Stage two," Jia continues. "You will cross the border by whatever means your new friends have devised. Captain Bang will follow as you make your way to Khaw's facility." Jia nods at Bang. "Captain?"

Bang takes a small plastic ziplock bag out of his pocket and tosses it onto the bed. Lu eyes it warily, then picks it up. Inside is a small lozenge-shaped device. "What is this?"

"Short-range tracking device," Bang says.

"What if Cho searches me? Am I supposed to sew it into the lining of my underwear?"

"You will swallow it."

"Swallow it? That's ridiculous."

"It's perfectly harmless," Jia says. "It will pass through your digestive system in a few days. But you'll want to wait until the last possible moment to ingest it, so you don't end up flushing it down a toilet before you reach your destination."

Lu figures he'll be able to get the tracker down without too much trouble, but what about when it comes out the other end? "Is this going to give me colon cancer?"

"The technology is perfectly safe." Jia sips from his can of beer and wipes his lips with a thick knuckle. "Once you have led Captain Bang to Khaw's location, he'll relay the exact coordinates to me by satellite phone. That is our first objective. The second is to gain some photographic evidence of Khaw's operation. The animal pens, drug labs, Khaw herself. And you'll want to establish that Fang is there, of course. My guess is he'll be laying low. It may be necessary for you to go looking for him."

"What if he's *not* there? Or he is, but I can't find him?"

"Then it might be difficult—perhaps impossible—to get him extradited."

"Can't you just digitally insert him into a photo of Khaw kicking a pangolin or something?"

"We could," Jia says. "But that wouldn't fool my superiors. I need irrefutable evidence to support an ironclad case."

"Well, just so you know," Lu says, "the cell phone Bang gave me went for a little swim."

"No problem. We expected that all personal devices would be confiscated before you cross the border."

"So how then do you expect me to come up with photographic evidence?"

Bang produces a second ziplock bag. "This is a self-contained mini-HD camera, with enough internal memory for approximately five hundred photographs." Bang rattles this off like the world's most boring electronics salesman. "It fits into a buttonhole like so." He shakes the camera out of the bag and fixes it to his shirt. "Normally such a device would be paired with a remote control. But because we expect you'll be searched multiple times, we can't take the risk of giving you extra hardware. So, we've configured this one to operate by voice command."

"A voice command," Lu says. "What voice command?"

"We tried to come up with something that didn't sound odd or suspicious," Jia says. "And that you could say repeatedly, as the need to take a photo presented itself."

"I can't wait to hear."

"The command," Jia says, "is '*ta ma de.*'"

"*Ta ma de?*"

"Yes. As in, *ta ma de*, it's hot today. *Ta ma de*, this beer is refreshing. *Ta ma de*, what a beautiful necklace you're wearing, Daw Khaw. *Ta ma de*, would you look at that magnificent tiger?"

"I get the idea," Lu says. "But never mind the remote—if they do search me, they'll find the camera, right? Unless you expect me to swallow it, too?"

"No." Jia smiles, a touch ruefully. "But there is one place on your person they are not likely to examine too closely."

It takes Lu a moment to understand. "Absolutely not."

"Inspector—"

"No!"

"Any minor and temporary physical distress you might experience is in the service of the greater good."

"Easy for you to say."

"Justice for the girl."

"You don't give a damn about her."

"No," Jia admits. "But I want Fang. And I'm going to get him. And you're going to help me."

"I'm not swallowing a GPS tracker, I'm not sticking a camera up my ass, and I'm not going to Myanmar."

"You are, in fact," Jia says, "doing all of those things."

"Get stuffed," Lu growls. "If you don't work for the NFGA, what do you care about Fang anyway?"

"The bare outlines of what I told you before are true. Fang has a compromising relationship with various officials, including some in both the NFGA and even the MSS. I can't trust anyone on the inside, apart from Captain Bang. I badly want to catch Fang, squeeze him, and root out the rotten apples."

"How noble. Maybe you're just looking for ammo against some department rivals."

"You misjudge me. I am a dedicated public servant." Jia drinks deeply from his can, then crushes it in his fist. "The hard part is already over. It remains only for you to take a trip down south, have some drinks, eat some exotic food—enjoy the local girls, if you like—and then return home."

"You're glossing over a few details there."

"In return for your service, I will see that you are reinstated as deputy chief. And when you grow tired of idling away your life in Raven Valley, you can choose your next posting. Nanjing. Shanghai. Even Beijing is not out of the question."

"I'm not that ambitious."

"How about when you marry and have children? I can arrange for them to attend one of the better schools. Don't underestimate the potential benefit my patronage can provide you."

"*Now* you sound like a *proper* ministry official."

Jia shifts gears. "Once Fang is in my hands, I promise you he will tell us what has become of the girl."

"Tan Meixiang," Lu says. "Her name is Tan Meixiang."

"I might even be able to arrange some sort of monetary disbursement for the Tan family. A sum confiscated from Fang's assets."

"Don't make promises you can't keep."

"Inspector, this is not a discussion. The operation is in motion, and you will see it through."

"Or?" Lu asks.

Jia stands. "I'm sorry to be so harsh, but the wheels are turning. *Po fu chen zhou.*" Literally: *smash your cooking pots and sink your boats.* "You are doing our country a great service. I wish you a safe journey to Myanmar."

Bang removes the camera from his shirt, drops it into the plastic bag, and tosses it onto the bed. He and Jia walk out of the room without another word. Lu locks the door behind them.

Only later, as he lies in bed tossing and turning, does it occur to Lu that Jia took his empty beer can with him, carefully removing any evidence that he was ever there.

TWENTY-SIX

The phone rings at dawn, startling Lu awake.

It's Cho: "Here's the deal. You will transfer a sum of three hundred thousand yuan to an escrow account as a gesture of good faith. The money will be offset against any purchases you make."

Three hundred thousand yuan is a tidy amount, equivalent to more than forty thousand US dollars. "That's a lot of money," Lu says.

"If you're not serious about this, then forget it."

"Does this mean my request has been accepted?"

"Transfer the money and then book yourself on the eleven forty-five a.m. flight to Jinghong."

"I'm not sure I can swing it that quickly."

"Then we won't be doing business. Got a pen? I'll give you the account details."

Lu jots down the information and hangs up. Now what? The cell phone provided by Bang is at the bottom of Cho's fish tank. How is he supposed to come up with three hundred thousand yuan?

Lu notices the message light on the hotel room phone blinking. He dials the line. There is a package waiting for him downstairs.

Lu showers, changes, and runs down to the concierge, where he collects a padded envelope. He can guess what's inside. He asks the concierge to help him book a flight to Jinghong and then returns to his room and opens the envelope. As expected, it's a new cell phone.

Lu punches in ten-zero-one-one-nine-four-nine. The phone unlocks.

There is one preset number listed as "Alex." Lu dials it. He hears a beep. "We need to talk," Lu says. He hangs up.

He is packing up his things when the cell phone rings. Lu answers: "Yes?"

"What?" Bang says.

Lu tells him about the flight and the money.

"Understood," Bang says.

"So, you will handle the money?" Lu asks. In response, all he hears is a dial tone.

Lu eats a leisurely breakfast in the hotel lobby, then checks out and catches a taxi to the airport. He passes through security without incident and discovers Cho and Bullethead sitting in the departure lounge. He gives them a nod but sits as far away from them as possible.

After a short wait, the plane boards. Lu sits in the back, Cho and Bullethead up front. The flight is just over an hour long and alarmingly bumpy. After disembarking, they meet in the baggage area. A car is waiting outside, and everyone piles in for the short drive to Jinghong proper.

"What's the plan?" Lu wants to know.

"Relax, Mr. Long," Cho says. "You're in the south now. Life down here moves at a slower pace."

Bullethead lights up a Hongtashan cigarette, a local Yunnan brand, known for its high nicotine and sugar content. Cho offers the driver a Marlboro Red and lights one of his own. Soon, the cab is filled with smoke and Lu is forced to crack the window. Warm, wet air ruffles his hair.

Lu doesn't know much about Jinghong, aside from the fact that it's the capital of the Xishuangbanna Dai Autonomous Prefecture in Yunnan Province. He recalls from his boring high school civics class that there are five autonomous regions in the country. Chinese law gives these regions the right to govern themselves in accordance with the cultural beliefs of their indigenous minority groups. However, in reality, as with all other levels of government, local leaders remain completely subordinate to the CCP.

They reach the city center. The atmosphere here is completely different from a northern metropolis like Harbin. The buildings are lower, many of them featuring the distinctive multitiered swooping roofs one associates with Thai temples. The streets are wider and lined with palm trees and flowering plants. Traffic consists of cars, trucks, the ubiquitous scooters, and motorcycles, but also something Lu rarely sees—*tuk tuks*. The Chinese call these three-wheeled jury-rigged contraptions *du che,* or "beep cars," for reasons which are obvious once you see their drivers, often hopped up on betel nuts or some form of cheap amphetamine, zip through traffic like they are being chased by a swarm of angry hornets.

The car turns down a side street and comes to a stop in front of a two-story building with a signboard that reads *The Golden Water Buffalo.* Everyone climbs out and collects their luggage.

They are greeted at the door by a plump woman in her late fifties, evidently the owner. She introduces herself as "Auntie Yang."

"You hungry?" she says. "Thirsty? Horny?"

Lu isn't sure he heard that last one correctly. When he enters, he sees the downstairs is a low-lit bar/restaurant, complete with karaoke equipment and a disco ball. A few girls are sitting around, dressed in shorts and halter tops, waving paper fans to shoo away flies.

"We'll have a late lunch," Cho tells Auntie Yang. "But first we'll put our stuff in our rooms."

Auntie Yang yells at a skinny youth, perhaps her son, to collect the bags. Lu hangs on to his, but Cho and Bullethead are happy to let the kid carry their things. The rooms are all on the backside of the building, overlooking a river the Chinese call the Lancang, but which Westerners know from its association with the Vietnam War by a different name—the Mekong.

"Bathroom at the end of hall," Auntie Yang tells Lu, pointing. She opens a door and waves Lu inside. "This is you."

"Downstairs in ten," Cho says.

Lu enters the room and shuts the door. It is spartan and cheaply furnished. A single bed, nightstand, a wooden wardrobe, an air-conditioning unit in the window, one solitary chair. The walls are painted uneven shades of light green. The only decorative accent is a giveaway calendar with a picture of some Dai girls in traditional costumes pinned to the wall.

Lu tosses his bag on the chair and looks out the window. He sees a ribbon of mud and marsh giving way to the wide expanse of the river. The water is greenish brown. A few boats drift lazily along with the current.

He switches on the air-conditioning and tests the bed. It feels like a thin layer of cotton set on top of a concrete slab. The sheets are stiff and scratchy. It's no Crowne Plaza, that's for sure.

Lu wonders how many desperately lonely men have had sex with one of the girls downstairs in this bed. On top of these very sheets.

He fishes the cell phone out of his pocket and texts his location to Bang. Then he erases the text.

The Golden Water Buffalo has the appearance of a low-rent operation, but Lu checks the room for hidden cameras and microphones anyway. He finds nothing, just a collection of dead, desiccated roach corpses under the wardrobe.

Lu isn't sure what arrangement exists between Cho and Auntie Yang, but he figures it's better to err on the side of caution and assume one of the girls will search his belongings while he's at lunch. He takes a pack of gum out of his pocket and crams a few sticks into his mouth. When he has a nice wet wad going, he extracts it and divides it into two pieces. He uses one piece to affix the miniature camera under the frame of the bed, and the other to attach the GPS tracker to the bottom of the wardrobe. He carefully arranges the zipper of his bag in a particular way. Then he walks down the hall to the bathroom. Inside is a toilet and a rust-stained sink. He washes his hands and splashes some water on his face, then heads downstairs.

Cho and Bullethead are sitting by the karaoke stage, drinking local beer and smoking cigarettes. Lu joins them. One of the girls comes over, leans casually against his chair, and rests a cool hand on his shoulder. "You want a drink?"

"I'll have one of those." Lu nods at the beer.

"Sure. My name's Jing."

"Thanks, Jing. I'm Ming."

"Ming and Jing," the girl says. "Sounds like fate. Maybe later we'll spend some time together." She strokes Lu's neck. "I can help you relax."

Jing brings Lu a beer. Lunch arrives. Chicken with bamboo shoots, shallots, ginger, and chili. Beef noodles. Lichen cake. Grilled fish slathered with chili paste. Deep-fried grasshoppers. The meal is surprisingly good, for a bar cum brothel.

"So, what's the plan?" Lu asks, for the second time, when they are on their second beers.

"We sleep here tonight," Cho says. "Tomorrow, early, we go across the border."

"How far is it?"

"Not far. A hundred and twenty kilometers or so."

"Why not just go this afternoon?" Lu asks.

Bullethead grins, his gold teeth flecked with grasshopper chitin. "What's your hurry, brother? Why don't you just chill out?"

"My employer is paying me to work. Not *chill*."

Cho wipes his mouth with a napkin. "I told you, Mr. Long. You're practically in Southeast Asia now. The weather is hotter. The pace is slower. People know how to take pleasure in the little things. A good meal. A cold beer. A warm girl." He pushes back from the table. "I'll see you boys later this evening." He heads for the stairs, collecting one of the girls on the way up.

Bullethead finishes his beer and bowl of rice and tugs at one of the other girls, leaving Lu alone at the table.

Jing comes over and sits in one of the empty chairs. "Had enough to eat?"

"Yeah."

"Ready for something sweet?"

"I'm pretty full."

She laughs. "That's not what I meant."

"Maybe later. I just need to lie down for a bit. Big lunch, two beers."

Jing rests a hand on his knee. "I'll help you sleep like a newborn baby."

"Later."

She makes a show of pouting. "You don't like me."

"I like you fine."

"Later, other men will come. You might lose your chance."

"I'll have to risk it."

Jing's pout deepens.

Lu wonders if this is a test devised by Cho. Jing is cute, although not exactly his type, even minus the fact that she's a prostitute. But what about Long Ming? What would *he* do in this situation?

"Tell you what," Lu says, pulling a wad of cash out of his pocket. He peels off some bills and slides them across the table. "This is an advance. I don't know what those other two have planned for tonight, but if I'm free, you and I can have some fun. Provided I don't get too drunk."

Jing takes the money and caresses Lu's cheek. "Don't worry about that. I can wake the dead."

Lu goes up to his room and checks the location of the GPS tracker and camera. They are where he left them, but the zipper on his bag is flipped in the other direction. He wonders who searched his things. Auntie Yang? The skinny kid? One of the girls?

He's worn out, but also wired. He lies down and attempts to catnap, but his mind won't stop churning.

Eventually, he gets up and finds a door next to the bathroom that opens to reveal a tiled stall with a water nozzle poking out from the wall. Lu rinses off and feels revived. He changes into a black T-shirt and white linen pants and heads downstairs. A couple of the girls are singing sad country songs on the karaoke set. One of them is Jing. Lu is surprised to hear she has a lovely voice. Given another time, another place, she might have had a career as a singer in a bar cover band. Instead, each night she sells her body for a fistful of cash.

Such is fate.

TWENTY-SEVEN

Lu steps outside into a blanket of thick, warm, soupy air. He ambles down the sidewalk, passing bars, restaurants, cheap hostels, stores selling clothing and souvenirs, a bike repair shop. As he walks, he hears a babble of languages. A few Caucasian tourists speaking something that Lu knows is not English. German, perhaps? Mandarin spoken in various accents. Some other Asian dialects that Lu cannot identify, but that sound like Thai. Lu assumes it is the Dai mother tongue.

He turns in the direction of the Lancang River, and, after winding through a couple of alleyways and detouring around a construction site, he emerges onto a leafy walkway overlooking mud flats, and beyond that, the river itself. A couple of old men stand in a shallow spot, fishing. A rusty trawler putts along the far shore.

Lu takes a long, slow look around. No sign of Cho or Bullethead. No sign of Captain Bang.

He takes out the cell phone provided by Jia and changes the settings to block its caller ID. He dials a number from memory. It rings and rings, and finally a girl's timid voice answers.

"Hello?"

"Meirong, it's me. Inspector Lu."

He hears a sharp intake of breath. "Did you— Have you—"

"No. Not yet. But I wanted to check in on you." Silence. "Are you there?" Lu pictures her in the shabby apartment, alone in her anguish, her father anesthetized on cheap liquor. "Meirong?"

"Where are you?"

"I'm . . . chasing down a lead."

"What lead?

"I can't say."

"Why can't you say?"

"The investigation is ongoing. I just wanted you to know that—"

"You keep telling me you're looking for her, but you won't say if you even think she's alive or dead! Can you tell me that, at least? Is she alive or dead? Is she alive or DEAD?"

Meirong's voice reaches a shrill crescendo. This was a bad idea. Perhaps it's just cruel to let Meirong believe her sister might one day come walking through the door. "The truth is, I don't know."

"You don't know anything!"

Lu is suddenly angry. "I know I'm putting my life on the line to find your sister!"

"What do you mean, putting your life on the line?"

Lu lets out a breath. "Forget it."

"But what do you mean?"

"Never mind, Meirong. I just wanted to call to check in on you. I probably won't be able to call again for a while."

"When are you coming back?"

"I don't know. Maybe a week." If *I come back*, Lu thinks. He sees movement out of the corner of his eye. A man, barreling toward him. An aggressive posture. Lu tenses.

Ta ma de. It's Bang.

"I have to go," Lu says.

"Wait!"

"Take care, Meirong."

"Wait!"

"What?"

"I . . ." Her voice chokes. "Come back soon."

"I'll do my best." Lu hangs up just as Bang is upon him.

"Who are you talking to?" Bang is dressed in a cap, sunglasses, jeans, hiking boots, a long-sleeve shirt unbuttoned over a T-shirt.

Lu hesitates, but it really doesn't matter if Bang knows. "Tan Mei-xiang's sister."

"Why?"

"To let her know I haven't forgotten the reason why I'm doing all this."

"What did you tell her?"

"Nothing," Lu says. "Just that I'm still on the case."

"That was a stupid thing to do. Give me the phone."

Lu hands it over.

Bang checks the phone log. "You'd better not have called anyone else."

"Or what? You'll spank me and send me to bed without supper?"

"Yes. I might just do that." Bang slips the phone into his pocket. "When are you leaving for Myanmar?"

"Tomorrow. Are you taking my phone to punish me?"

"You won't need it from here on out, anyway. And I don't want you making any more unauthorized calls. Such as to your girlfriend at the Red Lotus."

"That sounds vaguely threatening, Bang."

"Does it? Have they said where you'll be crossing over?"

"I could use some coffee. You want coffee?"

"Coffee?" Bang asks.

"Dark, bitter liquid."

"I know what coffee is."

"Let's get some." Lu starts to walk away. Bang catches his arm. Lu looks down at Bang's hand, then up at his own reflection in the lenses of Bang's sunglasses. "Let go."

Bang smiles. To Lu's recollection, this is the first time he's seen Bang express any emotion whatsoever. "Or?" Bang says. His fingers squeeze Lu's elbow, seeking a pressure point.

Lu rips his arm out of Bang's grasp, moves away, and takes a defensive stance. "Don't push me, Bang. I'm liable to just punch you in the face."

A group of old men pass by, carrying makeshift fishing poles. Bang glances in their direction. "As . . . entertaining . . . as that might be, a fist-fight would attract the wrong kind of attention."

"Then don't start shit with me."

"Don't walk away when I'm asking you a question."

"I have some questions of my own," Lu says. "What do you say we grab some coffee and talk like civilized human beings?"

"I don't think we should risk being seen together any more than necessary."

"Didn't you make sure I wasn't being tailed before you snuck up on me?"

Bang shrugs.

"Come or don't come," Lu says. "It's up to you." He turns and walks away.

Lu knows he's being unreasonable. But he's tired of feeling powerless. He wants to take a measure of control, no matter how trivial.

And besides, if all goes according to plan, he's shortly going to be stranded in Myanmar with Bang as his sole lifeline. It would be prudent to get some measure of the man.

Lu retraces his steps to a coffee shop he passed on the way to the river. He enters and takes a seat in the back. Bang shuffles in sixty seconds later. He sits across from Lu, his back to the door.

Lu scans the menu. "You look to me like a *maqiduo* kind of guy."

"What is a *maqiduo*?"

"Espresso with steamed milk."

"What's espresso?"

"Never mind." Lu signals to the waitress and orders two iced coffees with milk.

Bang twists around to eye the entrance. "Switch seats with me."

"No. Take off your sunglasses. You look like a hoodlum."

Bang puts his sunglasses in the pocket of his shirt. "Where are the camera and tracker now?"

"Safe."

"Safe where?"

"How about this?" Lu says. "You ask a question, and then I ask a question. We take turns, see? How did you come to work for Jia or whatever his name is?"

"That's classified." Bang says. "And we are not here to get better acquainted. I'm asking for a situation report."

"Did you volunteer for this gig out of a love of exotic animals, or because you're a mindless killing machine who does what he's told?"

"Classified."

"You're going to have to throw me a bone."

"Why?"

"Because if you're going to be my only backup, I want to know something more about you than your name, rank, and serial number."

"You should consider the possibility, however remote, that in the course of this operation, you'll be exposed and tortured," Bang says. "If that's the case, the less you know, the better."

"Way to set my mind at ease."

Their coffee arrives. Bang sips and makes a face of disgust. "I prefer tea."

"I'm sure you've seen whatever file MSS has on me," Lu says. "You know as much about me as my own mother. Return the favor."

"My personal history is irrelevant to this operation."

"I disagree."

Bang glances again at the entrance. "Switch seats with me."

"When you were in the special forces, you trained for months with the same team of guys, right?" Lu asks. "You knew each other inside and out. Trusted one another implicitly. You were closer than brothers. You'd give up your life for any one of them. Isn't that the warrior ethos?"

"This is not the special forces. And you are not a warrior."

"I'm not rappelling from a helicopter into an enemy position, but I'm still on a dangerous mission. How many times have you infiltrated hostile territory completely alone?"

"Classified."

"And I don't mind admitting that I'm scared," Lu says. "This is not what I was trained for."

"I'm taking an even bigger risk," Bang says. "At least you have a cover story. I'll be in hostile territory with my ass hanging out in the breeze. So, man up."

"You're a real bastard, you know that?"

Bang takes another sip of coffee, then pushes the glass away. "Part of the job description."

"Tell me how you came to join the military."

"No."

"Come on, Bang," Lu says. "The mountains are tall and the emperor far away. Jia's not risking his life. *We* are. If not friends or brothers, let's at least be allies."

Bang looks at the door once more, then back at Lu. He sighs. "I joined up after high school. It was either that or get a job in a factory. I figured, if nothing else, I'd at least have food to eat and a roof over my head."

"Straight into the special forces?" Lu asks.

"Infantry first. After I made corporal, my commanding officer suggested I submit an application. I did, and I made it through the training. Most did not."

"What branch?"

"Classified."

"Come on."

"Eastern Sword."

"Oh? Impressive." Lu doesn't know much about the PLA special units, but Eastern Sword is famous as the elite of the elite—a small force of highly trained individuals who are qualified for any kind of combat operation, land, sea, or air. "Ever kill anyone?"

"Classified. But yes." Bang smiles.

"Okay, so you achieved the rank of captain, and then what?"

"After some years, I was approached by the MSS. It seemed like the next natural step in my career."

"And Jia?"

"I was assigned to his department eighteen months ago."

"How well do you know him?"

"We don't go out for coffee, if that's what you're asking."

"You trust him?"

Bang shrugs. "He's my commanding officer now."

"You just follow orders and don't ask questions, is that it?"

"My turn," Bang says. "The tracker and camera?"

"Hidden in my room. Someone searched my bag, but I assume if they'd found the devices, I'd be floating in the Lancang River about now."

"Where are you crossing the border?"

"I don't know, but Cho said the crossing point is one hundred and twenty kilometers from here."

Bang asks a few more questions, about Cho and Bullethead, anything they may have said concerning the journey, what to expect on the other side. Then he leans in. "Be prepared for them to come for you before dawn. They'll want to catch you with your guard down. Keep the camera and tracker handy, but not in a place where they can be found. Is there a bathroom in your room?"

"We share one down the hall."

"Maybe find a hiding place under the sink. Choose carefully. Ask to use the bathroom just before you depart and . . . do what needs to be done." Bang sets a small square package on the table. Lu is scandalized to see it's a condom. "Lubricated," Bang says.

Lu slaps his hand over the condom and slides it off the table. "I'm going to pretend you didn't say that."

"From this point forward, we won't meet again," Bang says. "Unless something goes terribly wrong."

He insists on leaving first. Lu gives it five minutes, then pays the bill. He looks for Bang on the walk back to the Golden Water Buffalo, but, true to Bang's word, he is nowhere to be seen.

TWENTY-EIGHT

Lu delays returning to the Golden Water Buffalo for as long as possible, hoping that Cho and the others will be too drunk to take notice of him and Jing will have found a willing client for the evening. He eats dinner at a hole-in-the-wall joint, then wanders the streets until he grows weary and finally heads back, his feet sore and armpits sticky with sweat.

He's out of luck. Cho and Bullethead are holding court at one of the tables when Lu enters, along with several girls, including Jing. Cho waves him over. Jing rises and motions for Lu to take her chair. He does. She plops herself onto his lap. "I thought maybe you fell into the river," she says.

"Bring us a glass!" Cho shouts. The table is littered with snacks, dirty ashtrays, and empty beer bottles. A half-empty Suntory whisky bottle sits beside a bucket of ice. Cho stabs at his gums with a toothpick. "What do you think of Jinghong?"

Lu gently tries to lever Jing off his lap, but she's not budging. "Reminds me of Bangkok." Lu has never been to Bangkok, but he figures it's a place Long Ming would visit frequently. "Hey, darling, I'm a little sweaty," he tells Jing. "Hop off so I can run up and take a shower."

"Stay and drink with us," Cho says. Auntie Yang arrives with a glass. Cho fills it with ice and whisky and sets it down in front of Lu. *"Gan bei!"*

"I'd rather have a beer," Lu says.

Bullethead sneers. "We're drinking *whisky.*"

Lu figures he can stomach one glass. He sips. The alcohol tastes like bile.

Cho and Bullethead are already three-quarters drunk. They chain-smoke, make dirty jokes with the girls, and force everyone to imbibe copiously. Peer pressure to consume alcohol is a common feature of Chinese dinner parties, a way to quickly build an atmosphere of frivolity, but the way Cho goes about it is decidedly malicious. Lu is plied with two glasses of whisky in short order and then decides he's had enough. The next time Cho reaches over to pour, Lu holds his hand over the top of his glass. Whisky runs across his wrist onto the table.

"*Cao ni ma*, look what you've done!" Cho says. "This shit costs nearly one thousand yuan a bottle."

"No more," Lu says.

"Don't be rude," Cho says. "We're just trying to show you a good time."

"I'm having the time of my life," Lu says. "But I don't want to end up sleeping on the floor of the bathroom."

"Brother Long," Cho says. *"Gei wo mianzi." Give me face.*

The magic words. "Fine," Lu concedes. "One last glass." He shakes droplets off his hand.

Cho fills Lu's glass to the rim, then pours for Bullethead. Bullethead takes the bottle and pours for Cho. Lu sips and gags.

Bullethead attempts to light a cigarette, but he has left his manual dexterity at the bottom of his glass. One of the girls finally takes pity on him, removes the cigarette from his mouth, lights it, hands it back. Cho grabs the girl next to him and roughly attempts to kiss her. She giggles and playfully pushes him away. Lu takes advantage of these distractions to pour a measure of his whisky onto the floor. Jing, who has shifted from his lap to her own chair, watches him do so. For a moment, he's afraid she's going to rat him out. But, instead, she gives him a conspiratorial smile.

Somehow, Lu manages to finish the contents of his glass. Cho orders a fresh bottle. Lu shakes his head and stands, already finding his balance to be compromised. "I'm calling it a night."

"But it's early," Cho protests.

"I'm tired."

"Sit, Brother Long," Cho says. "You're ruining the mood."

"I'm done."

Bullethead reaches under his shirt and pulls out a gun. He slaps it on the table, rattling the glassware. The girls immediately stop chattering and eye the gun warily, but do not run away screaming in a panic. Lu assumes this is not the first time they've seen a firearm brandished at the Golden Water Buffalo.

"Put that away, you idiot," Lu says.

"You insult us by refusing our hospitality," Bullethead slurs.

"That's not my intention. I'm tired, is all. I want to take a shower and get some sleep."

"Sure," Cho says agreeably. "Just as soon as we've finished our drinks." Auntie Yang magically materializes with an unopened bottle of Suntory.

Lu considers his options. Cho is being an ass. The question is, if Lu just leaves, what will he do? Probably nothing. It would be bad form to kill a potentially lucrative client. But Bullethead's eyes are glassy and mean. In his state of drunken belligerence, he might do something stupid. Something both he and Lu would greatly regret. "This is a dangerous game you're playing," he says.

Cho pops the top on the bottle. "No game. I'm just trying to be a good host." Cho holds the bottle out. Lu responds with a cold stare. Bullethead slips his finger into the trigger guard of his gun.

Lu makes no move to pick up his glass.

Bullethead spins the gun a few centimeters to point the barrel at Lu.

The girls remain frozen in place—like garishly painted Roman statues in short-shorts and tank tops. Auntie Yang expertly fades into the wallpaper.

Cho motions insistently with the bottle. Bullethead bares his dirty golden teeth.

Jing breaks the impasse by picking up Lu's glass. She holds it out with two hands. Cho pours to the rim. He sets the bottle down and smiles. *"Gan bei."* This traditional toast literally means "dry your cup," and it can be taken as a challenge to finish all the alcohol in your glass in one go.

"*Sui yi*," Jing says, giving Cho the polite response for when you prefer to just have a sip. Despite this, she drains nearly half the glass, enraging Cho.

"I'm not here to drink with a whore!" he shouts. "Give it to Brother Long!"

Lu takes the glass and resentfully drinks. His stomach lurches.

Cho and Bullethead laugh uproariously. Cho says something to Bullethead in Burmese and Bullethead slips the gun back under the table.

The party resumes. Lu sinks into his chair and wonders how he's going to get the rest of that glass down without puking all over his linen pants.

Jing speaks softly to the girl sitting next to Cho in a local dialect. The girl takes Cho by the ears and sticks her tongue sloppily into his mouth. Bullethead slaps the table with glee. Jing takes Lu's glass and drinks a portion, then quickly passes it back. She wipes her lower lip with a finger and gives Lu a lopsided grin.

The evening wears on. Lu finishes the whisky with Jing's help. By this juncture, Bullethead is nearly comatose. He sits slumped over, eyes half-closed, an unlit cigarette dangling forgotten from his lips.

Lu senses an opening. He pushes himself up from the table. "Thank you for your hospitality, Brother Cho." He is aware that he is slurring his speech. "Now, I really must be going to bed."

Cho belches and clutches his chest. For a moment, it looks like he will be the one to vomit. But he quickly recovers and leers blearily at Jing and Lu. "You two make a sweet couple. Why don't you kiss her, Brother Long?" He motions for the girls around the table to join him in a chant. "Kiss! Kiss! Kiss!"

Lu figures, *What the hell*. He turns to Jing. Their lips meet. The whisky tastes better on her tongue than in the glass. The kiss goes on for longer than he intended. He finally breaks it off. He attempts to say a final good night, but only a stream of gibberish comes out of his mouth.

Jing takes his arm. "Come on."

She helps him up the stairs, down the hall, into his room. She closes

the door and puts her arms around his neck and kisses him again. Despite
his inebriated state, or perhaps because of it, he finds himself noticeably
aroused. Then he thinks of Yanyan, and the fact that Jing is a prostitute,
and an image of her entwined in a naked embrace with men like Cho and
Bullethead intrudes on the moment. He pulls away.

"What's wrong?" Jing asks.

"Shower. Water. Aspirin."

"I'll get you water." She pecks him on the lips and leaves the room.

Lu shuts the door and gets down on his hands and knees. He reaches
under the wardrobe and pats the rough wooden underside, his hand
scattering dead cockroaches. He locates the tracker and slips it into his
pocket. He rolls over and sticks his arm under the bed frame. He searches
for the camera and cannot find it and for a moment, he thinks he's been
found out. *Tian! They'll cut my balls off and drown me in the river.* But
no—there it is. Relieved, he slips the camera into his pocket and sits un-
steadily on the edge of the bed.

Jing returns with a bottle of boiled water and a glass. She pours and
Lu drinks and then holds the glass out for more. She refills it and presses
two tablets into his hand. Lu swallows the aspirin and drinks more water.
"Shower," he grunts.

Jing assists him down the hall. "First, piss." Lu closes the bathroom
door and locks it. He hunts for a spot to hide the devices. He lifts the lid
from the toilet tank. The water is green and murky and smells like it's
been pumped in directly from the Lancang. Lu drops the devices, still
in their ziplock bags, into it and presses them down to the bottom of the
tank. He adds the condom given to him by Bang. He replaces the lid and
pees and then exits the bathroom, only to find Jing waiting.

She pulls Lu into the shower room, turns on the water, and adjusts
the temperature. She tugs his shirt up. "I can do it," he says, pushing
her hands away. He removes his shirt with some difficulty. He starts on
his pants and nearly falls over. He steadies himself against the wall and
sees that Jing is already completely naked. "What are you doing?" he asks.

"Taking a shower."

Lu is too tired to protest. And too drunk to really care. He strips bare and ducks his head under the water. It feels sublime.

Jing comes up behind him and kneads his shoulders, runs her fingers down the groove of his spine, massages his lower back. Her strong hands wring anxiety and tension from Lu's body like water from a wet towel.

"I like your tattoo," Jing says. She moves closer and he can feel her breasts jutting into his back. She reaches around to stroke Lu's chest. Her fingertips trace a circle around his nipples, then slide into the V-shaped crease of his lower abdomen.

Lu violently twists the shower knob. The water quickly turns ice-cold. Jing squeals and jumps back. She says something, but Lu can't hear with his head under the spout. He endures the cold for thirty seconds, then turns the water off and snatches a towel from a hook on the wall. Jing is cringing in a corner, shivering, her arms wrapped around her chest, her skin puckered with goose bumps. She has a tattoo of a golden carp curving over the top of her right breast—a Buddhist symbol representing freedom and happiness.

"Why did you do that?" Jing says.

Lu hands her a towel. "I needed to clear my head."

Jing dries off, unashamed of her nakedness. "How old are you?" Lu asks.

"How old do you want me to be?"

"Seriously."

"Nineteen." She wraps the towel around herself and frowns. "I thought you were enjoying it."

"I need sleep." Lu opens the door. He walks down to his room. He feels a twinge of guilt for his abruptness, but he's dog-tired and conflicted and still befuddled by the whisky. His only desire now is to close his eyes and wake up back in his own bed in Raven Valley.

Lu puts on a pair of shorts. He shuts off the light and crawls into bed. His head spins like a pinwheel. Never a good sign.

The door opens. Shuts again. Lu feels a weight on the bed.

"I'm too tired, Jing. I'm sorry."

She slides under the sheets. He feels her hair, still wet, against his shoulder. "Can I sleep here?" she asks. "Just sleep?"

Lu grunts. He is clinging for dear life to a looping roller coaster fueled by alcohol. Tomorrow is going to be rough. Jing's warm breath blows softly against his neck.

He sleeps.

TWENTY-NINE

As Bang predicted, they come for Lu before dawn.

Lu is asleep, his limbs entangled with Jing's. The door crashes open. The light is switched on. Lu sits up and squints.

Bullethead is standing at the foot of the bed. He's wearing denim shorts, flip-flops, and a tank top. His gun is stuck into the waistband of his shorts. Cho hovers in the doorway. Even at this early hour, his hair and makeup are flawless.

"Morning, Brother Long," Cho says. "Sleep well?"

"What time is it?" Lu says.

"Time to be on our way."

Lu glances at the window. "It's still dark out."

"The fleet of foot are the first to the mountaintop. Get up. Get moving."

Lu's mouth tastes like silt from the Lancang River. His head throbs. Cho and Bullethead stand there, watching. "How about some privacy?" Lu says.

"No need for privacy among brothers," Cho says.

Lu groans and climbs out of bed. Jing remains huddled under the covers. Lu unzips his duffel bag and chooses a set of clothes. Bullethead comes over, his flip-flops slapping on the floor, and holds his hand out. Lu grudgingly hands the clothes to him. Bullethead carefully checks seams and pockets, then tosses them back. Lu turns to face the wall and slips out of his shorts.

He hears Jing squeal. He turns back, only to see that Bullethead has yanked the sheet off the bed to expose Jing's nakedness.

"Quit it!" Lu shouts.

"What's the big deal?" Bullethead says. "She's a whore. Everyone in Jinghong has seen her little 'abalone.'"

"Your mother's a whore, so why judge?"

"Watch your filthy mouth!" Bullethead snarls, taking a step forward.

"Enough," Cho admonishes. "We've got a long day ahead of us."

Bullethead tosses the sheet back onto the bed and Jing draws it up to her neck.

Lu finishes dressing. "I need to use the bathroom." Bullethead trails him down the hall. Lu reaches the bathroom door. "Are you coming in to watch me do my business?"

"Hurry it up," Bullethead says, sourly. He leans against the wall and shakes out a cigarette.

Lu goes inside, shuts the door, and locks it. He quietly lifts the toilet water tank. He reaches inside and fishes out the ziplock bags holding the tracker and camera. He dumps the tracker out of its bag into his palm. He tilts his head back and drops it into his mouth. He tries swallowing, but it sticks in his throat. He lurches to the sink and scoops water from the tap into his mouth, forcing the tracker down.

Great—now he'll probably get dysentery.

Lu retrieves the condom from the toilet tank. He rinses it off, tears the wrapper open with his teeth, and tosses it into the toilet. He slides the camera into the open end of the condom and ties a knot.

Bullethead raps on the door.

"*Qu ni ma,* I'm busy!" Lu shouts.

"Let's go!" comes Bullethead's muffled response.

Lu sits on the toilet and gingerly inserts the camera. He pulls up his pants and washes his hands and tentatively paces the small confines of the bathroom. It isn't painful, not exactly, but it's several degrees more disconcerting than having a stray piece of gravel in your shoe.

Lu flushes the toilet, replaces the tank lid, then unlocks and opens the door.

Bullethead blows smoke in his face. "Have a nice dump?"

"If only I could be rid of you so easily," Lu says.

When Lu returns to his room, Jing is gone and it looks as if his duffel bag has been searched—again. No matter. There's nothing incriminating to find. Lu heads downstairs, Bullethead his loyal shadow. Despite the early hour, Auntie Yang is awake and drinking tea at a table with Cho. A cool predawn breeze wafts through the open door.

Jing emerges from the kitchen door carrying a plastic bag. She offers it to Lu. "Breakfast for the road."

"Thanks." Lu looks at Cho. "I want to have a word alone with Jing." Cho shrugs. Lu takes Jing's elbow and leads her toward a corner of the bar. Bullethead follows. "Fuck off," Lu tells him.

"Give the young lovers a moment of privacy," Cho says.

Bullethead makes a rude gesture, then goes over to sit with Cho and Auntie Yang.

Lu gives Jing a wad of cash, almost all that he has. "Take this," he whispers. "Leave this place. It's enough for a couple of months. Find something else to do with your life."

"Like what?"

"I don't know." Lu closes her hand over the money. "Buy a food cart."

"I can't cook."

"If I ever come back through here, I don't want to see you working at the Golden Water Buffalo. Or anyplace like it."

Jing gives him a sad smile. "You think it's so easy?"

There is no time for a long debate, so Lu gives Jing a hug, collects his duffel bag, and walks over to the table. "I'm ready."

"Frisk him," Cho tells Bullethead.

"Seriously?" Lu complains. "You watched me get dressed, didn't you? And Bullethead practically wiped my ass just now."

"Go on," Cho orders.

Bullethead roughly pats Lu's clothes and gives him a sharp crotch-squeeze for good measure. "He's clean."

"Where's your cell phone?" Cho asks.

"What cell phone?" Lu asks, innocently.

Cho smiles. "Answer the question, Brother Long. Otherwise, I'll be forced to strip-search you. Again."

"It was a cheap burner phone. I tossed it into the river. I figured you'd confiscate it anyway."

A van waits outside. Cho sits up front, Lu and Bullethead in the back. The driver shifts into gear and speeds aggressively through the streets of Jinghong, rushing to catch traffic lights and working the brakes like a stock car racer. Before they've made it five city blocks, Bullethead cranks down the window, sticks his head out, and vomits. Cho laughs and lights a cigarette.

Once they make it onto China National Highway 214, the ride smooths out and both Bullethead and Cho fall asleep.

Lu opens the plastic bag given to him by Jing. Inside is a Styrofoam cup of tea, rice porridge with bits of pickled vegetables and pork, and a piece of fried bread. Lu drinks the tea and tries to find a comfortable sitting position.

He fails.

Two interminable hours later, the van rolls into the village of Daluo. The sun has only been out for forty-five minutes and already scads of Chinese citizens—99 percent men—are disgorging from massive tour buses.

The village is a humid, sleepy settlement on the banks of a river, known for its picturesque scenery, quaint Buddhist temples, and ancient banyan forest. It has served as a trading post between China and Southeast Asia since the seventeenth century.

But Lu knows the tourists aren't here for the historical interest or sites. They are just passing through on their way to less wholesome attractions. Perhaps a meal of bushmeat, chased down with shots of tiger-bone wine. Cheap jade and ivory and, if their pocketbooks are deep enough, medicinal rhino horn. A few rounds of gambling at a local casino, followed by a quick and dirty tryst with a young prostitute.

All these diversions and more are a scant twenty-minute motorbike ride through a porous jungle pass into one of the Wild West frontier towns of Myanmar.

Cho tells the driver of the van to park at the Daluo bus depot and let them out to stretch their legs. Lu waits in a long line for the bathroom, then buys a bottle of water. Back at the van, Cho and Bullethead are smoking and watching the tourists with undisguised contempt.

"Off they go, *gao, fu, shuai,*" Cho says. *Tall, rich, and handsome.* "And back they'll come, *ai, qiong, chou.*" *Short, poor, and ugly.*

"Aren't those your customers?" Lu says. "The ones who buy your animal parts and recreational drugs?"

Cho shrugs and tosses his cigarette on the ground. "Let's get moving."

They pass through several checkpoints manned by soldiers, both Chinese and Burmese. The driver of the van flashes some permits and doles out some yuan. Nobody bats an eye or asks to search the vehicle.

Before long, they arrive at a sizable town nestled in a basin amid lush green hills. The buildings are painted a garish yellow, pink, and blue. A golden-robed Buddha statue sits atop a hill, pointing a finger—benevolently? Accusingly?—down into the valley.

As the van makes its way through the streets, Lu spies several gaudy restaurants, seedy hotels, ostentatious nightclubs, outdoor markets, shopfronts, bars, and what appear to be gambling halls.

"Gambling is legal here?" Lu asks.

"Sometimes yes, sometimes no," Cho says. "When too many Chinese tourists lose all their money, the authorities shut off electricity and cell phone coverage until the casinos close up shop. But the operators just move deeper into the jungle and open their places bigger and better than before."

Lu sees a lot of unaccompanied girls on the streets, dressed in revealing clothes. Some of them look to be in their teens. Even a smallish township like Raven Valley is not without its hostess bars and massage parlors, so Lu is no stranger to the murky demimonde that is the Chinese sex trade.

In the People's Republic, poor women from the countryside essentially have two routes to upward social mobility: marry into a better situation or move to a city and find a higher-paying job. There currently exists a whole cottage industry of roaming marriage brokers who set rural women up with bachelors in other, slightly more desirable, rural areas. But these marriage brokers often lie and cheat their clients. A young woman might be told her husband, viewed only by photograph, is kind and handsome and owns a prosperous farm. When she arrives, she discovers he's a cruel drunk or perhaps suffers from a physical handicap and his farm is nothing more than a collection of stunted trees and scrubland.

A better option is to find a husband who has a decent job in the city. But China's mandatory household registration system, the *hukou*, presents a significant barrier for this type of match. Citizens from the countryside are not allowed to move to urban areas without state approval. The prospect of more desirable employment lures many to cities anyway, but even if they find a good job, they are barred from accessing urban health care, education, and housing benefits. And since children inherit their mother's *hukou* status, no self-respecting urban bachelor wants to marry a poor girl from the sticks—unless they are truly in love, and in which case, everyone lives happily ever after. Except for the woman and her children, who, because of their *hukou*, are essentially illegal aliens in their own country.

As for that perfect job in the city, all too often it turns out to be a nightmare. Lacking education or special skills, rural women generally end up in a sweatshop or factory, working twelve hours a day, living in a shoddy dorm "cheek by jowl" with their coworkers, poorly paid, subject to unattainable quotas, verbal abuse, and sexual harassment, with no job security and no chance of advancement.

It's no surprise, then, that many young women see the sex trade as a viable option. If you're young and pretty, you can find work as a hostess in a nightclub or bar. If you're a little older and less pretty, you can work the streets. The disadvantages are obvious: exploitative pimps, violent customers, sexually transmitted diseases, the psychologically damaging

nature of the work itself. But for girls like Jing, there are advantages that
make it difficult, or even impossible, to say no. A measure of personal freedom, shorter workdays, less physical labor, and in some cases, sex work
is the only way to make enough money to support oneself and parents,
siblings, and other dependents left behind in the village.

In any case, Lu doesn't pass judgment, and watching the girls trawl
the streets in their cheap platform shoes, smoking cigarettes, a look of quiet
desperation or, worse, numb indifference on their faces, his soul aches for
the awful choices they are forced to make.

Bullethead notices Lu staring. "You want a girl? You didn't get your
fill at the Golden Water Buffalo?"

Lu ignores him. In addition to the young girls, he sees many soldiers,
dressed in green fatigues, brandishing AK-47s, manning security posts, or
driving around in Ford 4x4 trucks equipped with chrome roll bars.

"Those guys are the local militia?" Lu asks.

"Yes," Cho says.

"They look well-outfitted," Lu remarks.

"Small arms, armored cars, surface-to-air missiles, howitzers, helicopter gunships—they've got it all."

"From where?"

"Beijing. Maybe Russia. And what they can't get elsewhere, they make
themselves. Those AK-47s are domestic manufacture."

"I guess the drug business is good."

"Drug business?" Cho says. "You misunderstand, Brother Long.
Drug cultivation was banned in 2005. People here make a living off rubber and tea."

"You're kidding, right?"

Cho smiles. "While we're in town, would you like to see some of the
sights? A Buddhist pagoda? Transvestite cabaret? How about the Drug
Eradication Museum? Admittance is free."

"I'm good, thanks."

They pass through a military checkpoint and stop for an early lunch
at a restaurant outside of town. Cho knows the proprietor and they are

shown into a private room and plied with beer and whisky. Nobody drinks the whisky.

The food is excellent. Pickled tea leaves mixed with cabbage, tomatoes, nuts, and beans, and seasoned with garlic and peppers. Pork curry. Deep-fried gourd fritters. Various types of noodles.

Lu eats sparingly. His stomach is unsettled from the night before—and the camera remains a mild, but ever-present, irritant.

Following lunch, they resume their drive. After another dozen kilometers, they turn off the main road and enter a roughly paved track leading into the forest. Cho says something to the driver, who stops. Cho leans over the back of his seat and offers Lu a black hood.

"What's that for?" Lu asks.

"You."

"Why?"

"You don't strike me as stupid, but you ask a lot of dumb questions."

"Look around you, Brother Cho. Do you really think I'll be able to memorize the exact shape of that particular bush or tree and find my way back here, even if I wanted to?"

"Put the hood on."

Lu complies. The van rolls forward.

THIRTY

Another hour, maybe a bit more—it's hard to measure the passing of time with a bag over your head—and they finally come to a stop. Lu is manhandled out of the van and frog-marched across sandy soil. The air is blisteringly hot and stinks of rotting vegetation.

Rough hands yank the hood off. Lu blinks in the bright sunlight.

In front of him is a short bridge, too narrow for any vehicle larger than a midsized truck to drive across. On the far side of the bridge is a concrete tower with a metal gate and walls curving off to either side. Beneath a camouflage canopy atop the tower, a group of soldiers mans a mounted machine gun. It's one of the rapid-fire, high-caliber, Gatling-style weapons used by the Americans on their attack helicopters. A gun like that will reduce anything short of a tank or armored personal carrier to scrap metal within seconds.

Lu hears a motor revving. He turns and watches as the van executes a three-point turn and drives away, leaving him alone with Cho and Bullethead, their luggage in a neat pile in the dirt.

"Let's get out of the sun," Cho says. He starts across the bridge.

"What about our bags?" Lu asks.

"Someone will collect them," Cho responds, over his shoulder.

The bridge spans a narrow canal of water that runs the length of the walls in either direction as far as Lu can see—a moat, just like an old-fashioned castle. Lu stops and peers into the brackish water.

"What are you looking for?" Bullethead asks.

"Crocodiles."

"Idiot."

When they reach the far side of the bridge, the gate opens. Lu pauses for one last backward glance. The dirt road extends about thirty meters before it curves into thick forest. He wonders about the radius of the tracking device he has swallowed. And how Bang plans to get this far undetected.

Bullethead gives Lu an unfriendly shove. "Move!"

An officer greets them at the gate. He's wearing green fatigues and a holstered automatic pistol on his belt. He and Cho exchange a few words in Burmese and then the officer leads them into a compound laid out like a military outpost, with living quarters, a corrugated shed where greasy mechanics tend to a variety of vehicles, a fueling station, storage depots, and various other buildings with less identifiable purposes.

Perhaps it is the heat, or the remote setting, but in contrast with the military facilities Lu has visited, the atmosphere here is decidedly lax. The grounds are unkempt. Soldiers lounge about in the shade, shirts off, smoking cigarettes and casually brandishing their firearms. Nonregulation facial hair, tattoos, mustaches, gold chains, and expensive wristwatches are very much on display.

But the faces of the soldiers are hard. They may not pass muster on a parade ground, but they have the air of remorseless killers about them.

At the far end of the compound is another gate. The officer unlocks it and ushers them through.

Inside is a narrow colonnaded courtyard, walls dripping with vines and flowering plants, leading to an ornate double door constructed of wood and brick, its surface painted red and gold and decorated with stucco illustrations of wild animals and Burmese dancers.

A young woman stands at the door. She is dressed in a dark sleeveless blouse and baggy knee-high *longyi*. Her hair is cut boyishly short and while she is small and slight, her calves and forearms are corded with muscle. She places her hands over her belly and bows.

Lu and the others follow the woman through the door and into a garden filled with miniature trees, flowerbeds, and large rocks and stones that appear to have been chosen for their unusual shapes and colors. Chirping birds and fluttering butterflies complete the bucolic scene.

At the far end of the garden is a small bungalow. The woman opens the bungalow door and bows again. "Please wait," she says, in accented Mandarin.

Lu is pleasantly surprised to find the interior a furnished room with a modern couch and chairs, and, even better, air-conditioning. In the back is a kitchenette with a wet bar and refrigerator.

"May I?" Lu says, nodding at the bar.

"Help yourself," Cho says.

Lu rinses his hands and face with cold water from the sink and feels greatly refreshed. He opens the fridge—it is stocked with beer and soft drinks. He chooses a bottle of water. Bullethead takes a beer. Cho has sufficiently recovered from last night's drinking to pour himself a glass of whisky over ice.

They sit. Lu is not sure what to expect. A business meeting, with a round of haggling? A goodwill tour of the facilities? To be interrogated with a blowtorch?

He wonders if Wilson Fang is here, somewhere, and, if so, if he's free to roam the grounds or is kept under lock and key for his own safety. Lu hopes the latter is not the case. He doesn't relish the prospect of hunting him down like an elusive bird or nocturnal marsupial.

Before long, the door opens, and three women enter. Two are dressed in traditional Burmese blouses and *longyi*; the third, in a Chanel pantsuit and Jackie O sunglasses.

Chanel-woman has the air of a once-young beauty who is gracefully, if reluctantly, transitioning into middle age. "You must be Mr. Long," she says, in lightly accented Mandarin.

Lu rises. "And you can be no other than Daw Khaw."

"You may call me *A Sao*." This is the Mandarin term for "older brother's wife"—but is also a common way for members of a criminal network to respectfully address the wife or girlfriend of a senior. Khaw seats herself in one of the chairs and crosses one leg over the other. Lu notes, with some revulsion, that Khaw is wearing the fancy Western high heels with the red soles known in Chinese as *Hong Di Xie*. "Ko Cho, fix me a drink."

"Of course." Cho hops up and goes over to the wet bar. Lu assumes "*Ko*" is a polite Burmese term for "brother" or the like.

"Sit, Mr. Long." Khaw rests her elbow on the armrest of the chair and props her chin on her fist. She wears a jade bangle around her wrist and rings with diamonds and precious gems on her plump fingers. Her hair is elaborately coiled and pinned in place with silver sticks. "I trust your long journey wasn't too exhausting?"

"Not at all. I had very pleasant company."

Khaw's lips curve into the barest hint of a smile. She accepts a glass from Cho and sips daintily. "As Ko Cho explained, I don't generally allow clients to visit me here. This is my home. It is not for outsiders."

"I greatly appreciate you making an exception in my case. Have you received the advance payment of three hundred thousand yuan?"

"Obviously, or you would not be here." Khaw extracts a metal case from her pocket and removes a hand-rolled cigarillo. Cho immediately produces his Zippo. Khaw puffs on the cigarillo, then waves smoke away from her face. "So, you work for Alex Ho."

"Yes."

"I've met him, you know."

"Oh?" Lu feels a tendril of cold sweat roll down his rib cage. "Strange. He didn't mention it."

"It was only in passing some years ago. We were introduced by mutual friends. I don't think he actually knew who I was, and he's probably forgotten all about it."

"I don't think anyone could possibly forget *you, A Sao*."

"How charming you are, Mr. Long."

"Please, call me Ming."

"Very well. By the way, I'm sorry to hear of Alex's medical issues."

"He's of a certain age," Lu says. "Drinks and smokes too much. Doesn't exercise. It's to be expected."

Khaw swirls the ice in her glass and stares at Lu. Her eyes are obscured by the huge sunglasses, rendering her face unreadable. "Tonight, you will join me for dinner. Tomorrow, after you have had a chance to see the quality of our merchandise, we will discuss terms. The following day, you will return to Jinghong."

"That sounds perfect. Thank you."

Khaw takes a last sip of her drink and hands the glass to Cho with a casual indifference. He takes it without protest. Lu can see who wears the Chanel pants in *that* relationship. "While you are here, please enjoy yourself," Khaw says. "But this is my home, not yours. Don't go wandering about or take liberties. Do I make myself clear?"

"As crystal."

Khaw stands. "Then have a restful afternoon and I'll see you tonight."

She departs in a mist of sweet-smelling cigarillo smoke. Lu notes that Bullethead has demonstrated silent deference for the duration of her visit. Just like a typical schoolyard bully. Eager to prey on a helpless junior, and content to lick the boot of the senior.

After a short wait, there is a knock at the door and a young Burmese man wearing a black Chinese jacket and ankle-length *longyi* enters. He speaks to Cho in Burmese.

"Let's go," Cho says.

"Where?"

"To our guest quarters."

The young man leads them outside and through a door in the garden wall. As they walk, Lu realizes Khaw's "home" is a sprawling compound consisting of dozens of buildings separated by courtyards, paved walking paths, and dirt plazas, with guard posts and defensive emplacements scattered about, interspersed with tall broadleaf evergreens and large swathes of camouflage netting, the entire complex encircled by irregular sections of wall and metal fences topped with razor wire.

After a circuitous route, they come to a large rectangular structure made of concrete and set two meters off the ground on thick stilts. The area below the structure is empty space. Stairs lead up to a narrow veranda, which extends across the structure's façade.

Lu knows some traditional country homes in Southeast Asia are raised above the ground to avoid damage from periodic flooding and provide a secure holding area for livestock, but neither requirement seems to hold here. So why the stilts?

Bullethead comes to an unpleasant realization. "Is he staying with us?"

"It would seem so," Cho says.

"Why?"

"We brought him here, so I suppose we're responsible for him." Cho looks at Lu. "You're not planning on causing any trouble, are you?"

"No, but I insist on the top bunk," Lu says.

"Idiot," Bullethead mutters.

They climb the stairs. There are three doors leading into the building, placed at evenly spaced intervals. Lu assumes they lead to separate rooms, like a hotel. His theory is bolstered by the presence of luggage in front of each door; Cho's knockoff Louis Vuitton at the far end, Bullethead's fake Gucci suitcase near the stairs, Lu's duffel bag in the middle. Bullethead picks up his bag and opens his door. "I hope you do cause trouble . . . so I can kill you." He disappears inside.

"Why does your friend hate me so much?" Lu asks Cho.

"He hates everyone. That's his job." Cho walks down to the end of the veranda and collects his bag. "See you later." He enters, leaving Lu alone on the veranda.

Lu picks up his duffel bag and opens the door to his temporary home.

Inside is a large, low-ceilinged sitting room, furnished with a couch and two armchairs, a teak coffee table, and an entertainment center featuring a television and DVD player. Mother-of-pearl-inlay Chinese folding screens, vases of fresh flowers, and a scattering of traditional Burmese art add a homey touch.

Lu checks out the movie selection—most are Burmese song-and-dance titles, but there is also a collection of Western action flicks, circa 1980s, and a smattering of Japanese pornography.

Tucked into a corner of the room is a kitchenette with cupboards and a sink, a small refrigerator, a breakfast counter, and a small round dining table with two chairs. A door at the back leads to a bedroom. Lu enters and admires the heavy teak four-poster bed. He runs a hand across the sheets. There is a single window looking out. Not much of a view. Just another structure on stilts, a carbon copy of the one Lu is in, across a narrow stretch of dusty ground. He discovers that the window is fixed—no latch, no hinge. And he notes it is the only window in the entire apartment.

Lu suddenly understands. One door. One window. Two meters off the ground, too high to jump down from or climb up.

The guest house is designed for security. It's a jail cell—comfortable, luxurious even, but a cell, nonetheless.

He goes into the bathroom. It's furnished with a huge tub, a double sink, and a Western toilet and is nearly as big at his entire apartment back in Raven Valley.

Lu spends twenty minutes hunting for hidden cameras and microphones. He comes up empty. He touches the mirror in the bathroom with a forefinger to rule out the presence of two-way glass.

Lu sits on the toilet. With a grunt of relief, he squeezes out the condom-wrapped camera. He rinses the condom off, tears it open, and dumps the camera onto the counter. He flushes the condom down the toilet and washes his hands. He takes the camera into the bedroom and chooses a shirt for tonight's festivities. He carefully inserts the camera into one of the buttonholes as Bang demonstrated. He hopes the damn thing works as advertised.

Lu returns to the bathroom and takes a long hot shower. Then he falls into bed and sleeps.

THIRTY-ONE

Lu wakes, disoriented. He was dreaming of lying beside Yanyan, running a finger along one of her thick caterpillar-like eyebrows, relishing the sound of her laughter. And then, to his dismay, her laughter began to fade and was gradually supplanted by primitive, discordant music. Warbling flutes and pounding drums. As the music grew louder and more insistent, Yanyan faded away, too.

When he opens his eyes, Yanyan is gone, but the music remains.

Lu looks at his watch. Almost 4:00 p.m. He's slept for nearly two hours. He goes to the window. A shadow cast by the guesthouse next door is slowly creeping its way across the sand. Lu is reminded of a poem by Li Shangyin:

> *The setting sun shines brilliantly . . .*
> *But dusk is approaching.*

He rinses his face with cold water in the bathroom sink and dresses, leaving the top of his shirt unbuttoned to show a hint of his dragon tattoo, with the camera just below his sternum. He helps himself to a bottle of water from the refrigerator and goes out onto the veranda. An afternoon breeze has taken the bite out of the day's heat. He hears voices from down below. He cranes his neck over the veranda and discovers two soldiers in fatigues and armed with rifles lounging in the shade beneath the building.

"Did you think escape would be so easy?" comes Cho's voice. Lu turns and sees Cho leaning in his doorway, smoking a cigarette. He is shirtless and his skin is milky white, apart from an assortment of tattoos, some quite elaborate and expertly rendered, and others that look like they were done by a cross-eyed sailor with a ballpoint pen.

"Why would I want to escape?" Lu says, innocently. "I just got here."

"Wait until dinner," Cho says. "And then we'll see if you feel the same." He tosses the cigarette over the railing and disappears back inside.

An old man comes to collect them at seven. He is dressed in the same uniform as the younger man who brought them to the guesthouse earlier—a black Chinese jacket and ankle-length *longyi*.

As they walk through the compound, Lu attempts to construct a mental image of its layout. Judging from the setting sun, the front gate, where they crossed the bridge spanning the moat, is to the east. Their guesthouse is in the southwestern quadrant. They are now heading northeast.

They soon arrive at a small rectangular plaza, enclosed on three sides by traditional wooden buildings, their multitiered roofs brightly colored red, blue, and green and handsomely decorated with gilt leaf. Their guide indicates a building on the left, bows, and makes himself scarce. A pair of servants—by now Lu has sorted the men in the compound into two categories, either servants or soldiers—flank the entrance. They open a set of doors and Cho steps through like he owns the place. Lu follows, a bit more tentatively.

Inside is a spacious banquet room with a high ceiling, polished teak floors, and walls painted with panels depicting the life of Buddha: starting on the left, the spoiled young prince leaves the sheltered confines of his boyhood palace for the first time, only to witness old age, suffering, and death; after a period of wandering in the wilderness, he meditates under the *pipal* tree while capering demons try desperately to distract him; following enlightenment, he gives his first sermon on the noble eightfold path; and so on, all the way around, until the final panel on the right memorializes his death at the age of eighty in a grove of *sal* trees.

Lu is surprised to see, placed in the center of the room, a one-meter raised platform with a padded surface. It reminds him very much of a *lei tai*—an elevated ring where *gongfu* matches were traditionally contested.

He sincerely hopes Daw Khaw isn't going to make the guests fight for their supper.

Low individual tables are arranged around the edges of the platform. Lu, Cho, and Bullethead are shown to their places and seated on floor cushions. A servant takes drink orders. Beers for Lu and Bullethead, whisky over ice for Cho.

Tucked unobtrusively in a corner, a troupe of musicians softly plies its trade on Burmese instruments—drums, flutes, gongs, and a boat-shaped harp. Lu is amused to realize he recognizes the tune—"Hotel California," by the Eagles. Then his amusement turns to disquiet as he recalls a snippet of lyrics about a feast, a beast, and an attempted stabbing—hopefully not a harbinger of things to come.

A few other guests are already seated at the tables, drinking, smoking cigarettes and cheroots, chatting with one another. Most are men, but there are one or two women. Everyone is of Asian ethnicity, apart from two Caucasian foreigners. Lu hears a variety of languages—Burmese, Mandarin, Cantonese, English.

"Do you know all these people?" Lu asks Cho.

Cho lights a Marlboro and takes a deep drag. "Most. The guy over there in the sunglasses and military fatigues—he's Colonel Ta, the senior military official for this district. The one in the Hawaiian shirt smoking a Cohiba—he runs Khaw's jungle casino. The skinny guy with the chin beard and skullcap is Khaw's veterinarian. As for the foreigners—Jacob, the handsome blond one, smuggles rhino horn out of Africa using Burmese and Thai whores as couriers. The big ugly guy is Andrei. He's a meth dealer out of Bulgaria or Romania or Serbia or some other country that ends in 'ia.'"

"I thought this was Khaw's home," Lu says. "Her inner sanctum. No strangers allowed."

"These people are not strangers. They are colleagues, employees, or valued customers. You're the only stranger here."

Hors d'oeuvres are served: pickled prawns; samosas with a filling of potatoes, peas, and onions; glutinous rice mixed with meat and wrapped in a banana leaf; skewers of grilled meat.

"Where is our esteemed hostess, anyway?" Lu asks.

Cho sips from his glass of whisky. "She likes to make an entrance. That's her place over there." He nods at a table set on a small dais.

Lu indicates the padded platform. "And that?"

"The evening's entertainment."

Conspicuously absent is Wilson Fang. Lu can't decide if he is relieved or disappointed. Despite Jia's assurances, Lu is still nervous that Fang might recognize him, but then again, if he must obtain photographic evidence of Fang's presence, a banquet attended by a rogues' gallery of Khaw's criminal network would be the perfect opportunity.

Speaking of which, Lu decides he may as well try to identify some of the other players here. "Any chance of being introduced around?"

Cho is immediately wary. "Why?"

"Networking."

"You're just here to buy some bushmeat, Brother Long. Stick to your lane."

"Sure thing." Lu turns his chest in the direction of Colonel Ta and says: *"Ta ma de."*

"What?" Cho says.

"Nothing." Lu shifts toward the two foreigners and knocks over his glass. *"Ta ma de."*

Following the hors d'oeuvres, Khaw sweeps in, flanked by two of her female bodyguards, dressed to impress in an ankle-length emerald-green *longyi* and a tight-fitting, brocaded silk blouse. Her hair is swept up and held in place with diamond pins and a jade flower clasp. Minus the big glamorous sunglasses, Lu can see her face more fully. He can't determine her age, but he guesses around fifty. And still a knockout.

Khaw acknowledges her guests with queenly smiles and personal words for a chosen few, then takes her seat. Conversation resumes, drinks are quaffed, cigarettes smoked, dainty morsels consumed.

Dinner consists of the ubiquitous tea leaf salad; rice balls with fish and turmeric; various curries; noodles in fish broth; a range of tropical fruits. Also: crocodile carpaccio; bat boiled in a ginger and coconut soup; bamboo rat stuffed with vegetables and roasted; and a hot pot consisting of pangolin, snake, and caterpillar simmered in a base of chicken broth, soy sauce, ginger, Shaoxing wine, and spring onion.

Lu passes on the bat, but lightly samples the other dishes. He contrives to take several photographs of Khaw, and as many of the other guests, as possible.

After the last course is served, a bodyguard approaches Lu's table. She has the face of a prizefighter—scar tissue around the eyes, a nose bent sharply to one side. "Daw Khaw would like you to join her."

"I would be honored."

Lu follows the bodyguard to Khaw's table. Khaw indicates a cushion to her right. Lu sits. A servant brings a pitcher and some cups.

"Have you tried *htan ye*, Brother Ming?" Khaw asks. "A local drink, made from the sweet sap of a palm tree."

Lu accepts a cup. The liquid is thin and milky and smells yeasty. He sips. He finds it sweet, but also a touch sour. "Interesting."

"Farmers drink it in the cool of the afternoon after a long, hot day in the fields." Khaw extracts a cheroot from her silver case. "Do you smoke?"

"Not as a rule."

"You must try one of these. Everyone in Myanmar, even grandmothers, enjoys a daily cheroot. They are traditionally filled with a blend of tobacco and *thanat* leaves. *Thanat* is famous for its medicinal properties."

Lu takes the cheroot. It is as thick as his thumb and about the length of his hand, wrapped in a yellow leaf and fitted with a homemade filter made of rolled-up corn husks. A servant produces a lighter. Lu sucks on the cheroot and gets a cloud of smoke going. It tastes sweet and mellow on his tongue.

Khaw lights up her own cheroot. "Your accommodations are acceptable?"

"Excellent, thank you."

"Did you sample the hot pot?"

"I did."

"Pangolin meat is very good for the kidneys, but the real value is in the scales, which are effective for alleviating skin issues, anxiety, hysteria, and promoting lactation."

"I'll keep that in mind next time I'm breastfeeding."

"The best way to prepare them is dried, roasted, soaked in a young boy's urine, and cooked with butter."

"Note to self: never, ever, ever eat pangolin scales."

Khaw smiles. "I enjoy your sense of humor, Brother Ming. Here, we have thirty-nine species of venomous snake, but an appalling paucity of wit."

"Perhaps everyone is just terrified of you."

"You think so? Good. More *htan ye*?" Khaw motions toward the pitcher and immediately a servant steps forward.

"I might switch to beer, if that's all right."

"Of course." Khaw gestures curtly. The servant runs off.

"How many staff do you have working for you, *A Sao*?"

"Oh, a hundred or so."

"A *hundred*?"

"I provide a living, one way or another, for everyone in this district."

"And the men in uniform?" Lu asks. "They belong to you?"

"Officially they are under the command of Colonel Ta." Khaw points out the man in aviator sunglasses and fatigues. "But the colonel eats at my table, same as the rest. I pay for the education of his five children overseas. I support the expensive shopping habits of his wife and mistresses."

"I see."

After the dinner dishes have been cleared away, Khaw signals to the band. They strike up a lively tune—drums, clappers, cymbals, harp, Burmese oboe, and bamboo pipe weaving a cacophonous melody that slithers and coils like a nest of serpents.

"Do you enjoy watching fights, Brother Ming?" Khaw says.

"As long as I'm not expected to join in." A servant delivers Lu's beer, ice cold, on a silver platter.

"You don't like getting your knuckles bloody?"

"I'm a businessman, not a fighter."

A side door opens, and two women enter, each followed by a team of men bearing stools, buckets, and towels. The women are dressed in silk boxing shorts and tight tops that leave their midriffs bare. Their hands are wrapped in gauze. The atmosphere in the room quickly takes a turn. Now that their gluttony has been satiated, the guests pivot to a new vice—bloodlust.

The women bow respectfully to Khaw, then go to opposite ends of the platform and begin their preparations.

"You are familiar with Thai boxing?" Khaw asks. "The art of eight limbs, so called because fighters strike with their hands, feet, knees, and elbows? Well, this is *Lethwei*. The art of *nine* limbs."

"Where are they hiding the extra one?"

"The ninth is the headbutt."

"Ah. Nasty technique." Lu has used it himself on more than one occasion.

The first fighter steps onto the platform, sticks her left hand under her right armpit, and slaps her left elbow.

"She is performing the *Lekkha Moun*," Khaw explains. "Both a gesture of respect and a challenge to your opponent, meant to resemble the flapping wings of a bird of prey before it swoops down on the attack." The fighter begins to shadowbox, punching the air, raising her knees high, then circling on one leg. "The *Lethwei Yay*," Khaw says. "Similar to the *Wai Kru* dance of Thai boxers."

Lu takes a long pull of beer. He resolves to quit after this one. The combination of the cheroot, alcohol, and stress are sending his heart rate through the roof.

Khaw nods at the fighter. "Her nickname is Pitiless Tiger, and she is undefeated in seventy bouts."

Lu realizes he recognizes her as the woman who showed them into the bungalow earlier. "That many?"

"I found her carrying bricks at a construction site eight years ago. She was just twelve at the time. An orphan. Underfed, underweight. Abused and filthy. But I could see the steel in her. I gave her a home, food, training."

"I noticed that all your personal bodyguards are female. Is it the same story with them?"

"I find the scraps. In the gutter. The cane fields. In the brothels and factories. I bring them here and give them a purpose. I forge them into weapons." The second fighter now climbs onto the platform and initiates her *Lekkha Moun*. "This one is Golden Krait. She is a relative novice. Only nineteen fights. But already she's killed two opponents in the ring. That's why I've matched her with the more experienced Pitiless Tiger."

"Killed two opponents? Aren't there rules in *Lethwei*?"

"Yes, of course. But a well-placed elbow or knee—it can happen in an instant."

"And where did you find *her*?"

"In a local prison. A group of men tried to gang-rape her. Big mistake. I think she was quite insane, even before that happened."

"And you still recruited her?" Lu asks.

"She is a born fighter. You don't blame a wild beast because it kills to eat. You just show it who its master is."

"Ah. Pitiless Tiger is here to tame Golden Krait, is that it?"

"Either Pitiless Tiger beats Golden Krait into submission, or Golden Krait kills her. Whatever happens . . . it should be an excellent fight."

THIRTY-TWO

Lu notices the other guests, even the two foreigners, excitedly exchanging bets.

A referee climbs onto the platform and summons the fighters. He provides instructions and they touch fists, then return to their corners. A gong sounds and the bout commences.

The fighters shuffle and feint. Lu understands that as they are not using protective gloves, they must choose their strikes judiciously to avoid breaking their hands.

Golden Krait suddenly pounces, winging an overhand right. Pitiless Tiger ducks, sidesteps, and hooks her fist into Golden Krait's face. Lu winces.

"Are you all right, Brother Ming?" Khaw says.

"I'm not a fan of watching women beat each other up."

"Only men are worthy of being fighters?"

Lu senses a trap. "That's not what I meant."

"Perhaps when a woman is on a stage, you prefer that she is dancing in high heels and taking off her clothes."

Golden Krait throws a few jabs and then a high round kick. The meaty slap of her foot against Pitiless Tiger's skull brings cheers from her supporters.

"Is fighting for the entertainment of an audience who wants badly to see you killed or knocked unconscious really better than taking off your clothes for money?" Lu says. "Certainly, the latter is less damaging to your health."

"I beg to differ, Brother Ming. A stripper is the object of a man's base desires. A plaything onto which he projects his lustful thoughts. These fighters are respected. And feared. Look at Pitiless Tiger. Look at Golden Krait. What man here would dare touch either one of them in a crowded marketplace? Rub his crotch against her on a bus? Eh?" Khaw makes a plump, bejeweled fist. "To be powerful, instead of powerless. That is worth dying for any day of the week."

Golden Krait clinches with Pitiless Tiger and throws a knee into her midsection. Tiger pounds Krait's torso with hooks and uppercuts. Golden Krait grunts and drops to the ground, but quickly pops back up.

Lu thinks perhaps it's best to shift the direction of the conversation. A bit of flattery will soften Khaw's sharp edges. "Speaking of power, I must say I am impressed with what you have built here. How did you do it? It can't be easy for a woman in this cutthroat business."

"In other words, who did I have to sleep with?"

"No—"

"That is your real question, is it not?"

"Not at all."

"Of course it is. You can't help it. You're Chinese, after all."

"Meaning?" Lu says, offended.

Khaw shrugs. "Chinese men have always considered women inferior."

The crowd reacts appreciatively as the fighters clinch, jockey for position, and exchange headbutts. Pitiless Tiger's eyebrow splits and blood pours down her face.

"You are being a bit unfair," Lu says.

"Really? Can you think of another country that mutilated its young girls in pursuit of some twisted idea of beauty for more than a thousand years?"

"What are you talking about?"

"Foot-binding."

"Oh. *That*."

Nowadays, every Chinese schoolchild learns of this practice as a particularly abhorrent relic of the evil old dynastic age. Starting at the age of four, upper-class girls were subjected to the daily torture of having the bones of their feet systematically bound and broken until they were re-molded into tiny misshapen lumps the approximate size of a small bird. Poems and sex manuals of the day extolled the erotic virtues of these so-called lotus feet, and the resulting crippled gait was even believed to promote the strengthening of vaginal muscles and increase sexual pleasure for male partners. It also had the added effect of making freedom of move-ment difficult and restricting women to the confines of the family home.

Lu is about to respond when Golden Krait and Pitiless Tiger exchange powerful kicks. Sweat and blood splatter. Khaw claps enthusiastically. Krait illegally rams her knee into Tiger's crotch. Tiger goes down on her knees. The referee steps in to issue a warning. The crowd boos lustily.

Lu waits until the din has subsided, then says: "Foot-binding was out-lawed long ago."

"If you consider 1912 a long time," Khaw says. "Which, given your country's extensive history, is a blink of a gnat's eye."

"Every nation has something shameful in its past."

"Do you know when the last recorded case took place, Brother Ming?"

The fight restarts. The women trade low kicks, then Golden Krait goes high again. Pitiless Tiger ducks under the kick, moves in, and un-leashes a vicious left hook. Golden Krait sprawls on the canvas.

"No," Lu says. "But I'm sure you're going to tell me."

"1957!"

"That must have been somewhere deep in the countryside. A society isn't transformed overnight, you know."

"Are things so different in China now?"

"Yes, of course. Our society has greatly evolved."

"How many women serve on the Politburo Standing Committee? How many women lead provincial governments?"

"Is the situation here any different? Is it so different anywhere in the world, apart from a few small outliers?"

Khaw shrugs. "Perhaps not. That is why I have created my personal kingdom of lost girls."

"I see." Lu nods at the fighters. "A feminist paradise."

"I wouldn't expect you to understand, Brother Ming."

Golden Krait stands and indicates that she is ready to fight, but as the two women square off again, a gong sounds, signaling the end of round one. The fighters return to their stools and cornermen sponge blood from their faces.

"I've heard you are half Chinese, *A Sao*? Is that true?"

"My father was a low-level drug smuggler and degenerate gambler from Yunnan. He was murdered in a Rangoon alley when I was three. I hardly knew him."

"Ah."

The fight resumes. Pitiless Tiger and Golden Krait continue to tenderize each other like sides of raw beef. Lu and Khaw watch in silence. By the end of the second round, both fighters have suffered broken noses, split lips, and swollen faces.

"How many rounds will the fight last?" Lu asks. He can't stomach much more.

"Five. If, at the end, they are both still standing, the fight is declared a draw. To win in *Lethwei,* you have to knock your opponent out."

The third round commences. Pitiless Tiger pummels Golden Krait with leg kicks and straight punches, cuts her forehead open with an elbow, and knees her in the throat. Golden Krait falls, gasping for air.

Colonel Ta leaps to his feet, waving a fistful of greenbacks. Bullethead, who must have placed his money on Golden Krait, is furious. One of the female guests, a plump matron in a dark silk pantsuit, screams: *"Hei loi, say bat poh!"* Lu's basic knowledge of Cantonese translates this as: "Get up, you damned bitch!"

The referee waves Pitiless Tiger to a neutral corner. He stands over Golden Krait while she struggles to recover.

"She will be given two minutes," Khaw explains. "If she cannot continue, the fight will be called."

Golden Krait takes the full allotment of time. Then she stands, wipes blood from her eye sockets, and nods to the referee.

"You see?" Khaw says admiringly. "That kind of heart cannot be taught."

The referee restarts the match. The tide quickly turns. Pitiless Tiger, perhaps wearied and dismayed that Golden Krait has eaten her best shots and come back for more, begins to flag. Golden Krait senses an opening. Her combinations are rudimentary, but powerful. She whips her shins into Tiger's legs and swings wildly at her head. Then she feints low and snaps a front kick directly under Tiger's jaw. Tiger is thrown clear off the platform. The back of her head smacks into Colonel Ta's table with a loud snapping sound.

"*Tian!*" Lu mutters.

The losers who bet on Pitiless Tiger pay out. The winners crow. Pitiless Tiger is carried out on a stretcher. Lu cannot tell if she is alive or dead. Golden Krait comes to pay her respects to Khaw. Lu can see bone showing through a two-inch gash in her eyebrow. Khaw gifts Golden Krait with one of the diamond stickpins from her hair. Golden Krait limps out of the room with the assistance of her cornermen.

Khaw rises and smooths the folds of her *longyi*. "I hope the meal was satisfactory and you enjoyed the entertainment. We'll talk again tomorrow after you've had a chance to tour my facilities."

Lu stands and bows. "It has been an evening I will not soon forget."

Khaw makes the rounds, exchanging farewells, then leaves with her bodyguards in tow. Lu returns to his table. Cho greets him with a sardonic smile.

"Have a nice chat?"

"Lovely," Lu says. "We discussed what pigs Chinese men are."

"Given sufficient opportunity," Cho says, "all men are pigs. That's how drug dealers and whoremongers make their money."

Lu yawns. "I'm bushed. I want to head back to the guesthouse."

Cho flicks ash from his cigarette into an empty whisky glass. "The night is young."

"I am not."

"You won't be permitted to wander unaccompanied." Cho turns to Bullethead. "Go fetch someone to escort Brother Long."

"Let him find his own way," Bullethead says.

"We are responsible for his conduct while he's here," Cho says. "Go fetch an escort."

Bullethead's face twists unpleasantly, but he gets up and does as instructed.

In due course, a servant arrives with two soldiers. "Remember to behave yourself," Cho warns. "Go back and get a good night's sleep. Don't attempt to stroll around the grounds. Don't make me lose face."

"Wouldn't dream of it," Lu says. "Especially with a face like that."

The soldiers return Lu to the guesthouse and take up a post at the foot of the stairs. Lu goes inside and hides the camera under the couch. He takes a long shower and climbs naked into bed.

He falls asleep quickly but dreams unpleasantly of Golden Krait violently forcing his feet into a tiny pair of slippers lined with broken glass.

THIRTY-THREE

A servant delivers breakfast early the next morning: *mohinga*—Myanmar's national dish, a noodle and fish soup served with vegetable fritters; fresh fruit; and toast with marmalade. Also, a pot of hot black coffee.

While he's eating, Lu hears distant shouting—the sound of soldiers drilling. After consuming several cups of coffee, he hurries to the bathroom where he's reasonably sure he passes the tracking device. He flushes it down, hoping by now it's served its purpose. He showers and dresses, fitting the camera into the buttonhole of his shirt. Then he waits for someone to come collect him.

A thin man with a chin beard and skullcap eventually arrives, in the company of two soldiers. The man, who Lu remembers from the banquet, introduces himself as Dr. Du. "I am Daw Khaw's veterinarian," Du says. "It will be my pleasure to take you on a tour of our facilities."

As they walk, Lu takes note of Du's beard and skullcap. "You are Hui?" he guesses.

The Hui are an ethnoreligious group of Muslims who live scattered throughout China but mainly in the northwest. Lu is not particularly knowledgeable about the Hui people, aside from the fact that most of them look Chinese and speak Mandarin but wear a *taqiyah*. They are not to be confused with China's other Muslim minority, the Uighurs, who speak a Turkic language and are regarded as a terrorist risk by the government.

"My ancestors came from China. They were part of the sultanate in Yunnan Province."

"A sultanate in Yunnan? That's news to me."

Du waves a dismissive hand. "It was a long time ago. Nineteenth century. There was a Muslim rebellion in Yunnan and the provincial Qing military was tossed out. An Islamic Kingdom of Yunnan was established and ruled in relative peace for ten years or so. Then the Qing returned with French artillery, and . . . well . . . you know how it goes. Muskets, spears, and rattan shields are no match for explosive shells. So, my ancestors fled south. And here we are, a hundred and fifty years later."

They make their way toward the western end of the compound, Lu keeping his eyes peeled for any buildings that might house a VIP like Wilson Fang. He asks Du more questions about his personal background.

"I was born not far from here," Du says. "My father was—like most locals—involved in the industry."

"Industry?"

"Poppy cultivation."

"Ah."

"But I wanted to do something different with my life. I worked very hard in school and against all odds for a poor kid like me from a small village, I managed to make it into our country's sole veterinary college."

"That's quite an achievement."

"Thank you." Du smiles, his pride evident. Then his face darkens. "Somehow I found myself back here anyway. Treating tigers for intestinal parasites, and pangolins with pneumonia."

They come to a rear gate with a fortified watch tower. Soldiers open the gate, and they cross a narrow bridge and start down a dirt path heading into the forest.

"You may have heard our government now allows the breeding of endangered species in private zoos," Du says. "Consequently, most of what I will show you today is completely legal. A year ago—not so much." Du lights a small cheroot. He offers one to Lu, who declines. "You may change your mind soon," Du says. "The smoke keeps the bugs away."

Lu sees wire barriers and metal fences tucked among the trees, ferns, and flowering plants. "I'm guessing the new regulations make it easier to 'launder,' as it were, the wild animals?"

"Correct. The government really has no way of knowing what's bred under the new regulations, what isn't, and what's poached. But my understanding is that your employer is primarily concerned with ensuring the *yewei* of his bushmeat?"

"Yes." Lu swats at a cloud of flying insects. Perhaps Du was right about the cheroot.

"Well, as you can see, even the animals we breed in captivity exist in a relatively natural state inside these pens and habitats," Du explains. "Although raised from birth, they retain the rich taste and medicinal efficacy of a completely wild animal. Look there—a tiger."

Du points. Lu squints, and yes, behind a tall wire mesh fence, among the dappled shadows of the thick underbrush, a tiger lolls in the tropic heat. It's not the most handsome specimen Lu has ever seen. It looks a bit thin and mangy, to be honest. And its enclosure, although relatively spacious, is littered with dried scat and devoid of any apparent means for the tiger to keep itself occupied. No climbing platforms, dens, or other diversions. Just a tin trough filled with murky water.

"There's no way he can escape?" Lu asks.

"Never say never," Du says. He laughs, then whistles. Immediately a young Burmese man in camouflage emerges from a concealed blind. He's armed with a .375 Ruger bolt-action rifle. "This is Kaung," Du says. Kaung bows and smiles broadly. "He and others like him are stationed at various posts, just in case the unexpected should occur. Thank you, Kaung." Kaung salutes and then disappears back to wherever he was hiding.

Lu wonders how many armed guards are hidden in the forest. He is growing less confident about Captain Bang's prospects for a successful infiltration by the minute.

They continue down the narrow trail. Du points out habitats for leopards, birds, and reptiles. Lu can't say the animals look in immediate distress, but the pens are crowded and dirty, and he knows that, while still in the prime of their life, these creatures will all be slaughtered and sold for meat, medicine, and other byproducts. After he mutters "*ta ma de*" under his breath for the third time, Du asks him if everything is all right.

"Oh, yes," Lu says. "I'm just a city boy, that's all. Tickled to see these exotic animals with my own eyes. I would have expected some elephants?"

"Oh, we have elephants," Du responds. "But they need a big area to roam, and they're quite destructive, so we keep them at a distance. Bears, too."

"Bears?"

"Of course. You northern cousins are crazy for bear paws and bile. Would you like to see our harvesting operation?"

They detour fifteen minutes up a slope to a large tin-roofed structure guarded by soldiers with AK-47s. Inside are a dozen filthy steel cages holding captive bears. The place reeks.

"Bear bile contains ursodeoxycholic acid," Du explains. "Excellent for treating liver and gallbladder disease."

"Do they suffer?" Lu asks.

"Eh," Du hedges. "We sedate them before we drain their bile. Not like some other facilities that just leave a drain permanently in place."

The cages are so small, the bears can hardly move. They look listless and thin. Many of them have missing or broken teeth. "Do you purposely extract their teeth so they can't bite you?"

"Ah, no. That's from them trying to gnaw their way out."

One of the bears begins to bang its head against the bars of its cage. Du at least has the decency to look embarrassed. "Shall we go?"

As they leave the tin-roofed structure, Lu sees another road leading farther up the hill. "Where's up there?"

Du hesitates. "That's where the *yaba* and ice are manufactured." By *ice*, he means high-quality crystal methamphetamine. *Yaba*—"crazy drug," a mixture of cheap meth and caffeine—is the drug that fuels Southeast Asian construction sites, day laborers, taxi drivers, and nightlife.

Lu knows from reading Interpol reports that despite the Burmese government's sporadic attempts to clamp down, meth production continues to fuel the local economy. And in addition to meth and *yaba*, heroin, ketamine, and, most recently, fentanyl are manufactured in high-tech jungle labs and then distributed to other parts of Asia, the South Pacific,

Canada, and the United States by Chinese triads, Japanese yakuza, and Australian biker gangs.

"Can we take a quick look?" Lu asks.

"It's not my area of responsibility." Du sniffs. "And I was told you are only here for the animals."

Lu decides he'd better not push his luck. "Quite right," he says. "I was just asking out of curiosity."

The tour concludes with a visit to the facility where animals are killed, skinned, deboned, their meat frozen or smoked, and their bones, sex organs, teeth, tusks, horns, and any other by-products considered medicinally useful or decorative are duly processed. It is a long corrugated building, with a slaughterhouse on one end and a meat packaging station at the other. As he passes through it, Lu can't help but feel as if he's traversing the Eighteen Levels of Hell. The Pit of Fire. The Chamber of Tongue Ripping. The Hall of Disembowelment.

The stench of blood, feces, offal, and chemicals is overpowering, but it doesn't appear to trouble the workers, who, naked apart from shorts and filth-encrusted aprons, their skin gleaming with sweat, conjure up a lurid image of Stone Age idol-worshipping savages. Lu even spies one or two with a necklace of animal teeth around their necks. Meanwhile, skins and animal parts are everywhere, hanging from poles or on meat hooks, as if in the aftermath of a gruesome industrial accident.

Du dutifully shows Lu the meat-processing stations: bloodletting, skinning, sectioning, refrigeration, packing. They stop to observe as a pangolin is prepared. The shy little creature is first stunned with a hammer blow to the head, then hung upside down and drained of blood. Next, it is descaled in a pot of boiling water. Finally, it is gutted, cleaned, sealed in plastic, and placed in a shipping container with dry ice.

"Where's this one going?" Lu asks, as a worker seals the container.

Du puts a finger to his lips. "We never tell."

"Of course."

When they finally emerge into the sunlight, Lu feels like falling to his knees in the dirt and thanking Guanyin, the Buddhist Goddess of Mercy, for releasing him from purgatory.

Du lights up another one of his cheroots. "Is there anything else you would like to see?"

"I think that covers it, Doctor. Thank you."

"Are you satisfied as to the quality of the product?"

"Yes."

"Would you like to join me in a spot of lunch?"

"Strangely, I'm not hungry. Perhaps it's the heat. I'll just head back to my room and bask in the air-conditioning for a bit."

"As you wish."

On the return trip, Lu and his escort of soldiers pass by several more guesthouses, all constructed on stilts. Lu hears music coming from inside one of them. He sees no guards below—the resident, whoever he may be, is obviously free to come and go.

Lu pauses for a moment to listen. He identifies the music as a traditional Chinese folk song called "Rainbow Sister":

Rainbow Sister, en ai hai you!
She's grown up so lovely, en ai hai you!
Lips like cherries, en ai hai you!

Lu thinks only someone who is nostalgic for his homeland would play such a hoary old tune.

When the soldiers deliver Lu back to his own quarters, he finds Bullethead, wearing only a pair of shorts, doing knuckle push-ups in the dirt near the stairs. Bullethead's beefy torso gleams with sweat. Tattoos cover his entire back, yakuza-style. The soldiers take shelter in the shade beneath the building and light up cigarettes.

Bullethead stands up and brushes sand off his legs. "Get your fill of tiger cocks for one day?"

"As if such a thing were even possible!"

Lu heads for the stairs, but Bullethead blocks his way. "I don't trust you."

"That hurts me deeply." Lu motions for Bullethead to move aside.

Bullethead doesn't budge. "Alex Ho is a snitch. I think you are, too."

"Who says he's a snitch?"

"People."

"People say a lot of things, don't they?"

"You know what Daw Khaw does to snitches? Feeds them to her tigers."

"Right," Lu says. "Got it. Now, if you're through trying to intimidate me, I'll ask you to get out of my way."

"Why don't you make me?" Bullethead's chin juts aggressively.

Lu looks at the soldiers. They are watching the proceedings with interest and show no inclination to intervene. Lu sighs. "Are we going to fight? Because if we are, I need to take a piss and get a drink of water first."

Bullethead's teeth glint dully. "Not now. But maybe soon." He steps aside.

Lu goes upstairs and strips out of his sweat-soaked clothes. He showers and lies spread-eagled on the bed.

What a day.

THIRTY-FOUR

After tossing and turning for an hour or so, Lu gets up and dresses. He threads the camera into the buttonhole of his shirt. He helps himself to water and fruit in the kitchenette. He watches thirty minutes of *Rambo* on DVD. It's worse than he remembered, and he finally shuts it off. A servant comes to collect him at seven.

Cho is already waiting at the foot of the stairs. He's wearing a traditional *longyi* with the folds tucked in at his hip, a red silk blouse, a brightly colored scarf, and a purple headdress. His face is fully made up—lipstick, rouge, eye shadow. Lu must admit he looks gorgeous—but he wonders what would induce Cho to go full-on drag.

Cho makes no explanation. He greets Lu with a nod and then starts walking, leaving the servant to trail behind.

Lu catches up. "No Bullethead?"

"No," Cho says. "Tonight, you and Lady Khaw negotiate terms. That is above his pay grade."

"He's just good for cracking skulls, is that it?"

"Sometimes you need a scalpel and sometimes a cudgel. Bullethead is a cudgel."

Lu can't help but ask. "What's with the outfit?"

Cho pauses before answering. "I am a *Nat Kadaw.*"

"A what?"

"Nat Kadaw."

"Is that the Burmese word for a guy who likes to wear women's clothes?"

"No. A *Nat Kadaw* is a . . . How do I say it? A person who communes with spirits on behalf of the living."

"A medium?"

"More or less."

"What spirits do you talk to? Dead relatives? Can you get a message to my grandmother? Tell her I miss her rice congee."

"It is not a joke."

"No, of course not." They trudge along in a silence for a bit, and then Lu asks: "So, what spirits *do* you talk to?"

"The *Nats*."

"The *who*?"

"*Nats*. They are nature spirits, but also humans who lived long ago. Kings and queens. Warriors. And some commoners. There are thirty-seven Great *Nats*. They all met untimely ends and, in so doing, acquired supernatural powers."

"What kinds of things do these *Nats* reveal to you?"

"Whatever they wish. Advice regarding business or a person's love life. The future. Sometimes nothing."

"But why the women's clothes?"

"*Nat Kadaw* are consorts to the *Nats*."

"Consorts. Like brides."

"Yes . . . but a *Nat Kadaw* can be male or female. It is not dependent on gender. Or sexual preference, for that matter. And I did not choose to be a *Nat Kadaw*. When I was sixteen, a *Nat* appeared to me in a dream and said we were to be married. I resisted for a long time. Then I got very sick. I had no choice but to acquiesce. That's why I eventually left this country and moved to Kunming. The *Nats* are less powerful there. But when I return home—the pull is strong."

"So which *Nat* are you married to?"

"What do you care?"

"Is it a secret?"

"No, but I won't be the object of your ridicule."

"You misjudge me, Brother Cho. I ask out of a desire to learn, not to mock."

Cho produces a pack of cigarettes from somewhere in the folds of his clothing and sticks one in his mouth: "The Lord of the Great Mountain. Also known as Mr. Handsome."

"Cool nickname."

"He was famously strong, able to break an elephant's tusk with his bare hands. Because of this, the king felt threatened and had him burned alive."

"Beware the despot with an insecurity complex. But I notice you didn't dress like this for the banquet last night. Why now?"

"Lady Khaw likes to consult Mr. Handsome when concluding business arrangements."

Lu doesn't like the sound of that. He has never heard of these *Nats* or *Nat Kadaw,* and he's not generally superstitious, but over the years he's witnessed phenomena he could not easily explain. Temple mediums being possessed by gods and so on. "That doesn't quite seem fair. It's like insider trading."

"You have nothing to fear. Unless you have reason to fear something."

"What are you, a fortune cookie?"

"A what?"

"Never mind."

They eventually pass through an archway and enter a courtyard, this one containing a pool of shallow water surrounded on all four sides by a roofed colonnade. A narrow arching stone bridge leads across the water to a pavilion in the center of the pool. Lu notices a handful of Khaw's female bodyguards positioned in the shadows of the colonnade.

The pavilion is square in shape, with a multitiered ceiling that telescopes upward into successively smaller levels. The supporting beams are richly carved and painted. The walls are decorated with bits of shiny glass and sparkling stones. Inside, a small dining table lit with candles has been set.

Lu immediately recognizes the interior of the pavilion from the screensaver on Wilson Fang's computer—it was here that Fang was photographed with a mysterious woman whose face was obscured by a raised cup. Lu now knows Khaw was that woman. He doubts Fang will show up for dinner, but at least this is a chance to obtain some circumstantial evidence that Fang was once here and has a past association with Khaw. He lines up a shot and says, *"Ta ma de."*

"What's the matter?" Cho asks.

"I am overcome by the beauty of the setting."

Cho and Lu sit across from each another, leaving the head of the table—Khaw's rightful place as hostess—empty. A servant takes their drink orders. Cho asks for his customary whisky over ice. Lu inquires if there is Shaoxing wine and is delighted to hear that there is. The drinks are brought quickly. Cho sips from his glass, leaving a bright semicircle of lipstick on the rim. Lu tries the wine. Not bad. Not great, either.

After a short wait, Khaw sweeps in, along with two of her bodyguards, one of whom, Lu notes, is Golden Krait. Golden Krait walks with a limp and wears the traces of the *Lethwei* match heavily on her face.

Khaw takes her seat. She is dressed casually tonight—a loose, flowing *longyi* and black blouse with a keyhole neckline. The skin of her neck, chest, and shoulders sparkles with some kind of shiny powder. Lu finds the effect alluring. She lights a cheroot and offers Lu one, but he declines. Cho smokes his Marlboros. Food is served in tiny porcelain dishes. Small talk is exchanged, although Cho doesn't join in.

Khaw uses a pair of wooden chopsticks with pearl inlays to place a tidbit of food into her mouth. "Dr. Du tells me you were satisfied with the quality of my product."

"I will give Alex a glowing report."

"I'm glad to hear it."

"He will be interested in perhaps receiving a monthly shipment of varying items." Lu samples the pickled fish. "Will that be an issue?"

"No issue. But prices will fluctuate, depending on supply, demand, and how aggressively the authorities are targeting the trade at any given time."

"What about transport?" Lu asks.

"We guarantee delivery."

"But how do you do it?"

Khaw sets down her chopsticks and sips from her glass of foreign wine. "We use commercial transport with fake papers. Human couriers. We send it by post. Many ways."

Lu coughs as a wave of cigarette smoke blows across his face. Cho is eating sparingly, smoking furiously, and drinking glass after glass of whisky. "What if it gets stopped?"

"You don't pay. Naturally, you'd be wise to use a third-party shipping address that cannot be traced back to you."

Logistical matters settled, they turn to pricing. Lu knows no money will change hands, but he bargains hard to make a good show of it. Khaw proves a shrewd and relentless negotiator. Afterward, Lu knows how one of her bears feels after it's been milked for bile.

Toward the end of the meal, a band sets up at the entrance of the pavilion and begins to play. Cho sways gently in his seat. He appears quite drunk.

Khaw calls for a bottle of champagne and pressures Lu into drinking several celebratory toasts. She is in an expansive mood. Lu decides this is the best opportunity he's going to have to probe for information regarding Fang.

"You know," he says tentatively, "I recently heard an interesting rumor."

"Rumors," Khaw says, "are stories little people whisper about those they are envious of."

"True. Forget I said anything."

Khaw taps ash from her cheroot into a porcelain dish. "Don't be coy. Out with it."

"Well, it involves someone who I believe is a customer of yours. A restaurateur from up north. Wilson Fang."

Khaw's expression hardens. "How do you know Wilson?"

"He's famous. Or at least his restaurant is. It's said you can get anything you want there, as long as you're willing to pay." Khaw's answering grunt is not encouraging. Lu presses on anyway. "It seems he pissed off the wrong people and they tried to kill him."

"*Shen bu you ji,*" Khaw mutters. This phrase, usually preceded by *ren zai jiang hu,* means something like "bad shit happens" and refers to the dangers inherent in the life of an outlaw.

"Do *you* know who tried to kill him?" Lu prods.

"What's it to you, Brother Ming?"

"Nothing," Lu says. "Just . . . gossiping."

"Foreigners have a saying. Perhaps you've heard it. 'Curiosity killed the cat.'"

"You're right. It's none of my business."

"No, it's not."

"The funny thing is—" Lu starts, but Khaw's look tells him he's gone too far. He smiles and shrugs and turns to Cho, hoping to incorporate him into the conversation as a distraction, but Cho's eyes are half-closed, his chin resting on his chest. Lu is surprised. At the Golden Water Buffalo, he saw Cho drink nearly a bottle of whiskey by himself and still maintain his wits. Then again, he's barely touched his dinner this evening.

"Well, go on, then," Khaw says, after a moment. "Finish your thought."

"It's really not important."

"Speak!"

"If you insist. Rumor has it that Fang has fled China and is currently holed up with a powerful friend. A friend who lives in a hidden location somewhere in Myanmar."

"Who is spreading this rumor?"

"Come now, *A Sao.* There are few secrets in the *jianghu.*"

The term *jianghu*—"rivers and lakes"—is shorthand for the criminal underworld. Inspired by Chinese martial arts novels, it represents a fictional universe in which righteous outlaw heroes fight for justice against a corrupt government.

"It would be foolish of me to harbor a fugitive from Chinese law enforcement," Khaw says. "We depend on the goodwill of our friends to the north. To jeopardize that would put me in a very uncomfortable position with my own people."

"A friend in need . . ."

"There are no friends in this business, Brother Ming. You would do well to remember that."

"No doubt." Lu lifts the bottle to pour more champagne as a peace offering, but Khaw puts her hand over the top of her goblet. His clumsy attempt to gather intelligence has soured the mood.

It is almost a relief, then, when Cho abruptly rises from the table. He lurches to a corner of the pavilion, raises his arms, and begins to spin in a circle. The band responds by increasing the tempo of its music. A female musician approaches and respectfully hands Cho a green leafy branch. He takes it and waves it around like a kid at a rave with a fresh glow stick.

Mr. Handsome has finally joined the party.

THIRTY-FIVE

The female musician warbles into a microphone. Cho capers, his awkward movements lying somewhere between the precise choreography of traditional Southeast Asian dance and a drunk grandmother cutting the rug at a wedding.

A servant takes the bottle of whisky from the table and pours a measure into Cho's mouth, then lights one of his cigarettes and places it between his lips. Lu can't tell if Cho is intoxicated, possessed, or faking the whole thing. Khaw, however, has no such doubts. Her expression is enraptured. A true believer.

Lu has an unsettling realization. With a few choice words in Khaw's ear, Cho has the power to have him bled out like the unfortunate pangolin he saw during his tour.

The music gets louder and faster. Cho pogos up and down, his face damp with sweat. Khaw produces a huge wad of American cash and holds it up. A servant runs over to accept it. He pokes a huge safety pin through the center and Cho stops gyrating long enough to allow the servant to pin the money to his clothes.

This goes on for quite some time. Cho is continuously plied with cigarettes and whisky and cash is pinned to clothes or stuffed into the waist of his *longyi*. At long last, he waves Khaw over.

She goes to him. He rests his arms on her shoulders and speaks, but Lu cannot hear what he says. Even if he could, he assumes they are speaking Burmese. Lu takes advantage of Khaw's focus on Cho to take a series of pictures of the two of them together. After a few moments, she nods and bows and returns to her chair. Lu searches her face for any warning signs. Her expression betrays nothing.

Cho beckons Lu. He pretends not to see.

"The *Nat* is calling you," Khaw says.

"I'm not interested, thanks."

"It is an honor. Not everyone is chosen."

"I don't believe in it."

Khaw's eyes flash. "Go!"

Lu reluctantly gets up and approaches Cho. Cho grips Lu's shoulders, his fingers like talons. A bead of sweat drips from the tip of his nose. "Brother," Cho says, after a pregnant pause. "You are on a dangerous road."

Lu's breath catches in his throat. The Mandarin word for road is *lu*. The Chinese character is written differently from Lu's surname, but still— could Cho be signaling that he knows something more than he's letting on? Is he toying with Lu?

"I'm happy to take a detour if you think it best," Lu says, carefully.

A servant pops by to stick a lit cigarette in Cho's mouth. Cho takes a few puffs, then spits it onto the floor. "If you make it back home, seek peace . . . and thereby find what you seek."

"What do you mean *if*?"

Cho rattles off a long continuous string of what sounds like gibberish. It takes Lu a moment to realize he's speaking Burmese. "You'll have to use Mandarin if you want me to understand you."

Cho belches rancid booze breath into Lu's face. "Remember this— one swallow does not a summer make."

In Chinese culture, swallows are the harbingers of spring, and a symbol of matrimonial bliss. It so happens Yanyan's name also means *swallow*. What is Cho trying to say here? He and Yanyan are doomed as a couple? "Speak clearly," Lu snaps, annoyed. "Enough riddles."

Cho appears on the verge of another mystic pronouncement, but then he collapses. Lu catches him before he can hit the floor. Servants rush over to convey Cho back to his chair. They mop sweat from his face and give him water to drink.

"Take him back to his quarters," Khaw orders.

Cho is assisted from the pavilion, his feet dragging, his head lolling. The band soon packs up and departs.

Lu is alarmed by Cho's condition. "Is he going to be all right?"

"He'll be fine," Khaw says. "Just terribly fatigued for a day or so." She seems in a better mood now. She holds out her goblet for a splash of champagne. A servant rushes over, but Lu waves him off and pours for Khaw himself.

"If I might ask, what did Mr. Handsome tell you?" Lu says.

"That I am unlucky in love but fortunate in business."

"I'm sorry to hear that."

"I consider it better than the other way around."

"Not a romantic, eh?"

"Love and beauty fade, Brother Ming. But gold lasts forever. What did the *Nat* tell *you*?"

"That I will become your number-one customer."

Khaw laughs. "Surely he must have had something more interesting to say."

"The cynic in me believes so-called mediums like Cho know that if you keep it sufficiently vague, people end up filling in the blanks themselves."

"Perhaps in your country, there are no gods left. Your Communist government has shooed them away. Here, they still exist. And sometimes, they draw aside the curtain for a quick peek into the next world."

Lu lifts his glass. "Let's hope the view is a pleasant one, *A Sao*."

They drink. Khaw leans closer. "Speaking of pleasant views, you're not half bad-looking."

"A high compliment indeed."

"You might not know it to look at me now, but in my day, I was a great beauty."

"You're still a beauty."

Khaw raises a plump finger. "But even when I was a girl, naive, wet behind the ears, I refused to be possessed or controlled by anyone. Some had to learn the hard way."

"I believe it. But you never . . . fell in love?"

"Oh, many times. And when I set my mind on someone . . . the heat I generated was sufficient to set any man's bed ablaze." Lu laughs awkwardly, embarrassed, but Khaw doesn't notice. She's too busy smiling up at the ceiling at some private memory playing there like an old black-and-white film. She comes back to earth and looks at Lu. "Or any woman's bed, for that matter."

Lu wonders where this is going. Khaw is not young, but she exudes a sexual allure that is hard to deny. Sleeping with the enemy was not part of the job description, however, and he's not sure he's up to performing under that kind of pressure.

Besides, there's Yanyan. There's always Yanyan.

Khaw rests a hand on Lu's arm. "Shall I tell you a secret?"

"Well," Lu says. "I suppose?"

"The truth is—nowadays I'd rather just curl up alone in bed with a glass of wine and a good movie." She laughs boisterously. Lu joins her, relieved.

Khaw dabs at the corners of her eyes with her napkin, then grows serious. "I'm glad we could come to terms. And I will admit I have enjoyed your company, Brother Ming. But from this point forward, Cho will be your sole point of contact." She rises from her chair. "We will not meet again."

Lu stands. "Thank you for everything, *A Sao*."

"You will never speak of what you saw here."

"Understood."

"If you do, I will hear of it. And the termination of our business relationship will be the least of your worries."

"Understood, *A Sao*."

"Good night."

"Good night."

Khaw departs, Golden Krait and the other bodyguard at her heels. Two soldiers appear at the foot of the arched bridge. They escort Lu back to the guesthouse and take up position at the foot of the stairs.

Lu enters his apartment and goes into the bedroom to gaze out the window. The moon is three-quarters full, bone white in a velvet sky. A perfect night for drinking outdoors with friends.

But Lu has no friends and no wine and more importantly, if he's leaving tomorrow as planned, no more time.

There's no way around it—he's going to have to go looking for Fang.

THIRTY-SIX

Lu switches off the lights and lies in bed, his thoughts churning, heart racing, until the stroke of midnight. He gets up and takes his duffel bag into the bathroom. He closes the door, switches on the light, and searches among his clothes for something suitably dark and loose-fitting. He settles on a black T-shirt, sweatpants, and a pair of knockoff Gucci low-top sneakers. The buttonhole camera goes into a pocket. He switches off the lights and exits the bathroom and waits for his eyes to adjust to the dark. Then he goes out to the veranda.

He listens to the night hum: the chirp, buzz, and whir of a billion insects; the distant trill of flutes and thump of drums; the soft murmur of the guards posted at the foot of the stairs.

He returns to his bedroom and strips the sheets off the bed. He knots them together and winds them into a makeshift rope. He goes back out to the veranda and ties one end around the railing opposite the stairs. He drops the other end over the side, behind a concrete support post.

Lu takes hold of the sheet and steels himself. *Last chance to* not *do something incredibly stupid*, he thinks. He takes a breath and climbs over the railing.

He shimmies down the support post, hidden from view of the guards, and drops the last meter into the dirt. He flattens himself against the post. He gives it a moment, then crawls across open sand to the underside of the neighboring guesthouse, where he huddles in the shadows. So far, so good, but there is the matter of the sheet dangling suspiciously from his veranda. Anyone who happens by and isn't legally blind can see it. He'll have to move quickly.

Lu threads his way through the compound to the building where he suspects Fang is sequestered. He squats under the stairs and watches and waits. Voices approach. Lu lies prone in the dust.

A pair of soldiers walk past, guns carelessly slung over their backs. They pause to light cheroots. One of them makes a comment and the other one responds with a high-pitched giggle. They continue onward.

Lu crawls up the building's stairs to the veranda. He sees there are only two doors. He chooses the farthest one. He figures he's got a fifty-fifty chance of it leading to Fang.

The door is unlocked. Lu knew it would be. The guesthouses are de-signed to prevent people from getting out, not the other way around. Lu enters and quietly shuts the door.

He smells cigarette smoke. Old food. Stale liquor. He shuffles forward in the dark and bangs his shin into a table. He pats the table and touches drinking glasses, aluminum cans, liquor bottles. Whoever is staying here isn't big on housekeeping.

Lu makes his way by feel to the bedroom. He opens the door. The singular window admits a rectangle of moonlight, illuminating a dark fig-ure splayed on the bed. Lu edges forward, fumbling for the camera in his pocket.

When he gets closer, he sees the bed is occupied by a man, lying on his back, mouth open, snoring. Shirtless, with a big belly that gleams like the underside of a slug. His skin is crisscrossed with tattoos of skulls, a bearded *Yesu* nailed to a cross, nautical stars, Cyrillic letters.

It's not Fang, it's the meth dealer—Andrei.

Ta ma de. Who would have thought European gangsters liked Chi-nese folk tunes?

Lu backs away toward the door. One step. Another. His heel strikes a bottle lying on the floor. It rattles loudly.

Andrei's eyes pop open. He gives a shout of alarm and leaps out of bed, taking Lu by surprise. He clamps his hand around Lu's neck and shoves him into a wall. Lu corkscrews a fist into Andrei's face. Andrei grunts in pain and stabs his thick fingers toward Lu's eyes.

Lu whips his knuckles into a pressure point inside Andrei's elbow. Andrei jerks his hand away. Lu follows up with a liver punch and a right hook to the jaw. It's a solid shot; Andrei drops to his knees.

Lu spins around behind the big man and wraps a forearm around his throat. Andrei lurches to his feet. Lu jumps on Andrei's back, wraps his legs around his waist, and locks in the choke. Andrei tries to shake him loose, and when that fails, turns and body-slams Lu against the wall.

Lu's teeth rattle in his skull. But he keeps the pressure on, not forcing, not straining, just squeezing, cinching the noose ever tighter.

Panicking now, acutely aware of the danger he's in, Andrei tugs frantically at Lu's arm. As blood ceases flowing to his brain, he grows dizzy and finally falls. Lu clings to Andrei's back, choke sunk deep, long after Andrei stops moving. One minute. Two minutes. Lu holds it until he can hold it no more.

He finally lets go and sits against the wall, catching his breath. His arms are like rubber. He shakes them out. The other foreigner, the one from Africa, must be in the neighboring room. But perhaps the pair of them got rip-roaring drunk before bed. Otherwise, he surely would have heard the struggle.

Lu checks Andrei's pulse. There isn't one.

Gan! What a cock-up. Worst-case scenario. Not only has Lu failed to locate Fang, he's gone and killed one of Khaw's guests.

But he doesn't have time for recriminations. Or even exultation at still being alive. His sheet is still dangling from his veranda in open view. He's got to get back before someone sees it.

Lu slinks through the compound. He finds the sheet dangling just where he left it, the guards seemingly none the wiser. He climbs up to the veranda, unknots the sheet from the railing, carries it inside. Leaving the lights off, he feels his way into his bedroom, unties the sheets, and shakes them out. The cleaning staff may wonder how he got them so dirty, but that can't be helped.

Now—he needs a drink. Does he ever. He turns to go into the living room.

A figure stands silhouetted in the bedroom doorway.

"Don't make a sound," the figure says in a low voice. "It's me." A flashlight snaps on. Lu sees a flash of swirling green and brown skin before the light flicks off.

"Bang," Lu says. "How . . . ?"

"Did you find Fang?"

"Come into the bathroom," Lu says.

"Why?"

"So we can talk." Lu goes into the bathroom and waits. He hears a rattle and thump of equipment and a few seconds later, Bang steps inside. Lu closes the door and switches on the light.

Bang is dressed in dark clothes, combat boots, a black knit cap. His face is smeared with camo paint. He smells like he hasn't taken a shower for a couple of days.

"Where's Fang?" Bang asks.

"How did you know what building I was in?"

"The tracker, obviously. Is Fang here or not?"

"I looked but couldn't find him."

"Where did you look?" Bang says.

Lu explains the layout of the compound as he's reconstructed it mentally. "He may be in another one of the houses. Or maybe he's staying wherever Khaw has her own apartments. I don't know where that is, but I'm guessing the northern quadrant."

Bang curses. "I have to find him."

"I killed a man tonight." Lu tells Bang about Andrei. "I left his body there—hopefully, when they find it, they'll think he just took a drunken fall in the night or had a heart attack."

"It doesn't matter," Bang says. "It'll all be over by morning."

"How so?"

Bang doesn't answer. He draws his sidearm, a Chinese QSW-06 automatic pistol. This model is known as the *weisheng shou qiang,* or the "low-noise handgun." Bang removes a suppressor attachment from a pocket and starts screwing it onto the barrel of the QSW.

"What are you doing?" Lu asks.

Bang doesn't answer. Lu wastes a few precious moments doubting his own eyes until it is almost too late. Then he reaches out and gets a hand on the gun just as Bang brings the barrel up. They fight for control of the weapon until Bang jams the fingers of his free hand into Lu's throat. Lu gasps and raises his hands to his neck. This is the opening Bang wanted. He thrusts the gun into Lu's sternum. Lu twists to the side, parrying with his arm.

The gun barks, as loud as a small dog. A bullet thuds into the wall.

Lu clamps onto Bang's gun wrist with both hands. Bang responds by ramming his left fist into Lu's ribs, then comes over the top with an elbow, striking Lu above the ear. Lu sees a flash of stars. He pushes, pulls, and twists Bang's hand violently, driving him up onto the bathroom counter. Bang's head smacks into the mirror, cracking the glass.

Bang shoves Lu away, levels the gun at his face. Lu deflects Bang's wrist with his forearm. The gun fires into the ceiling.

Lu leaps forward and headbutts Bang, cracking his nose. Bang grabs Lu by the throat, hoists him nearly off his feet, and hurls him into the tub. He aims downward. Lu lashes out with a foot and the gun goes flying.

Bang scrabbles for it. Lu pops out of the tub and does the same. Bang reaches the gun first. From behind, Lu knees him head-first into the wall. Bang aims backward under his armpit—Lu sees the round hole of the barrel and turns sharply as Bang fires, punching a neat hole in the bathroom door. Lu grips Bang by the back of his shirt, lifts him up and then slams his face into the toilet seat. He is rewarded with a painful grunt. He wings an elbow toward the back of Bang's head, but Bang ducks. Lu's elbow hits the top of the water tank, cracking off a sizable chunk of porcelain.

Bang rears back and sneaks in an elbow of his own into Lu's ribs. He pushes off, pivots, brings the gun into play again. Lu scissors Bang's wrist between his forearms—hard. The gun flips end-over-end into the tub.

They abandon the gun and focus on killing each other the old-fashioned way, careening around the bathroom in a savage embrace, ripping the towel rack from the wall, cracking tiles with their fists. But Bang is heavier and stronger, and his wrestling skills are high-level. Lu isn't sure what technique Bang uses, but one moment he has his hands locked around the back of Bang's neck and is stomping Bang's combat boots with his Gucci sneakers, and the next he's flying backward into the bathroom door. The latch pops and Lu spills onto the bedroom floor.

Bang reaches into the tub for the gun.

Lu gets up and runs.

THIRTY-SEVEN

Lu's objective is the front door, even though he knows fleeing to the safety of the soldiers downstairs will raise questions he may not be able to answer. But as he comes out of the bedroom, his foot kicks an object leaning against the wall. It rattles to the floor. Lu can't see it clearly, but he knows instinctively what it is. He snatches the object up, races across the room, and dives over the back of the couch just as Bang emerges from the bedroom, gun at the ready.

There is a moment of heavy silence. The light in the bathroom is on, but it barely reaches the dark recesses of the sitting room and Lu thinks maybe Bang didn't see him leap over the couch. He runs his hands across the object. There's a lever sticking up from the top. He pulls on it and hears the satisfying metallic chunk of a round feeding into the chamber. "I've got your rifle," he shouts.

"This is all a misunderstanding," Bang says, hastily.

"You mean you weren't trying to kill me just now?"

"Of course not. You suddenly attacked me." Bang's voice is muffled. Lu figures he's ducked behind the breakfast counter.

Lu gets to his knees. "You just needed someone expendable to show you the way in, is that it?"

The QSW coughs. A bullet zips through a couch cushion, close enough for Lu to feel a puff of air displaced by its trajectory. Lu drops and rolls and then pops up from behind one of the armchairs. He squeezes the trigger of the rifle. It belches rapid automatic fire.

Unlike the QSW, the rifle is not fitted with a suppressor—and it is astoundingly loud. Spent shell casings roll across the floorboards. Lu ducks back behind the chair.

"You idiot!" Bang shouts. "The entire compound will have heard that!"

What Bang says is undeniably true. Lu understands he has made a serious error. But it's hard to think clearly when someone is trying to kill you.

He hears Bang's boots beat a retreat. The door to the bedroom slams shut. Lu gets up, pursues. He's not sure what the plan is—or if he even has one. Shoot Bang? Or beg him to exfiltrate them both?

Lu hears glass breaking. He throws opens the bedroom door, pokes the muzzle of the rifle inside. He feels a whisper of cool night air. He runs to the window. Broken glass crunches underfoot. He looks out.

Shouts and flashlight beams rip through the darkness below. There is no sign of Bang. How could he have jumped from this height without breaking a leg?

Lu has just enough time to flush the camera in his pocket down the toilet before the front door crashes open and a dozen soldiers rush in.

THIRTY-EIGHT

Dawn finds Lu locked into a heavy steel chair, his ankles and wrists shackled, a metal tray pressing down firmly on his thighs. Aside from turning his head, he can scarcely move at all.

Similarly medieval contraptions are found in Public Security Bureau stations across the People's Republic and in "black jails" where dissidents and other undesirables are detained—without legal proceedings—by the MSS. Officially known as "interrogation chairs," they are touted by the authorities as a safe and humane means to restrain criminal suspects during questioning.

Those who have had the unfortunate experience of sitting in one call them "tiger chairs."

In comparison to being shocked with a battery cable or having your fingernails yanked off by a pair of pliers, a tiger chair is not so bad. Until you are immobilized in one and left for hours or even days with a harsh light shining in your face, no food or water, no bathroom breaks, not even allowed five minutes' sleep—that is torture, even if it does not result in burn marks or broken bones.

Lu estimates he has been sitting here for perhaps two, maybe three hours. His buttocks are numb, his mouth dry, and he has a powerful need to relieve his bladder.

Earlier, after the soldiers burst into the guesthouse, Lu was made to sit on the couch while his apartment was thoroughly searched. Colonel Ta arrived, dressed in fatigues and carrying a pearl-handled .45 automatic in a side holster. As it is the middle of the night, he is not wearing his mirrored aviator sunglasses, and Lu can see that he has sustained a serious injury to his left eye sometime in the past. The skin around the socket is puckered and scarred, and the eye itself sits in the middle of this crater, watery and discolored, like a soft-boiled egg.

Ta questions Lu. Lu tells the colonel he woke in the night and went to use the bathroom, where he was attacked by a stranger dressed in dark clothes. He relates the particulars of the actual fight much as they happened.

"Why would someone break in here to kill *you*?" Ta wants to know.

Lu shrugs. "Mistaken identity? They thought I was one of Daw Khaw's other guests? Maybe they were after those two foreigners I saw at the banquet?"

Ta isn't buying it.

While this is going on, the compound has become a beehive of activity. Lu wonders if Captain Bang can reasonably expect to escape an army of several dozens. He thinks of the soldier hidden in the jungle—Kaung—and others like him.

Ta orders Lu to lay flat on the floor. Lu, playing the aggrieved guest, refuses. There is yelling and the pointing of weapons. Lu thinks it is very likely he might be killed if he doesn't comply, so he gives in. His wrists are tied, and he is marched to an isolated corner of the compound, put into this dark room, and placed in the chair.

And here he sits.

The room has a cement floor, brick walls, and a wooden roof. The walls muffle sounds from outside, but Lu can hear distant shouts and the faint crow of a rooster. *"Ge-ge-ge. Ge-ge-ge."*

He also hears the intermittent crack of gunfire.

As he waits for whatever terrible thing is going to happen next, he puzzles out why Bang might want to kill him. The simplest explanation is that Lu completed his primary mission—helping Bang infiltrate Khaw's lair for the purpose of obtaining GPS coordinates—and now he represents a security risk and therefore must be eliminated. It seems a cold and calculating trick to recruit a pigeon to do your dirty work and then murder him to cover your tracks, but the MSS is not known for placing a high value on human life.

The other possibility is that Lu's true purpose all along was to guide Bang in so he could simply kill Fang. All that talk about extradition was a ruse. This makes perfect sense if Jia figures Fang's *guanxi* or leverage over his colleagues in the MSS will ultimately protect him from prosecution. In such a scenario, the discovery of Fang's body would immediately place suspicion on Lu. Rather than taking a chance of him cracking under interrogation, it would be prudent to ensure he is in no position to reveal the details of Jia's plot.

Either way, Jia has gone to great lengths to eliminate Fang. It seems to Lu that maybe there is more going on here than a case of a loyal civil servant determined to see justice served.

What if Fang has something on Jia? Perhaps Jia makes an appearance in one of those restaurant videos. And this whole thing is just a cover-up attempt by one man with an axe to grind and the terrifying powers of MSS at his disposal.

Lu attempts to ease the pressure on his buttocks, but it's hopeless. The need to urinate is reaching an excruciating crescendo and he is almost relieved when the door finally opens. He squints against the bright rectangle of sunshine. Shadowy figures enter. One, two, three. The door shuts. A ceiling light is switched on. Lu's eyes slowly adjust.

He finds himself facing Colonel Ta. Daw Khaw.

And Wilson Fang.

Khaw is furious. "You turtle's egg." She slaps Lu across the face.

"*A Sao*—" Lu starts, but Khaw grips the skin of his cheeks with clawlike fingernails. "You will soil yourself in terror and agony before I grant you the mercy of death, that I promise you." She lets go of his cheeks and slaps him again. She packs a surprising wallop.

"I haven't done anything!" Lu protests.

"Who has a knife?" Khaw shouts, freshly enraged by Lu's denial. "Give me a knife so that I can cut off his balls!"

"Let's find out what he knows first," Ta says. "Then you can cut off all his little dangling bits."

Wilson Fang steps forward. "*A Sao*. May I?"

Khaw waves angrily and stalks off into a corner to gather herself.

Fang takes his time lighting a 555 cigarette. He takes a deep drag and squints at Lu. "You look familiar. Have we met?"

"No," Lu answers, carefully.

"Lady Khaw says you were inquiring about me."

"I heard rumors you were here, that's all. Everyone's heard those rumors."

Fang blows smoke toward the rafters. "Tell me who you are really working for."

"Alex Ho."

Fang reaches out and taps ash from his cigarette onto the top of Lu's head. Lu shakes it off.

"Alex Ho would sell his own mother to a Syrian brothel for pocket change," Fang says. "He is a two-faced, untrustworthy, turd-eating dog's prick."

"How dare you speak about him that way!" Lu says. "And how dare you treat a guest in this manner. I'm here to do business in good faith and suddenly some madman breaks into my quarters and tries to kill me and the next thing I know, I'm strapped to a chair and being accused of . . . I don't know what exactly!"

"Amazing coincidence," Ta says. "You arrive. You inquire about Mr. Fang. And then comes a shooter who displays all the signs of being a highly trained military operative."

"What kind of idiot conspiracy do you think I'm involved in that requires someone to break into my apartment and kill *me*?"

"Ding sent you," Fang says. "Didn't he?"

"Ding?"

"This is a waste of time," Khaw says. "I'm going to fetch a knife."

"You heard the lady," Fang says. "Better talk while you still have a tongue. And a nose. And testicles."

"Call Alex if you don't believe me!" Lu shouts.

"Suit yourself." Fang tosses his cigarette on the floor.

They leave Lu alone to stew in the dark.

A span of time passes. Perhaps an hour. Lu works his wrists in the restraints but succeeds only in rubbing off a layer of skin. The urge to pee has become an agony. He holds out for as long as he can, but then the inevitable happens. He lets go—the relief is sublime but short-lived. Afterward he's disgusted with himself. How low can he possibly get?

He fears he'll find out soon enough.

Another interminable hour passes and then two of Khaw's female bodyguards enter, followed by Colonel Ta. The bodyguards begin to free Lu from the chair.

"What's happening?" Lu says.

"We caught your shooter," Ta says.

Lu is pulled to his feet. His legs aren't working properly. He falls and the bodyguards make no move to catch him. They tie his hands behind his back, then pick him up and drag him outside. Hot sunlight stabs into his eyes. The bodyguards muscle him along. Lu realizes they are heading west—toward the back gate.

Lu wants to know what Ta knows. "Did he say why he was trying to kill me?"

"Men like him do not talk." Ta wrinkles his nose. "You smell like piss."

They soon reach the back gate. It is manned by a handful of soldiers who stare at Lu with a mixture of indifference and hostility. They cross the bridge and walk along the dirt track leading toward the animal pens.

Lu is reminded of Bullethead's warning: *You know what Daw Khaw does to snitches? Feeds them to her tigers.*

Before long, they come upon a knot of people: Khaw, flanked by two bodyguards and a servant who shields her with a bamboo parasol. Wilson Fang. Half a dozen soldiers. Dr. Du, looking decidedly queasy. Cho and Bullethead.

And Bang—on his knees in the dirt, arms tightly bound at the elbows and wrists.

The bodyguards drag Lu over to Khaw and force him to kneel in front of her. "Is this the man who tried to kill you?" she asks.

Bang's head hangs low, a stream of blood drizzling from his broken nose into the dust.

"Hard to say," Lu says. "It was dark. I didn't get a good look."

Lu feels a twinge of sympathy for Bang, but mostly anger. He and Jia, with their twisted machinations and dark plots, are to blame for all this. And Bang would have killed Lu without a second thought. Still, Lu isn't going to make things worse for him than they already are.

Khaw gives a signal. Soldiers step forward and lift Bang to his feet. They haul him into the edge of the forest. Bang's right leg drags—he's been shot in the thigh. Khaw speaks sharply to Du. Unhappily, he follows.

The group approaches a wire fence. The soldiers callously drop Bang to the ground. He lies there, limp, unresisting. Weak from blood loss and in excruciating pain, Lu expects.

Du shades his eyes and peers into the enclosure. He unlocks the gate and motions for the soldiers to move quickly. They carry Bang inside and toss him down. They bump into each other in their haste to get out. Du locks the gate.

Lu doesn't want to see this. He looks down but hears the scrape of metal and feels the touch of something cold and hard under his chin. It's the tip of a machete, held by Golden Krait.

"You watch," Golden Krait says.

"No," Lu mutters.

"You watch!" Golden Krait turns the blade edge-up on Lu's skin. Lu reluctantly shifts his eyes over to the pen.

Bang worms across the ground to the fence and slowly, painfully, gets to his feet. He glares at Khaw. His face is cut and bruised and bleeding, his lips swollen, one eye nearly shut. But his defiance transcends all that.

Lu can't help but be moved by Bang's spirit. What a waste.

There's movement in the underbrush behind Bang. Lu closes his eyes. Golden Krait's blade nicks his throat. Lu feels a droplet of blood run down his neck. He opens his eyes and looks at her with hatred. She jerks her head toward Bang.

A tiger glides out of the shadows, its ropy muscles bunching beneath orange and black fur. It bares its teeth. Lu feels its low, menacing growl deep in the pit of his stomach.

Bang surely knows the tiger is slinking up behind him, but he never turns, never takes his eyes off Khaw.

Not even when the tiger pounces, sinking razor-sharp claws into Bang's shoulders and clamping its jaws onto his skull. Blood gushes down his face. He crumbles under the tiger's weight. At first, he does not cry out, but in the end, he cannot help but scream in agony until the tiger mercifully rips out his throat. The beast savages Bang's body, licks its bloody chops, and finally drags him back into the underbrush.

Lu wants to vomit. His body shakes.

He will be next.

THIRTY-NINE

Lu hears Khaw say, "Take them." He waits for cruel hands to drag him toward the enclosure. Then he thinks, *Them?*

Lu looks up and sees Khaw pointing at Cho and Bullethead.

"Lady—" Cho starts, but Khaw cuts him off with a sharp gesture.

"You brought a viper into my home," she snaps. "Out of malice or ignorance, it doesn't matter." She motions at the soldiers. "Go on!"

The soldiers hesitate.

"What's wrong with you?" Khaw shouts. "Do as I say!"

Cho drops to his knees in the dirt and presses his palms together at his forehead. He rattles off a long stream of Burmese. Whether he is praying or begging, Lu cannot say.

Bullethead, true to his nature, does not take this turn of events lightly. He backs away—then draws a gun from his waistband and, before the soldiers can raise their AK-47s, he fires. One of the soldiers goes down. Bullethead aims for Khaw. He shoots, but a bodyguard leaps in front and takes the bullet. Bullethead fires several more rounds and then runs.

Golden Krait pursues, limping badly, her leg still injured from her *Lethwei* match. One of the soldiers has the presence of mind to level his AK-47, but wary of hitting Golden Krait, he hesitates.

Colonel Ta steps forward, .45 in hand. Bullethead is racing down the dirt path as fast as his thick legs can carry him. Ta shouts, the commanding tone of his voice honed by decades as a military man. Golden

Krait immediately sinks into a squat. Ta extends his arm and sights down the barrel of his gun with his one good eye. He exhales, squeezes the trigger.

The top of Bullethead's skull explodes. He drops like a sack of bricks.

There is a moment of shocked silence, broken only by the sound of Khaw's wounded bodyguard wheezing. Khaw drops to her knees and cradles the bodyguard's head in her lap. The dying woman looks up at Khaw, adoration in her glazing eyes.

Ta shouts orders. A pair of soldiers pick up their wounded comrade and hustle him back toward the compound. One holds his rifle on Cho. Another pair rushes to take the bodyguard away, but Khaw angrily waves them off.

The bodyguard coughs wetly. Blood streams from her mouth. Khaw murmurs softly. She shields the bodyguard's face from the sun with her hand. Nobody moves until the bodyguard breathes her last.

Khaw caresses the bodyguard's cheek, then gently lowers her head into the sand. She stands. Her blouse is wet with blood. She nods at Cho, her voice thick. "Take him now."

The remaining soldiers avoid her eyes.

"They are afraid of the *Nats*," Colonel Ta says.

Khaw scoffs. "Would a true *Nat Kadaw* be so easily fooled?"

"The *Nats* decide what they reveal. They are contrary that way."

"I want him dead!" Khaw stamps her foot in the dirt. "Now!"

"Do it yourself, then," Ta says.

Khaw curses. "Useless. All of you!" She snaps her fingers at Golden Krait. It takes Golden Krait a moment to understand what she wants. The machete. She hands it over. Khaw marches over to Cho. "Look at me."

Cho does. His flawless face is artfully smudged with dust—like a 1950s matinee idol in a movie western. He is calm now. Perhaps Mr. Handsome has whispered comforting words into his ear.

Khaw swings, grunting with effort. Cho's head plops into the sand. Blood spurts. His body topples sideways.

Khaw wipes the blade on Cho's pants. The servant carrying her parasol has recovered his courage enough to rush over, but Khaw pushes him away. She walks over to Lu and places the tip of the machete under his chin.

"I'll tell you everything," Lu promises.

"I know you will," Khaw says.

FORTY

Lu is rushed back through the compound and locked back in the tiger chair. Stools are brought in for Colonel Ta and Wilson Fang. Khaw snaps at a soldier: "I won't squat on a stool like some roadside betel nut hawker!" Once seating that befits her station is brought in, the door is closed, and Golden Krait takes up a post in front of it.

Colonel Ta lights a cheroot. Fang, a cigarette.

"Can I have some water?" Lu says.

"You are working for Ding," Fang says. "Let's start there."

"Who is Ding?" Lu asks—but he's pretty sure he knows who Ding is.

Fang shows a flash of anger, then reconsiders and pulls a cell phone out of his pocket. He unlocks it and shows Lu a photograph of a group of men seated around a banquet table. The setting looks like Fang's restaurant. The men are red-faced, drunk, all smiles. Fang stands with his hand resting on the shoulder of a man seated just right of the center. The receding hairline, broad shoulders, and thick forearms are unmistakable.

"Right," Lu says. "First he led me to believe his name is Jia and that he works for the NFGA. Then he told me he works for the MSS but wouldn't give me his real name."

Fang leans in and stares at Lu's face. "Wait . . . I do know you. The hair really threw me off." He snaps his fingers. "Lu Feng, Raven Valley PSB."

"Lu Fei. The name is Lu Fei."

"A cop?" Khaw hisses.

"Don't worry," Fang says. "I'm sure Ding set up some bullshit cover story and no one even knows he's here. But why *you*?"

"The girl you murdered," Lu says. "Tan Meixiang. She's from my hometown."

Khaw leans forward in her chair. "What is he talking about, Wilson?"

"A girl who worked for me," Fang says. "But I didn't kill her."

"Then where is she?" Lu says.

"Oh, she's dead all right," Fang says. "But I didn't kill her. Ding did!"

"Liar!" Lu growls.

"I guess he didn't tell you he was one of my best customers. In once a month, at least, drinking Hennessy, eating his fill of contraband meat, half the time with some cheap tart or another he'd picked up at a local hostess bar. Is that really why you're here? A dead *waitress*?"

"She's from my hometown," Lu says again, as if that explains everything.

"Hold on!" Khaw rises from her chair. "You!" She points at Lu. Her fingers are still stained with blood. "Start at the beginning."

Lu takes a breath. What does he have to lose at this point? "I'm a PSB deputy chief from a town outside of Harbin. A girl came to me—fifteen years old. She said her sister was missing. The sister—Tan Meixiang—worked at Fang's restaurant. When I started poking around, I got the runaround from Fang and a lot of heat from my superiors. Then Jia—Ding—contacted me out of the blue. He said he was part of the National Forestry and Grassland Administration and wanted to bring Fang down for illegal animal trafficking. But because the NFGA was compromised, he needed to run a shadow operation outside of normal channels. He later admitted he was MSS, but his objective was the same."

"And what was your role in this operation?" Khaw says.

"Ding assumed Fang was here, but he needed proof to convince his superiors. He wanted me to pose as a customer."

"To what end?"

"To find a way in so he could . . . get a fix on your location." Lu doesn't mention the buttonhole camera. And he hopes no one checks the plumbing in the guesthouse. "I believed him when he said the end goal was to extradite Fang. Obviously, that was a lie."

Khaw curses under her breath. "And now this Ding knows where my facility is?"

"Bang—he's the guy you fed to the tiger—that was his department. I don't know if he ever relayed the coordinates to Ding, and even if he did, it doesn't matter. Ding doesn't care about you. It's Fang he's after. And it's all because of the dead girl, Tan Meixiang."

"This girl," Khaw says. "What happened to her *exactly*, Wilson?"

Fang chooses his next words carefully. "Ding came to my restaurant, got drunk, as usual, and put his hands on her. Things got rough and he knocked her around. Then he turned remorseful and offered her money as compensation. She told him to get stuffed. So, he killed her, or had her killed, I don't know, I wasn't part of that."

"Killed where?" Khaw asks. "At your restaurant?"

"No. Of course not."

"Then where?"

"I don't know. He took her away." Fang drops his cigarette to the floor and immediately lights another. His shirt is sticky with sweat.

"And you just let him?" Khaw asks.

"What was I supposed to do? Ding is MSS. I don't have to tell you what that means. And I couldn't go to the authorities. I operate a restaurant that offers illegal off-the-menu items. That's ten years, easy."

"Tan Meixiang doesn't have ten more years," Lu says. "She doesn't have ten more seconds."

"Shut up," Fang says. He looks at Khaw. "Ding's gone insane. He tried to kill me in Harbin and now he's compromised your operation. We need to take him out."

"I think the question you need to ask yourself," Lu tells Khaw, "is *why* Ding wants Fang dead so badly."

"You said so yourself!" Fang snaps. "Because I can implicate him in the girl's murder."

"Let's say for the sake of argument Fang has a conscience," Lu says, focusing on Khaw. "Which he obviously does not. He could very well go to the police and report Ding. But his word against an MSS official? Please. All that would accomplish would be to put a target on Fang's back. Fang knows this. Ding knows it, too. So why would Ding go to all this trouble?"

"He's a paranoid nutcase!" Fang shouts.

"The reason why Ding had to create an elaborate scheme to get to Fang," Lu says, "is because Fang has his restaurant wired for surveillance. He's got the whole incriminating incident on video!"

Fang snorts. "That's a lie!"

Lu presses on: "Imagine you're a high-ranking official who tried to rape a waitress in a banquet room. Think of the leverage someone would have if they had it all on tape. Even if they didn't use it to blackmail you, it would be like a dagger hanging over your head, held up only by a single hair. I doubt I'd sleep well at night if I were Ding."

"The cameras are just so I can make sure my employees aren't stealing from me!" Fang protests. "I don't keep recordings. That would be stupid, given the fact that my clientele largely consists of rich and powerful people!"

Lu keeps his eyes on Khaw. "Fang might have been able to intervene if he'd been so inclined. Convince Ding to let the girl go. Persuade her to accept a payout. But Fang is a smart businessman. And he knew that Tan Meixiang was more valuable to him dead than alive. So, he stood aside and let it all happen."

Fang tosses his cigarette in a corner. "That's a nice fairy tale. But Ding killed the girl, not me. And now he wants me dead so I can't tell anyone."

Khaw frowns. "But if what he says is true, you're in no position to go to the authorities. So why would Ding take the risk of sending men down here to kill you?"

"I told you," Fang says. "He's crazy."

"I still don't buy it," Lu says. "That Fang didn't kill her himself."

"Nobody cares what you buy or don't buy," Fang says. "You're a dead man, anyway."

"There's a simple way to find out the truth," Lu says. "Watch the video."

"I've said it a thousand times," Fang snarls. "There isn't one."

"Of course there is," Lu says.

"Where?" Fang snaps. He turns to Khaw. "Do you think I'd be so stu-pid as to upload highly incriminating videos into the cloud? Did you see me show up on your doorstep with a hard drive tucked under my arm?"

"How about a thumb drive?" Colonel Ta says.

"Stay out of this!" Fang shouts.

"My guess is he had to flee his restaurant pretty quickly when the shooter Ding sent showed up," Lu says. "He was probably too scared to go home, pack a bag. He grabbed some cash and made his way down here with the clothes on his back. But make no mistake, he brought an incred-ibly powerful computer with him. One fully capable of storing hours of video securely. A computer otherwise known as a cell phone."

Fang rolls his eyes. "Ridiculous."

"Give me your phone, Wilson," Khaw says.

"You don't believe him, do you?" Fang asks.

"I don't know what to believe," Khaw says. "Your phone."

Fang's face cycles through a range of emotions. Then he smiles tightly. "The phone is useless to you, *A Sao*. I switched the SIM card the first chance I got so it wouldn't be traced."

"Switching the SIM won't affect downloaded files," Lu says.

"Aren't you a clever monkey?" Fang sneers. "Do you moonlight Saturday nights at the cell phone store?"

"Give it," Khaw says.

Fang takes a cell phone from his back pocket and hands it over.

"Password?" Khaw asks.

"Ten, four, eight, eight."

Khaw punches it in.

"You might find some photos and videos of a . . . private nature," Fang says. "I hope you won't think less of me."

"Colonel," Khaw says, "would you mind remaining here to watch over things?"

Colonel Ta draws his pistol and places it on his thigh. "Have someone bring tea."

"Where are you going?" Fang says. "I've given you the phone. Look for yourself."

"If such a video exists," Khaw answers, "I'm sure you wouldn't be careless enough to leave it where it could easily be found. But don't worry. We are not so primitive down here that we lack the technology to hack a phone."

Fang's face darkens, but he doesn't reply.

Golden Krait opens the door for Khaw. They leave and the door shuts.

Fang lights a cigarette, mutters angrily, and wipes sweat from his forehead. He finishes his cigarette and lights another. There is a knock at the door and a servant enters with tea for Colonel Ta. Nothing for Fang or Lu. The wait resumes.

Ten minutes. Fifteen. Ta looks like he might be asleep—it's hard to tell with his eyes hidden behind the sunglasses. Fang watches him on the sly. Lu thinks he's considering going for the gun. He's about to shout a warning when the door crashes open and half a dozen soldiers rush in. They encircle Fang in a scrum and take him down. Colonel Ta barely twitches.

Fang is dragged out of the room, kicking and yelling. Two soldiers remain behind. They salute Ta. One of them motions at Lu and says: "Daw Khaw wants us to take him."

"Then by all means, take him," Ta replies.

The soldiers free Lu from the tiger chair and shove him down onto the floor. They bind his hands. They tug a hood over his head and drag him outside.

FORTY-ONE

There is a bumpy car ride, a long one. Lu is sandwiched tightly between the two soldiers. They do not speak a word, and they reek of cigarettes and jungle rot.

He wonders where they are going. Why haven't they just tossed him in with one of the tigers? Or put a bullet in the back of his head? Maybe Khaw has some particularly awful death in store for him. Trampled by elephants. Slathered in honey and tied to an anthill.

Eventually the road smooths out and the driver begins to make liberal use of his horn. *Traffic*. Lu understands they are entering a populated area. A town. Perhaps the one with the Buddha pointing accusingly down into a wicked valley?

The vehicle periodically halts, and words are exchanged, sometimes in Mandarin, sometimes in Burmese. The discussions are perfunctory. A greeting, a response, and then the vehicle rolls on.

Checkpoints. Are they crossing the border?

After a time, the road turns bumpy again. By now, Lu is suffering the suffocating effects of the hood. And a dire thirst. He fidgets uncomfortably until one of the soldiers elbows him sharply in the ribs.

Just when he thinks he is about to go crazy with fear and claustrophobia, the vehicle slows to a stop. The driver switches off the engine. The door opens and Lu is tugged out. He's marched across dirt under the broiling sun and into a shady spot.

The hood is removed. Lu blinks.

He is surrounded by a small troop of soldiers. Colonel Ta is present, in his aviator sunglasses. Golden Krait, with her bloody machete. Khaw, changed into fresh clothes—loose cotton pants, combat boots, a military-style blouse, a wide hat. And Fang, like Lu, blinking in the sunlight, hands tied behind his back.

"Where the fuck are we?" Fang rasps.

Excellent question. Lu sees a dirt road, a scattering of buildings on either side of it, and a backdrop of thick impenetrable jungle.

"Wilson," Khaw says. "You know I have a tolerance for a certain level of bad behavior. After all, I make my living in a way many people would consider immoral. But I have my limits."

"*A Sao*—" Fang starts.

"Quiet." Khaw takes Fang's phone out of her pocket. She enters the passcode, swipes, and shows it to Lu. "Watch."

She's cued up a video. There's a date and time stamp on the top-left corner. It's hard to read on the small phone screen, but Lu can just make it out: *7/11. 19:34. Friday.*

This is the night Tan Meixiang went missing.

On-screen, the door to an empty banquet room opens and Ding appears, dragging a woman in with him. Ding flicks on the light and shuts the door. Lu is 90 percent sure the woman is Tan Meixiang—he's never seen her in the flesh, just in photographs.

Ding pushes Meixiang up against the wall. She shoves him off. They speak, but the video does not feature sound. Ding grabs Meixiang's breasts. She slaps him. Ding touches his cheek, his face contorting with anger. He punches Meixiang in the belly. She doubles over. He strikes her in the side of the head. She drops to the carpet.

Ding stomps her once, twice, then comes to his senses. He kneels and turns her head to the side. He thumbs open an eyelid. Lu can see blood on Meixiang's face. Ding stands and collects himself. Smooths his hair back, tucks his shirt in. Then he opens the door and leaves.

So far, there is nothing here to contradict Fang's version of that night's events.

Khaw swipes, advancing the speed. She stops when Fang and another man rush into the banquet room, followed by Ding.

The third man is wearing a white short-sleeved smock. His arms are heavily tattooed. It's the cook. *Lao Ping*.

Lu watches as Ping helps Meixiang into a chair. He uses a towel to dab at the blood on her face. She pushes his hands away. Ding stands in the corner like a naughty boy. He speaks. Meixiang shakes her head. Fang makes shushing motions. The discussion goes on for some time, during which Meixiang becomes increasingly agitated. Fang waves Ding outside. Once Ding is gone, Fang pulls up a chair and has a long exchange with Meixiang.

Ping leaves the room and returns with a bottle of water and an ice pack. He gives the water to Meixiang. She is crying now. Fang leans forward, speaking calmly. Meixiang isn't having it. Fang sits back, the frustration plain on his face. He stands and motions for Ping to follow him. They go out into the hall.

Khaw advances the video again.

Ping returns. Alone. His face grim. He walks over and stands in front of Meixiang. Looks down on her.

The video ends.

Lu shrugs. "What does this prove?"

"For a cop, you're not too bright, are you?" Khaw says.

"For a nuclear physicist, I'm not too bright. For a cop, I'd have to say I'm pretty smart."

"Do you see Ding murdering this girl?" Khaw asks.

"No. But Fang already said Ding didn't kill her on the premises." Lu feels odd for defending Fang.

"It's clear that Wilson ushered Ding out and told him he'd handle it," Khaw says.

"No!" Fang says. "That's not how it went!"

"If he opens his mouth again, cut out his tongue," Khaw says. Golden Krait draws her machete. Fang gives her a hateful look but shuts his mouth. Khaw motions to one of the soldiers. "Free him."

The soldier produces a knife and cuts Lu's wrists loose. Lu isn't sure where this is going, but for the moment, it doesn't appear that he is going to be summarily executed. He works his hands open and shut to get the blood flowing.

Khaw gives Lu the phone. "It just so happens, I have access to a handful of contacts at various ministries in Beijing. I was able to obtain a phone number for Ding. I phoned and we had a chat."

Fang makes a sound like he's choking on a piece of gristle.

Khaw dabs sweat from her upper lip with an embroidered kerchief. "I informed him his little assassination plot failed and that I'm very put out he sent agents to invade my home. He assured me it was nothing personal—his only objective was Fang and the video. He offered me quite a large sum of money to hand them both over. Quite a *large* sum."

She pivots on her bootheel. "Wilson, as far as I'm concerned, you and Ding are equally culpable for the woman's death, regardless of who actually cut her throat. He assaulted her, and you took advantage of the situation to obtain leverage over him."

"Not true," Fang squeaks.

Khaw turns back to Lu. "And you . . . you came to my home under false pretenses, compromised my security, betrayed my trust and hospitality, and intended me grave harm."

Lu doesn't bother arguing. Everything she's just said is absolutely true.

"I've also weighed the fact that you were lied to by Ding, and your intentions were, in their own way, quite noble," Khaw says. "You thought you were helping to extradite a man who murdered an innocent woman. You put yourself at great risk on her behalf. That says something about your character." She holds her two hands up like the pans of a scale and balances them out. "For that reason, I've decided to let you live."

Lu lets out a long breath. He feels as if the soles of his shoes are lifting off the ground. He's lighter than air.

But not so fast. Khaw's not going to kill him. Great. However, there is almost certainly a catch.

"What about me?" Fang asks.

"Yes, what about you, Wilson?" Khaw says, heatedly. "What about you is this—I made a deal with Ding. And I told him where he could find you and your phone."

"You can't trust him!" Fang says. "He'll assume you have a copy of the video. He won't stop until you're dead, too!"

"Of course I don't trust him," Khaw says. "But we've agreed, for both parties, it's best to declare a truce and stick to our respective sides of the border." Khaw looks at her watch. "I expect he'll be along in, oh . . . two hours or so." She waves at the scattering of buildings. "This village has been abandoned for going on twenty years. Bad air, the residents said. Harmful vapors. The nearest settlement is thirty kilometers in either direction." She motions to one of the soldiers and he hands over an automatic pistol. Khaw shows the gun to Lu. "You know how to use one of these?"

"More or less."

"Ding will come armed. But I told him you're dead, so he'll be expecting to find Wilson, defenseless and alone." She gives Lu the pistol. "Get your justice for the girl, Mr. Policeman."

"*A Sao*—" Fang starts, but Khaw turns and walks to the waiting SUV without a backward glance. Colonel Ta follows, and then Golden Krait. Their SUV executes a U-turn and heads south. A soldier frees Fang's wrists. Another leaves a Styrofoam chest by the side of the road, then they all pile into the remaining vehicle and drive off in a cloud of red dust.

Lu examines the gun in his hand. It's a Chinese-made QSZ-92. A poorer cousin to Bang's QSW.

Fang hocks and spits into the dirt. "What now?"

The gun makes a dull click as Lu chambers a round. "I guess we wait."

FORTY-TWO

Ding has taken up temporary residence in Jinghong—to be closer to the action—when he receives Khaw's phone call. He's alarmed that she was able to obtain his number. She must be more connected than he realized. And he's dismayed to learn that Bang has been killed. Bang was a good man, a good soldier.

As far as Lu's death goes, Ding couldn't care less. He was just a tool to be used and discarded.

"A trade," Khaw proposes. "Fang and the phone."

"In return for?"

"You will make no further attempts to violate my security or interfere with my business. And should any intelligence regarding me cross your desk, you will be good enough to let me know."

"I have no desire to interfere with your business. It's none of my concern."

"Then you agree?"

"In principle. But how do I know you didn't make a copy of the video?"

"You don't. If you stick to your side of the border, we won't have any problems, you and I."

"Give me the coordinates of where I will find Fang."

He jots down the information, then hangs up. He looks at his watch. With any luck, Fang will be dead by dusk.

And he will find a way to deal with Khaw later.

Ding makes a mental list of what he will require. A suitable vehicle is no problem. Appropriate weapons will be a more difficult matter.

But Ding is resourceful.

As he plots his next move, a sensation he has not felt for many years courses through his veins. Excitement. Anticipation. Even a tinge of nervousness.

The thrill of the hunt.

FORTY-THREE

Lu takes a closer look at his surroundings. He sees an abandoned village of perhaps a dozen buildings, mostly huts, one or two with concrete walls and the others made from wood and thatch, vines snaking up their walls. A single narrow road cuts through, running north to south. Any approaching vehicles will be easy to spot. But if Ding parks at some distant point and makes his way through the jungle, all bets are off.

Lu walks over to the Styrofoam chest. He nudges the lid off with his foot. Inside are bottles of water and beer, packed in ice.

Lu fits the lid back in place and picks up the chest. He carries it into the nearest and least ramshackle of the buildings. This one has cement walls, a partially caved-in roof, a doorway minus a door, and windows on three sides with broken glass lining their frames. Lu finds a plastic stool lying among the detritus and takes up station by the window that offers a sightline to the north. He helps himself to a bottle of water. He finishes it, finds that he is still thirsty, and helps himself to another.

Fang steps inside. Lu watches him from the corner of his eye, the gun resting on his knee. Fang squats against the far wall. His once-white shirt is now liberally stained with red earth. He's wearing the same crocodile shoes Lu first saw him in. Fang extracts a dented pack of cigarettes from his pocket and shakes one out. A scatter of crushed paper and tobacco drops into his hand. He curses and widens the mouth of the pack until he finally locates a smokable cigarette. He lights it. "What's in the chest?"

"Beer and water."

"Toss me a beer."

Lu considers telling Fang to take a hike, but instead grabs a can and underhands it across the room. Fang fumbles the catch. Now that Lu's rehydrated, a beer does sound refreshing. He takes one and pops the tab. It's a common brand that can be purchased, cheaply and generally lukewarm, at any roadside stand. He swallows a big mouthful. It is the best damn beer he has ever tasted.

Fang opens his own can. It sprays over his pants. He curses bitterly, then puts his mouth on the opening and slurps. He belches. "I have a lot of money."

"Good for you."

"I'm happy to share."

"I don't want your money."

"What do you want?"

"I want Tan Meixiang alive and back with her sister. Can you give me that?"

"You didn't really come all this way to pinch me for a murder I didn't even commit."

"I did. And you did."

"Ding killed her."

"I saw the video. It was your man, Ping. On your orders."

Fang lights another cigarette and smokes in silence for a moment. He finishes the beer, crushes the empty can, and tosses it in a corner. "I had no choice. Ding's MSS!"

"The girl didn't have to die," Lu says.

"She was going to report Ding."

"Like you said, he's MSS. He would have skated."

Fang shakes his head. "In this anticorruption political climate, who knows? Ding wasn't going to take that risk. And I was put in an impossible situation."

"One that gave you an opportunity to slip a high-level MSS official into your pocket."

Fang smokes his cigarette down to the butt, then tosses it aside, stands up, and brushes off his pants. "Ding's going to kill both of us. I hope you understand that."

"He's going to kill *you*. Me, he doesn't know about."

"He will once he gets here. He's ex-military. You'll be dead before you even know he's behind you."

"Maybe I'll just stake you to the middle of the road like a goat and use you as bait."

"And then what?" Fang asks. "Ambush an MSS agent? Do you know what they'll do to you?"

"Ding's gone rogue," Lu says. "If he dies here in the jungle, even his own people won't have a clue what happened to him."

"Are you that much of a badass?" Fang asks. "To go one-on-one with a trained and experienced operative? Because I can tell you one thing . . . for Ding, this counts as a slow day at the office."

Lu finishes his beer and drops the empty can back into the Styrofoam chest.

"And what about me?" Fang says. "You're okay with him murdering me in cold blood?"

"Pretty much."

"I'll give you a million yuan," Fang says.

"I told you, I don't want your money."

"Two million."

"Keep talking," Lu says, "and I'll shoot you right now."

"Two against one stand a better chance than just you alone."

"What do you suggest? We take turns with the gun?"

"Are you a good shot?"

"I'm a cop," Lu says.

"So then, no," Fang says.

"*Qu ni ma.*"

"I'm an excellent marksman," Fang brags. "An experienced hunter. Give me the gun and I'll deal with Ding."

"No."

"What's your plan, then?"

"My plan is for you to shut up. I'm listening for the sound of a car engine."

"Idiot!" Fang growls. "We're both going to die here." He paces, his

feet crunching on shattered roof tiles and dried palm fronds. "Screw this."
He heads for the doorway.

Lu abruptly stands. "Where are you going?"

"Away from here."

"You heard Khaw. There's nothing around for thirty klicks. You won't get far on foot with no water, no supplies."

"But we're sitting ducks!"

"We have one advantage. Ding doesn't know about me."

Fang looks at the gun in Lu's hand, then at Lu's face. It looks like he's going to make a run for it—but then he returns to his corner to slump resentfully against the wall.

They wait.

FORTY-FOUR

Early afternoon edges into late afternoon. Lu's rumbling stomach reminds him that he hasn't eaten for twenty hours or so. He glances up at the sky through a gap in the ceiling tiles. He sees swaying palm fronds against a purpling sky. It'll be dark before long.

He weighs the QSZ in his hand. He recalls from his firearms training that it holds fifteen nine-millimeter rounds.

Fifteen rounds versus whatever Ding will be bringing to the party.

Fang's head suddenly lifts. "What's that?"

Lu hears the incessant chatter of birds and buzz of insects. Nothing more. He looks through the window. The road to the north is clear as far as he can see, which is about fifty meters.

"Hear it?" Fang asks.

"Shh!" Lu listens. Yes, now he does. A low purr. The sound of a car engine. Lu's mouth is suddenly dry. "Go out on the road where he can see you."

"Are you crazy?"

Lu points the gun. "It wasn't a request. Go do it."

"Is that the best strategy you can come up with? Have me stand in the open so he can take aim and hope that you're a better shot than him? Because I guarantee you aren't."

"Honestly, Fang, I'm winging it. Now, get your ass out there where Ding can see you."

"Sure. Whatever you say." Fang stands and slaps dirt off his pants. He goes to the doorway and pokes his head out. He looks at Lu. He makes a rude gesture with his fingers and runs.

"Ta ma de!" Lu goes to the doorway and watches Fang sprint across the road and around the back of a hut on the other side. He wouldn't have credited a guy in fancy crocodile loafers with the ability to move so fast.

He returns to the window and watches a vehicle slowly approach. It stops near the edge of his sightline down the road. He estimates that the QSZ has the accuracy to hit a target at that distance—but Lu isn't confident that *he* has the accuracy to hit a target at that distance. He squats down and watches from the corner of the sill.

The door to the vehicle opens and a man rushes into the foliage on the side of the road.

Ding isn't taking any chances. He'll approach using the jungle as cover. But at least it looks like he's come alone.

Lu wonders if he can make a run for the vehicle and just get the hell away. Unlikely. Ding probably has the key in his pocket. And even if Lu does escape, that won't be the end of it. Ding won't stop until he's dead.

Lu ducks below the sill and pricks his ears for the crunch of shoes moving through cane grass.

Minutes pass. Lu hears insects, birdsong. The rattle of palm fronds in the breeze. The sound of blood pounding in his ears.

Ding should be close by now. And what about Fang? Is he making a run for it? Or hiding behind that hut with a plank of wood in his hand?

Lu wipes his palm on his pants, regrips the pistol. What in Buddha's name is taking Ding so long? The stress of waiting is excruciating. When he can take it no longer, he lifts his face toward the windowsill, his knee joints cracking.

He spots Ding squatting behind a palm tree, five yards distant, carrying a bull-pup assault rifle.

Their eyes meet.

Lu drops down.

A burst of automatic gunfire rips across the side of the building. Bullets spray through the window, shattering the few remaining shards of glass, peppering the far wall. Lu crawls for cover. Another quick burst rattles the rafters.

Lu tucks himself into a corner. He eyes the north window. The doorway. The east window. He's made a serious tactical error. Trapped himself in a box. If Ding sticks the barrel of his gun through one of those openings and squeezes the trigger, he can't miss.

Lu hesitates, paralyzed by indecision. Then a small black object flies through the window and bounces across the floor. It resembles a Shaoxing clay wine pot. It takes Lu a second or two to identify what it really is:

A grenade.

Lu runs and leaps headfirst through the doorway. A violent concussion rips across his back. He lands face-first in the dirt. Cement, tile, and wood patter to the ground like hail.

Lu doesn't know if he's been hit by shrapnel. And it doesn't matter—his more urgent concern is that he's exposed out here on the open road.

He scrambles up and sprints. He registers the sound of automatic gunfire and the buzz of bullets zipping past his right shoulder. He crosses the road and dives around the back corner of the nearest hut. He remembers, too late, that this is where Fang has fled to. He is rudely reminded when Fang smashes a chunk of brick into his head.

Stunned, Lu falls to his knees. Fang drops the brick. He swings a fist. Lu reflexively ducks under it. Fang's knuckles thunk into the edge of his forehead. Fang yelps in pain and shakes out his hand. He reaches for the QSZ. They wrestle for it. Fang kicks at Lu and wrenches the gun away. He aims at Lu's face and pulls the trigger.

There is a click—but to Fang's immense disappointment, there is no bang.

Fang quickly realizes what the problem is. The safety is engaged. He searches for the mechanism, flicks the switch.

Shots ring out from across the road, ripping into the side of the hut. Fang cowers. Another burst sends him racing across open ground and into the surrounding jungle.

Lu flattens his back against the wall of the hut. He feels a trickle on his temple, wipes it away, sees blood on his hand. He hears the distinctive metallic *chunk* of Ding loading a fresh magazine into his rifle.

Lu knows he can't stay here. Fang is only ten meters away, hiding in the bushes. An easy shot if he's anywhere near as good as he said he is. The hut is made of bamboo and thatch, but it's better than nothing. Lu crawls through the back entrance and rolls out of sight.

The layout of the hut is simple—a long rectangular room, four walls, dirt floor, a flimsy front door facing the road. Moldering shutters on the windows. A tattered and disintegrating bamboo screen divides the room in the middle, but there is no furniture, no bed or tables, nothing substantial to shelter behind.

Lu casts about for a weapon. A rusted machete. An abandoned farm implement. A sharp stick. There's nothing.

The walls are thin and riddled with cracks and holes that admit tiny pinpricks of dying sunlight. As Lu watches, he sees a shadow moving across the front of the hut.

Ding. Heading for the door.

There's an old Chinese saying: *Yi gong wei shou.*

Attack to defend.

Lu scoots forward, then crouches. When Ding is just outside the door, he springs up, leaps and crashes through it with both feet.

FORTY-FIVE

Lu feels the impact travel in a direct line from his heels to his jaw.

The door flies off its hinges and crashes into Ding. Lu scrambles up and tosses broken door slats aside. Ding lies stunned. Lu tries to take the rifle, but it's looped around Ding's shoulder with a strap. Ding pushes Lu away. Lu hits Ding, feels a satisfying crunch and Ding goes limp.

Lu yanks the gun strap over Ding's shoulder and backs away.

Ding stirs, blinks, sits up. He rubs his chin and works his mouth open and shut. "Easy. Don't do something you'll regret."

"I won't regret a thing. Keep your hands where I can see them."

"Where's Fang?"

"Hiding out back, in the bushes."

"He'll kill you," Ding says. "First chance he gets."

"He said the same about you."

"Give me the gun. I'll let you go. This is between him and me."

"Fang said that, too. And it's a lie. You've dragged me down into your shit and now I'm in it up to my neck."

Ding licks blood from his lips and glances at the corner of the hut. "We can't sit here arguing."

Lu nods at the doorway. "Get inside."

Ding crawls over the threshold. Lu follows. They slink over to the back wall and take up posts on either side of the rear doorway. Lu peeks through a crack in the bamboo. He can see nothing of Fang.

Ding massages the sides of his jaw. "Khaw said you were dead."

"Surprise!"

"Fang is armed?"

"Unfortunately, yes."

"With what?"

"QSZ."

Ding finds his own crack to peek through. "The sun's going down soon. He'll have freedom of movement under cover of darkness. We need to take him out before that happens."

"Speaking of freedom of movement—where's the key to your vehicle?"

"In my pocket."

"Toss it over."

"I can't let you take my only means of transportation. Help me kill Fang and we'll leave together."

"And that will be the end of it, right? I'll just return to my boring small-town life. You'll go back to raping waitresses and having them killed."

Ding snorts. "I didn't kill her."

"Key!"

Ding is wearing black tactical pants with voluminous thigh pockets. He slides his hand into the pocket on his right leg.

"Stop!" Lu says.

"Make up your mind," Ding says. "Do you want the key or not?"

"You'd better not pull a gun out of there."

"I only have the rifle. *Had* the rifle." Ding grips the outside of the pocket with his left hand and rummages inside with his right.

"Careful," Lu warns, his finger on the rifle trigger.

Ding slowly withdraws his hand and shows Lu a small object dangling from his finger. He tosses it over. It falls in the dirt. Keeping one eye on Ding, Lu reaches down and scoops it up. It's not a key.

It's a grenade pin.

"Listen carefully," Ding says quietly. "I've got my left hand on the safety lever of a grenade. If you shoot me, you'll have about four seconds before it blows."

"You stupid bastard!"

"I'm going to take the grenade out of my pocket now. Be very still. It's a delicate operation."

Ding slips his right hand back into his pocket and carefully transfers his grip. He withdraws the grenade and holds it up. This one is smaller and more cylindrical than the Shaoxing pot device he tried to kill Lu with earlier. Lu doesn't recognize the make—it looks of foreign manufacture.

"How many of those did you bring?" Lu asks, mentally kicking himself.

"Just the two. Even for me, explosives and guns are not easy to come up with on the fly. Give me the rifle."

"So you can shoot me? Go to hell."

"If you don't, I'll toss this grenade in your lap."

"Then we'll both be blown to bits."

"I'm not afraid to die, Inspector. Although given the choice, I'd prefer not to. The rifle, if you please."

"I think I'll hang on to it, thanks."

"To be perfectly honest, you're no threat to me. No one will believe a wild tale about you going undercover to some hidden fortress in the jungles of Myanmar. They'll think you're completely insane. That ridiculous haircut isn't going to help your cause, either. Throw me the rifle and I'll take care of Fang. You want him to die, don't you?"

"What happened to Tan Meixiang?"

"I don't know. I swear that's the truth. Fang said he'd handle it. And he did. Maybe that cook of his chopped her up and put her on the menu. I didn't kill her, and I didn't order Fang to kill her, either."

"But you tried to rape her."

"*Rape* is a strong word. I fell prey to a moment of drunken indiscretion. She should have just taken some money and moved on."

"You're a prick."

Ding squints through a hole in the wall. "I can also be a good friend. You want your old job back? Or something better? I will make it happen."

"I can't be bought."

"Everybody has a price," Ding says. "I just need to find what yours is."

"Tell you what. I'll give you the rifle in exchange for your car key."

Ding smirks. "Toss over the rifle, and I'll toss over the key."

"Key first."

"I'll have to reach into my pocket again."

"If you pull out a gun, I'll shoot you and take my chances with the grenade."

"Fair enough." Ding reaches into his left pocket. He withdraws it and shows Lu a small black remote car key. "Catch." He throws it—through the open mouth of the doorway. "Oh. Sorry."

"Get it," Lu growls.

"No way. Fang's out there and you say he's armed."

"Get it or I'll blow your head off."

Ding gives the grenade a little shake. "My friend says you don't give orders around here."

"Bastard," Lu says. He sidles up to the doorway. The key is an arm's length across the threshold.

"Good luck," Ding says.

Lu lunges for the key. He hears the crack of gunfire. His fingers scrabble in the dirt. Another shot—this one takes a chunk out of the wall near Lu's head. He snatches the key and rolls back inside. Two more shots pepper the side of the hut. Lu scrambles into a corner.

The shooting stops. Silence. Then Ding laughs. "That was close."

Lu puts the key into one pocket and removes Fang's phone from another. "Recognize this?"

"Is that Fang's phone? Give it here!" Ding reaches out, like a toddler demanding a treat.

"Go fetch." Lu tosses it through the doorway.

"*Gan!*" Ding curses. "What have you done?"

"Fang!" Lu shouts. "I just tossed your phone out. Did you see it?"

"Quiet!" Ding hisses.

"I'm in here with your buddy Ding," Lu yells. "I have his rifle. He's unarmed. I've decided to let the two of you settle this matter one-on-one."

"What do you think you're playing at?" Ding growls.

"How do I know he's unarmed?" comes Fang's answer, muffled by distance and foliage.

Lu runs his hand under the stock of the rifle, finds the catch, pops the clip out. "Are you watching, Fang?" He throws the clip outside.

Ding is apoplectic. "You idiot!"

Lu yanks on the charging lever to eject the rifle's chambered round. He tosses the rifle through the door. "See that, Fang? All clear."

Ding squeezes the grenade until his knuckles are white. For a moment, Lu thinks he's going to throw it.

"All part of the plan," Lu tells him.

"What plan, you moronic jackass?"

Fang calls out: "How do I know he doesn't have another gun?"

"If he did," Lu yells, "do you suppose I'd still be alive?" Lu looks at Ding and lowers his voice. "Fang will come for the phone. He must. Khaw has tossed him out on his ear. And he's got no other hand to play. He'll come for the phone. And when he does—you throw the grenade out. Boom. Problem solved."

Ding glares but doesn't say anything. Lu can see the infernal machinery in his head clicking and whirring. The plan is logical.

"Good luck." Lu slowly crawls backward across the dirt floor. Ding watches him go.

"Lu Fei!" Fang calls. Lu ignores him.

When Lu is almost at the front door, Ding says, "See you soon, Inspector."

Lu leaps through the doorway. And starts running.

FORTY-SIX

The smart thing would be to make a beeline for the vehicle, start it up, and drive north. Find the nearest working phone. Call Deputy Director Song. Tell him the whole crazy story. Hope that Song's *guanxi* will be sufficient to insulate Lu from any reprisals Ding might cook up. Pray that Ding won't risk coming after Lu and exposing his own crimes.

But this is unlikely. Ding won't rest easy knowing Lu's out there, even if he figures Lu will fail at any attempts to bring him to justice. Just the hint of scandal, a whisper of the sordid tale Lu has to tell, would potentially be enough to derail his career.

No—Ding will send another Bang. Or come for Lu himself.

Lu makes it ten yards down the road, then ducks behind the nearest structure, a tin-roofed shack. He crawls inside and pries open the back door just enough to view the open space between the hut where Ding is sheltering and the edge of the jungle where Fang is concealed.

Fang will crack soon. Lu is sure of it. He'll go for the phone, regardless of the risk. It's his only lifeline. Minus the video, he's got nothing to bargain with.

Sure enough, thirty seconds later, Fang shouts: "Ding! Let's talk about this."

Ding doesn't answer.

A minute passes. Two minutes.

"Ding!"

Silence.

"Ding, damn you!"

Crickets.

Eventually, the inevitable occurs. Fang slithers from the underbrush. On his belly, like a snake. He advances a meter, stops. Lu can almost see him flicking his tongue out, tasting the air for threats. Another meter. And another.

Lu tenses. He's watching a man crawl, literally, to his death. He can put a stop to it by simply yelling a warning.

He keeps his mouth shut.

When Fang is within spitting distance of the phone, he makes a lunge for it. In the deepening dusk, Lu doesn't see a dark cylindrical object pop out of the hut. But he knows it's coming. He retracts his head into the shack. Two seconds later he hears an explosion and feels the concussion through the soles of his shoes. The roof of the shack rattles.

Fang shrieks.

Lu throws open the door and runs toward the carnage.

Ahead, Ding emerges from the hut. He and Lu converge on the same patch of churned-up turf, both looking for the rifle.

Ding wins. He snatches it up and searches for the clip. He realizes he won't find it before Lu is upon him, so he reverses his grip and swings the rifle like a club. Lu dodges, scanning the ground for the QSZ pistol while trying to avoid getting brained by the rifle.

Lu and Ding circle around each other, Fang's shattered body acting as the center of their orbit. Ding soon tires of this and steps directly over Fang, his face contorted into a murderous mask. Lu crouches. Ding swings—Lu springs at his front leg, cups the back of Ding's ankle with his hands, rams his shoulder into Ding's leg just below the knee. As Ding falls, he cracks Lu across the back with the rifle.

It hurts like hell. But Ding goes down.

Lu stands, cinches Ding's ankle between his armpit and the crook of his elbow, wrenches hard. Ding screams as his ankle pops. Lu backs away. Ding clutches his leg in agony. Lu snatches up the rifle and goes hunting for the pistol.

He finds it near Fang's body. He tosses the empty rifle on the ground and picks up the pistol. It's scratched and scuffed, but in one piece. Lu

test-fires it into the hut. It works. Lu looks at Fang to confirm he's dead.
He is.

Lu walks back over to Ding.

"You broke my ankle!" Ding moans.

"I doubt it. Just gave it a nice twist. I'm going to frisk you now. Don't
mess about or I *will* break it. The other one, too." He rolls Ding over and
pats him down. He finds only a folding tactical knife, which he throws
into the jungle.

Ding sits up and massage his ankle. His breath hitches in pain as he
probes it with his thick fingers. "What now, Inspector?"

"I take you to Jinghong."

"And then?"

"I don't know. Right now, I just want to get the hell out of *here*."

"You've rendered me unable to walk."

"I'll find something for you to use as a cane." Lu searches around,
finds a serviceable branch. He helps Ding to his feet. "You can put your
arm around my shoulders, but be a good boy or I'll just kill you and be
done with it."

"I want to get out of this place as badly as you do," Ding says. They
start hobbling, then Ding stops. "The phone."

"The grenade destroyed it."

"I want to be sure. Please. If you don't mind."

Lu returns to the blast area. In the rapidly failing light, it takes him
several minutes to locate the cell phone. The screen is spiderwebbed
and the case is cracked, leaking electronics. Lu brings it over and shows
it to Ding.

"May I have it?" Ding holds out his hand.

"Don't be ridiculous." Lu puts the phone in his pocket.

They limp down the road to Ding's vehicle. Lu props Ding against
the front grille, then uses the remote key to unlock the door. He quickly
searches the interior. No guns. He does find a cell phone, a large envelope of cash, bottles of water, and a plastic bag with snacks. "Got any duct
tape?" Lu asks. "Any rope?"

"I need to sit down," Ding says. "Please."

Lu helps Ding around to the passenger side. He props Ding by the front wheel well, opens the door.

He hears a gunshot. Loud. High caliber. And very, very close by.

Lu ducks. Liquid splatters against the windshield. Ding drops to the ground. Lu sees a neat round hole in his forehead.

Lu leaps into the SUV, tugs the door closed, and climbs over the gear-shift into the driver's seat. He stabs the ignition button, and the engine starts right up.

He shifts into drive, expecting another bullet to punch through the side of the car at any moment. Ahead, he sees headlights approaching from the south. Two vehicles. Blocking the road. Lu shifts the SUV into reverse. By reflex, he glances in the rearview mirror.

A man stands a few meters from the back bumper, illuminated in the red glow of Lu's taillights. He's pointing a rifle directly at Lu's head.

Lu experiences a moment of panicked indecision. Then he understands he's not going anywhere. He shifts into park. Turns off the engine. He takes the QSZ pistol out of his pocket. And waits for what happens next.

FORTY-SEVEN

The headlights stop five yards away. Doors open. Doors shut. Lu climbs out of the SUV, the QSZ held low. By now, it's full dark.

Shadows pass in front of the headlights. First comes Golden Krait. Then Colonel Ta. Ta whistles. The man standing at the back of the SUV marches forward. He's holding a .375 Ruger and he smiles genially at Lu. It's the young soldier Du introduced him to near the tiger pen—Kaung.

"Weapon?" Colonel Ta says.

Golden Krait holds out her hand. Lu gives her the QSZ.

Ta gives a signal. Khaw emerges from the shadows. She gives Lu a careful once-over. Backlit by the headlights, Lu can't read her face. "Wilson?"

"Back there." Lu says. "What's left of him."

"You killed him?"

"Ding."

"And the phone?"

"In my pocket."

"Hand it over, please."

Lu pulls out the phone, gives it to Golden Krait.

Khaw takes her time lighting a cheroot. "So . . . you got your justice for the girl."

"This might be your idea of justice, but it's not mine."

"Men like Ding and Fang are beyond the reach of the law. They'll never see the inside of a courtroom. A more rudimentary solution was called for."

"Would you include yourself in that category?"

Khaw smokes in silence. The tip of her cheroot glows red. "You really don't belong here, darling. Take Ding's vehicle. Head due north. Don't look back."

Lu can't believe it will be that easy. He suspects Khaw will allow him to drive twenty meters up the road and then Kaung will blow his brains all over the SUV's dashboard.

Khaw holds out her hand. "You'll need this."

Lu sees that it's his identification card, in the name of Long Ming. He puts the card into his pocket.

Khaw steps closer. Now he can see her face. "I know where you live, Inspector Lu Fei of Raven Valley Township, Heilongjiang Province. You'd do well to remember that." Her expression softens and she unexpectedly reaches out to touch Lu's cheek. "Safe travels."

She throws her cheroot in the dirt and walks off into the darkness behind the headlights. Colonel Ta gives Lu a mock salute. He and Golden Krait follow. Doors slam, engines start, vehicles reverse and drive away.

Lu slowly turns. Kaung is gone. Melted back into the jungle.

Lu climbs into Ding's SUV, starts the engine, makes a shaky U-turn, and speeds as quickly up the dirt road as he dares, hunched over, his knuckles tight on the steering wheel.

Waiting for the bullet.

He makes it a kilometer. Two. Three. The bullet does not come.

Lu travels twenty minutes without passing a car, a village, a single sign of civilization. He pulls over and turns off the engine. He opens the door and stands on the side of the road and screams into the black night.

Calmer now, he uses handfuls of dirt to scrub Ding's blood off the side of the SUV. He pops the cap on one of the water bottles and rinses his hands and face. His clothes are filthy, but there's not much he can do about that. He tosses the empty bottle into the vegetation along the side of the road and opens a fresh bottle. He drinks half, then relieves himself in the dirt and continues on his way.

In due course, he reaches a paved road and passes through a series of small villages until he finds a sign indicating the way to Highway 214. From there, it's a smooth ride. He arrives on the outskirts of Jinghong in the wee hours of the morning and cruises around looking for a small hotel—the kind that won't ask too many questions of a man who looks like he's just crawled out from a hole in the ground. He finds a suitable place: an establishment near the train station, painted a garish pink with a neon sign advertising its name: the Pink Swan.

Lu parks and goes inside. An older woman sits behind a glass counter. Behind her, a variety show blares on a portable TV. She gives Lu a disinterested once-over. He smiles politely and requests a room.

"Hourly or nightly?" the woman asks, stone-faced.

"Just for the night."

"Theme?"

"Excuse me?"

"We have a dungeon room, garden room, chalet, jungle room."

"No jungle!" Lu says, more strongly than intended. "Your simplest room. I'm alone."

"You want company? I can call a girl. You like tall, thin, young, old, skinny, fat—"

"No."

"You want a boy?"

"Just the room."

The woman shrugs. She checks his ID. He gives her cash from Ding's envelope. She gives him a key card. "There's a machine down the hall for a prepaid movie card. One hundred yuan, unlimited movies for twenty-four hours. Third floor. Take a left out of the elevator. Enjoy your stay."

Lu goes up and unlocks the door to his room. Inside is a tiny sitting area with a couch and a flat-screen TV. A bed behind a black gauzy curtain. A shelf holding a variety of erotic aids—massage oils, fluorescent condoms, honey drops. Lu pokes his head into the bathroom and sees a large jacuzzi tub. Perfect. He turns on the tap and walks down the hall to the vending machine alcove. In addition to movie cards, there are drinks, snacks, and even cosplay outfits—naughty nurse, policewoman, schoolgirl, maid. Naturally, none of the costumes are designed for men.

Lu buys two cans of beer and a variety of snacks and goes back to his room. He scarfs down the food, cracks a beer, strips, and climbs into the scalding-hot bath. He lies in a state of torpor, moving only as much as is necessary to pour more beer down his throat. Then he rises and towels off, brushes his teeth with the hotel amenity toothbrush, and climbs into bed with the second beer. He falls asleep before he can finish it.

Lu wakes with a start, disoriented. He sees the gauzy curtain, the geisha wall prints, the condoms on the bedside table. *Right*. He checks the bedside clock. It's nearly nine in the morning. He dresses in his filthy clothes, drinks water from the sink, and calls China Air to check flights to Harbin, with a layover in Beijing. He'll have to go to the airport and book it in person, since he doesn't have a credit card. Then he calls Information and obtains the phone number for the Criminal Investigations Bureau headquarters. He is patched through and requests to speak to Deputy Director Song. He gives his name and rank and states that he's calling on official business. Song is unavailable, and Lu doesn't trust the minion on the phone, so he asks if CIB's chief medical investigator—Dr. Ma Xiulan—is available. After a few clicks, she comes on the line.

"Yes?"

"Hello, Dr. Ma. This is Lu Fei, from Raven Valley Township."

"Inspector Lu! What a nice surprise. Are you in town? Calling to take me up on that tour I offered?"

Lu smiles into the phone. "I wish. I'll be passing through Beijing very briefly this afternoon and I was hoping to meet with the deputy director. Is he in town?"

"Oh, how disappointing. You're just using me to get to Song."

"I . . . Well . . ."

Ma laughs. "You're just too easy, Inspector. It's a wonder how you deal with criminals all day."

"To be fair, most of them are farmers and factory workers, not distractingly attractive forensic geniuses. Anyway, I will make a proper trip to Beijing soon, but I'm in kind of a bind here, so—"

"I get it. Song's in the office today. Probably in a meeting. Shall I ask him to call you back?"

"I don't have a phone at the moment, but I'll be at the airport for a quick stopover this afternoon." Lu gives Ma the flight details.

"Very mysterious, Inspector."

"I'll tell you all about it next time I see you."

"Deal. I'll make sure Song gets the message."

Lu rings off and goes downstairs, pays the phone bill with Ding's cash, and hops in Ding's SUV. He doesn't have much time, so he finds the first suitable clothing shop and buys himself underwear, socks, a shirt, pants. He changes in the car and drives to the airport. He purchases a ticket at the counter, passes through security, and eats at a noodle shop in the terminal. Then he boards the three-and-a-half-hour flight to Beijing.

Song is waiting for Lu at the gate when he arrives. He looks very put out. "This better be good. I canceled all my afternoon appointments and rushed down here and you're thirty minutes late and I'm dying for a cigarette."

"I'm sorry. Let's find a spot where we can talk."

They sit in a corner and Lu gives Song a rushed summary of what he's just been through. Ding, Bang, Fang, Khaw.

Song listens with his mouth open. "Unbelievable," he says, when Lu is done.

"It's true. Every word."

"You have a way of getting yourself mixed up in some unbelievable shenanigans."

"And yet all I crave is a peaceful life of drinking and chasing wayward chickens."

"I need a cigarette to process all this," Song says.

"I have to catch my next flight."

"How can you expect me to consider such a complicated matter without a cigarette?"

"You're right," Lu says. "What was I thinking?"

They go to a glassed-in smoking lounge. Song smokes his *Chunghwa*, thinking furiously. He finishes, stubs out the butt, and they leave to find another quiet corner.

"My advice is, forget about it," Song says.

"About what?"

"The whole thing. Just go on with your life like it never happened."

"That's it? That's what I flew to Beijing for?"

"Fang and Ding are dead. This Khaw—she's in Myanmar. Untouchable, unless someone in our government wants to take her out, and if that were the case, she'd be gone already. Fang's restaurant will close down. We already know he's either bribed or compromised various cops and officials, so there won't be any follow-up investigation. There's no case to make."

"What about the girl? Tan Meixiang."

"Like I said, Fang and Ding are dead. If they'd gone on trial and been convicted, they'd have been executed. The result is the same, no?"

Lu doesn't like it. Song puts a hand on his shoulder. "Listen, Lu Fei—it's harsh, but this is the way of the world. All things considered, despite the circumstances, justice was served." He looks at his watch. "I've got to get back to the office and you'd better hightail it to your gate."

They shake hands and part ways. Lu boards his flight. He decides to get properly drunk on the way to Harbin. And does he ever.

FORTY-EIGHT

Lu arrives in Harbin around midnight. He's too tired and inebriated to contemplate taking the train to Raven Valley, so he checks into the nearest airport hotel. He sleeps fitfully.

He wakes the next morning uncharacteristically hungover. He buys a cup of strong tea and two steamed pork buns in the hotel restaurant. Then he takes the shuttle bus to the railway station and boards a train for Raven Valley.

He makes it home by noon. He goes up to his apartment and falls into bed and sleeps the afternoon away. When he wakes, it's almost 7:00 p.m. His hangover is gone, but his overwhelming sense of disillusionment and disappointment remains.

He takes a long hot shower and scrubs away at his tattoos until his skin is raw and red but succeeds only in reducing their vividness by a few degrees. He removes the earring lent to him by Monk. He phones Yanyan. "I'm back."

"I'm so glad to hear from you."

"Really?" Lu is suddenly on the verge of tears.

"Of course, why wouldn't I be?"

"I don't know."

"How'd it go? Your undercover job?"

"It was awful."

"I'm so sorry. Are you okay? Are you hurt?"

"Can I see you tonight?"

"Sure. I'm at the Red Lotus."

Lu sighs. "I'd really like to see *you*. And not at the bar."

There is a moment of silence. "I'll close up and meet you at my house in an hour?"

"Are you sure?"

"Yes."

When Lu arrives at Yanyan's house she opens the door and takes one look at his face and pulls him into her arms. Then she takes his hand and leads him to the kitchen. She heats a pot of Shaoxing wine.

"Do you want to talk about it?" she asks.

"It's better if I don't."

"I understand. Are you hungry?"

"I want you to cut my hair," Lu says. "I don't want to walk around looking like this."

"I'll have to give you a buzz."

"Whatever it takes."

"All right. Have some wine." Yanyan pours wine into a rice bowl, then sets down the pot. Lu drinks. Yanyan disappears and returns with a towel and clippers. She drapes the towel over Lu's shoulders, plugs in the clippers, and starts running the blade through his hair. When she's done, bits of yellow hair are sprinkled about like dirty snowflakes. She stands back to appraise her work.

"Well?" Lu says.

"It's . . . different." She stifles a smile. "You can have a look in the bathroom mirror when you're done with your wine."

Lu finishes his bowl, then enters the bathroom and looks at himself. He runs a hand over his skull. It feels fuzzy and weird. The area where Fang brained him with the brick is scabbed over, but still sore. Yanyan leans in the open doorway.

"I look like Monk," Lu says.

"I think you look handsome," Yanyan says.

"Oh?" Lu runs a hand over his skull again. "Maybe I'll keep it."

"Let's not be rash," Yanyan says.

"Aha. The truth comes out."

"Why don't you take a shower and wash those bits of hair off? I'll make us some dinner."

"I don't have any other clothes."

"I might have a robe laying around. Just leave your clothes outside the door and I'll go hang them on the line and give them a good beating."

Lu pictures a silk kimono with pink peonies with a hemline that hangs just low enough to cover his "little brother." "That's okay, I—" Lu starts, but Yanyan is already gone. Lu shrugs to himself and shuts the door and turns on the showerhead. He strips and tosses his clothes on the floor outside the bathroom, then rinses off. He dries off and finds a simple cotton robe hanging outside the bathroom door. He puts it on and knots the tie. It fits reasonably well. Lu assumes it once belonged to Yanyan's deceased husband.

He follows the smell of food to the kitchen. Yanyan is huddled over the stove. She turns when he comes in and for a moment, the sight of him in the robe makes her face twist in some unreadable manner and she quickly returns to her task.

"Sit," Yanyan says, a little too brightly. "This will be done in just a minute."

Lu feels like an imposter wearing another man's skin. He sits glumly at the table. He pours the remainder of the Shaoxing wine and drinks. It's gone cold.

Yanyan sets down a steaming dish of stir-fried noodles. "Beer?"

"Sure."

Yanyan collects a Harbin lager from the fridge, pops the cap, and brings it over with two glasses. She pours for Lu. He takes the bottle and pours for her. They drink. Yanyan uses chopsticks to portion out the noodles onto two plates.

"Looks delicious," Lu says.

"It's just a little something." Yanyan takes a bite and chews, her eyes downcast. She notices that Lu is not eating. "What's wrong?"

"I'm not hungry."

Yanyan sets the chopsticks down. "Me, either." She drains her glass and holds it out for more. Lu pours. They finish the bottle and another, in silence.

Lu yawns. He's never felt so drained in his life. "I'm sorry. I can't keep my eyes open."

"Come on." Yanyan holds out her hand. Lu hesitates, then takes it. She leads him upstairs to the bedroom. She opens her wardrobe and takes out a pair of shorts and a T-shirt. "I'll just be a moment." She disappears through the door.

Lu stands there for a moment, unsure of what to do next. Then he sloughs off the robe and slips under the sheets. He rests his head on a pillow. He shuts his eyes.

By the time Yanyan returns, Lu is softly snoring. She smiles, shuts off the lights, climbs in beside him. She lies there for a long moment, listening to Lu breathe. She turns and picks up the framed photo of her wedding day from the nightstand. She kisses her fingertips and presses them to the glass, then sets the frame facedown.

She snuggles up behind Lu, wraps an arm around his waist, and rests her cheek against his back. She sleeps.

FORTY-NINE

Lu opens his eyes shortly after dawn. He watches a beam of sunlight from the window slowly inch its way up Yanyan's sheet-entangled body. He wants to wake her up, but her expression is so childlike and serene he is loath to disturb her.

He eventually slips out of bed, puts on the robe, and goes downstairs to retrieve his clothes. He dresses and writes her a note, which he places on the dining table. It's a snippet of a poem called "Spring Sleep" by Bai Juyi:

> *The pillow is soft, the blanket warm, the body at peace.*
> *Sun shines across the threshold of the door, the curtains not yet open*
> *The flavor of Spring lingers*
> *It visits often while you sleep, but only for brief moments in time*

Lu returns to his apartment and makes himself tea. He calls Chief Liang.

"Sorry, kid," Liang says, when he answers. "A date for the hearing hasn't been set yet."

"That's fine," Lu says. "I'm pretty worn out. A forced vacation isn't such a bad idea."

"You all right? You sound . . . strange."

"I'm fine. But, Chief, listen—"

"Uh-oh. Here it comes. First you say something reasonable, but then you say something extremely unreasonable. Can we just leave it at the reasonable thing?"

"I have a lead on Tan Meixiang."

"No, Lu Fei. No. I'm going to hang up now."

"There was a cook at Fang's restaurant. Ping something. He was wounded in the shooting. I want to talk to him."

"Kid—"

"Chief, please. This one last thing. I won't cause a ruckus. I'll just talk to him and if there's something there, I'll call you and you can decide how to handle it. I promise."

"Bad idea."

"If I'm going to lose my job over this case . . . I'd at least like to wrap it up. You understand?"

"I understand, but—"

"I could always just start calling hospitals in Harbin. As far as they know, I'm still deputy chief. Or worse . . . I could call a Raven Valley reporter like Annie Ye to help track Ping down. I'm sure she'd find the whole story very compelling."

"You wouldn't."

"Of course not," Lu says. "Because I won't have to."

Liang hisses loudly into the phone. "I don't like dirty tactics. I'm going to kick your ass for this."

"I will gladly submit to an ass-kicking in exchange for the name of the hospital."

Liang hangs up without saying goodbye.

He calls back ten minutes later. "Ping was discharged yesterday. Got a pen? Here's his home address."

Lu writes it down. "Thanks, Chief."

"Don't make a mess of it, kid. I'm warning you."

"I won't. I'll just talk to him."

Lu dresses in his police uniform. Since he's essentially barred from showing up at the station, he has no way to obtain a firearm. He hopes that won't be a fatal issue.

He calls a car service to take him to Harbin. When the driver arrives, he gives Lu a strange look. "Don't you guys have your own vehicles?"

"It's in the shop," Lu says.

The driver takes him to the ass-end of Harbin. Ping's residence is a massive apartment building, dating to the 1980s, drab and gray. Lu goes inside and inquires about Ping from an old man sitting behind a desk in the lobby.

"Yes, I know him," the old man says. "He came back yesterday, looking like death wrapped in calamity."

"Alone?"

"Yes, he lives alone."

"Don't alert him that I'm coming up, Uncle. Understand?"

"I won't."

Lu takes the elevator to the twenty-third floor. He walks down a poorly lit hallway with scuffed walls and tattered ceiling tiles. He knocks on Ping's door, and steps to one side. There is no response for a long time, so he knocks again. Finally, the door opens. Ping looks out.

"Public Security Bureau," Lu says. "Show me your hands."

Ping holds his hands out. They are empty. "I remember you."

"You alone?"

Ping nods.

"Move back," Lu says. Ping shuffles away and Lu enters. He sees a living room combined with a kitchen and eating area. He shuts the door and nods at the couch. "Go sit down. Put your hands on your knees and keep them there."

"I don't have a weapon. I'm not looking for trouble."

"Do it!"

Ping complies, moving slowly, favoring his side. He's wearing a white T-shirt and pajama pants. He was skinny to begin with, but now he's positively skeletal.

Keeping one eye on Ping, Lu pokes his head into the bedroom and bathroom. Satisfied, he comes over and stands in front of the couch. Ping sits quietly with his hands on his knees as directed.

"Your boss is dead."

Ping nods. "I'm not surprised."

"So is Ding."

Ping smiles slightly. "Good. He was a bastard."

"I saw the tape. Ding, Tan Meixiang. You."

"Then you know everything. So, what happens now?"

Lu is suddenly furious. "What happens is, you confess to killing the girl and disposing of the body. And then you're convicted, and you get a bullet in your brain."

"Ah." Ping shifts on the couch, clutches his side, and winces in pain. "But what if . . . there is no body?"

FIFTY

Over the years, many scandalous rumors about Ping have circulated among the waitstaff at the Hoist the Big Banner restaurant.

Miss Lin, the most senior waitress, claims that Ping spent ten years in prison for murdering his wife and lover. "He discovered them doing it in the bushes in Zhaolin Park," she says. "He chopped up the lover with a cleaver and drowned his wife in the lake!"

The head busboy chimes in: "I heard he worked for the yakuza in Japan and accidentally killed a little kid during a shoot-out, so they made him cut off his finger!"

Lao Yang, who operates wok number four in the kitchen, snorts derisively. "Nonsense. The truth is, Lao Ping was a hitman for the government, eliminating internet agitators, but then one day he was given an assignment to kill a student who was posting criticisms about the Communist Party and when he saw the address, he realized it was his own son! He had to kill him anyway, of course, but after that, he retired to the simple life of a cook."

Tan Meixiang is aware that not all of these rumors can be true. But where there's smoke, there's fire, and although she has never spoken to Ping or interacted with him in any way, she finds his cold, unsmiling demeanor deeply unsettling.

So, when Ping returns to the banquet room on the evening of July 11th and stands looming over her, his face set like stone, Meixiang assumes she's going to die.

"Come with me," Ping says.

"Where?"

"Come. Now."

Meixiang considers fighting, screaming, clawing—but in the end, she just acquiesces. Ping takes her downstairs and through a back entrance. He flags down a taxi. The driver asks them their destination. Meixiang expects Ping to name some remote no-man's-land along the Songhua River suitable for dumping a body, but after a moment's consideration, he designates a hotel she's never heard of.

Now she's convinced Ping is going to rape her before killing her. She begins to cry. Ping tells her to shut up.

They reach the hotel, a seedy establishment near the train station frequented by itinerant salesmen, prostitutes, drug addicts, and hustlers. Ping books a room, then takes Meixiang upstairs.

"Sit," he tells her, once they are inside.

"Don't hurt me," Meixiang begs, starting to cry again.

"Stop crying. Sit down and listen carefully." Meixiang just stands there, hands covering her face. "Sit!"

The room contains only one chair and one bed. Meixiang takes the chair. Ping glances out the window, then walks over and sits on the bed.

"Your life is in danger," Ping says.

Meixiang would have thought that was obvious.

"But I'm not going to kill you," Ping says.

"You're not?"

"No. I am not a murderer. Despite gossip around the restaurant." Ping grimaces ruefully. "And even if I were, I wouldn't kill someone who has done nothing apart from attracting unwanted attention from a drunken asshole."

Meixiang thinks Ping is perhaps playing an elaborate joke. Getting her to lower her guard before he takes a cleaver out of his waistband and starts chopping her limbs off.

"But you're going to have to lay low for a while," Ping continues. "I don't know how long. A week. Two. Maybe longer. I'll tell Fang I . . . took care of you. He won't ask for details. But if someone sees you . . . there will be hell to pay. Understand?" He rummages in his pocket, counts out some cash, lays it on the bed. "This is all I have on me. It's enough to start. Don't use your bank card. I don't know if Ding will go so far as to monitor your transactions and phone calls. Just in case, I'm going to ditch your phone far away from here."

"I need to call my sister—"

"No. You're going to book a train ticket and then text your sister that you're taking a trip. That's it. No more contact until this blows over."

"But—"

"No buts."

"How long will that be?"

"I don't know."

"We talk almost every day. She'll think it's strange I'm going away."

"Let her worry. Let her think it's strange. Better that than she gives away your location. And if they're watching her, her reaction will only add to the ruse that you're dead."

"If they're *watching* her?"

"I don't know what Ding is capable of. I just know he's connected. So, for your sister's safety as well as your own—do as I say."

Once Meixiang has reserved a train ticket for Dalian and texted her sister, Ping takes her phone. "I'll come by when I can, bring you money and supplies."

"But—"

"I didn't sign up for this, but now my neck's on the chopping block, too. If Fang finds out I'm hiding you, they'll kill the both of us. So do exactly as I say."

As promised, Ping comes every other day, bringing her cash, toiletries, take-out food, and leftovers scrounged from the restaurant. Aside from sitting in the lobby when the maid cleans, Meixiang never leaves her room. The waiting is excruciating, not least because she frets about how Meirong is dealing with her absence. Since the death of their mother, Meixiang has become something less than a parent, but more than just a sister to Meirong.

And then a day passes—two, three—without a visit from Ping. By day four, Meixiang has run out of money. She starts to panic. What if he's been found out? Tortured and murdered? How long before she can expect a knock at her door?

She thinks about making a run for it.

But without a phone, money, a bank card, she's not going to get far.

So, she waits.

And waits.

And then, as she feared, there is a knock on the door.

FIFTY-ONE

"Public Security!" a voice calls out.

A male voice.

Meixiang hears a key sliding into the lock. She panics.

There is a hot water thermos for making tea on the nightstand. She snatches it up and runs into the bathroom. She slams and locks the door.

After a moment, the voice calls through the bathroom door: "Meixiang?" It doesn't sound like Fang, but Meixiang knows he wouldn't come himself. She raises the thermos. It's not much of a weapon, but she's resolved to fight this time. They'll have to kill her right here in the bathroom or drag her kicking and shrieking through the lobby.

"I'm a police officer," the man says. "Open the door."

Sure you are, Meixiang thinks.

"It's safe to come out," the man says. "Fang and Ding are dead."

The doorknob jiggles, there is a click, and the door opens. Meixiang nearly hurls the thermos, but then she sees a man standing there, dressed in a PSB uniform. He's holding a bank card in his hand, which he's used to pick the bathroom lock. He smiles. "Meirong and I have been looking high and low for you."

It takes some time for Lu to convince Meixiang he's telling the truth. And then he is obliged to wait out a prolonged bout of tears. Finally she collects herself, washes her face in the sink, and is ready to go.

He takes her downstairs, through the lobby, outside. She turns her face up toward the sun and breathes deeply.

Lu fiddles with his phone. "I'll have to summon a car service."

Their car arrives and they go to Meixiang's building. Her roommate is out working, so Meixiang leaves her a goodbye note and packs up. She doesn't have much—just clothes, some electronics, a few knickknacks. And the photograph on the refrigerator.

They take the car to Raven Valley. Meixiang weeps intermittently on the way. The driver keeps glancing in his rearview mirror, uneasy, but too intimidated by Lu's uniform to ask questions.

It is midafternoon when they arrive. Lu is relieved to see the neighborhood kids are elsewhere. Perhaps they have found stray cats to torment. Old ladies to pelt with rotten vegetables.

"Wait here," Lu says. He figures Mr. Tan is probably drunk on the couch and he doesn't want anything to cast a pall over the occasion.

The door leading to the lobby is propped open. A few elderly residents sit inside, enjoying a bit of a breeze. Lu gives them a polite nod and takes the stairs up to the third floor. He knocks on the apartment door. After a short wait, Meirong opens it. Her expression initially reads panic, then numb resignation.

Lu takes her hand. She complacently allows herself to be led downstairs. Her gaze never leaves the floor.

Meixiang is waiting outside. When Meirong sees her, she lets out a piercing scream and launches herself into her sister's arms. The two of them nearly topple backward off the front steps. They spin around and around, vacillating between laughter and tears.

Lu's vision blurs. He wipes his eyes and his knuckle comes away wet. Must be the summer pollen.

The girls' happy reunion reminds him of one of his favorite poems— "Qiang Village" by Du Fu—which goes something like this:

I return from a thousand li.
My wife and children are amazed to see me.
By good fortune I have come back alive.
Late at night, we bring out candles.
And stare at each other, as if in a dream.

ACKNOWLEDGMENTS

Thank you to the wonderful team at Minotaur: Keith Kahla, Alice Pfeifer, Hector DeJean, Martin Quinn, and the many others who toil quietly behind the scenes. Thanks also to my agent, Bob Diforio. A huge shout-out to Chris Alexander and Nicholas Sigman for their invaluable critiques and suggestions. Heartfelt gratitude to my friends and family for the encouragement, support, and love. And to those of you who enjoyed *Thief of Souls* and are back for more adventures with Lu Fei—多謝, 多謝.